3/23

The ★ FAREWELL ★ TOUR

The
FAREWELL TOUR

★ *A Novel* ★

STEPHANIE CLIFFORD

HARPER

An Imprint of HarperCollinsPublishers

This novel is a work of fiction. Any references to real people, events, establishments, artistic works, organizations, or locales are intended only to give the fiction a sense of authenticity and are used fictitiously. All other names, characters, locales, and events portrayed in this book are the product of the author's imagination.

FIRST EDITION

Designed by Kyle O'Brien

Library of Congress Cataloging-in-Publication Data has been applied for.

ISBN 978-0-06-325113-7

23 24 25 26 27 LBC 5 4 3 2 1

For Bruce, with love: Rough new prizes

We who must act as handmaidens

To our own goddess, turn too fast,

Trip on our hems, to glimpse the muse

Gliding below her lake or sea,

Are left, long-staring after her,

Narcissists by necessity

> —"A Muse of Water," by Carolyn Kizer (b. 1925,
> Spokane, Washington)

Old train, I can hear your whistle blow, but I won't be jumping on
again

Old train, I've been everywhere you go, and I know what lies
beyond each bend

Old train, each time you pass you're older than the last

And it seems I'm too old for running

> —"Old Train," as recorded by Rose Maddox, 1994
> (written by Herb Pedersen and Nikki Pedersen, 1972)

The
★ **FAREWELL** ★
TOUR

★ PROLOGUE ★

I wouldn't have recognized the farm. Almost didn't. Charlie nearly drove our tour bus right by it.

The farmhouse seemed small and unremarkable, not the place that had reared at me in memories I'd struggled to forget, the place that I'd run from for so long. Its white paint was badly chipped. Rangy weeds clung to its sides. The step to the front door looked like it had sunk in a rainstorm, and nobody had bothered to pry it back up. There was junk where the kitchen garden used to be: a hubcap, a rusty lawn mower.

Hen must not live here anymore; she never would've let it decline to this state. Still, I could hear her voice, telling me: "All girls sacrifice for their families." And then: "Don't speak, you won't remember."

The last time I'd seen this land, I'd been ten years old and had a different name.

"This it?" Charlie asked from the driver's seat of our tour bus.

My stomach roiled, and I pressed it against the plastic of the bus's dashboard, hoping the pressure would settle it down.

When Charlie and I left Walla Walla town behind, nothing had been the same as when I was a kid; the streets were paved now, crossing north and south over the main road on what had been horse paths. The land was divided into small lots, and where I'd once marked distance by the golden wheat and the red vines, by the brown-and-white Herefords of the farm next to us and the dapple-gray Percherons of the farm two down, now there were strip malls and stoplights. We took a few wrong turns, went north toward Pedigo, and had to spin around. When we got to heading west, and Washington's golden hills rose and shimmered, I felt I was recollecting it from a dream.

Then I saw the farmhouse, and a phrase from "Bo-Weavil Blues" burbled up. *Hey, hey, bo-weavil.*

My body stiffened.

Charlie, noticing, made a hard left and pulled up on a side road. He shut the bus's engine off. I heard a metallic drumbeat. I smelled chicken manure.

He opened the bus door and I stepped out, steadying myself against the weather-beaten wood of our old fence. I'd gotten a splinter when I jumped this fence barefoot as a kid, taking the shortcut to run cream down to the Melgaards' in exchange for some side meat. Mother had to slice my skin with a knife tip to get the splinter unstuck. It was my sister who suggested we douse my foot in rubbing alcohol. When Mother poured the alcohol over my foot, I'd screamed, and Hen pushed me into the milk shed as punishment.

As far back as I can remember, it's been Hen I've sung to. Hen on the ballads, when it was just me and my left hand stretching long for barre chords and my picking hand working the guitar strings. I thought if she heard, if she knew it was me, she would at last feel guilt. She would at last feel bad for making Mother do what Mother did, for telling Mother *"Arga katter får rivet skinn."* Hen, now, certainly, living in a beautiful brick house in Walla Walla town, with her pretty hands, like Mother used to talk about. Such elegant hands, Mother said. Long fingers.

Mine: stubby, dirt-smeared.

That Hen was an old woman now seemed preposterous. When I thought of her, late at night, before the whiskey washed the memories clean, I see her as she was the summer I left. There's Hen in her tidy larkspur-blue dress, and me busy wondering where Mother found the time to let out the old dress so it still fit her. Mother had used matching thread, I could tell, so I knew that Mother had paid egg money, sour-cream money, to buy that thread for Hen, and I was thinking how many milkings it took me to get that cream when—

But no. It does no good. I left, that is all.

Hen haunted me as I moved from Walla Walla to Tacoma to Bakersfield to Nashville. Had she heard me on the radio? Did she recognize it was me? Did she see me on television, feel a cattle prod of recognition in her body? Did she know my songs were sung to show her who I was, how far I'd come?

She was an unresolved note in a chord I couldn't quite master, waiting for me, the songwriter and performer, to get it right so the audience could applaud and I could end my performance and go home.

"This is it," I said now, hoping my voice sounded composed.

There was no point in delaying anymore. When I learned time was running out, I'd known what I needed to do to tie things up.

I needed to go back.

Back to her. Back to this farmhouse. Back to Washington.

Back to the West.

★ 1 ★

Rossville, Georgia
June 1980

"You're not taking photos, right? I don't have my face on," I said to the young reporter as we sat at a picnic table at an amusement park just outside Chattanooga, Tennessee, four hours before the kickoff show for my farewell tour. I was only wearing foundation, blush, eyeliner, and lipstick.

No photos, she assured me; they'd use a file photo of me singing at a WDOD Country Music Spectacular in '66. The reporter said she usually covered society for the *Chattanooga Times*, but this piece could be syndicated nationwide if she could find a good hook.

"If I'm a good hook, you're in real trouble," I said. Though it was arguably still breakfast time, the air smelled of hot peanuts and cotton candy, and the screams of kids on the Tilt-A-Whirl and kiddie bumper car rides drowned out the end of my sentence.

She took out a notebook and asked how it felt to be back on tour after all this time. I gushed about my excitement at opening at Lake Winnepesaukah, an old-fashioned-in-a-good-way park that had been running since the twenties. Lake Winnie regularly hosted country singers, and had just opened a new concert space called Country Junction, where I was to play a one-hour afternoon show, followed by a southern-rock singer. The evening performances, of course, drew more of an audience, but an eighteen-year-old girl I'd never heard of had landed that slot.

"How do you feel about the new generation of female country singers? Crystal Gayle, Debby Boone, Barbara Mandrell?"

The women I'd come up with in the business, Dolly Parton and Loretta Lynn and Tammy Wynette, were all still charting. I wanted to point out that there was something in the longevity of gals like us, but I thought I'd better be diplomatic. "I'm glad to see so many women on the charts these days; when I was young, record companies would sign one girl singer and that was it."

"Do you like the new music?"

Their songs were sappy nonsense compared to Tammy's voice swollen with emotion, Loretta's bluster and originality, Dolly's songwriting and showmanship, and the hard rhythms and tough lives in my songs. They—we—had moved the genre so far forward, it had only bare chords in common with the country and western I'd heard as a young woman in the West. "Their music is sweet enough, but it's pop; it isn't country."

She scribbled this down, and I knew the quote would make me sound like an envious old thing. "You stopped touring in '75, after that notorious performance in Memphis, isn't that right? So why a farewell tour? Why now?"

I touched my throat almost automatically before snatching my hand away, hoping the reporter hadn't noticed.

I'd known something was wrong since my performance at Fan Fair the year before. I don't mean wrong as in the dozens of things in my life that the good churchgoing people who made up my audience would judge me for if they knew about, how fast and hard and ugly I'd had to be to make it in this business. No, this was something physical. A year earlier my manager, Stanley, had booked me a performing slot at Fan Fair, the annual get-together at the Nashville Municipal Auditorium where country music fans meet the stars. Loretta Lynn and Connie Smith and Barbara Mandrell had two-hour waits at their signing tables. In my prime, I had a great spot, too. But I stopped performing after the '75 Memphis appearance this reporter had already asked about. Racked by a letter I'd just received, I laid into my own fans. So what if I'd once played huge venues as part of package shows—the Charlotte Coliseum or Cobo Hall in Detroit, ten thousand people or more—and packed my solo shows with two thousand? I was now trying to break back into the business in my fifties, playing church basements or chicken restaurants. I was always a bit of a novelty in my day, anyhow, with my old-time honky-tonk sound, and the genre had moved on to slick sounds and performers who dressed like Hollywood stars. So my signing table was in the far back of the auditorium, next to a six-year-old Elvis impersonator. One woman holding a Barbara Mandrell souvenir book, apparently remembering that Memphis dustup, pointed it at me and said, "Shame on you!"

I still wanted to put on a good show for Fan Fair, and, getting ready for performing, I'd been singing for hours a day. My voice felt increasingly strained, my throat irritated. During my Fan Fair performance, I was in the middle of a hit from '63 when my voice cracked on a B. When I went up a key, I couldn't hit anything above a C. I sounded raspy and dry, like I was a baton-twirling rodeo sweetheart who'd never used a mic before.

Though I'd been able to finish my Fan Fair performance, more vocal problems followed. I'd gotten shooting pains between my ears and an ache in my throat, which aspirin barely soothed. My voice developed a growly smoker's overtone, and I sucked on cough drops constantly. When Stanley noticed the aspirin and the packets of cough drops I carried around, he told me, all schoolmarm-like, that he wasn't going to book me any more dates until I saw a doctor, which I finally did this spring.

Singer's cancer, we called it in Nashville: the specialist I saw said I had a polyp on my vocal cord. He'd seen it before, given he worked in the country music capital of the world. It wouldn't kill me, but it could, I knew, end my career. He prescribed immediate vocal rest, then surgery. Vocal rest, as if I would stop working now. And as for surgery, I knew one gal with the prettiest voice, sweet and clear as a flute, who went under the knife and sounded like Orson Welles afterward.

How long do I have before my voice gets so bad I can't sing? I asked the doctor. Through the summer?

He didn't say no. I took that as a yes.

I went straight to a bar when I left the doctor's office. If I could sing through the summer, that meant I could fit in one last tour. On my third whiskey, I hit on the idea of calling it the Farewell Tour. The title would be a gimmick, as far as anyone else knew. I wouldn't tell Stanley, wouldn't tell anyone, about the diagnosis, would say that I was calling it my last tour just to gin up ticket sales.

But I knew it'd be my last. And I knew where I had to finish up.

It was April when I made the plan, which gave me and Stanley just enough time to set up summer dates, hitting the county-fair circuit and ending at the Southeastern Washington Fair in Walla Walla. One more time. One last time.

Now, to the reporter, I gave a saucy answer as to why-now: "I don't think anyone wants to see me swishing my skirts when my knees are this wrinkled. It may be time to hang up my hat."

I thought she'd tell me I looked fine for my age, but she nodded like I'd uttered a universal truth. "I understand you're finishing up the tour in Washington State, where you were born, right? During the Walla Walla flood of '31?"

"That's right," I said, hearing her repeat the tale I'd told for years.

"Now, I had our librarians look up birth records in that county from March 1931, but there wasn't a Lillian Waters that they could find."

I winked. "Why, you aren't accusing a lady of shaving a year or two off her age, are you?"

"There weren't any Waterses out in that area at all."

No, there weren't. I scrutinized the reporter—snooty accent, fancy jewelry—and figured she'd buy a story about how backward a place I came from. "You know how it is in the Wild West. I'm not sure Billy the Kid's records are all stored in one neat file folder, either."

"I've never been out West, but that makes sense." She crossed her legs, her patent-leather pumps shiny. "You've talked before about how you left your farm pretty early."

"At seventeen, with a guitar and a dream." I'd said this so often it had stopped sounding false, even to my ears. It was a decent answer; seventeen sounded old enough that no one raised an eyebrow.

"Why'd you leave home?"

"We were a family with two girls, so one of us had to work; let's just say when it came to brains . . ." I tapped my temple, as I had so many times delivering this line, and put on a honey-soaked southern accent for the follow-up. "And to think that I was blessed with the intelligence and the beauty, too; my poor, dear old sister." If I landed the emphasis on the *old* just right, I'd get a chuckle and the person asking the question would move on. But the reporter didn't pick a new subject, to my annoyance.

"Yet you've never gone back to Walla Walla?"

"When I first moved to Tacoma, Walla Walla was so far away—Washington is a big state—that it was tough to go back when I was so busy working. And then returning became something I wanted to save for . . ." I nudged my tongue into a gold filling on my molar. "For a very special homecoming, and that homecoming is now."

The reporter wrote down my answer and flipped a page. "I hear you're not touring with any new material? That it's all the old songs?"

"Fan favorites," I said through a tight jaw.

"Have you written anything new?"

I recalled when the songs poured out of me like boiling water from a kettle, when I always kept a little notebook on me to scrawl down conversations, thoughts, images, *life*. When the hard part was finding the time to sit and give the songs a little space to grow and breathe.

I stopped writing that kind of stuff when I moved to Nashville, so I could churn out the hits my producer wanted, ones that fit with the sexy-divorcée image he created for me. Then, after he dropped me, all I could come up with were bland words like *grass* or *sky* that conveyed no feeling. Yet I kept writing phrases from "Bo-Weavil Blues," an old song I learned as a kid, one of my father's favorites. I didn't even think I still knew the words to it—yet there they were, scrawled in my handwriting on scraps of paper, napkins, notebooks scattered through my house.

I listened to the rumble of a roller coaster making an ascent and then a quick drop, with riders' concurrent shrieks. I wished I'd put a fifth of whiskey in my purse so I could run to the bathroom and have a glug mid-interview. Since that wasn't an option, I did what I used to do when Hen told Mother to put me in the milk shed. I kept my face calm, my body rigid, and waited for time to run out. "Should I put no comment?" she said finally.

I didn't speak, so she couldn't even no-comment me.

"How will you feel going home? Do you think you've achieved what you wanted to in your life, your career?"

"I've had nine number-one singles, and if you want me to tick off how many CMA and ACM awards I've won—"

"But that was a while back. At that '75 TV appearance in Memphis, you said, quote, about your fans: 'Nashville sells it and you all buy it, because you're that simple.' There was a huge blowback from the country-music audience, and your label dropped you—alcohol and pills were also part of the problem, reportedly—and you haven't put out a record or toured since."

I winced. "I've apologized to my fans, and I'll keep apologizing," I said. "I didn't mean what I said, and I've regretted it ever since. The fans are the best thing around." This, I didn't need to lie to her about. As for her other question, the truth was, those years after '75 hardly existed for me. The day of that Memphis performance, I'd received a letter from Bank of the West, with something inside it that I'd been running from for decades. I drank to wipe it out, and only remember shards of my show that night and my TV appearance after. My label dropped me, and for the only time in my life, I gave up. "And I thought this was going to be a conversation about my new tour," I said.

She put her pen down like she was confiding in me. "This *is* about your tour. You decided to come back on the road and back into public view, and you agreed to this interview. You can't be a public person and just decide which parts of your life you talk about and which parts you don't."

Like hell I can't, I thought. I've been doing that my entire career. But before I could come up with a zinger, she leaned in, her voice all soft, like we were trusting pals now. "Miss Waters, are you really ready for this tour?"

My stomach moved with the unsettling feeling I'd gotten regularly since I was a kid, as if wheat stalks were waving inside it. Ticket sales were agonizingly slow, I hadn't been on the road in years, my songs were outdated, and my voice was weak and unreliable. The reporter hadn't even asked about my band, but it wasn't in good shape. I'd never played with my guitarist, a Nashville type named Chip or Chick who I knew through Tootsie's, the music-industry hangout there. I didn't know my fiddler, someone Stanley had scared up. The Farver brothers—my bassist and steel guitarist—were old industry friends, but they'd just called to say they'd hit a road closure on the way to Chattanooga, while the guitarist's flight was delayed, meaning we wouldn't have time for a rehearsal or even a sound check before we went on. The musician I really wanted for the band, Charlie Hagerty, was currently in Nashville and not speaking to me.

And, however badly the tour went, I'd committed to ending it in Walla Walla. Though I'd hoped to see Hen one more time when I was at the top of my game, it was looking like I'd roll into town a flop, just the way she always treated me.

I stood up, straightened the collar on my minidress, and told the reporter that I'd forgotten about a previous engagement. She tipped her chair back, looking unfazed, as I stalked off toward a pavilion shaped like a cake with birthday candles on top of it.

As I wound through the park, I bought a can of Coke for our tour manager and driver, Patrice, at a snack stand and popped it open because he liked his Cokes flat. I found our rented tour bus parked near the concert space. It was a beast of a thing, with an olive-and-chrome exterior. I'd nicknamed it the Green Giant, and I left the open can on its dashboard for Patrice before locking myself into my bedroom in the back. Back in Nashville, I'd bought a few notebooks at the five-and-dime, hoping I'd be filling them up by now. But they were still in my suitcase, untouched. I took one out and opened it to the first page.

I don't want no man to put no sugar in my tea . . .

This was the problem with writing. An unsettling day or a late night, a blank page, and I couldn't control what memories might poke their way in. Phrases in Swedish I hadn't heard since I was a child, perhaps, or images of the farm, or the grunts of the Judge. Those I could handle, but then others landed: the smell of curdled milk, the slide of a metal bar, the bank man in his town hat, the lyrics to "Bo-Weavil Blues." And Hen, with that look on her face, telling me that girls must sacrifice for their families.

For the story of the West was the story of men, printed in our faded primer books, creased and thumb-oiled, passed from student to student right to left across our classroom when we were children. It was told at our county fairs, at our Pioneer Days, at our rodeos. It was the men who hitched oxen to wagons and traveled the Lewis and Clark trail, men who brought liniments and whetstones, augers and kingbolts, reflector ovens and salt, who left and never stopped, for time meant food and food meant oxen and oxen meant getting over the Blue Mountain pass or not.

It was the men who traded fur, who camped and logged and fished, who homesteaded and built fences, who laid down railroad tracks, who herded cattle and planted wheat and coaxed apple trees up from seed. The West was where they reinvented themselves. It was adventure or opportunity, exile or salvation, new, dangerous, dirty, wild, unconquerable, different. I once had to memorize an early-1900s passage from a pamphlet advertising Walla Walla to easterners for a high school elocution competition. "The Pacific Northwest," I'd enunciated, "is one of the few sections of America that represents a virgin field of wonderful possibilities for men and capital."

And the women?

Look carefully, and you can see us at the edges of brown-ink sketches of early Washington, leaning over an oven, bending over a broom in our sun-faded aprons. We bloomed into relevance when it was time to bear children who would soon labor or adventure themselves, depending on if they were girls or boys, then quickly receded. If we stepped into the sun once more, it was to call our men to supper and to give them a dose of God and home and country, to shore them up for the next day's trials and see them off from our posts behind our wooden doors.

The women's trials, those stayed behind those doors.

"Sacrifice," I heard Hen instructing me, and then those lyrics I could never escape bubbled up: *I don't want no man to put no sugar in my tea . . .*

I took no photographs when I left the farm, for we had no photographs, I think, other than the one of Hen that Mother kept on her dresser, where my sister wore her pretty larkspur dress with its lace bib. I am left with only memories of the people and the place, negatives almost half a century old that a wash of chemical solution will never properly develop. Not after all this time. The Bank of the West mortgage in the bread box. Hen in her blue dress in the parlor, doing nothing. The milk shed with its door shut, reeking of rotten cream.

I'm a lone bo-weavil—I'm a lone bo-weavil—I'm a lone bo-weavil . . .

I threw down the pen and unzipped a pocket in my suitcase, pulled out a bottle of whiskey, and twisted open the top. I plopped on the bed, shoving the notebook to the floor. As I gulped down a sip, my answers to the reporter careened in my head. So many damned stories I had to tell to make myself palatable to the world.

But I'd been telling tales since I was a girl. It was the only way for me to explain why I left home.

★ 2 ★

Walla Walla, Washington
1924–1929

I was born Lena Thorsell on a farm west of Walla Walla town.

By the time I was four, I spent most of my summer days with Hen, for she was home from school and our parents were out in the fields. Mother often left us fruit smash on bread for meals when she was out working, and Hen, who was eight, would wipe raspberry juice from my chin while she outlined the day's plan. Once we did our chores, we could play, as long as Mother wasn't back yet. We might choose Annie Annie Over or hide-and-seek, and we'd sing to each other, bars from "Bo-Weavil Blues." Father had taught the song to us, and since we had weevils in our flour from time to time, Hen and I immediately loved it. "Hey, bo-weavil, don't sing the blues no more," we'd warble when we went to our basement cold room to scoop flour for Mother, or retrieve the beautiful jars of food we had put up the summer before, deep-red beets next to yellow-orange peaches. "I'm gonna sing these blues to ease the bo-weavil's lonesome mind."

We also sang it to work up our courage, like the day Mother left us alone and we decided to explore the abandoned milk shed, one of the falling-down structures about a hundred yards behind the farm-house. Mother had gone out to pull mustard weeds from the wheat fields, leaving us baked apples not just for breakfast but for dinner, so we knew she wouldn't be back for some time. Hen and I decided to venture to the milk shed.

We used the other outbuildings, the outhouse and the chicken coop, but the shed had always been more forbidding, especially in the back, where purple thistle grew around a western juniper. The build-ing had been left there from when Father's father briefly raised dairy cows and sold cream and milk. Mother told me and Hen we weren't allowed to explore it, but we weren't sure why; we supposed there was poison ivy.

The shed was made of brick painted white, with a sloping roof, and it stood barely taller than a grown man. The slats on its wooden door were just wide enough apart that Hen and I could peek through them, and its small, high window had long been boarded up; it was too dim for us to see much from the outside.

"I'm gonna sing these blues," I sang in a quiet voice.

Hen clutched my arm as she scanned the fields to make sure Mother was still away. She slid back the door's long metal bar, which served as an exterior lock, and blew up her cheeks with breath.

"I'm gonna sing these blues," I repeated.

"To ease my lonesome mind," she responded.

"No, it's 'To ease the bo-weavil's lonesome mind,'" I corrected her.

She opened the door, letting go of me, and we each took a tentative step inside.

It was about half the size of our small bedroom, laced with cob-webs and covered with paint flakes and crumbles of brick. To our right was a narrow metal tub, rusted out at the bottom, and old milk cans and jugs littered the place. It smelled of sour milk and dust, and I was afraid the door would slam shut and keep us in there forever. I willed Hen to give up on our mission.

"I s'pose we've seen that," she said.

I let out a sigh of relief.

"Now around back," she said. I shifted from foot to foot. She squeezed my hand tight as she led me outside to the patch of thistle surrounding the prickly juniper tree. The ground was covered in ivy. But that was all we saw: thistle and juniper and ivy.

"What's she so worried about?" Hen said. "That's regular ivy, not poison ivy. What baloney. Why, it's just like the rest of this farm. Just dirt and nothing else."

I knelt down and lifted the ivy vines. "Maybe there's buried treasure."

"If Mother knew there was treasure here, don't you think she'd have dug it up by now?" Still, Hen joined me on the ground, pushing the ivy aside. Then she gasped. "Lena. Look."

Underneath the ivy were two small gray, flat stones with letters and numbers on them. "B . . . a . . . b," I began sounding out; I wasn't in school yet, but Hen, who was four years older than me, had taught me the alphabet.

"'Baby boy, 1918,'" Hen read for me. "'Baby boy, 1919.' Lena, don't you see? Jimmy Bove told me once that Mother had had babies before me, and I asked where they were, and he said they had passed before they were born. This must be them. Oh, Lena, these are our brothers!"

"We don't have brothers," I said.

"We must have," she said. "Nineteen eighteen, 1919, and then I was born in 1920. And they died before they were born!" She did not look particularly stricken by this, but then Hen could handle a sheep's throat being cut without blinking.

"You can't die before you're born," I said.

"You can! Teena Watterson's mother was supposed to have a little brother or sister for Teena, but it died inside her body and came out dead." Hen's eyes lit up. "Mother never talks of the babies, of course, and that's why we can't come back here! Oh, Lena! Do you think they visit us at night?"

Wanting to stop her, I made the highest noise I could, and so loudly it hurt my own ears.

"Lena, Lena," Hen said, taking my shoulders. "Oh, Lena, stop, it's all right."

"They're ghosts!" I shrieked.

"Don't cry. Lena, don't cry! If they were ghosts, they'd be kind ghosts, anyhow." She paused. "Think of it, a terrible, terrible secret." That had been enough to send me into another fit of screams. Hen had grabbed me tight. "Shhh, shhh, shhh, Lena."

"Hen, are they really ghosts?" I said into the thin fabric of her sackcloth dress, touching a faded red dot on it.

"'Hey, hey, bo-weavil,'" she sung softly. I looked up, sniffling. Her cheeks were flushed, and I knew she hoped that the babies had become ghosts, and that she'd get to see them.

"They won't visit us, not really, will they?" I said.

"They would only come to help us," she said. She continued to sing as she led me back to the house. She didn't bring up the ghosts to me again, though for a good three weeks I saw her drawing ghost babies on scraps of paper and had to look away. Neither of us returned to the milk shed; even when we played hide-and-seek, we had an unspoken agreement that it, and the eerie stones behind it, were off-limits.

The summer was happy, Father home, Mother busy with the farm, Hen and I working and playing and singing, made even better when the Boves had a party one night. Hen and I wore our best gingham dresses, and the adults shoved back their chairs and tables and got everyone dancing, and Mr. Bove put "Bo-Weavil Blues" on his Victrola. I'd internalized the song as a simple tune, hardly different from "Pop Goes the Weasel" or some other children's song. When the Victrola played it, though, I heard a woozy wailing instrument against a slow beat, and my whole body tingled. Then Ma Rainey came in with the first word, "Hey," pulling five notes from that single syllable, and from her deep, weary voice, I understood the song was a melancholy warning. I pressed one ear against the Victrola's wooden body, listening.

Father leaned over me to lift the Victrola needle and play the record again. He hollered the lyrics, Hen joined in, and I tried to imitate Ma

Rainey's voice, us girls moving to the music in our gingham dresses. Mother had been helping Mrs. Bove fill a punch bowl; when she came into the living room and saw me and Hen next to the Victrola, she set the bowl down on a table so hard the juice spilled over. Then she slapped me clean across the cheek. She smelled not of punch but of the astringent sweetness of her aquavit. "That's a race record," she said. She pushed me and Hen outside, leaving our family's horse and wagon tied up outside the Boves', and marched us the mile and a half home. There, when my sister saw Mother pull out her boar-bristle brush, Hen hollered at me to run upstairs and dashed after me. She shut the door to our bedroom, jammed a chair under our doorknob, and gestured to me to lean all my weight against the chair with her. Mother yelled and whacked the brush against the door, but Hen held my hand tight, and after a time we heard Mother's footsteps recede. We left the chair wedged against the knob, just in case.

Later, safe in bed, I brought up the image of that record the moment before Leon Bove played it: the gold eagle perched on top of the world, the "Paramount" in fat golden letters against the purple label, and the unbelievable idea that Ma Rainey—a singer, a woman—had written and recorded a song, and I could hear it from a phonograph in a farmhouse in Walla Walla.

Father stayed late at the party that night, and the next morning I heard him whistling "Bo-Weavil Blues" as he rode to the fields. It became our secret code, me and Hen and Father, our quiet mutiny against Mother. "I'm a lone bo-weavil, been out a great long time," we started greeting each other when she wasn't nearby.

It was harvest time when Father—back then, he was still working the farm—came into our room one morning. "Wake up, girls," he said, kneeling on the floor beside me and nuzzling my nose with his. He lifted Hen from her bed and set her, yawning, on the floor. We reached for our gingham dresses, thinking we were going to town and perhaps Father would buy us chocolate ice creams like he had a month or so earlier. Father winked, though. "*Nej, nej*, it's a working day," he said. Hen and I widened our eyes at each other in excitement and put on sackcloth work dresses instead, Hen's a hand-me-down from the Boves' younger girl, mine a hand-me-down from Hen.

Father toasted slices of bread for breakfast, and we followed him outside as the sun rose. He pulled us onto his draft horse, me in front of him, Hen behind, and we trotted to our wheat fields, passing crops to harvest and brown-green patches of summer fallow, the wind strong and gritty. It was hard to tell where the wheat ended and the dust-blasted air began. In Walla Walla it was like God took the earth and the sky and pushed them together so they cragged up like raw dough pressed between hands. Our clouds hung so heavy and close, I felt I could touch them.

Father told us to wait for a surprise, and I heard it before I saw it: the clatter of hooves on hard ground, a roar. Then mules appeared, fine and shining in the sun, row after row. Hen counted aloud: thirty-three mules in all, noses flared, harnessed and pulling a giant machine across our hill. At the front a mule skinner, holding the lead animals' reins, perched on a metal seat that stuck out from the machine, and a handful of men balanced themselves on its body. Straw shot from a thresher spout as the machine cut and separated the stalks, leaving a track in the hills like the path of a finger through apple butter.

"It's a combine," my father said to us, flicking a speck of wheat dust from his face. "Think, they figured out a way to do the reaping and threshing and winnowing at once. Gets next to no straw and just the heads. This one's rented from Harris, in town." He reeled off numbers; Father had a good memory for them, as he'd once been a timber cruiser, wearing through seven pairs of shoes each season as he measured and estimated the size of Shevlin-Hixon Lumber's holdings around Oregon. Though he'd come back to run the farm, he retained a cruiser's ease with figures: a such-and-such-inch cylinder, this many sheaths per hour.

I grabbed the horse's mane, stretching forward as the combine took the top of the hill. I'd never seen such a majestic thing, harvesting heaps of wheat in minutes even on the Walla Walla hills, notoriously difficult because the slope wasn't constant. "It's magic," I said.

That afternoon, when the three of us rode back to the farm on the horse, sweaty and covered in bits of wheat, we burst into "Bo-Weavil Blues" again. "I don't want no man to put no sugar in my tea," we bellowed. "Some of them so evil, I'm 'fraid they might poison me."

At the house, Mother smoothed Hen's pretty dark-brown hair, leaving my straw-colored tangles alone, then shooed the two of us out the back door to the kitchen garden to pull carrots for the hired men's dinner. Through a window we could hear our parents fighting, again, about the farm, and I could feel the waving wheat stalks I'd just seen on the hills moving inside my stomach.

The farm had been my father's father's. He was a tenant farmer who'd emigrated from Sweden. He'd come west because of the Homestead Act, planting 160 acres with wheat, which grew well in the Touchet loam, as we called our soil, along with alfalfa for a rotation crop. When the Homestead Act limits were raised, and when he bought, on mortgage, some nearby parcels, he pulled together almost 900 acres. My grandmother died in childbirth when my father was a few years old. When he was fifteen, my father left home for the lumber company job, until his own father died of some sickness or another and he had to return to run the farm. To pay off his father's debts, he sold a third of the land to Hunter Fruit, which converted it to apple orchards that stretched to the west of us. That left my parents with 600 acres and a monthly mortgage payment to Bank of the West.

My mother came from Sundsvall, Sweden. She had the bad luck to be the youngest girl in a family of eight children, so of no use to anyone. When my mother was five, her parents sent her with her childless aunt and her uncle to Oregon, where my uncle was to work for Grande Ronde Lumber. My mother only went to school until fourth grade, and after that she helped her aunt take in sewing and babysat children. She never saw her parents or siblings again.

When America entered the Great War, towns with railroad depots were desperate for workers, and my mother moved north the eighty or so miles to Walla Walla and found a job at the steam laundry in town. My father was a customer of hers, and he liked that a good, hardworking Swedish girl that he hadn't known his entire life had suddenly appeared. He wooed her with his singing voice, which she loved back then. And marrying my father meant that she no longer had to send back most of her wages to Sweden, as single girls did. She became Mrs. Thorsell in early 1918, when my father, at twenty, was too young for the draft. My mother joined him in working the wheat, and Father careened between timber jobs and our fields. Mother had Hen in 1920, and, four years later, me.

With the right kind of attention, the farm could've done fine, though 600 acres wasn't quite sizable enough to support a family plus the required equipment and supplies, not to mention the hired men paid every year to help with harvest. The bigger problem, though, was that my father felt the woods in his blood still. He'd go to a tavern and hear someone talking about the money to be made in the Okanogan or out in the Olympics, and ride back to our farm singing his logging songs. I'd run across the bedroom floor and jump into Hen's bed, and we'd jam up the window she slept next to so we could listen to him: *Our logs were piling mountains high/ Jeer up jeer up / Steel's gonna be the death of me, Lord / Way, rye-o.*

The songs are still as familiar to me as the lines on my palm.

Gone half of the year, my father lost money on the farm, and Mother always worried about making the mortgage payments.

Though I knew Father was happiest logging, I preferred when he was home, as that was the only time there was any music at all. For one, we got to go to church: Father handled the farm on Sunday mornings, so as long as the roads weren't too muddy or snowy for our temperamental draft horse, Mother dressed me and Hen in our gingham, piled us into the wagon, and we attended a service on the edge of town. I liked the choir and the organ and sang along with the hymns as loudly as I could. On top of that, Father's logging songs filled our house. When Father went off to work the timber, though, Mother oversaw the farm on Sunday mornings, so there were no hymns, and of course there was no music of any other kind either. Instead, she read us passages from her Swedish Bible. I could only understand a few words of it, and it wasn't any substitute for the harmonies of the choir. Music was the only promise that there was something in the world for me here, now; everything else in my life, we rationed, we pickled, we preserved, we jammed, we dried, we stored, we saved for another day. And it was the only thing that made me feel I could be something more than just an Anna.

That's what the girls from Walla Walla town, those daughters of Daughters of Pioneers of Washington, called us farm girls: the Annas. Not just me and Hen, but all of us. To them we were interchangeable, with lank hair and dirty fingernails. We might be Swedes or Danes or Norwegians, but our families had arrived in Washington later than theirs had, and so we were all called Anna, pronounced the Nordic way, "Ah-nah." The Annas, and we worked at their fathers' stores; the Annas, and we cleaned their mothers' kitchens. Our own mothers spoke with accents, their *s*'s lingering too long between their teeth, their soft *v*'s replacing the firm American *w*'s, so *weather* became "veather." Our fathers were not the jolly men at the sporting-goods store, or the butchers bantering as they carved up a neck of lamb. Our fathers' pants were stiff with dirt, and they talked to other Nordic farmers about rain, about rye, about feed.

They called us the Annas when they mimicked us on hot squares of pavement at recess, saying "Ay thoss shickens" and "Yoss," pretending that was how we sounded. These were things we did not really say. We Annas took care to say "Oh, those chickens" and "Yes." They called us the Annas, and we did not correct them, even when they did not distinguish Ragna Sigmundsdottir, a dark-haired and humorless maid to the president of Whitman College, from Kiersten Urdahl, a pale and bold hired girl in the home of Walla Walla's mayor.

The boys in our families were allowed their own plans. Karl joined Junior ROTC and planned to go into the Army, and Tor played first base and hoped to try out for the Pacific Coast League. Trygve won for sheep showmanship at the Walla Walla fair and droned on about Rambouillets versus Cheviots. Bill became hairy and stinky and smoked at the billiards parlor.

Not for us. Not for the Annas. We stayed the Annas during harvest, when we were excused from school and our skin reddened in the sunshine of our fathers' fields, and the Annas in winter, trudging into class with sloppy boots and thawing our hands, frozen from the walk to town, in buckets of cool water. We should have taken our callused hands and closed them tight and punched the girls who called us that. Instead we let them make us feel shame for where we came from, for the strange foods we ate and the shabby things we wore.

Our parents came from Jutland and Småland, Trondheim and Malmöhus, and when they met outside our homes they spoke in quiet tones about their cold and faraway homelands, and assured themselves that life was better here. But we have land, they said. But we can keep the harvest ourselves, and live our own lives, and there is no aristocracy, they said. But we have choices, they said. Inside our homes, though, our parents tossed aside these claims as they fought over food, money, the future.

We, their daughters, knew our own future already. We would either continue to work for our families on our farms, or we would become hired girls in town and work for our families that way. It was a fine, respectable thing to do domestic work to help your father pay for cattle feed, or allow your brother an extra year or two of school before he started farming—but never to improve your own situation.

The Melgaards' girl died from pneumonia. The Boves' daughter had to marry a cousin. The old-maid daughter of the Thompsons was washing men's laundry the last time I passed her on the road.

"You think you're a Drumheller, Erik? You think you're a Hunter? These men's daughters, you think they're called Annas?" Mother shouted at Father the day of the mule combine, as I crouched outside, listening. "What cause you got to rent a combine when we have equipment, have hired men already? And you say it's a surprise, but now I have to find water for these animals, and food for the men running the machine?"

"You tell me to give up timber and take over the harvest, and then you tell me how I'm doing the harvest wrong? The folks at Harris said the combine was an investment, and it is. Think how fast we'll harvest with it, how quick we'll get the wheat to market. You'll see, Alma."

Hen, beside me in the kitchen garden, stepped on a pitchfork to loosen the carrots from the soil. I was supposed to be shaking them off and stacking them in a crate, but I just stared at the kitchen window as I listened to Mother and Father. My sister set her pitchfork down, then patted me on my head. "Lena?" she said. "Let's see who can find the tiniest carrot."

When Father rode back to the fields, Mother sent me and Hen to fill pails of water from the creek for when the crew broke. We hauled up a few buckets' worth, and by our third or fourth trip we were dusty and exhausted and had sweated through our dresses. Hen motioned for us to sit and rest on a smooth rock. "I went downtown and bought me a hat," she sang to me with a mischievous look.

"I brought it back home, I laid it on the shelf." I carried on with the song, trying to harness Ma Rainey's grown-up sound. We sang "Bo-Weavil Blues" over and over, quietly, for we weren't certain where Mother was and how far our sound would carry.

Hen touched a plant drooping with full green and red berries. "Dare you to eat this," she said, plucking a lone fruit. I shook my head no. Hen popped it in her mouth. "Fraidy-cat," she said, and I was awed: though I was only four and Hen was eight, I knew we were not supposed to eat the plants by the creek. "Fraidy-cat," she repeated, pulling off a few of the fruits, shaped like tiny, colorful eggs, and passing them to me.

"Not hungry," I said.

"You're a fraidy-cat."

"Am not. They look sour. I don't like sour."

"Fraidy-fraidy-fraidy-cat."

"Am not." I took the pile, put it in my pocket. "I'll eat them later. With sugar." I wasn't entirely sure I would be brave enough to eat them like she had, though. "Say, 'Bo-weavil's here . . .'"

When we returned to the farmhouse, we saw that Mother had left fruit smash on bread for us to eat while she served dinner to the crew in the fields. It'll taste all right that way, I thought, and crushed the berries from my pockets into the smash.

Then I remembered that Hen had left the pitchfork in the garden, and Mother might step on it and get whacked in the head and take the boar-bristle brush to the both of us. I left the smash-covered bread on the kitchen table and hurried outside, found the pitchfork, and dragged it to a storage shack. The air was layered with smells of grass and metal.

Then: time elapsed, going achingly slow then at a fast clip, and I was sent away, to a room where a paper-faced woman recited prayers about flesh and sin. The hard floor chapped my knees.

When I was returned to the farm, Hen wasn't there, and Father was working the Kapowsin timberlands, west of the Cascades and several days' travel from us. Wheat prices fell, and the harsh summer brought a drought to the late crops. My gingham was gone; I wore sackcloth instead. I didn't know where Hen had been sent. Mother smelled more and more of her aquavit that reeked of cleaning solution and herbs; it made her breath sour and her eyes blank.

We never spoke about any of it. Conversation was a luxury reserved for those who sat needlepointing in front of hearths, not people trying to coax wheat from a strong-willed land.

Hen returned on an afternoon in late spring when I was five. I'd started school by then, and I came home one day and there she was, standing outside the house. She wore her favorite larkspur dress with its lace collar. Mother must've washed and pressed it for her. Her dark hair shone in the sun.

"Hen?" I said. My yearning for her didn't reveal itself in a hug, a kiss, though I was so excited my breath hitched. I wanted to tell her how, since that night of the mule combine, Father had rarely come home, and Mother had grown strange and silent. I wanted to say how I found Mother looking out a wide-open window during a snowstorm wearing just a thin cotton nightgown. How I heard the glug-glug from her bottle in the mornings now, too. How, sweeping up the hallway, banned from the kitchen, I noticed Mother uncap a bottle of ammonia, rather than vinegar, and pour it into a jar of sliced beets that she was pickling. I could do little but wait until she put on the jar's ring and lid and placed it in boiling water; I then ran in so fast I knocked the whole pot to the ground and broke the jar's glass, earning me a burn along my thigh and a boar-bristle brush on my backside. How once, I slept and dreamed of the mule combine cutting through the fields, and when I awoke Mother was sitting on my bed with sewing shears, and my long hair was cut off and pooled around me.

With my sister home, Mother would be happy again, I thought, and so would I. Hen and I would adventure to the fields together, sing, sit by the creek. We would sneak bread slices at night, she would help me with my reading, she would hold my hand in hers, tight and warm.

"Mother said you took my bed," was all she said.

During the time Hen had been away, Mother had put away Hen's things, and our shared room now had just one bed; we must've sold the other.

I followed Hen into the house. We had four rooms on the ground floor: a hallway, then at the back of it, a parlor with armchairs repaired so often that they had seven different colors of thread and horsehair stuffing erupting. A dusty shelf held our two books, the Swedish and English Bibles. The English one was all I had to read other than the Sears Roebuck catalog. To one side of the hallway was our kitchen, a drafty room with a wood cookstove and a rear door into the vegetable garden, and to the other side, our parents' room. A staircase in the hallway led to the small room under the eaves that Hen and I shared.

Where before that night of the mule combine, I had trailed Hen like a puppy as she gathered eggs or helped with milking, now I had to do it alone, navigating iced-over dirt in the dark, even though she was back.

In our shared bed, Hen opened the window and dared me to jump out. Everyone would be happier without you, she told me.

Rossville, Georgia
June 1980

I strummed a B-flat chord, but the sound was way too bright. Shifting in the booth at the front of the Green Giant, I lowered the treble knob on my amp, then moved the selector on my Telecaster guitar to get a muddier, darker sound. I was trying the chord again when a pair of feet, strapped into leather sandals, slapped up the steps of the bus and into my line of sight. Though I increased the volume on the amp and played the chord again, the feet just stayed there. They belonged to a petite girl with long, loose black hair parted in the middle, whose frilly white tank top was so thin I could see she wasn't wearing a bra. Though she was skinny, she had the muscled limbs of an athlete.

"Lillian," she said in a calm voice as soon as my chord died out. Presumptuous to call me by my first name, I thought. I figured she was someone Stanley had dispatched to the Lake Winnie show to make sure I wasn't drinking too much. "Busy," I said, leaning over the amp, a vintage Fender Twin Reverb I'd bought for the tour.

"I'm Kaori Tanaka," she said.

I looked pointedly at my Tele.

"I'm your fiddler," she continued.

Good thing I was sitting, my guitar in my lap, because otherwise I would've dropped it on the floor. "That a joke?"

She smiled like she was expecting precisely that response, which annoyed me. "No."

"You're a kid."

"I'm older than you were when you started performing."

"What do you know about when I started performing?" I unwrapped a cough drop, considering the exact unladylike words I'd use when I reamed Stanley for sending this child my way.

The girl picked up a fiddle case I hadn't noticed was by her feet, took out her fiddle, and played the opening notes to "Water Lil," then swerved into "Deep River Blues." A little flood joke. And she was actually pretty good at fiddling.

"You from around here?" I said, sucking on the cough drop, once she finished.

"Minneapolis."

My manager had been living there until recently. "That's how Stanley found you?"

"He lived next door to my family before he moved to Nashville. My father was his doctor."

I gave her a look meant to wither. Instead, it seemed to amuse her. "You've got something in your hair," I said. This was true—there was a bramble in it—but she kept her hands on her fiddle. "You ever played country before?"

"I have a bluegrass group at school."

"Lord, you're in high school?"

"College."

"That's not much better."

"Well, I'm not enrolled now, and I'm not sure if I'll go back, honestly. I write music, too, and sing, and this is what I want to do. Country music." The directness that she said it with reminded me of Charlie, all those years ago in Tacoma, saying the reason he'd moved there was to play country and western. Kaori leaned against the dashboard, all loose limbs. "I've been studying your albums, of course. Some of your songs are terrific."

Some of my songs. "I'll alert the fan club."

"I wanted to ask about phrasing on 'Memphis Bound.' I was thinking, in the bridge—"

"If I wanted a music critic, I would've hired one."

"I meant phrasing for when we play tonight. Patrice said we're not doing sound check."

"We'll go over all the songs before the show, once the rest of the band gets here. And the phrasing will be how it's always been."

"Maybe I could talk to the bandleader?"

"You're looking at her," I said. Truthfully, I wasn't much of a bandleader, not schooled enough in theory and not good enough at managing people for the job. But neither were the Farvers, and Chick-Chip was way too green, so I'd have to do it. If I'd succeeded in getting Charlie Hagerty to come along, I'd have had a real bandleader. I tried—sort of. At that bar after my vocal diagnosis, drinking my fourth, maybe my fifth, whiskey, I convinced myself that the only way Stanley would get excited about a tour was if I got a great musician on board that promoters and venues loved. So I called Charlie. The problem was, he was in the middle of a recording session. I told the receptionist it was an emergency, the liquor fueling the notion that I had to arrange this immediately, and asked her to tell Charlie to meet me right away. It was an emergency, for me, but when Charlie hurried over, I didn't tell him about the diagnosis. Instead, he found me toasted and babbling about playing county fairs, and he'd gotten so mad at me we hadn't spoken since.

"I see," the girl said. There was a hint of a laugh underneath her words, which made me want to kick this college girl in the shins. She replaced the fiddle in its case. "We're ending in Washington State, right?"

"Last I checked."

She seemed to be waiting for me to ask a question, but I wouldn't give her the satisfaction. Finally, she said, "I've never been there. My mom's family was from near Kent."

Kent, not too far from Tacoma, had been farmland when I knew it. "They raise crops there?"

She gave me a strange look. "Not anymore. You're from out west, right?"

Out west: the phrase of someone from the East. "I'm from no-where," I said. I put the Tele in its case, rose from my seat with what I hoped resembled regal flourish, and waited for her to take the hint. Once she was safely off the bus, I locked myself in my bedroom, pulled out a whiskey bottle from my suitcase, and raised it in a toast to myself. "New tour," I said, taking a long swig, "same old Lil."

★ 4 ★

Walla Walla, Washington
1929–1934

It was Hen's idea to put me in the milk shed.

She came up with it that spring she returned. Mother was overseeing the planting, and had hired a Nez Perce woman to bake bread and sweet rolls for the crew. I watched from my bedroom window as the woman, whom my mother called Ellen, rode up with her husband on an Appaloosa. She had a wooden item resembling a tray strapped to her back, and leaped easily from their horse before her husband had fully reined it in. I was meant to be upstairs darning, but instead I tiptoed to the kitchen and stationed myself at the doorframe. I was not supposed to be in the kitchen, not since the night of the mule combine, but Mother wasn't there to prevent me.

While my mother's baking was restrained, a teaspoon of this and a pinch of that, the Nez Perce woman mixed everything in a blizzard of flour and sugar, punched down yeasted dough, scattered seeds over the top of loaves in explosive handfuls, and roughly scored the dough with a knife. The wooden item she'd brought was a bread peel, and no sooner would she draw out a finished loaf from the oven and slide it off the peel than she'd stoke the fire, plop raw dough on the peel again, and bake the next loaf. I thought she hadn't seen me at all, but when she took out her second or third loaf, she motioned to me. "You help me with this," she said, passing the peel to me after she'd moved the finished bread from it. "Flour," she said, and I understood, and I scooped a small handful of flour and patted it on the peel.

After we'd finished a few more loaves, her husband rode by on their Appaloosa. He shouted to her—though he used another name, not an English one—and she hurried out with a sack of warm bread for him to take to the men. When the woman returned to the kitchen, I asked her what the Appaloosa was named. "Not 'Appaloosa,'" she corrected. "Your word. We say 'Maamin.'"

"'Maamin,'" I repeated, wondering where she lived, what her own real name was, and why my mother didn't bother to use it, but it was impertinent for a child to ask an adult that.

She did not keep me away from the kitchen like Mother did, and I tried to be useful, preparing the bread peel for her and covering the finished loaves with tea towels. I was squinting against the sun beating through the kitchen window when a sound from outside made me duck below the counter. Mother's work boots came close. She grabbed my wrists tight, flipped up my palms. "You've been cooking," she said. She yelled at the Nez Perce woman, and the woman just dusted herself off and left without a word.

Mother grabbed the collar of my dress and pulled, and, aware I only had one other dress that fit and couldn't ruin this one, I didn't resist. I let her drag me outside, where I thought she'd shove me away from her and tell me not to come back for a while.

She was about to do that, except Hen materialized, prim in her blue dress. How it made me jealous, that Mother had found the time and money to let it out so that my sister could always wear her beloved dress. "You aren't supposed to be in the kitchen," I heard Hen say. "You think about what you did." Then I saw that Hen was looking at Mother, and pointing to the milk shed. I hadn't been in it since that day when Hen and I explored the inside and discovered the gravestones in the back.

One hand gripping me, Mother slid the milk-shed door's metal bar to the side. Just before she threw me inside and slid the bar to keep me there, I heard Hen cackling behind Mother. *"Arga katter får rivet skinn,"* Hen said. *Angry cats get scratched skin.*

Then the milk shed went dark.

Alone and locked in, the first thing you do is yell "Mama," that first word that babies learn, because if you call that, so something in your body thinks, someone will come. Someone will help.

Someone does not.

"Hen!" I tried.

I sat against a wall, wrapping my arms around my knees, trying not to think about the dead babies buried so close to me. The milk smell must've been gone by that point, as it hadn't been a working shed for years, but I swear I could smell it, thick and curdled and sour. I sweated as the day baked hot, and shivered when the sun set and it grew cold. When I could see it was dark outside, I heard the slide of the metal bar. I stood, the paint chips and dirt clinging to my behind, my heart beating fast.

Mother threw in a blanket, barred the door, and left again.

I banged at the door, screaming that I hated them, that I was leaving. No one responded. I balanced on the galvanized tub to see if I could reach the window, but I lost my footing and crashed down. I wished that I would be struck by lightning, get measles, that our fields would catch fire or our chickens escape, so that they would have to speak to me. In my head I shrieked, *I'm here, see me,* but they didn't.

After that day, I began to get put in the shed for all manner of things, for I had a darkness inside me and it spilled out like vomit. I was put in when I did not find the last egg from a chicken and it rotted, or when I slopped milk over the side of the pail on the way to the house. When my footsteps sounded like buffalo, and this distracted Mother, or I was too quiet, slipping into the room like a cat and startling her so she missed a stitch. When she saw I'd used cursive on a school assignment when we had not learned cursive yet.

When I wasn't as good as Hen.

I learned to scan the situation, to listen under the kitchen window to assess what I would be facing whenever I returned home. If Mother was washing dishes, and the touch of a dish to the counter was especially hard, then I knew that Hen would suggest I go in the milk shed again. My heart raced, my stomach gurgled, the wheat moved, and I felt a loose rush of waste about to release. I knew I'd have to burn sage leaves to get rid of the stink I was going to leave in the outhouse.

I tried to not be too late or too early, too loud or too quiet, to stay out of Mother's and Hen's way. I sometimes succeeded. More often, they'd put me in the shed and go to bed, and as I rocked on the floor, grit against my legs, silence would settle on the milk shed like a damp quilt.

★ ★ ★

"Lena," Mother said, flapping a pair of peach-colored stockings over the washtub where my arms were elbow-deep in water. "What else, wash and dry them."

It was May of 1934. I was ten years old. And though other ladies may have worn stockings regularly, I did not know Mother even had a pair, and couldn't imagine why she might have bought them.

I took the wilted stockings from her and added them to the wash. I'd been at it for three hours already, taking buckets of creek water to the house, heating the water in a pot on the stove, then emptying those into the washtub. I grated more lye soap into the tub, my hands stinging, and rubbed it into the stockings. As soon as Mother left, I resumed singing, as I always did, my only way of resisting Mother and Hen. I'd listened to our hired men, passing through from Mexico, China, Quebec, Denmark, or Oklahoma, as they helped with the harvest, and added their songs to mine. I sang on the walks to school and the walks home. I sang when I gathered eggs. I sang to the cow. I knew about parties, even if we no longer attended them, and after everyone else was asleep in our house I'd slip out to Leon Bove's or Erik Eriksen's to hear them play records on their Victrolas or improvise on guitars and harmonicas. At night, Hen asleep next to me, I drummed out rhythms on my legs.

I sang through March 1931, when a huge snow fell and then a Chinook wind melted everything in sight, plunging water into Mill Creek, which flooded downtown Walla Walla. Alder Street became a choppy river, Poplar a mudbank, and Birch had water deep enough to canoe on. The water slurped up lawns and fences, even those belonging to the fine mansions on South Palouse and around Whitman College. Cars and trucks were swept away. Trout swam downtown. We all went to town to help, going after runaway animals and sloughing mud from buildings, and I gave out hard rolls and mugs of coffee and tried to keep everyone's spirits up by singing.

I sang through the bank failures. In 1932 People's State Bank on Main went broke and closed. The next year, Union Bank and First National shut their doors for two months too. Our teacher, who'd bitten her cuticles so much she was bleeding, let us throw spitballs in class that day. I came home to share what I thought was good news with Mother. The other banks closed, I told her excitedly when I found her standing outside the house, gazing vacantly at a broken gutter. The Bank of the West, which sent us letters about our mortgage, had not.

Mother sank, letting her forehead smash hard against the winter-hard ground.

As '33 rolled into '34, the county sheriff seized the Zumschneiders' farm and sold it off at auction, along with their two hundred head of cattle. Some neighbors refused to bid, while others thought it was better to have another farmer buy it than a bank. Down the road, the Melgaards' farm was in receivership, and we no longer saw little Bob Melgaard at school; we heard they'd gone back to Missouri to live with family. Hunter Fruit bought up land, and we heard little more of the

families that once farmed there. Foreclosure, default: my mother muttered these words during the day as she reviewed letters and ledger
books and our mortgage, a single sheet of type and signatures that she
kept in the bread box. The rare times Father was home, she shouted
the same words to him at night.

The years ground on. Bad harvests. Falling wheat prices. Father
coming home less and less. Tractors replacing mules so rapidly that
whatever money Father spent on the new technology of the mule
combine, he might as well have thrown in the oven. We always had
enough food, thanks to the kitchen garden, our Holstein, and our
chickens, so I did not fully comprehend what was happening. In early
'34, I took eggs to town and didn't get the price Mother wanted. Everyone has eggs to sell, I told her, and besides, the other farm people
have gone mad. They were selling their pots and pans on Main Street
for the price of penny candy, chairs and tables in exchange for a loaf
of bread.

She and Hen put me in the milk shed. We needed that money for
the mortgage payment, they said.

That mortgage, ever present. Mother talked about it as though it
were a living thing. In May 1934, the day after I washed and dried her
stockings, Mother pinned up her hair, fixed a cloche hat I'd never seen
to her head, like she was a lady going shopping at Jensen's, and put on
the stockings and pumps. She said she had an appointment at Bank
of the West. I knew what it had to be about. Once she left, I opened
the bread box and read the mortgage document. The bank's logo, a
sunrise over a jagged mountain, filled the center top. Below it, impos-
ing lettering declared "Bank of the West." "On May 19, 1934, without
grace, for value received, I promise to pay to the BANK OF THE WEST, on
order, the sum of, Five Hundred Dollars with interest thereon at the
rate of Seven Percent, according to, and secured upon, Land in Walla
Walla County, Wash., those certain parcels including W 1/2 NEW 1/4
of Section 30. . . ."

I didn't understand exactly what it meant, but I knew it wasn't good to have promised to give the bank five hundred dollars when our wheat had sold at forty-three cents a bushel the year before. The *Almanac* wasn't favorable for this year, and we had months of work and costs ahead of us to get to market. There'd be no harvest to sell by May 19. Five hundred dollars; I doubted all the safe-deposit boxes in the Baker Boyer Bank held that much money combined. For five hundred dollars, Father could buy the train line from here to Pasco. There was no way.

A few days later, Mother received a letter and went straight to town, again wearing her stockings. I read the letter once she left, examining first the envelope, the line drawing of a mountain and a rising sun above the return address. The letter was written in baffling language: "The Court will sell all tax-deeded . . . those certain parcels of land . . . W 1/2 NW 1/4 . . . If not redeemed . . ."

When she returned, orange dust on her stockings, she told me she'd tried to reach Father in the mountains via a telephone operator and then a wire, but hadn't succeeded. Hen tried to tell on me for reading the letter, but Mother didn't seem to understand anything Hen said to her, and Mother's words were muffled, herb-scented, sloppy. "Go to the Sorensons' place," she directed me, "and see when Gustav is next going in." Gus was a teenage neighbor who occasionally gave me rides to town when I had a load of things to sell, and he told me he'd be going there that afternoon. When I reported back to Mother, she piled up just about everything in our pantry into a crate: all those jams and jellies and preserved fruits and pickled vegetables. "There's a special on pectin at Purity," she said. "Buy more pectin and I can make more jams to sell." She gave me a gunnysack bag and sent me to the chicken coop, telling me to grab five chickens and as many eggs as I could. Mother even hurried down to milk the Holstein, though I'd milked the cow that morning, and then she added one bottle of watery milk to the crate. "Get as much as you can for it, Lena," she told me.

Gus dropped me off at the poultry market, where I hauled in my bag of squawking chickens and a dozen still-warm eggs, receiving a dollar for the chickens and fifteen cents for the eggs. I already knew a bottle of milk was worth nothing, so I gave it to a man waiting outside the YMCA with a bedroll for his turn to shower. I then dragged the crate of preserves over to Purity Grocery. The counterman said he could only take them as barter, not in return for cash, so I picked out boxes of pectin and baking soda, plus a few other goods, and put them in my crate.

It was a harsh sunny day, and too hot to wander around. I knew Gus always spent afternoons playing billiards at Lutcher's, so I lingered in the bit of shade that Purity's awning offered. A few steps away, two men whose shoes were almost as worn as mine leaned against the store. One had a long angular face, and sweat rolled down it and caught in its crags. The other wore a flat cap in a checkered pattern. They shared a paper sack of peanuts, shooting shells from their mouth so they ricocheted off the sidewalk.

The door to Purity opened, and a round-faced, red-cheeked woman came out, carrying a package of brown paper tied with string. One of the men took off his hat; the other kicked the shells against the storefront. "Hello, Doris," the men said, and they all greeted each other, nice and friendly, and then the cap man asked why she was at Purity herself.

"Another of the hired girls has up and left us, so here's Doris carrying around groceries like a pack horse, when I should be preparing dinner for the Feasleys," she said.

The men asked if she wanted help with her package, but Doris said no. "It's just ham and grapefruits, so none too heavy, even for me. Oh! Here's the judge now. He'll be wanting to know the order arrived fine. Excuse me, fellas." She bustled off to meet her employer, who was leaving the shoeshine parlor. He used a cane.

The craggy man cracked another peanut. "Ham and grapefruits," he said. "Weren't cans of grapefruit or ham, neither. Both fresh."

The man in the hat spit out a long string of phlegm. "No one's got money for groceries except for the judges, I guess," he said. "Poor

Doris, she's not even going to get a taste of it even when she cooks it up for him."

Ham, grapefruit, a cook: this Judge was rich. I hoisted my crate to my shoulder and hurried after him as he went into a hat store. Though Doris kept walking, I waited. When he left the store, I saw a man who seemed as old as a grandpa, with lines etched deep from his nostrils to his mouth, but they didn't look like smile lines at all. His eyebrows clamped close together, and his horn-rimmed glasses were black on top, clear on the bottom.

I stayed behind him as he turned on South Palouse, passing the Carnegie Library and Wa-Hi on his left. On the right were houses that got finer and finer. They had balconies, columns, carriage houses, wooden footbridges over creeks. My crate rubbed against the scratchy fabric of my dress as I took them all in.

I'd never been this far down South Palouse; it couldn't have felt more off-limits to an Anna like me if it'd had a rope across the middle of the street. Just before the road curved at Juniper, the Judge's cane paused at the biggest house I'd ever seen. It was made of brown wood crossed with planks of white, liked an iced gingerbread cookie, and had iron gates, and lit gas lamps though it was daytime.

The Judge left his front door open for a few seconds as he called to someone, and inside I could see thick rugs and a bright light, what I would later learn was called a chandelier. I lingered outside, collecting more useful information. On the second floor, I saw a little boy's face at one of the windows, and then a stern young woman behind him, too young to be his mother, holding a baby. After a while I saw a different woman step outside wearing a green suit, a triple strand of pearls around her neck and a green hat on top of her washed-and-set hair. This had to be the Judge's wife: she was dressed exactly as I guessed a woman who ate grapefruit and ham all day would be dressed. Her eyes darted left and right as though she thought a hobo would attack her here on her shiny sunny street, and she drew her purse against her belly. Though I did not know what I wanted from that house, the phrase Doris had used returned to me, perhaps the only framework available that could fit someone like me into a place like this: *hired girl*.

As I made my way back to Purity to meet Gus Sorenson, I memorized the house's address.

When I returned home, I gave Mother the little money we'd made. It wasn't enough to save us. The note came due, and I was gone within a month.

★ 5 ★

"I'm sure glad to see all of you out there this afternoon," I said into a mic from the stage of Lake Winnie's Country Junction. Empty seats gaped at me like missing teeth. Barely fifty people had showed up to an outdoor venue that could've held ten times that, and they appeared more interested in their bags of popcorn and beers than in me. "It's nice to be back on the road again. I'm Lillian Waters, better known as Water Lil, and we're gonna start with one of my favorites, 'Three-Quarter Time.'"

I'd meant to have just a couple more sips of the whiskey in my bus bedroom, a balm to soothe the chafing from the reporter's questions, Kaori's inexperience, and my nerves, but then I had a glass of it, followed by another, and two felt so good that I had a third. The day before, when Patrice Aguillard picked me up at my house on Old Hickory Lake, outside Nashville, and got my things onto the Green Giant, he'd noted how heavy my suitcases were. I'd told him it was because of all the liquor bottles inside, which he thought was a joke. Patrice, a short, broad-shouldered man with a booming baritone, had also loaded in my two old trunks, filled with costumes, shoes, makeup, and wigs that had all been in storage since 1975, relics of me at my peak. Patrice was a math teacher during the school year, but spent summers with country bands, driving the bus, helping with equipment, and keeping everyone on schedule. He and I had become fast friends after deciding to change the letters on the front of the Green Giant, the ones that usually say the band's name, to read "Here Comes Trouble."

While he drove the bus north, I'd worked on my set lists, but all the songs seemed stale. "Three-Quarter Time," which I'd sung in a duet with Tammy Wynette for the '68 Country Music Awards; "Water Lil," my first number 1 hit, which I'd sung at every gig I'd ever played. Who'd want to hear me now, at fifty-six and gone from the scene for five years, which in music might as well be three centuries, singing my old warhorses with a scratchy voice? What was I doing? Pursuing some idea I had of sweeping into Walla Walla and causing Hen to fall to her knees in regret, as though that would fix everything? Meanwhile, though I'd always been the one who worked harder than anyone else, I hadn't even bothered to rehearse my band.

Between the whiskeys, I listened to Patrice call out updates through my locked bedroom door at prompt five-minute intervals. The Farvers had arrived only half an hour earlier, with barely enough time to unload and plug in. Chick or Chip, the guitarist, had finally gotten here and wanted to run through chords. I told Patrice everyone would have to wait, and tried to figure out what to wear. For my recent penny-ante shows arranged by Stanley, I'd been wearing headscarves, palazzo pants, and spangled sweaters, since my old getups didn't fit; for this tour, though, I'd vowed to wear my old costumes, and had put myself on a diet of whiskey and carrots.

I pawed around the bottom of a trunk for a girdle, and the one I tugged out smelled of old skin and talcum powder. I sucked my torso in and hooked it on. It pinched, but with one more gasp I got the final hook in. Over it I zipped up a Nudie Cohn dress, floor-length and sleeveless, beige with colorful flowers bursting across the bodice.

In a mirror I could see bulges on my back and hair that had never recovered from the years of Atomic Fire Ball–red dye jobs, so I rooted around until I found a stocking cap and a wig of red ringlets, and fastened both of those on. Then I did my best to mimic the hair and makeup that my stylists used to do for me when they accompanied me on tour. *"Dumskalle,"* I told my unprepared, unrehearsed self.

We'd been allotted an hour onstage at Lake Winnie, to be followed by the southern-rock singer. Behind the stage I spotted the Farvers—Gene and Tommy Reed, my bass player and my steel guitarist—both sunburned to a bright red, but didn't have time to hug them or even shake Chick-Chip's hand. I ran through the set list in three minutes, describing what I wanted for each song, the feeling and the rhythm and the key, while ear pain started and I wished I'd brought whiskey to drink during our set. Kaori, still braless, played a few notes on her fiddle. Chip-Chick asked about time signatures and again about keys. "For Pete's sake," I said, "I thought you could play, so play." It was only when I took my Tele from its case that I realized none of my Nashville-era performance costumes had pockets in them for my guitar picks, as my Nashville producer hadn't let me play guitar. Panicking, I stuck a couple of picks into my wig.

As the promoter introduced me, I felt sweat pool between my breasts and start trickling down the backs of my legs. I gulped in air, took the stage to scattered applause, plugged my guitar into my amp, greeted the audience, and played the first notes of "Three-Quarter Time." It was about a gal messing around with a married man, and the "three-quarter time" referred to the period he spent with his wife and not with her; the song's rhythm was, of course, three-quarter time, a waltz. I'd written and recorded it in '71, when it charted at number 2. The beginning sounded shrieky and off, as if none of us had tuned our instruments, but settled into the right sound—almost. It wasn't until Chip-Chick tried a melodic line a few phrases in that I could tell he was playing in the wrong key. I tried to catch his eye, but he was looking at his guitar like it was in charge of him and not the other way around.

"Stop," I said. "Stop." It rang out into the mic. I faced Chip-Chick, so the audience couldn't hear me. "Get in the right goddamn key," I told him. To the audience, I said, "Sorry about that. We're gonna take that up one more time. And a one-two-three." Though Chick-Chip stopped playing for some reason, and the song sounded hollow without the rhythm guitar, a body without a spine, we got through it.

When we finished, I glared at Chip-Chick, my back to the mic. "You ready to actually play?"

"I was ready before. You gave me the wrong—"

"I gave you the wrong nothing. You figure out how to play guitar in the next couple of minutes, or I'll boot you out of here. You ever performed in your life?"

"You gonna sing?" yelled someone in the audience.

I needed a fast song. I looped my finger in a circle, signaling to the band—or at least to the Farvers, who'd played with me many times—that I was switching up the set list. "Next up, I'm gonna play an old favorite that I hope you'll stomp your feet to," I said.

The microphone sneered into a squeal, a casualty of having skipped sound check.

"Fix your microphone!" someone shouted from the crowd.

"It's, ah, it's called 'Jackson,' and you might've heard Johnny Cash and June Carter give it a go, and here's our version." I patted my hair until I found a guitar pick, extracted it, and played the opening notes with a combination of picking and plucking with my free fingers. I hoped that Tommy Reed or Gene would be intuitive enough to fill in the lines Johnny sang, so I could take June's.

The guitarist, now red-cheeked, strummed slower than me, neither of the Farvers picked up the vocals, and two lines in I was flailing. I pointed at Tommy Reed so he'd take over with a steel-guitar solo, then eyed Chip or Chick. "What in the name of . . . ?"

"Guess I never performed in my life," he said, with a meant-to-look-dumb smile on his face.

"Amateur."

I ran through "Jackson" almost automatically while I thought through what to play next. A hefty man in the audience held a silver beer can, moving his forearm back and forth from the elbow, as though he were about to hurl it right at me. "Sing Debby Boone!" he shouted.

Fine, I thought. Debby Boone was inoffensive, at least. I thought of the song of hers that had been all over the radio for months now, "Are You on the Road to Lovin' Me Again." Since I'd been a kid, I'd been able to hear a song once and recall near all of its lyrics. How'd this one start? Those silly synthesized chimes opened it, I recalled, and then "Are you here, just to pass the time of day?"

My band would wonder what I was doing, but at least I wouldn't get a beer-can dent in my forehead.

I finished up "Jackson," a stew of overcooked sound, and whirled around. The Farvers were both sweating. "Can you pick up 'Are You on the Road to Lovin' Me Again?'" I asked.

"Gene and I can," Tommy Reed said.

"Kaori?"

"I'll improvise," she said.

I didn't bother asking the guitarist; if he didn't know it, then he couldn't mess it up.

"Key of C," I said. "I'll kick it off."

Into the mic, I said, "I hear y'all, you want modern tunes!" I used the pick to strum a C chord and jumped into the song, and found my left hand knew where to go to keep the song moving, from C to F, from D7 to G7. Tommy Reed matched me on steel, Gene kept a good rhythm, and Kaori figured out embellishments. Chip-Chick set his jaw and gazed at the horizon rather than looking for cues from me, but at least he was keeping up with the chords. When I got into the second verse, I saw the old boys in the audience clanking the heels of their boots against the ground—to someone else's song.

"You get ready to sing along, all right?" I called as we launched into the chorus, and a few of the audience members did. The crowd actually clapped when we finished, so I followed up with Crystal Gayle's "Talking in Your Sleep," then a few songs from Barbara Mandrell and all the modern pop-country crooners I'd just told the reporter weren't worth a dime. Two guitar picks flew out of my wig as I shimmied around the stage and told jokes between songs. Finally, mercifully, in my peripheral vision I saw the Lake Winnie manager raise his arm: our hour was up. I was about to douse the Farver boys in celebratory whiskey for having survived the gig when I noticed the reporter in the second row. She twisted her head around on her long neck, taking in the audience's reaction.

I'd forgotten she was there. It could be syndicated nationwide if it was newsworthy, she'd said. Her story would be something about how not only had I torpedoed my career in '75, but on my first tour in years, I'd ripped off contemporary acts I'd just dismissed as no good. Stanley would call in a snit. Promoters who'd lined up other shows in other towns would read the piece and see that I was washed up and messed up. I'd be bad Lillian, difficult Lillian, no-wonder-she-can't-get-any traction Lillian. *Arga katter får rivet skinn*, as Hen used to say. It might become a taunt: Hey, Water Lil, whose music you're gonna play tonight?

I kept my eyes on the beat-up ground the whole way to the bus and poured myself a double whiskey into a paper cup as soon as I was inside.

Tommy Reed came in as I was returning a whiskey bottle to the bus's front cupboard. He looked at it but didn't say anything.

"Some way to kick off a tour," I said.

He grunted, took a packet of chewing tobacco from his pocket, and climbed into his bunk, one of several in the middle of the bus, then drew the privacy curtain across.

When his brother climbed up the bus stairs, I asked, "Where's that guitarist?"

"Having a smoke," Gene said.

"Go get him, would you?"

He sent the guitarist in but didn't return himself. Chip or Chick loomed in the bus's doorway, pinching a cigarette.

"You got nothing to say to me after that show?" I said.

He took a drag and puffed the smoke from his mouth. "Three of my buddies said no to this gig before I took it, and they said I'd regret it," he said. "They said Lillian Waters has a hell of a reputation, that she's out for herself and chews through everyone around her, and I didn't listen to them."

"Says you? You can't even tune a damn guitar."

"You said key of A for 'Three-Quarter Time.'"

"I've been singing that song for more than a decade. You think I don't know what key it's in? Then playing off tempo on the second song? You don't mess with an audience like that when they paid money to see your show."

"I'm pretty sure they weren't paying money to see *your* show. Didn't you see how many of them were wearing T-shirts for the next act?"

I'd hurled the drink at him before I realized it. The whiskey splashed onto my shoes, and the paper cup sailed to the ground in a soft, unsatisfying arc.

He tramped down the bus stairs. "Enjoy your drinking. You don't have to fire me; I quit."

"Get out," I said. It came out between a shriek and a cry, feeling like it stripped my vocal cords even further. I rubbed my neck hard as he left.

"Lil." Tommy Reed was in his bunk with the curtain drawn, so his voice was muffled.

"What?"

"That boy was out of line, but you did tell him that 'Three-Quarter Time' would be in A."

"I've never played 'Three-Quarter Time' in A. I've always played it in G."

"That's what I thought, but I started in A, and had to adjust real fast to G. Your fiddler did, too. That's why it sounded so strange at the start."

I sat down in a booth, facing the windshield. I was sure I'd said G, not A, but Tommy Reed didn't get things like this wrong. Now Chip-Chick could add that to whatever tales he'd tell around Nashville: Lillian Waters, washed up, drunk, as impossible to work with as ever, and doesn't even know the keys to her own songs. "Tommy Reed," I said. "You know any good guitarists?"

"I know a dozen of 'em, but you need a bandleader, Lil," he said. "Gene and I play as good as anyone, but we can't translate what you're saying half the time. I get that you want the music to be a certain way, but how you're telling it to us, it don't make sense."

The bus's door was open, and I heard the crowd roar. The southern-rock singer must be up. We were parked too far back for me to hear what he was saying, but the audience laughed, and I wondered if he was warming them up by making fun of me. It took me right back to being a little girl at school in Walla Walla, when I had to take my shoes off to get my feet measured and everyone saw the soggy cardboard in mine meant to cover the holes in the soles.

"You gonna fire me, too, for telling you that?" Tommy Reed asked.

"Nah, you're like a weed, Mac; if I tried to cut you, you'd just crop back up in Owensboro or Louisville or wherever we're playing next. Besides, you can play steel guitar better than most."

"Figure so." His voice sounded faded, that slow talk before someone drifts off to sleep.

"Tommy Reed, you and Gene came on this tour because we've played together so much, and you know me and I know you and we all get along. But I couldn't hire a fiddler I knew. Couldn't get a guitarist. You think I chew through people, like that boy said, that I'm just out for myself?"

I waited for a response from his bunk, but only heard a snore.

I went to the bedroom, I unpinned my wig, and fluffed up my real hair. My plain-Jane Swedish hair had started out flaxen and darkened to dishwater as I aged. I'd learned how to do pin curls when I worked at the Judge's, and in Tacoma, I used rollers. Later, when I made enough money, I graduated to salon wash-and-sets before upgrading to my personal hairstylist. Now, I couldn't grow it beyond a couple inches of dry brownish-gray tufts. I unclipped mother-of-pearl earrings that hung like fat teardrops from my sagging earlobes, so giant that they could be seen from the cheap seats, and put them in the trunk's tray. In the mirror, I pressed my cheekbones, which were still high, and touched my jawline, sharp enough to slice a Granny Smith. But age had carved canyons under my eyes, my eyebrows had all but disappeared, and my neck was a wrinkly mess.

Pressure was setting in between my ears, which the doctor had said would keep happening unless I got my vocal cord cut up. I tapped out three aspirin from a bottle, letting them dissolve into a bitter mash on my tongue, and pressed my knuckles against my temples.

I changed into trousers and a shirt, put a cough drop in my pocket, and tied a scarf around my hair. I'd passed a pay phone on my way back from meeting with the reporter, and as I left the room, I tucked my address book under my arm. I needed to call someone.

★ 6 ★

Walla Walla, Washington
1934

The night I left, I slept in a work dress, waiting in bed for Hen's breathing to even, wishing Father wasn't on the road so I could sing with him one last time. But I had to go.

Sunset. The farrowed rows of the hills glowed red. Ducks' shrieks lifted from the creek. I counted our hills, the near ridge, the far ridge, the camelback ridge to the East, the old Melgaard farm to the west. The mountains blued. Chickens nestled in hay and sheep folded themselves in neighbors' fields. The air smelled of cold, clean water and toasted hay.

The moon cast silver light on Hen's face. I wanted to grab a fistful of her thick brown hair. I wanted her to bleed like I had bled. I wanted to stop time that day I found Mother and Hen in the parlor with the man in the city hat, dirt on my hands.

It was too late, though. Life moves forward, not backward.

I slept only a few hours. I woke when it was time.

"All girls sacrifice for their families," Hen had said to me. I'd done my part.

I reached under the bed and tugged out a flour sack I'd sewn straps onto earlier in the week. It contained the other dress I owned, underclothes, winter boots, a sliver of soap, a hairbrush, and fifty cents I'd stolen from Mother's cash box. It was three miles to town, and I planned to walk there before it got too hot or too light. I tiptoed down the stairs and out the kitchen door, grabbing an almost-ripe zucchini from the kitchen garden in case I needed food. Despite my early start, I was sweating and covered in grit when I arrived on the outskirts of town. At the Northern Pacific switching yards I cleaned myself up as best I could, using ice left over from the re-icing stations for the refrigerator cars. I pinched my cheeks, smoothed my hair, and went to wait downtown until it became a reasonable hour.

As I walked on East Main, which I chose because it kept me a safe distance from Bank of the West on Alder, I realized that I needed to do two other things. First, I'd better get myself a new name so no one connected me with the Thorsell farm. The Liberty Theater was advertising a movie called *Hell Bent for Love*, and I picked Lillian from the name of its star, Lilian Bond, adding an extra *l* because it sounded more solid, respectable. Then I added Waters, as Walla Walla meant "many waters" in one of the Indian languages. Second, I saw a sign in the window of the drugstore for an assistant registered pharmacist, and it said "Letter of Reference Required." I knew about these—a senior hired man had come with one—so I waited until the Book Nook opened, bought a sheet of paper and borrowed a pen, and wrote a letter in my best cursive recommending Lillian Waters as a hired girl. I signed the letter with a made-up name and the town of Waitsburg, Washington. I knew Waitsburg was a place the train ran and hoped it was far enough off that Judge Feasley wouldn't bother verifying it.

It was less than a mile to the Feasleys' grand brown-and-white house. I knocked on the side door and recognized the woman who answered as Doris the cook. I told her that I'd heard from the Shady Lawn milkman that a hired girl had just left and they might need household help, and Doris fetched Judge Feasley. After some time I heard the tap of his cane, and he reopened the door and examined me through his glasses.

The trick was to look plain and poor and proper, which I could do easily: I was plain and poor, and proper—well, I could look the part. I told the Judge I'd lost my mama at birth and my daddy died logging. I said I'd been a hired girl in Waitsburg, and came here after my Waitsburg employer moved to Seattle, and I presented the letter I'd worked up that morning. I worked hard and for cheap, I said.

"I suppose we could use another girl," the Judge said.

★ 7 ★

Rossville, Georgia
June 1980

At a pay phone outside a bank of restrooms, the scent of chili dogs and bleach in the air, I opened my address book to H. On that page, I found a name with dozens of crossed-out numbers and addresses beside it. I put a bunch of coins in the phone's slot and dialed the most recent number, one with a Tennessee area code.

I popped a cough drop in my mouth as the phone rang. "It's Lillian Waters," I said as soon as Charlie picked up.

Seconds ticked by, but he didn't respond; he was about the only person who could wait me out. Eventually I said, "I'm sorry."

"What's that?"

I pushed two fingers against my throat. "I said, I'm sorry. For interrupting your recording session."

"Lillian," Charlie said, "I know this is your first time apologizing in your whole life, so here's how you do it: 'I'm sorry for pulling you out of your recording session, Charlie. I'm sorry I worried you by saying it was an emergency. That wasn't right and I shouldn't have done it.'"

Thing was, had I gotten up the nerve that day at the bar to tell

Charlie about my diagnosis, I don't think he would've minded missing half his session. Instead, I'd let him think that I'd interrupted his recording just to chat about some cockeyed notion of a tour that I had. I hadn't even worked up the courage to ask him to join it before he'd stormed off.

"How's my dog behaving?" I said. Red the Fourth wasn't actually mine, but since I'd been there the day Charlie took her home, I felt I had some claim to her.

"She's fine. She's the best. Stole my ice cream cone straight from my hand yesterday. You're not changing the subject. Go on with your apology."

"You gonna make this hard?"

"And enjoy every minute."

"Okay, I'm sorry for calling you out of your session. Wasn't nice of me."

"Because?"

"Because musicians don't interrupt each other's sessions, especially when it's not a real emergency."

Silence, again. A kid with a pinwheel lollipop passed me and stuck out his tongue, which was dark purple from the candy. I stuck out mine right back at him.

"Isn't it your turn to say something now? Like, 'I accept your apology?'" I said.

I could hear Charlie chewing something, and he took time to swallow before he responded. "Well, I never expected an apology from you, so I'm not sure what to say."

"Before you accept it, I got something else to ask you."

"Christ, Lil, what have you done now?"

"I haven't done anything." I heard noise from the stage. "Well, I've kind of done something. I'm on the road. Just played my first gig."

"You're actually touring?"

"I'm calling you from Lake Winnie, where I just about got booed off the stage tonight, so yeah, looks that way."

"Hah." Charlie made a half-chortling, half-coughing sound when something intrigued him. "About time. How does it feel?"

"It feels like I don't know how to sing and play anymore."

"Keep going. It'll get easier."

"That's the thing about tours, Charlie. Nowhere to go but to the next date, right? I'm working the road in style, anyway. I rented a tour bus and I got us a road manager and driver, Patrice. I'm calling it the Farewell Tour."

"Good gimmick, though I know you; you're not giving up performing."

I balled up the cough-drop wrapper. "Course not, but I'll say anything to sell tickets. The problem is, I just fired the guitarist—"

"Lillian—"

"And the band needs a leader. I understand exactly what I'm telling them about the music, but it's not getting through."

"Well, Lil, you can't just yell when something sounds bad. You got to give them cues and rhythms. They're musicians."

"Sorry I'm not as learned in the way of music as you are," I said, pronouncing *learned* in two syllables. "I'm not calling to complain, though. I'm calling to ask you to come on tour with us. Like I said, I need a bandleader, and you know my songs sound better when you're on guitar. Or harmonica, mandolin; you can play whatever you want."

"I can't, Lil. I just got a call about playing on the new Sylvia album. She's recording in two weeks."

"Excuse me, I think I have the wrong person. I wanted to talk to Charlie Hagerty, the country player? Sylvia's pretty much singing disco these days. You didn't say yes, did you?"

"Not yet, but—"

"So you're available."

"Also, Donna'd kill me. I was just doing sessions morning to night, and I promised her we'd take a vacation when I was done."

"Donna won't kill you, at least not until you've made an honest woman of her."

"I proposed to her last week, actually."

I pressed a finger to my throat again, sure I felt something unyielding this time. I'd expected Charlie to put off proposing to his latest girlfriend, a young thing with a Lady Di haircut and a habit of phrasing sentences as questions, for a while longer. The one declarative thing she'd said in the time I'd spent with her was that she preferred chocolate-dipped ice cream to plain. I'd named her Donna the Dip in my head.

"Third time's the charm, they say," I said, forcing an onstage smile, even though Charlie couldn't see me. "Anyway, that's good news; if you've proposed, then you got leeway with Donna. Charlie, come on. This is summer on the road, decent pay, and the main thing, real country music. Like we used to play." I laid it out for him: after Lake Winnie, dates in Tennessee, Kentucky, and Missouri, then west and even farther west to Bakersfield, California, the nexus of Western country music, where I'd once lived and performed. "And Tacoma, Charlie. We're playing Tacoma. Think of that. We can go to the honky-tonks we used to play at, go around town, see the port again. We'll do a bunch of my old songs; we can work in any stuff you want, too. The Farvers are here. It'll be like it used to be. Egads, you don't want to be playing synthesizer for Sylvia. You want 'Foggy Mountain Breakdown,' 'Take Me Back to Tulsa.' Come out on the road with us. You're the best musician I know. The best bandleader."

"Like you'd know. You've never had a good bandleader because you want to be in charge of everything."

"I'm saying I'll let you do your thing."

"That means you have to step back sometimes, let me take over."

"I hear you."

"Do you?"

I examined the phone dial, wondering what committee had made the decision to assign three letters to each number.

He took another bite of whatever he was eating, talking through a full mouth. "You finishing up in Tacoma, then?"

"No. The last concert's in Walla Walla."

He whistled. "No kidding. You're finally going back?"

"Well, we're performing at the fairgrounds, and I figure it's my last, best chance to be queen of the Southeastern Washington Fair."

"Will you see your sister, then?"

I'd long had a clear notion that Hen was living in a mansion on Boyer Avenue, near Whitman College. Sometimes when I was on tour I passed those big newspaper kiosks that had every paper from all over the world, and I'd buy a *Walla Walla Union-Bulletin* and read it straight through. I'd always be expecting to find a mention of Hen, but she never made the papers. I could've hired an investigator to track her down, I suppose, but I had no interest in seeing photographs of her or finding her address. I wanted to show up, in person, and find out why she'd done what she'd done to me. "See her, perform for her, kick her in the shins, one of the above," I said. I flattened a kernel of popcorn with my toe. "Charlie . . . Charlie, will you come?"

As the silence stretched, I had the awful sense I might cry. I held the receiver away so he couldn't hear me if I did.

"Doggone it, Lillian," he said finally. "I do like being on the road, and I don't know that I can say no to the thought of you having to actually listen to me for once."

"You just want to see if I still play better guitar than you," I said, but my smile was so big all I could see in my reflection in the pay phone were my teeth.

"'Still?'" he repeated, laughing. "When did you ever play guitar better than me?"

He told me he could get there for our Friday date in Owensboro, and when I gave him the name of the venue, he was nice enough not to mention how long it'd been since he'd had to play a high school.

Charlie hung up, and I cradled the receiver against my ear, listening to the even buzz of the dial tone. I bought another snack-stand Coke, opened it, and gave it to Patrice when I got back to the bus. He was ready to start for our next stop; Kaori, Tommy Reed, and Gene were in their bunks, rustling around but not talking.

I washed the gunk off my face, brushed my teeth, and got into bed. It was light out, but the day had sucked the energy from me, and we wouldn't be stopping for dinner for a few hours. As soon as Patrice hit the gas, I relaxed into a nap despite the swaying of the bed. Even if it felt like I was in the ricketiest cradle in the whole world, at least I was moving once more.

★ 8 ★

Walla Walla, Washington
1934–1940

Work at the Feasleys was easy for me compared to what I'd had to do at the farm. I took delivery of ice blocks from Tausick and Kauffman in the mornings and put them in the icebox, then brought in milk and cream from Shady Lawn. I cooked the Feasleys breakfast—eggs and bacon—and made coffee, as Doris did not arrive until eight. I helped her serve dinner, and washed dishes. I did laundry with the Feasleys' new electric machine. I swept, I mended, I drained the icebox. I did anything the housekeeper told me to do, and helped Doris when she needed a hand, or Elsbeth, the Swiss au pair looking after the Feasleys' two young children. The only task I detested was putting out the empty Shady Lawn bottles, which reeked of sour milk no matter how thoroughly I rinsed them.

If the Feasleys weren't hosting or attending a party on a Saturday night, Mrs. Feasley went to her bedroom after dinner and the Judge went to his study. Once I cleaned up from the meal, I was allowed a couple of hours off. I spent it looking for music. In the Judge's neighborhood, when folks left their windows open, I could sometimes hear foxtrots or big bands from their phonographs and radios. What I wanted was closer to what I'd sung with Father or the hired men, music that conjured up hand clapping and feet tapping instead of a fussy ballroom.

I found it up near the Northern Pacific tracks one Saturday evening. Kids playing jump rope and marbles filled the streets, so I could wander among them without being noticed. Several of the houses were playing the same radio program, all at full volume. I heard the announcer shouting about Alka-Seltzer, then a fiddle sawing away.

A little girl skipped toward me. "What's this program?" I asked her.

"*Barn Dance*," she said. "It's on every Saturday night."

I sat down on the curb like I had every right to be there. There were songs about cowboys, there was a vibrating hoo-hoo singing called yodeling, there was Patsy Montana and the Girls of the Golden West. I wished I'd brought paper so I could write down all the songs, all the lyrics, all the names.

I came back the next Saturday I had free, scouted out a willow tree, and sat underneath it, its drooping branches covering me. At the stroke of seven o'clock I heard, "Hello, hello, it's *National Barn Dance* time." I kept returning. One night, I heard fast fiddling and saw teardrops on my arm and understood I was crying for the first time since leaving the farm. I wasn't sure why until the singer began the lyrics to "Bo-Weavil Blues." I wanted her to stop right away, and I wanted her to sing forever, and then the first stars were coming out and I needed to get back to the Judge's and it felt like I was a piece of laundry wrung out to dry.

Though I'd gotten myself from my farm into town, I didn't yet have a plan for getting out of town. My wages mostly went to school supplies and clothes and the occasional candy; what I had left at the end of the week was barely enough to pay for a horse opera at the Roxy.

Then, when I was twelve or so and had been working at the Judge's for two years, I heard Lulu Belle and Scotty on *Barn Dance*. I knew from Ma Rainey that women could write and sing songs, so I wasn't startled to hear Lulu Belle's voice. This time, though, the announcer said, "That was our Lulu Belle on guitar." A woman could play guitar: that, I didn't know. Whenever I had a few minutes after an errand after that, I lingered at Bendix Music on East Main, studying the guitars in its windows. One week a new one appeared. Unlike the others, which had violin cutouts at the sides, this guitar had a round hole in the middle and shiny light wood, deepening to dark wood at the outer edges. It cost forty dollars, an unfathomable amount for me; I made a dollar and a quarter a week.

After a few weeks of gawking, I followed a rich-looking family into the store so the Bendix owners would assume I was with them, and asked about the guitar. A young salesman gave me a catalog from the maker, Gretsch, and said I could come back and read it anytime.

I took him up on that, studying the catalog's description of the guitar I wanted, the Gretsch Model Forty Hawaiian, every time I passed Bendix. "Six-string Hawaiian Guitar. Auditorium-Special size. Its tremendous depth, power, and richness of tone have made this model an outstanding favorite among recording and broadcasting artists." I can still recite every word of it: smoked-pearl headpiece inlaid in mother-of-pearl, ebony bridge, flat top of old spruce.

I knew that Gretsch would be my escape. I needed it, and I would get it.

I was in ninth grade at Wa-Hi by then, and I was twelve years old, but since I'd lied about my age to the Feasleys, I was officially fourteen. Wa-Hi was the only high school in town, and when I started there, I scurried along the hallways, always ready to duck into an empty classroom if I spotted Hen. Sometimes, as I did my work at the Feasleys', I thought of the farm. I imagined Mother and Hen fretting about me, Father returning and quizzing them: How could you let her go? Why weren't you kinder to her? Why didn't we see how much she did? I thought of Hen's delicate hands chafing from washing with lye soap, and wondered if she was getting locked in the milk shed in my place.

These were dreams. When I was being truthful with myself, I wasn't sure Father was planning on coming back at all, and if Mother or Hen wanted to find me, they probably could have. I didn't want to chance running into them, though, so I avoided the road into town that Mother or Hen would've used, and if Doris asked me to go to Purity Grocery, I went to Beck & Winans instead.

At Wa-Hi, though, there was no trace of Hen. I mentioned the name Henrietta Thorsell to one or two teachers, but it didn't seem to mean anything to them. I knew she couldn't have been so forgettable. When finally I thought to look at the school's annual from the year before, Hen's perfect face with the round eyes and the glossy brown hair was not on the class-officer pages, nor in the social clubs. I could only guess that Mother must've sent her away to school, to Boise, to Seattle, so that when Hen returned to Walla Walla she would no longer be thought of as an Anna, and could marry a town boy instead of a farm boy.

In a Wa-Hi hallway, a boy who'd gone to my grammar school stopped and said "Lena?" I bent my head so my hair fell around my face, and said "Who?" I saw he wasn't moving on, so I threw my head back and scowled. "You mean me? No, I'm the fire-eater; if you're looking for the peep show, that's two tents down." He didn't talk to me again. I had no interest in these high school boys nicknamed Ozro and Jitterbug, in any case, not even when I grew taller, when I had to buy bigger brassieres every six months, not when my hips added flesh and my waist seemed to shrink. My hair was a lank dark blond, my skin and eyebrows overly pale, and my clothes were ugly and didn't fit, but these were things that could be fixed, and the boys didn't care so much about them. When they looked me over, though, I didn't reciprocate. They spent their free time playing vermin safari at the dump, shooting at rats. They could no more afford a guitar than I could.

I was not friends with the girls, either, but I found them more in-structive. Most of them didn't pay attention to me, given my drab hair and my faded dresses. Even when my body changed, I was practically invisible to them, which let me observe them. I watched one false-faint like a movie heroine in the girls' bathroom, and another whisper and widen her eyes at every word spoken by her baseball-player boyfriend. Then, about six months after I first saw the Gretsch, I picked up Mrs. Feasley's dry cleaning one afternoon. On the way back I passed a tavern on the edge of Mill Creek and saw a popular brunette just a grade above me sitting at a table and sipping a bright drink from a cocktail glass. She was with an older man who I recognized from one of the Judge's dinner parties; it was not a relation of hers. She dropped a handkerchief, covered her mouth in a giggle, then bent over, her backside to the man, to pick it up. I noticed the way he stared at her rear end, like a cattle dog ready to mount.

That night, in the attic room I shared with Elsbeth, the au pair, I sweated through my sheets. I had violent dreams about a subterranean bordello, its doorframes lined with red satin, the brunette describing to me what things the women in each room specialized in as I tried to run away. A hallway led down one empty dirt corridor to another; it was a closed rabbit warren, a trap. I woke myself up with my cries, but the warren was waiting for me as soon as I thrashed into sleep again.

In the dining room the next morning, I poured coffee for the Judge, and as he reached for the china cup's handle, I jerked the coffeepot toward me, splashing hot liquid across my bare forearm, but I did not make a sound. Later the burn blistered in a line, oozing with liquid thick as Vaseline. I burst it with a pin as I told myself: Go on. Just go.

And I did. I spent my meager savings at Penney to buy a close-fitting shirt and a brassiere that lifted and pointed my breasts. I hemmed a skirt Elsbeth had handed down to me so it would show more of my legs. I told her as she shut off the lights one night that I was sweet on a boy from Wa-Hi, and she took me to the five-and-dime and helped me buy products. In our room, she demonstrated how to pin-curl my hair overnight, and how to use the tip of my new lipstick to create a bow mouth, and how to use the same black drawing pencil I used for art class to create a thin arch on top of my light eyebrows. As I imitated her, she teased me in her gentle Swiss accent. "He is fair or dark?" she asked. "You prefer eyes which are blue or brown?" I blotted the lipstick like she indicated, avoiding eye contact, for I thought if she looked at me directly, she would realize what I was planning.

★ ★ ★

It was a Saturday night. The Feasleys were home, Mrs. Feasley in her bedroom, the Judge in his study. I'd served them dinner and cleaned up. I could've had the night off, could've been listening to *National Barn Dance*, but instead I ran a comb through my pin curls, applied lipstick to my lips and cheeks, and put on my brassiere, new shirt, and short skirt.

I knew the Judge would be working on his manuscript in his study. He was writing about Marcus and Narcissa Whitman, a missionary couple who'd come from the East to Fort Walla Walla in the 1830s. The Judge was awfully proud of his connection to the Whitmans, who were distant relatives of his, and whenever the staff gathered for things like Christmas or Easter, he tended to lecture us about them. They were revered throughout town, too; Walla Walla's private Whitman College was named after them, and our history lessons began in 1836, the year they arrived here. They didn't seem to be very good missionaries, though, and kept squabbling with the Indians and complaining about them. Distrust spread, and after a measles outbreak, some Cayuse suspected Marcus, a doctor, was poisoning them rather than helping them. They killed him, Narcissa, and other white people at the mission. That pushed Congress to establish the Oregon Territory, open the area to white settlers, and eventually force the area's tribes onto reservations. Now, when the Cayuse and Nez Perce and Palouse came to town for Pioneer Days, they marched in their tribal finery along Main Street, which had been a Nez Perce trail. Town ladies hoisting portraits of Narcissa walked ahead of them. Of course, the Sons of the Pioneers, led by Judge Feasley, were first in line.

I'd just finished blotting my lipstick when I heard Mrs. Feasley's door close on the floor below, which meant she'd be taking her sleep tincture and be out within minutes. I sprayed on a bit of Elsbeth's perfume, hoping it would settle my nerves, but the scent was overwhelmingly buttery.

My stomach lurched and I leaned against the wall, feeling trapped in the milk shed on the farm again, fumes of rotten cream enveloping me, Hen barring the door: "Don't speak, you won't remember," she said. I squatted and lifted Elsbeth's rag rug, rubbing an edge of it along my wrist until my skin was red and pulsing, trying to get the smell off me. I rose, checked myself in the mirror, fixed my curls. All I had to do was move.

My soles clicked against the bare pine boards of the servants' floor as I went down the back stairs to the kitchen, where I took a broom and dustpan from the closet. I headed for the Judge's study, letting my shoes sink into the lush Oriental runner that lay along the second-floor hallway, and stopped outside his closed door.

Go on, Lillian, I told myself. Go.

The air was flavored with the Judge's sugary pipe smoke.

Go.

The Judge coughed, and the broom jumped from my hand and clattered to the floor. "Who is it?" he called. I heard his cane coming closer, and then he opened the door, his pipe bobbing in his mouth, just as I picked up the broom. "Whatever are you doing?"

My mouth opened and shut as I held up the broom in inane reply. I had no good answer ready.

"Anna, really, I'm not to be interrupted while I work," he said.

That made me straighten up, that "Anna." That was the name they used for the hired girl who had preceded me, who I hadn't met, and whose name I doubted was Anna at all. "It's Lillian, Judge Feasley," I said. I lowered my voice, purring like I'd heard the girls do in the school hallways. "I'm awfully sorry. I was planning to give your study a little extra care tonight, but I thought you and Mrs. Feasley were out." I stepped from the hallway's shadow into the rectangle of light coming from his study, pulling my shoulders back to stick out my chest in its new brassiere.

"I suppose," he said, not taking his eyes from me. "I suppose you might as well sweep up there."

"Yes, Judge." I tried to move like the brunette at the bar had, bobbing and swaying as I took mincing steps toward him. "Oh, Judge, but you've spilled a little ash," I said. I bent over next to his desk so he could see my body parts hanging. It was absurd that the suggestion of a buttock or a breast would stir a man, but when I looked back his tongue was stuck at the side of his lips.

The wheat waved in my stomach, frantic, warning me to go upstairs.

No. That would keep me where I was. I had to move.

I asked the Judge what he was working on, and he said it was a section of the book about Narcissa's early life. Though I knew the answer, I asked him where Mrs. Whitman had come from, and got an earful about her western New York hometown, and how she had wanted to be a missionary but wasn't allowed to as a single woman, so arranged a marriage for herself with Marcus. It was the only thing I'd ever heard about Narcissa that made her sound likable, and the rest of my questions weren't ungenuine. Before long the Judge asked me to sit down, so I did, lowering my eyes and thrusting an ankle forward. Though the wheat shivered, I forced myself to check and make sure his thing was poking a triangle in his trouser fabric before I left.

I went back the following Saturday, late. Judge Feasley seemed to be expecting me. He had extracted a scrap of fabric that he'd preserved under glass and wanted to show me; it was a fragment from a quilt Narcissa Whitman had made. The Saturday after that, when Mrs. Feasley was out at a supper for the ladies' auxiliary of the American Legion, he laid a moist palm on my thigh. I spun around so that he could not see my face as I moved his hand up, could not see me screw my eyes shut so I could pretend it wasn't happening. Then I sucked in a sharp breath, for his thing was inside me and I felt red raw pain.

I'm a lone bo-weavil, been out a great long time

I pressed my arm against my eyes to keep tears from falling onto his desk.

Afterward, while all my body wanted to do was run fast and far and plunge into a cold clear lake, I let him stroke my hair and said, "A man like you must appreciate music, don't you, Judge?"

★ ★ ★

I lay underneath my bedspread the next morning, thinking of his panting and his stomach flesh hot against my back. But I could not be late, so I rose and dressed, went downstairs, and set the breakfast table. When Mrs. Feasley said good morning, acid bubbled in my throat. The Judge came in and told me the butter was too cold and I should have taken it out earlier.

That helped. This is work, plain and simple, I told myself.

The next night, there was a note slipped below my pillow in the Judge's handwriting. Look underneath your bed, it said. I waited until Elsbeth went for her bath and pulled up the bedskirt to see a guitar case. I pulled the case out and opened it. It was the Gretsch Hawaiian.

I took the Gretsch out gingerly, pressed it against my body, and breathed out. No one could touch me with this as a shield. No one could get to me.

It was the first beautiful thing I had ever owned.

I couldn't tune it yet, nor play it, but I could sit with it, its indent on my thigh, and coax music from the strings. I figured out that if I pressed here with my left hand and pulled here with my right, I could play two notes together that sounded good, then moved my hand up and down the neck until I was picking out little melodies. Music had been something I'd had to seek out, and it was now sitting here, available to me. I slipped it back under the bed before Elsbeth returned.

On my free Saturday nights, I began going to the Edgewater, a dance hall near the creek. I'd hang out near the stage and beg whoever was playing guitar to show me tuning and chords. I told the Feasleys' housekeeper that I'd received the guitar from a California cousin, and was joining the Wa-Hi orchestra—it played classical music, and had no modern guitarists, but she didn't know that. That gave me cover to go from school to the Whitman College campus with my guitar and join students playing music on the quad, quizzing them about fingerpicking patterns or harmonies.

The summer before tenth grade, I took the Feasley boy to the Walla Walla fair. We were wandering through a pavilion that was holding a coffee-cake contest when I heard swing music coming from the far end. Behind glass panes, I saw horns, a piano, an upright bass, and a sign: "KUJ, Walla Walla's Only Broadcasting Station: Serving the Northwest's Richest Agricultural Area." There were microphones, and other equipment I didn't recognize, and a large sign showing wheat, oat, and lard prices on the Chicago Mercantile. As the band finished its number, I recognized a trombone player from Whitman and ran after him, asking how he'd gotten a spot on the radio. He told me the assistant station manager at KUJ was looking for morning-show players for the farm broadcasts, and gave me the manager's name. Two weeks later I had a job as a country and western girl singer at the station, where on Sundays at 5:00 a.m., between reports about weather and Winnipeg wheat prices and Chicago hog markets, I sang songs as the sun came up to the farmer that I used to be.

Because the ice man and the milkman took Sundays off, and even the housekeeper slept until eight on Sundays, the housekeeper allowed me to fit in two hours' work at KUJ, which broadcast from the Marcus Whitman Hotel, before hurrying the mile back to the Feasleys to do my morning chores. I then pretended to attend the Lutheran service while the Feasleys went to the Presbyterian and Elsbeth and the housekeeper to the Catholic. Instead of church, though, I wandered through the Whitman campus with my guitar, hoping to find people to play with.

Judge Feasley often reminded me of his belief that the KUJ work was due to his generosity—it was he, after all, who had given me the Gretsch. For the next three years, he collected his payments in his study on Saturday nights, which sometimes seeped to Wednesday nights, or Fridays, making me spin increasingly outlandish stories for Elsbeth about some housekeeping crisis that had kept me from our bedroom. I learned to drink, learned that a slug of whiskey prior to visiting his study would make it seem even less like me in there with him, and when sweat beads dropped on me from the wrinkled sacs below his eyes, I could prevent myself from wiping them away.

In spring of my senior year, 1940, with Japan and China fighting on one side of us and Europe at war on the other, training flights roared over the Blue Mountains, and we took our exams to the sound of B-17 engines overhead. The Judge squeezed the soft part of my thigh in his study, which reeked of sweet tobacco. "I'm taking you on a special trip as a graduation gift," he said, "to Lake Coeur d'Alene. Just you and me for a whole weekend. And when we're back, the housekeeper is moving to Kennewick, and I've arranged for you to take her position. What do you think of that?"

The whiskey I'd had earlier rose harsh in my throat. I had thought that with my graduation, this arrangement would end. I didn't have a new job, not yet, but I'd been reading the classifieds to find work outside of town. I had to keep moving.

Later in my life, people who'd visited Washington would ask me why I hadn't stayed there, for my home state always shocked newcomers with its beauty. It wasn't what people thought of as the West, not the Dakotas, or Oklahoma, or Nebraska. It wasn't sun-baked Arizona and New Mexico, eerie and red and harsh, nor California with its walnuts and oranges and highways. It was greens so varied they were innumerable, Douglas firs with trunks so thick a class of schoolchildren could hardly encircle them. It was cool forests with thick raindrops falling quiet on the dirt. It was sand dollars on gray beaches, salt in my nostrils, kelp curled at my feet. It was the jagged cut of the Cascades splitting us into Eastern and Western Washington, country and city, growers and buyers.

That question showed how little they understood the West. I'd always moved, and knew I always would. For I'd been born in Washington. I had not been put on a train from the other coast, had not seen smoke-choked cities through the train window, had not shrunk back at the grasping hands of beggars when I changed trains in Chicago. I knew Washington's heavy apples, our sweet onions, our jammy gooseberries and our sweet pea pods as produce I could pick. I did not know that mountains elsewhere were mere foothills, that other fields were not painted gold. I did not know to mark the clouds shot through with violet light at sunset, the clear fresh air that filled my lungs each day. I did not know that I would not find that again.

But it wasn't a place I could stay. For I was a daughter of the West, and we did not settle, not for long; when we left, we made no plan to return. We knew in our bones that when we raised a hand in farewell from a train, we might never again see the figure blurring on the platform. For in the West, we are on the land only temporarily. A bad harvest or a bad bet at the American Legion might mean a farm is no longer yours. And it's not always about money, but about restlessness. When I was a child, a three-way trade between ranchers we knew meant that the Oregon Gustafsons took the Wynns' place, and the Wynns moved to Willow Creek, and the Millers at Willow Creek went over the border to Oregon. The families didn't do it for financial reasons. They did it because they couldn't stand to stay still.

In the East, I came to understand, people anchored themselves to their homes. If they left, they sent cards and letters, and returned for Christmases and summer holidays, and made sure their children swam in the same lakes they did, sledded down the same hills. In the East they paved roads and built neat rectangles of fence to tame the land. In the West, we know the earth will reclaim all that when she wants to, through fire, flood, or drought. She will set a roaring forest fire. She will send a spring with no rain. She will whip down the harvest and dry out the wheat, she will wither the berries on their vines. She will send snow before market time, she will freeze and parch and flood. The earth is not ours, never was, and she will not submit.

And so far, she'd made it clear that movement was my only hope of finding peace.

So I saw, when the Judge laid out his plans for me, that the dream I'd had of the rabbit warren, the inescapable bordello, was prescient, that the exit doors would close unless I left Walla Walla right away. He wouldn't give me a reference for another job if he wanted me to stay in this house and be available whenever he wanted me. He thought that by giving me the Gretsch, he had gotten me in return. He wasn't aware that I was the one who'd set up the deal.

★ 9 ★

Owensboro, Kentucky
June 1980

An hour before load-in the Green Giant pulled into Owensboro, giving us time to grab a bite before meeting at the high school. Kaori, who had been up at daybreak doing calisthenics, of all things, went off in search of vegetables, and Patrice and the Farver boys planned to drive to the edge of town to a meat-and-three, so I had Patrice drop me off downtown outside a burger joint that looked decent. I'd spent the day sewing pockets for guitar picks on to all my '60s and '70s costumes. To reward myself I ordered a hamburger loaded with tomatoes and onions, and a whiskey. The whiskey was going fast; I'd promised myself just one before the show, but was about to signal for another when I heard from behind me, "Two things we got to get straight."

My lips curved up. "What's that?" I said.

Charlie Hagerty slid into the booth opposite me. His darting light-blue eyes were now creased around the edges, and the stubble along his jawline was silver, but he still had the red hair and freckles that made him resemble a kid in a cartoon strip. His button-down shirt flopped open so I could see the notch in his collarbone from when he'd broken it as a kid.

"First," he said, "onions don't belong on a burger. Pickles do."

I stuck out my tongue. "You'd put pickles on your oatmeal if you could. You know I can't agree to that. What's second?"

He picked up my whiskey glass and tipped it toward him. "None of this," he said. "Not on nights we got gigs, anyway."

"One glass isn't even gonna do anything, Charlie."

"I don't care. I read that article, that review, whatever you want to call it, from Lake Winnie, and if people got their guns out for you and are thinking you can't handle the pressure of touring without booze and pills, then don't put a target on your own back, Lillian. Especially not one shaped like a bottle."

"I didn't— Hang on a minute." I pulled out a pen from my purse and scrawled "target shaped like a bottle" on a paper napkin. "I didn't read the article," I said. "How bad was it?"

He spun the whiskey glass and didn't answer.

"Why do men get traction at this age while the country music world is trying to wring my neck and stew me overnight till I'm tender?"

He twirled the glass the other way. "Because audiences don't mind seeing hard-drinking old cowboys, in fact they kind of enjoy seeing them go off the rails, but . . ."

"Not a woman."

"Don't give them reasons to not like you."

I held up my burger, offering him a bite, but he waved it off. "How'd you find me at this joint, anyway?"

"We've spent half our lives running around the US. You think I haven't learned how to track you down?" He signaled to the waiter and ordered a coffee. "Hard to miss that bus. 'Here Comes Trouble'? Flagged it down, said hello to the Farvers, met Patrice, moved my gear over, asked where you were. Donna dropped me off—she says hi, by the way—and she wanted to head back to Nashville before it got dark."

"Hi, Donna. There's another band member, too. A woman. Kaori. A fiddler."

"She good?"

I added another slice of raw onion to my burger and took a big bite. "At fiddling, yeah, actually. But she's a kid. I'd be surprised if they let her into some of the joints we're scheduled to play."

"I remember when you weren't even old enough to go into the parts of honky-tonks where beer was sold."

"True, but at least I wore a bra, unlike her. Also, she does *exercises* in the morning. She was up at six or seven today, jumping around outside the bus like a circus act."

The waiter set down Charlie's coffee. "Thanks, pal," Charlie said, adding sugar and then looking at me. "We got a deal on the whiskey?"

"Fine. Not before a gig. Two things I got to get straight with you, then."

"Shoot."

"If I don't drink the nights we got dates, fine, but neither can you and the boys."

He was holding in a grin. "And?"

"And shave your face before we go on, for Pete's sake. You think I want a hippie band? You're the bandleader now; you got to look re-spectable."

He rubbed his stubble. "Deal."

"Good." We locked eyes, and that old feeling spread from my chest across my body. "So Donna let you hit the road, huh?"

I was hoping he'd say something about how Donna and he weren't understanding each other these days. Instead he said, "Yeah, had to move up the wedding to keep her happy, though. You free in September?"

I examined my burger. "September," I said. "A singer can't miss her bandleader's . . ." I couldn't get the last word out, so I took another bite instead. "I'm serious about the shaving."

Once we'd finished, Charlie went to the high school, and I took a stroll around the block. I'd figured out marriage wasn't for me after just the one try, yet here Charlie was on his third attempt. Donna, dip though she was, couldn't be that thick if she'd gotten him to not just propose but set a date in the near future. I was deep in this circle of thought when Patrice, coming out of a soda shop, told me I'd better head to the venue with him, as Charlie was about to start sound check.

The large high school gym we were playing in had a shiny wooden floor with basketball-court markings on it. Above us, banners with the high school's titles hung from the wall. Our audience would sit in bleachers that ran along one side of the gym, and we'd play from center court, which could be tricky, given how sound bounced around in a gym. Inside, Charlie had already switched up the stage plot to improve the acoustics, so we went straight into sound check, working through "Water Lil" on an easy beat. Patrice, who had a great ear—his father had played accordion in a Cajun band—jogged up and down the bleachers to test out how the music carried.

"What else you want to try, Lillian?" Charlie said.

"Why don't we do 'Three-Quarter Time,' since we couldn't seem to get it right in Lake Winnie."

Charlie edged up to me, out of the mic's range, so the rest of them couldn't hear. "You got an empty gym, no audience, a full hour till the show, and you want to do a song you've sung a thousand times? Try something new."

"Like what?"

"Like something you've been thinking you'd be good at but aren't sure yet."

I moved my hand up my fretboard, thinking. We could try blue-grass, or gospel, or maybe an old song by one of the performers I loved. "'John Henry,'" I said. The version I'd first learned was the one my father sang, but great performers had recorded their own versions of it, too. "You think we can get the feeling of the Big Bill Broonzy recording?"

He whistled. "Setting the bar high."

I spoke to the rest of the band. "Let's give 'John Henry' a try," I said. "Quick and hard-driving."

"How many verses?" Charlie asked.

I moved my hands over my guitar, calling up the versions that my father had sung, Big Bill Broonzy had recorded, and that I'd heard from other folk, country, and blues singers. "I can come up with five; I'll make up the words I can't remember exactly."

"Only verses, no chorus, right? It's four/four time. What key do you want, Lillian?"

"Let's do—" I tried singing "He pulled up his hammer and he hit that piece of steel" in a couple of keys; on the higher ones, I could feel my voice straining. "Plain old D."

"Plain old D, and you want to do the intro, or you want me to?" Charlie played a ringing take on the melody, his guitar pick between his thumb and forefinger.

I grinned. "Well, playing like that, I think you want you to, so it's all yours. Tell you what, you play lead, I'll play rhythm on this one." That meant a reversal of our usual roles; lead guitar was the show-off part, with rhythm the steady backup.

Charlie shot a look to the Farvers. "Lil voluntarily giving up a lead guitar part? Tommy Reed, I didn't see the newspaper today, but I'm guessing the headline was 'Hell Freezes Over,' right?"

"Sounds about right," Tommy Reed said, chuckling.

I crossed my arms. "It's for the one song. Don't get used to it."

"Wouldn't dream of it," Charlie said. "All right, Farvers, ready?"

They both took out paper and pencil.

"So it'll be me on the intro, and then on the verse it'll start on the one," Charlie said. He reeled off the whole song in the Nashville Number System, and the Farvers scribbled notations as he spoke.

"Kaori, for you, it's gonna be D, C, G, A on the turnaround in the middle of the verse." He gave her the rest of the chords, then said to me. "What about singing? You want me to back you up after verse four, Lil?"

"I'll do it," said Kaori loudly.

"You sing?" I said.

"I told you that when we met."

Charlie looked at Kaori, then me.

"Rather have her just fiddling," I said.

"Lillian." Charlie's voice had a warning in it. "Could you sing a verse of something?" he said to Kaori.

She rested her fiddle in the case, did a few of her strange giant arm circles, then picked the fiddle back up. "We said sing—," I began, but Charlie shushed me.

Kaori launched into "Wabash Cannonball." It's notoriously difficult to sing and play a fiddle at the same time, because singing fiddlers have to drop their instrument from its usual position between their chin and shoulder and jam it against their armpit instead, not to mention the breath control it takes to project your voice while your arms zip around the fiddle. Yet Kaori did it well. She was too dramatic, slowing the song down and adding pop-music vocal frills, but her voice was strong and sure and she could hold a note.

"That's good," Charlie said, tossing me a look. "That's real good." He directed the two of us to work through the verses of "John Henry" so she could learn the words and sort out harmony. When we were all ready to go, Charlie played the intro on his guitar and the whole band launched into the music as I sang the first verse. I stopped them. "Got to be heavier," I said. "I want it to feel like we're holding the hammer and it's smashing against steel."

The rest of the group looked to Charlie. "Hit the downbeat harder and up the tempo a hair," he said. "Lil, on 'Steel's gonna be the death of me,' I'll snap a couple strings on the offbeat, and why don't you do a little run up and down the fretboard. And on solos, everyone, so we don't compete with Lil's voice, stay out of her range, and take it up an octave."

We tried again, and this time, it sounded all right, even if it wasn't Big Bill Broonzy.

That night, I could've sung the alphabet and it would've been an improvement over Lake Winnie, but even so, I thought we did a couple of the songs with real style. I kept myself from correcting any of the band members, even when I wanted to, and didn't push my voice too high or too loud so it wasn't obviously shrill. I joked with the friendly Owensboro audience. "John Henry" sounded great with Charlie's adjustments, and when I threw in a song of mine from '65 that the Farvers had recorded with me, it was like a couple decades fell off each of those men.

After the show, Patrice drove while Kaori slept in her bunk and the boys played rummy up front. I wanted a bath, but the Green Giant bathroom only had a sink, and we weren't yet far enough into the tour to rent a single motel room that we could all shower in. Later on, if ticket receipts were good enough, we might pay for individual hotel rooms. Instead I washed my face in the bathroom, leaving rivulets of black and peach makeup in the sink. In my bedroom I dabbed on too much cold cream, and extracted a tissue from my purse to wipe it off. What I thought was a tissue, though, was the napkin from the burger joint. I read what I'd written on it at dinner: "Target shaped like a bottle." That didn't quite work. Target like a bottle, I sang to myself, but that wasn't it. Bottle target. Nope. I played around with the phrase for a bit, but couldn't quite harness it. I took out an untouched notebook and wrote "Target shaped like a bottle" on the first page, then left it in my bedside drawer, hoping a song might crawl out from it in the night.

Tacoma, Washington
1940–1941

What I took:

A letter of recommendation from KUJ Radio, Walla Walla, attesting to my work as a morning girl singer on the station, stating that I'd showed up on time and played guitar to boot. I deserved the letter, and yet when I asked the assistant station manager for it, he closed his office door, and I'd recognized the glint of dull expectation in his eyes.

My Gretsch, now paled at the top from my arm resting on it while I played.

Day clothes that the Judge had picked out and bought, all in browns and greens that he thought suited me, just right for an Anna. He'd bought other things for me to wear at night. I threw those in a garbage can at the depot.

Thirty dollars in singles and coins, the wages I'd put aside after six years of daily work.

Molex Pills, which were no longer for sale at the drugstore but which a friend of a friend from the Edgewater had sold to me, plus Lysol to use as a douche. Even if I was leaving the Judge behind,

I knew what awaited me, and I wanted to avoid the worst consequences of it.

A piece of paper with the destination I'd written down in careful
letters as that Coeur d'Alene weekend with the Judge loomed. I heard
a KUJ news report on how preparing for war meant West Coast port
cities were full up with jobs, and there was an Army base in Tacoma
called Fort Lewis.

A one-way Northern Pacific Railway ticket to Pasco, where I'd
change to a Tacoma-bound train.

* * *

It was May 1940. I was sixteen years old.

I left in a hurry a month before high school graduation, telling the
housekeeper I had to go see a dying aunt. I ran out that same morning
with one suitcase and my guitar, not even saying goodbye to Elsbeth.

As the train entered the tunnel at Stampede Pass to cross under
the Cascades, the land was shrubby and dry. When we came out on
the western side of the mountain range, it was transformed. Gray
skies, green trees, rain-wet grass, as though a painter with a limited
palette had explored every variation of those colors with each daub:
the nimble light green of the new-grown grass and the knowing green
of the hundred-year-old firs, the shaded grays of swollen clouds and
the pale clear grays of the morning.

When we pulled close to Union Station, I thought the train was
leaking fuel, but I'd learn it was the smell of Tacoma itself, muddy,
sulfurous, and industrial, topped with diesel. Every local had a theory
on what created the Tacoma Aroma: the oil refinery, the Simpson pulp
mill, or the canal of the City Waterway, which ran between the city
and one side of the port. It suited Tacoma, though; this was a work-
ingman's town.

I had to run to keep up with the crowd as we stepped onto the platform and up several sets of stairs to the Union Station waiting room,

set under a gleaming white dome filled with light. I had no idea where to go, so I fluffed up my pin-curled hair, put on a new coat of lipstick, and approached a newspaper vendor. "Excuse me, sir, but I need to get to Fort Lewis. I don't suppose you could tell a girl how to walk there?"

"Miss." His face was kind. "You can't walk. It's a good ten miles south. Why are you going there?"

I said to find work, and he said I'd be better off downtown anyway. He directed me to a table against a wall in the waiting room; there were so many new arrivals needing housing, he said, that volunteers had set up an information table matching would-be boarders with Tacomans who had space in their houses. "And take this, no charge," he said, pulling out a city map and pointing to a spot. "This is downtown: you'll want to start there looking for a job. All the stores and restaurants are looking to hire. Good luck."

I thanked him, and went to the table he'd referenced. The woman volunteering there listened to my (made-up) age and (made-up) profession (I said I was a nurse), slotted me into a house in a neighborhood called Old Town, and wrote down bus directions to it. "Welcome to Tacoma, dear," she said as she gave me the information.

Outside, the streetfront appeared reassuringly like Walla Walla, with advertisements in white lettering on black backgrounds painted on brick buildings. Here, though, they were for F.S. Harmon Mfg. Co., West Coast Wholesale Grocery, and Hunt & Mottet Co. Wholesale Hardware rather than ladies' millinery or men's shoes. I didn't think to check behind me, where I would've seen my first glimpse of the Cascades and the City Waterway, a sludgy canal drawn from Commencement Bay, which was itself drawn from the Pacific. Instead, I gaped as cars and people and buses tangled together. I did not know so many people could exist in one place, especially in a place that was in Washington State. I soon saw, to my utter relief, the bus the volunteer had mentioned, and I boarded it, trying to look like I knew what I was doing.

When I reached Old Town, I found my assigned place was in a one-story bungalow that belonged to a grim landlady. Her idea of hosting boarders was slapping four thin mattresses onto bedframes in her freezing concrete basement. Another boarder was fixing herself up for work as I arrived, and gave me a brief rundown of the situation: the landlady worked as a receptionist at the huge Centennial Flour mill on the bay, and prohibited the residents from using the house's only bathroom from six to eight a.m., when she might be getting ready for work, and seven to nine p.m., when she might be getting ready for bed. The other girls had jobs waitressing, cleaning, or typing, and since they'd been here longer, they had priority in the bathroom schedule. I wasn't bothered; I didn't plan on boarding here too long.

Once I'd deposited my stuff under my bed, I fixed my hair and makeup and put on walking shoes, bound for downtown and a job. Outside, it smelled of seawater and rotten eggs, and seagulls shrieked and dipped overhead. In front of me, down a hill, I spotted what I thought was a lake dotted with large green-tree islands. When I read the map, it was clear that it was Commencement Bay, to my north. To the east, I could see from clouds of opaque steam rising up from the far side of the hill that that must be the port. I headed for it, uphill. As I got to the heights of what the map called Stadium and started the downward slope to downtown, I saw slices of the port, its own little city, with canals set into land like strips of fabric, and cranes and factories and piles of sawdust and stacks of paper spreading over the port, the Cascades far beyond it.

And then, out of nowhere—I almost yelped—giant, beautiful Mount Rainier appeared on the southern side of the city, her base framed by the industry of the port.

That Mount Rainier. She'd slide up all over the southeast side of the city, moving like she was on roller skates, here peeking up over North Slope, here vanishing when she should've been right behind the flour mill. I'd soon learn that Rainier was useless as an orientation point, given her inexplicable retreats and reappearances; instead, I'd use the always-visible smokestack puffs from the port to figure out where I was.

I checked my map and maneuvered down the steep pitch of a street called St. Helens Avenue, pausing at a five-way intersection. Broadway, spanning out from where I stood, was crowded with people, shops, and neon lights. Ladies with purses and men in hats bustled in and out of shops and restaurants as bus horns, train whistles, and clanging metal from the ports added to the buzz. To my left, a hill led down to the port; I saw on the map that the nearby Eleventh Street Bridge connected people and vehicles to it across the City Waterway. A stream of longshoremen and laborers, in thick canvas pants stained with oil or paint, were coming from and going to the port, as were trucks and cars.

I stepped into the intersection and was almost clipped by a car that then squealed to a stop. "Sorry, miss," the driver called out, though it was my fault. "Are you all right?" I waved to her, and she smiled back. When I turned backward, I saw a building with a Help Wanted sign on it. It was a seafood restaurant, Triton's, and in fact it resembled the prow of a boat. The restaurant was triangular, a marquee at the narrow point in the front, and on both sides floor-to-ceiling glass flooded the place with light. The marquee read "Triton's—Coffee—Breakfast—Seafood All Day."

I went inside and suddenly understood seasickness, though I'd never been on a boat. The restaurant floor was even, but given the crazy angles of the neighborhood, someone entering from the St. Helens Avenue side had to take—I counted—a fourteen-step staircase down to reach the floor. Triton's was packed with people, taking all the seats at a counter that fronted a kitchen on the St. Helens side, and filling the tables lined up along the Broadway windows. A small woman in a neatly pinned sailor hat, her skin a dark brown similar to that of a girl from my Wa-Hi class who headed the Library Club, passed me, carrying napkin-wrapped silverware. "Excuse me?" I said.

"Hi, there. It'll be about half an hour for a table," she said, setting down the rolled silverware, telling a customer his halibut would be out shortly, and whirling back toward the kitchen in a dainty pirouette. Her face was diamond-shaped: a sharp jawline, prominent cheekbones, and a tiny forehead, and her build thin and straight up and down.

"I'm here about the Help Wanted sign," I said.

"Do you waitress?"

"Not yet."

"What's your experience?"

"Cleaning, serving, cooking, sweeping, washing dishes, all of it."

"So you can work. Come back at five, when the manager will be here. I'm Althea."

"Lillian," I said, but she was off, materializing half a minute later with a plateful of pink bug-like things that I later learned were shrimp.

I came back at five, and the manager promptly hired me to start at Triton's the next morning. I'd be working a five-to-eleven morning shift, the same as Althea Williams, the waitress I'd met. I picked up the lingo and the rules of the place fast. Once I could reel off "Eighty-six it" or "Flop two, over easy," I started thinking about my music again.

One morning I brought my guitar to my shift, stashing it in a utility closet. When I finished, I walked over and down to the Rust Building, where the radio station KVI was located. I hoped to waylay the director of the noon show once that segment ended. When I got there, a receptionist told me to wait, as I was the third person hoping for an audition that day. She had black hair, a black jacket, and a black skirt, making her giant red hexagonal glasses—they stretched from mid-forehead nearly to the tip of her nose—stand out all the more. She didn't have a nameplate like the executives did, but as KVI men streamed into the office, all of them said "Hello, Mrs. Hideshima," and she responded "Hello," almost always adding a useful tidbit: "Mr. Robinson seems eager to speak to you," or "Miss Gentry's mother has taken ill, so she won't be in till half-past, and I can help you with anything in the meantime."

"It shouldn't be much longer," Mrs. Hideshima told me, typing with her right hand while she flipped through papers with her left. She picked up the phone, without pausing in her typing. "Good morning, KVI Radio, how may I direct your call?" It was my first time seeing a woman in an office, and I was intrigued by how she addressed the men—as though she were their equal. After some time, her intercom crackled, and she stopped typing for the first time and led me back to a production area. In Walla Walla, the on-air host had handled the control console, fixing his own sound levels. Here, the host was on one side of a pane of glass, while an engineer on the other side ran the console and adjusted levels. The DJ had two turntables instead of one, plus a phone. An "On the Air" button was lit up, and the host sounded smooth and assured. A transmitter the size of several over-size Frigidaires, with dials and pipes and buttons and vents, loomed in the background.

"Miss Lillian Waters, here to audition," said Mrs. Hideshima to the program director, who sat in an office just off the production area.

He thanked her and half-gestured at me. "Go ahead, sing."

I took out my guitar, trying not to be distracted by the DJ's patter being piped in overhead, and played "My Adobe Hacienda," a new song by Louise Massey that I figured sounded sophisticated enough for this city. The program director threw up his arms. "Stop, stop," he said. "What are you singing? We're in Tacoma, Washington. No one knows what a hacienda is. You want to be a girl singer on our country show, we need you singing about Mama and sweethearts and God bless America. Know what I mean?"

I strummed a D to a G, thinking, and picked out the start of a Monroe Brothers tune.

"Give me an intro like you're on the radio and you're talking to the boys at Fort Lewis and Boeing," the manager said. "I'll cue you in: 'Now, we got a special treat, a new girl singer here at KVI Radio.'"

I sucked in a breath, channeled the manner of the *Barn Dance* performers as best I could, and said in a high and friendly voice, "Hi there, this is Lillian Waters out of KVI Radio, Tacoma, Washington, and I've got a special song for all you Army and Navy men, and the Air Corps and shipbuilders and everyone else here in Tacoma helping out." I launched into "Sailor Boy," and the manager let me get through two verses before interrupting me.

"Next time, skip the verse about the sailor boy being at the bottom of the ocean, but you got the idea," he said. "We could use you on the noon show, *Country Canteen*, Thursdays, noon to two p.m."

I wanted to cheer but just buckled my guitar case shut, imitating Mrs. Hideshima's professional manner, and thanked him. The timing was just right: I could do the opening-and-breakfast shift at Triton's and slip out just before noon to run the two blocks to KVI. Maybe I could fit in mid and dinner shifts, too, for extra money and fill in on other shows if KVI needed it. Hello, Tacoma, this is Lillian Waters.

★ ★ ★

A strand of hair fell out of my white sailor-style cap, and I repinned it as I studied a man at the Triton's counter. As the new girl, I was assigned to the counter station; it was where the frugal customers usually sat to avoid the forty-cent minimum at the window booths. At my counter, customers ordered a fifteen-cent egg or a ten-cent coffee, and if they left any change for me, I was lucky. I'd gotten to know my regulars, usually tired men just off their graveyard stints at the Port of Tacoma, or brighter-looking men on their way there, and occasionally one or two fellows who'd spent the whole night drinking nearby. I also developed a clientele of girls from the brothels on Whiskey Row, who spoke in thick Polish or Yugoslavian or Norwegian accents when they came in for a fried egg and a coffee, worn out after a night's work. I always gave them free toast.

The man at my counter this morning wasn't a regular, but he'd sat here silently three days in a row, choosing the worst seat in the house each time. The corner stool he sat on was ripped; it was next to the passage where we ran in and out with coffee, and so close to the kitchen it smelled like deep-fried ocean. He had red hair, wide enough shoulders that his shirt pulled a little at the buttons, and deep parentheses in his cheeks that made him seem like he was smiling when he wasn't.

The other morning men had the *Tacoma Times* or the *News-Tribune* spread out in front of them, carrying news of the war in Europe, but this man didn't. Instead his hands danced around the counter, over the open Triton's menu, his left one curled up, fingers moving in a fast pattern, his right going back and forth like he was scribbling with a pencil.

"I said, your order's up," Althea said. She leaned close enough that I could see the bobby pins that fixed her own hat to her black curls. Althea was a head shorter than me, but a slight narrowing of her eyes could ward off any customer who might've called her "sweetie" or "hon" more than once. She followed my gaze. "Ooh, a logger."

He wasn't a logger. I knew timbermen's hands, and though they were big, they were usually scarred from handsaws and slow from injuries, not quick like this man's. "This is his third day in that seat," I said. "You think I need to watch out for him?" Althea, who was older than me, had warned me about customers who hung around too long, and yesterday she'd accompanied me to the top of Stadium at the end of my shift after a man who stank of beer asked me if I didn't want a little company after work.

"You'll be watching out for him if you're lucky," she said. The doorbell jangled, and a pair of Black longshoremen came in. She adjusted her cap. By unspoken agreement, Althea, who was Black, seated the Black customers, and I the white ones; it got us both better tips. "Don't let your order wait too long; you'll get the kitchen riled up," she said. "And no, I've never seen him around here before this week."

While she greeted the customers, I retrieved my order of two fried eggs and served them to a mailman reading the sports pages, leaning over the counter farther than I needed to. "There you go, nice and sizzling," I said, my voice artificially high and feathery. The mailman widened his eyes and flushed pink, and I hoped he'd tip me better than the day before.

I shimmied my shoulders to shift my blouse down before I addressed the redhead. "Morning, pal. What'll it be?"

"You work here every day?" he asked.

"What?" Althea had tried to get me to say "Pardon me," but it hadn't caught yet.

"Just I've seen you every time I've been here."

"A girl likes to be noticed."

He wasn't responding like the mailman had, though, and seemed more interested in the menu than in me. "So, what'll it be?" I asked.

"Coffee, to start with."

"Cream?"

"Just sugar."

"Good," I said under my breath; I still hated the smell of milk, and dreaded pouring cream or milk into little silver pitchers for customers who took it. The few times the cream had been off, I'd had to run right to the toilet and heave. I guess I said it louder than I thought, because he said, "Why is that good?"

"The coffee's good, I meant," I said.

"Hah," he said. It wasn't quite a laugh, more a combination of clearing his throat and chuckling. He read the menu. "How about the butterhorns? Do you make them fresh?"

"We make them, sure; as for fresh, depends on your definition." I winked.

He just said, "I'll have one of those."

"If you order the number-two special, you get orange or tomato juice alongside coffee, and the butterhorn for the same price."

"Number-two special, then. Thanks. Tomato," he said, and ran a finger so callused it looked like he'd dipped it in hot wax along the menu's edge.

When his roll and juice came out, I slid them across the counter. "Why do you sit at this corner?"

He checked right and left, as if he'd just noticed where he was.

I tipped my chin down, so my eyes appeared bigger. "Isn't it hard to concentrate?" I said with a teasing grin. "Waitresses going in and out?"

"I guess because there's no seat next to me." He tore a piece of his butterhorn and chewed slowly. The usual routine I relied on for tips was having no effect on him; he sounded like he was talking to his aunt. "So I can practice while I eat."

"Practice?"

He lifted his hands and positioned them across his torso, where I instantly saw what I hadn't before: he'd been practicing playing a string instrument. He opened his mouth to elaborate, but I beat him to it. "Banjo," I said, dropping the act and the breathiness in my voice.

His left hand hit a chord position, his right moved an invisible bow. "Fiddle," he said.

I squinted at him as though I could see the thing. "Country and western?" I asked.

"Country and western, yup." His blue eyes crinkled for the first time, and I felt like I was sitting in front of a fire in winter. "Surprised to hear you call it that. Lots of people would call it 'hillbilly.'"

This was a description sophisticated folks used to dismiss country music, and I'd heard it as a put-down from a couple of the snooty people at KVI. "Lots of people would call me a hayseed, so I don't care much for what lots of people think," I told him.

Althea bumped me with her hip as she moved behind the counter with an empty water pitcher. "Lillian," she said, and gestured to the front door, where a white customer waited. At the register, someone needed to pay, and the mailman lifted his coffee cup for a refill. By the time I'd seated the one, made change for the next, and refilled the third, the fiddle player was gone, leaving me a tip of a dime on a forty-cent bill. I picked up the coin, ran out the door, and spotted him going down South Ninth. I crossed the street after him, yelling out "Hey!" (another word Althea disapproved of). He stopped midway, and I caught up to him, pinching the dime he'd left for me. "I'll give you this back if you tell me where you play country and western," I said.

He told me to keep the dime and asked, not unkindly, what I knew about country and western.

I answered by singing him a bar from Ernest Tubb, this time with my own fingers flying over a make-believe guitar.

"Hah." His eyes brightened. "Guitar."

"That's right. Where do you play?"

"We play all around, but my band—we're Johnny T. and the Paper Boys—has got a regular gig the first Friday of the month. That's coming up this Friday, but the place is kind of rough: you know what a honky-tonk is?"

" 'Course I do." I didn't. "So you're Johnny T.?"

He laughed at that, a rich, deep sound. "No," he said, those smile lines deepening. "No, my name's Charlie Hagerty." He lifted two fingers in a sort of salute and ambled down toward the port.

★ ★ ★

Honky-tonks, it turned out, were my kind of places: bars with live country music for dancing that were meant for workers drinking beer, not city people drinking cocktails. After I met Charlie Hagerty, I went to Johnny T. and the Paper Boys performances at a few joints around town, going alone each time. My only real acquaintance in Tacoma was Althea, but she'd been born in Louisiana, and couldn't get over that a girl born and raised in Washington was playing the sort of music she, too, called "hillbilly." The one time I'd asked her to come with me to a honky-tonk, she'd laughed so hard she almost tipped an entire platter of crab legs to the floor. Besides, she spent her free time with her boyfriend, Claude, a candymaker at a Hilltop shop.

At the bars, the few other women in the crowd swayed drunkenly and leaned on men. I didn't meet any of the fellows' eyes, though, and I waved them off when they asked to buy me a drink. I was there for the music. The Paper Boys were a bare-bones band, with Johnny T. on guitar, Charlie on fiddle, and a fellow whose name I didn't know on bass. Johnny T. mostly sang other people's songs, like Bob Wills's "New San Antonio Rose," but the tunes sounded much less polished and more ragged than Bob Wills or Gene Autry or whoever it was. Even when the crowds were wild and loud, stomping their feet, Johnny T. had a good clean sound that carried over the noise. He sang into a microphone, which should've drowned out his instrument, but the guitar stayed defined, and I couldn't figure out how he got that effect.

One Friday I swung by the Triton's kitchen as I finished up a double shift. "Anything good for me today?" I asked Marko, a dishwasher I was friendly with. He pointed to a plate of almost untouched broiled clams from a customer on a shelf above his sink, though that was technically against Triton's rules; I did the same for him, siphoning rolls or fruit from plates before I put them in the sink. Before Tacoma, I'd eaten fish now and then, but it had been river trout my father had caught or mysterious hunks of white fish left over from the Feasleys' dinners. The first time I saw the piles of fresh seafood in one of Triton's industrial refrigerators, I was shocked. Giant orange king crabs with studded shells; glistening salmon cut in half, the skin silver and glinting and the interior a rich red-orange; stacks of oysters, bowls of black mussels, translucent gray shrimp, and dark-brown halibut with pouting mouths. When, early on, a customer ordered a crab cocktail and hardly touched it, I whisked it to the kitchen and picked up a piece of the slippery pink crab, not bothering with the cocktail sauce. It punched into my mouth, salty and slippery and delicious, and from then on I siphoned off whatever I could from customers' plates. I knew that however much steak or roast beef Hen was eating on the other side of the mountains, she wasn't getting these kinds of delicacies.

My belly full of clams, I walked on Broadway, passing Woolworth's and a jeweler's and a malted-milk shop, then through Nihonmachi, the Japanese American section of town, with its hotels and grocers and florists and tailors. Though I could take a series of buses to get around, I preferred walking. Even when it was wintry and rainy, the sun made an appearance each day, and the rain was rarely heavy; with a Salvation Army raincoat and a Woolworth's rain bonnet, I was usually fine.

Plus, walking let me encounter Tacoma's surprises. The first time I went back to the bungalow via North Slope, I gasped when I glimpsed a second set of snow-covered mountains to the west. For a second I thought Rainier was playing another trick on me, but when I asked around, I learned Tacoma was set between two huge mountain ranges, the Cascades in the east and the Olympics in the west.

"You'll Like Tacoma," a sign near Old City Hall used to announce to visitors, and I did.

From Nihonmachi, still tasting the garlicky clams on my tongue, I zipped down to Union Station, turned right into the warehouse district, and after a few blocks made a left onto Puyallup Avenue and into a honky-tonk where the Paper Boys were on stage. When they took a break, Johnny T. stepped down from the makeshift stage, a platform of nailed-together wooden planks. "You again?" he said. He had golden skin and a presidential sort of jaw, and when he eyed certain ladies in the crowd and got them excited, their men knew to take them home, and then the ladies and men both came back for more. Music came too easy to him, though. There were guitar licks that would be natural fits in his songs that he never added, because licks took work to get right. He just played easy, standard chords and relied on his charm to win over the audience.

Charlie, sweating from how fast he'd been playing, stepped off the platform after Johnny. He'd continued to get breakfast at Triton's a couple mornings a week after his graveyard shift as a shipping clerk at the salt plant, a job that made him smell like chlorine. He stuck with the number-two special with tomato juice, and I peppered him with questions: what fiddle he had, what songs he listened to, how he got gigs. I'd told him about my KVI show, and though it aired in the middle of the day when he was meant to be sleeping, this week he'd told me he liked how I'd played a Patsy Montana song on the air. "Wish Johnny could pick like that," he'd said, and that gave me an idea: if Charlie thought I was as good as Johnny, maybe I could join their band and get some experience in front of a live crowd.

"Me again," I said to Johnny as Charlie wiped his brow.

"Well, now you've met me," Johnny said. He eyed a corner of the room, where a redhead slumped against the wall, her eyes half-closed.

"And here I thought you'd be pretty glad about meeting me," I said, pressing my arms against my chest to make my breasts balloon. "Especially when you heard I can play backup guitar and be your girl singer."

His eyes flicked past me to the other woman. I stretched an arm out so he couldn't pass by. "Every band could use a little feminine charm, don't you think? I'm already doing the Thursday noon show at KVI. Cowboy Canteen."

"Where you fresh off the bus from?"

"The train, thanks. Walla Walla. I sang on the radio there, too."

"Walla Walla's got itself radio waves now? Honey, a pretty girl like you should be sitting in the audience, not pretending at playing guitar," Johnny said. "Tell you what, though, I'll be glad to show you a few musical tricks anytime." He popped a toothpick in his mouth, bobbing it up and down between his teeth.

Charlie shot me a worried look, and I thought he was going to put a stop to the whole thing—he didn't like Johnny much, and was always telling me not to go to honky-tonks on my own because I could get myself into a bad situation, to which I thought, Brother, I just got myself out of a bad situation. Instead, Charlie said, as though he'd never met me, "Might as well hear her, Johnny. We could use a girl singer."

"Oh, well, if the *musician* says so. Let's see what you got, honey. You know 'You Walk By?'"

I did, but I didn't understand. That was a croony, tinkling song, and this audience was full of servicemen and shipyard workers, roaring and drinking. They wanted beers and a beat. "Isn't that slow for this crowd?"

"If we really need a girl singer, we need a girl singer who can do sweet stuff."

Charlie started to say something, but I spoke over him. "Fine."

"You'll need to accompany yourself," Johnny T. said.

"Johnny . . . ," Charlie said.

"I can do that," I said, not willing to let Johnny T.'s resistance get me down. "I'll need to borrow your guitar."

"Oh, of course," Johnny T. said, friendly at last. "You wait here." He maneuvered in front of some tall men, so I couldn't see the platform as he climbed back on. I heard shuffling and squeaking as he moved things around. The crowd was getting restless, and a beer bottle shattered against the floor. "All right," Johnny shouted to them, though he sounded quieter than before. "We got a little girl here who says she wants to play you all something, so we told her we're gonna let her do a number."

The audience cheered.

I'd never gotten nervous before my radio shows, and when I felt something running down the back of my legs I wondered if an audience member had spilled something on me before I figured out it was sweat. I plucked my shirt away from my chest to keep it from getting soaked and stepped onto the platform, where Johnny passed me his guitar. I strummed but couldn't hear it over the crowd, and I hoped it was tuned. As soon as I said, "I'm singing 'You Walk By' tonight," I realized Johnny T. had unplugged the mic. It was a dumb trick, but I wasn't about to let it stop me. It took my mind off the sweat, at

least. "Here we go," I shouted. I didn't like the song, which was syrupy sweet, but that wasn't the problem. My strumming and picking
were too quiet; the sound wasn't reverberating as it had for Johnny T.
Before I got four words in a wave of boos came at me.

I raised my voice and forgot about the picking to strum as hard as I
could, but it was still too quiet. Someone shouted, "Get out of here!"
from across the room.

I raised a hand, half surrender, half wait-a-minute, and stepped off.

Johnny T. stood away from the platform, drinking from a gin bottle he'd pulled from somewhere. "What did you do to the sound up
there?" I said.

He wiped his mouth. "We got a hot pepper here."

"You'll have a hot pepper in a place you don't want to think about
if you don't tell me what you did." I angled the guitar's neck at him
like it was the blade of a knife. "You want to see me foul up, fine, but
let me try my best first. What'd you use to get your sound out there?"

Charlie, who'd gotten pushed back in the crowd, charged at us then
and took the guitar from me. His shirt opened when he did, and I saw
a healed break on his collarbone that made the backs of my knees fizz
like they did when I drank whiskey. "Johnny's Gibson goes into an
amplifier," he said. He pointed to a big brown cube that resembled a
suitcase. "You got to plug it in to get much of a sound. You didn't plug
it in, Johnny?"

Johnny slurped at the gin bottle.

Charlie clenched and unclenched a fist. "Johnny," he said, but then
he looked at me. "Can you do something lively?"

"What about 'Oh! Susanna?'" I said, naming the first fast song I
could think of.

"That'll be fine," he said. "Here, Johnny's gonna loan you his guitar
again, aren't you, Johnny? I'll back you up on fiddle." Johnny stroked
his gin bottle as I followed Charlie back onstage. When the crowd saw
me again they jeered, and though my cheeks were burning, I wiggled
my hips. Charlie plugged in the mic and the amplifier, connected the

guitar to the amplifier, and handed the instrument to me. "We had a sound problem there," he said into the mic. "Sorry about that, folks, but it's fixed now. If you could give Lillian here a real Tacoma welcome, she'll sing you an old favorite in return."

I touched the guitar body and told myself that it was a shield, just like my Gretsch had been in Walla Walla. I felt dizzy and everything was whirling, but I must've gotten the words and chords out, because as soon as Charlie did a solo, I had a moment to check out the crowd, and they were paying attention. Their energy lifted me up, and I wanted to give it right back to them. I jumped back into the song when Charlie finished his solo, and together we hauled away on that music. On the last chorus I threw my strumming arm around my head like a lasso, signaling for the crowd to join in, and people were dancing and laughing like they were happy, like I had made them happy.

When I finished, half of me wanted to jump into the crowd and hug each and every one of them, and the other half wanted to crack Johnny T.'s guitar over his head. Instead I gave a little curtsy and a wave, as the men cheered and the women clapped, and practically skipped offstage.

"Well," Charlie said. "I guess we got ourselves a girl singer."

★ 11 ★

Jefferson City, Missouri
June 1980

Who knows what day it was on the road: Wednesday? Friday? We played our first of two shows in Jeff City, where Charlie mixed in traditionals and folk songs in new arrangements. When he'd met us in Owensboro, he'd packed Donna's car full of his instruments, which he'd transferred to the tour bus: fiddle, electric guitar, acoustic, harmonica, autoharp, accordion, banjo, washboard, dobro, mandolin, even a zither. And whenever we played a location that had a piano, or an organ, or anything unusual—in St. Louis, he borrowed a tuba because he wanted to try out a strange old polka number—Charlie layered those in, too.

We parked for the night in Jeff City, and I set my alarm for a quarter to five, so I'd wake up in time for another round of radio interviews to promote the second show. It wasn't my alarm that woke me, though, but a slapping sound outside my bus window. Pain shot between my ears, and I rubbed my neck and sang do-re-mi. My voice had been sore and sounding rough, especially by the end of each show, but I stayed as quiet as I could during the day to recover. I took three aspirins and sucked a cough drop, pulling my curtain open to see Kaori under the lights of the still-dark parking lot, squatting down and jumping up, squatting down and jumping up. I observed her for a good ten minutes, until the cough drop was gone, and then slid open my window and called out, "You in basic training?"

Red-cheeked and sweating, she jogged over to the bus and peered up at me. "Care to join me?"

"I start the day with a coffee, thanks. What's all this about?"

"Watch." She dropped out of sight. I leaned my head close to the window and saw her doing push-ups on the pavement at a rapid pace. When she sprang back up, she looked at me expectantly.

"Search me," I said.

"When you play your guitar, your arms are below your heart, so it doesn't get your heart rate up. Fiddling, your arms are up here"—she demonstrated—"So the blood's got to pump harder, and when you add singing . . ."

"You can't catch your breath."

"Right. Unless you train your body. I didn't think I'd be able to jog on the road, so I got some exercises from the track team at college."

"You've been doing this every morning."

"Some people are natural talents, some just—"

"Work harder." I frowned in approval. "Keep at it. I'll get you a muffin on the way back from my interviews."

After our second Jeff City date that night, while Patrice drove us southwest for some Arkansas dates and Kaori headed to the back of the bus, Gene, Tommy Reed, and Charlie sat in the front booth, Gene shuffling cards for rummy at the table. "You in, Lil?" Gene asked.

"I would clean the floor with you three, and it wouldn't be lady-like," I said as I opened a cupboard, searching for the decaf Folgers I'd brought. Instead of a coffee tin, I saw four giant jars of dill pickles. I groaned. "Charlie. Still?"

"Yep. Hand me a jar, will you?"

I passed one to him. "This bus is going to smell like vinegar for the rest of the tour," I said. He unscrewed the top and popped a pickle in his mouth.

"I could go for a pickle, too," Patrice said, glancing in the rearview.

"Don't do it, Patrice," I said. "You're probably long past being shocked by musicians, but just wait, and—yep." Charlie plunged his hand into the pickle juice. "Never, and I mean never, eat a pickle from one of Charlie Hagerty's jars." I located my jar of decaf in a drawer and put on a kettle. "Lord, you probably just went on this tour so you could get back to Tacoma and load up on Nalley's pickles."

"I do plan on bringing a crate or two back," Charlie said.

"I bet it wasn't just the Tacoma pickles," Gene said, dealing out the cards. "I think he went on this tour because it's your farewell tour, Lil. We all did, probably. Very last chance to see Water Lil live onstage."

"Oh, the very, very last," Tommy Reed said, a wad of chewing tobacco between his lower gum and his lip. "She'll never sing again."

"It couldn't be a ploy to sell tickets," Charlie said, fanning out his cards with his unpickled hand.

"Lillian Waters doesn't even like the stage," Gene said, making a neat stack of leftover cards in the middle of the table and flipping the top one over.

"Or performing," Tommy Reed said, spitting tobacco juice into an empty pop bottle.

"Or yelling at her band," Charlie said.

"That true, Lil?" Patrice asked. "This isn't really your last tour?"

The kettle whistled. I busied myself with it. "You gonna trust those fools over me?"

Tommy Reed reached for the upturned card, and the rummy game started. As I poured water into a mug and stirred in coffee crystals, the men moved on to their other frequent topics of conversation: whether MCA was getting better songs out of Merle than Capitol had when he was signed there, and how did Charley Pride's cover of Hank Williams's "You Win Again" compare with the covers by Jerry Lee Lewis and Ray Charles. I took my mug and joined Kaori in the back of the bus, where she was scratching something on a legal pad.

"It's the same talk with those boys every night," I said, sitting down.

"If MCA would just get Merle writing good music again, we could resolve it once and for all," she said.

"What are you writing there?"

Her eyes flicked to the ceiling, then back at me. "Lyrics."

"Right, that's right. You said you write songs."

"Do you have any advice?"

Advice, as though I were in a place to give it to anyone. Still, I told her that back in Tacoma, Buck Owens had counseled me not to make the process precious. Hear something interesting and get it down in a song, that was what he did. I'd kept notebooks in my purse—or I had, before the days wandering around the Old Hickory Lake house—for when I heard anything intriguing. A good lyric, or a fine tune, shows up as quick and fleeting as a passing cloud, and you've got to be ready when it comes. I'd rolled my eyes at the men who believed that to write a song they had to be, well, take your pick: Alone in a cabin. Fishing for bass on a stream. Drinking for the third night in a row at a honky-tonk café, while their wives made their meals and handled their bills and got their children to school. No. It came when it came—*it*, not *she*, for to me the muse was no rival woman but a spark of connection. If I didn't write it down that very moment, it was gone, the memory of a dream.

"You know Thoreau?" I continued.

"*Walden?*" Kaori said, her surprise obvious.

"Don't look so shocked. I've read books, too. Yeah, *Walden*. I had to memorize one of his poems in high school. 'I did not, when I wished to die, discover that I had not lived.' I thought that quote was terrific, thought Henry David Thoreau and I thought about the world the same way. Later on, guess what I found out? While he was off living his solitary life in the woods, his mother came each week to pick up his laundry."

She whistled. "You're kidding."

"Men get to live deliberately, and we get to do their laundry. So? We can complain, or we can write while the clothes are drying. Write while you're in line at the grocery store, write when you're at a stop-light, it doesn't matter. Just write." It sounded so simple coming out of my mouth, but I hadn't written anything in years. "You want some coffee? Water should still be hot."

She looked surprised. "Sure. Thank you. With milk, please."

"We don't have milk."

"I bought some in Jeff City."

I put a hand over my mouth. "You'll have to throw it out when we stop next. The smell, the taste—I just never have it around."

She widened her eyes. "Okay."

"Let's have a drink instead. Are you even of age? No, don't answer that. You're on the road, you're of age. I'll make you a drink."

She studied me, wary. "That's all right. I can do it. Would you like whiskey?" I nodded, and she went to the front and returned with two cups, a bottle of whiskey, and another of rum.

"Thanks, about the milk," I said, pouring a bit of whiskey into my cup. "So how'd you come to country? Was it on the radio much in Minnesota?"

"Record sorting for Stanley."

"What's that?"

She explained how her family had lived next door to Stanley and his wife when they'd lived in Minneapolis, and her father had been his doctor. Stanley used to pay her a dollar an hour to do tasks like filing his papers and organizing his records. Part of that involved listening to each record all the way through to see if it was scratched, and then whether it should go under "country" or "pop" or "jazz." "He had a basement study, and I'd be in there for hours, listening," she said. "I couldn't believe I got paid for that." Her parents had put her in violin lessons at age five, and she'd hated them, annoyed by the precise sheet music and the strict instructor who chided her for tapping her foot in rhythm. When Kaori listened to one of Stanley's records and heard the crowd break into wild applause after Suzi Arden fiddled faster than she thought was possible, she taught herself fiddling on her violin. Her parents wanted her to go to college and become a lawyer or a doctor; she had other ideas. In college she recruited some other kids and started her own bluegrass band, playing mostly traditionals but also some original pieces she'd written.

We sipped our drinks. "What do your parents think of it?" I said.

"Well, my sister's in med school, and my brother's a lawyer. I'm a fiddle player and college dropout, so I'm throwing my life away." She shook out the rum bottle, but it was empty.

"The world has plenty of doctors and lawyers. If it isn't you, you can't make it you." I slid the almost-full whiskey bottle toward her. "Move on to this, if you want. I'm gonna turn in."

"Good night, Lillian." She examined the liquid in the whiskey bottle like it held an answer.

In my room I opened the drawer of my bedside table, where I'd left a notebook. *Just write*, big talker. I kicked off my shoes and sat on my bed, still wearing my show outfit, a blue satin dress with flouncy sleeves. I ripped off the sheet where I'd written "Target shaped like a bottle" and placed it on top of my quilt, then pulled a pencil from a drawer and held it in the air for a second.

Target, bottle. Bottle, target.

Bottle target. I could do something with that. I hopped off the bed and grabbed my beat-up acoustic from the closet. On the bed, I leaned over my guitar to scribble lyrics. I started off with a 4/4 rhythm: "You got a bottle target on your back. You said you'd quit the drinking and come back," I sang. Not quite it. But there was a kernel.

The bus hit a rut in the highway, sending my pencil skittering onto the bed. "Doggone it," I muttered.

The rhythm felt too plodding. I tried to think back to the moment when the country music I sang became danceable and rhythmic. It had been in Tacoma, of course. I sat back against a pillow and conjured up the city in the forties. The smell of the Waterway, and the pitch of the hills, and people crowding into taverns in their oil-splattered work clothes after a shift, places so loud you could hardly hear the instruments.

The music was spreading then, out from the migrant camps and down from the mountain towns, over radio waves, into jukeboxes. The people sang it working grapes in Porterville and picking apples in Yakima. They strapped bass fiddles on their cars and drove the kerosene circuit to county fairs, to courthouses, to church basements, to schools, to square dances. They took mandolins to their waitressing jobs, and after serving burgers and milkshakes to hungry customers, they sang and played. They recorded acetates and delivered them to radio station DJs.

Then the soldiers carried the music farther, bringing it with them on trains to Army bases, and as the country mixed and migrated, the music did too. Stationed at bases with jukeboxes, some Americans heard the music for the first time. House bands charged a dollar cover, and honky-tonks served beer and pop and hot sausages. And if a band didn't make people dance, it'd be booed right out of there.

So: "Bottle target" would want a brisk beat, the sound of work boots on a hard floor, one and a two and a three and a four.

I picked it up, crossed out, rewrote, tried different chords, heard the Farvers and Kaori go to bed and Charlie noodling on his guitar up front. The Green Giant drove west, hours passed, I slapped my thigh to figure out the rhythm, and I filled the notebook's pages. "Charlie," I said, finally looking up, but my door was closed. I leaped from the bed, opened the door and ran down the bus aisle, barefoot, holding the notebook. "Charlie," I said, waving it in the air. "Charlie, I wrote a song."

★ 12 ★

Tacoma, Washington
1941–1945

"My Lord," Charlie said, surveying the music library at KVI, which I'd discovered a few weeks prior. I was now on *Country Canteen* five days a week, and if I had time before my second shift at Triton's, I listened to records from the station's huge collection. Charlie, who'd agreed to play with me on air that day, touched the albums' spines, some alphabetized on shelves, some so fresh from the record labels they were in mailers. He jogged to the classical section and pulled out a Brahms, then trailed his free hand until he got to jazz, and tipped out a Django Reinhardt record. "Lillian, you get to mess around in here all day?"

I snorted. "Yeah, because I've got nothing but free time." I woke at four each day to open at Triton's, and if I was covering dinner, I wasn't home until midnight.

"I mean, you can listen to anything in here?"

"Sure I can. They let me pick a couple tracks for the show, too."

He whistled. "Should've gone into radio. What're you listening to now?"

I lifted the record-player needle to replay a song. "It's the new Bob

Wills single. I just can't figure out what Eldon Shamblin's doing on guitar to get that sound."

When the song finished, he said, "It sounds like he's using jazz chords."

I didn't listen to jazz, figured it was the kind of thing sophisticated Chicago and New York people listened to, not people like me and Charlie. He gestured for me to give him my Gretsch, checked the tuning, and in a few seconds he was mimicking the song's guitar sounds near perfectly.

"I thought you played fiddle," I said.

"I've been teaching myself guitar, too. You should listen to—hold on." He stood up, went to the jazz section, pulled out a Benny Goodman record called "Flying Home," and put it on. He told me to listen for Charlie Christian, who was playing an amplified guitar called a Gibson ES-150.

Charlie dropped the needle. The beginning sounded like the new kind of jazz that had been catching on lately, with a swing beat and an energetic piano. I slapped my leg in time. That opening was followed by instruments I couldn't quite identify; one sounded like a mallet hitting a xylophone, but with way more vibration than usual. And then, about fifty seconds in, I heard it: Charlie Christian, playing his amplified guitar as easily and melodically as if he were skipping over piano keys. Johnny—I now played with the Paper Boys regularly— had an amplified Gibson, too, but he handled it just like I played my Gretsch, same notes, same strumming, a little picking. Charlie Christian was making a new sound. I darted to the record player, one ear cocked so I could register every detail. I'd always considered a guitar an accompanying instrument, filling out a singer's voice with rhythm or chords. But Charlie Christian made the guitar the star.

When the solo ended, I moved the needle back to hear it again. This time I moved my own fingers on imaginary strings to see if I could sort out what Christian was doing, but it wasn't making sense. "What's the secret?" I said.

Charlie held up his palms. "Don't know. I think you'd need to work it out with an amplified guitar and an amp."

I recalled seeing both in the office of Stewart Spencer, Sales, as I thought of him. I'd never once heard him play the guitar, and I figured he'd gotten them as a freebie from a KVI advertiser. I told Charlie we should borrow them.

"We can't. You'd lose your job," he said.

"We're not stealing. We're just testing them out. He won't be there; he's out on sales calls every afternoon. Come on." Once I hit the corridor and crossed into the hallway of executives' offices, I imitated the pronounced hip sway of their secretaries, trying to appear like I'd been sent on an important errand, Charlie a few paces behind. Stewart Spencer, Sales, had left his door open, and inside was the guitar, glossy and gorgeous, its dark edges sliding into sunny maple at the center.

"Oh," Charlie said, his voice weak. "That's what Christian plays. A Gibson ES-150."

"Then it's meant to be," I said.

"Lil, we shouldn't."

"Why? Because Stewart Spencer has it and we don't? This is a fellow who says 'Hello, Mrs. Hideous' to Mrs. Hideshima every time he gets here."

"He gets away with his hide?" Upon arrival at the station, Charlie had been reprimanded by Mrs. Hideshima for wearing wet work boots into the reception area.

"Not much she can say back, I guess. He's a big deal around here. So we don't need to feel bad about borrowing something he doesn't even know how to use. You're telling me you don't want to play that thing?"

Charlie squinted as though he were staring into the sun.

"There's my answer." I picked up the guitar and pointed to the amp. "You can carry that."

We took our plunder back into the library, no one seeming to notice what we were doing. Charlie set the amp on the floor and shut the door, and we both exhaled. I rotated my old guitar so its strings faced the wall. "Don't look," I said to the Gretsch. "She's prettier than you."

Charlie tuned the ES-150, plugged it into the amp, plugged the amp in, too, and played the opening chords to "A-Tisket, A-Tasket," which had a similarly jazzy feel to the Benny Goodman record. By now I knew the sound of Johnny T.'s amplified guitar well, but this had a different sound, bright, like a slice of sun through Tacoma clouds. I closed my eyes, and a moment later felt Charlie put the guitar in my lap. "Your turn," he said.

The notes I tried sounded jarring. "Could you play the Charlie Christian record again?" I said.

As it played, I slid my left hand up several frets, toward the body of the guitar, trying to figure out his approach. I tried a chord that should've sounded good, but it came off as muddy. "It's higher," I said. "He's playing higher up the neck, I think." I experimented, trying different chord shapes up the fretboard with my left hand and picking out individual notes with my right.

He narrowed his eyes. "This is really the first time you've heard Charlie Christian?"

"Yeah, why?"

Charlie took the guitar back from me and moved his left hand up to where mine had been. "Because I've been trying to figure this out for a few weeks now, and I think you just did it in five minutes. You're right, I think, that he's playing all the way up here. It would mean less distortion and give a clearer sound. If you think about the dominant chord there—"

I looked at him blankly.

"Where did you say you were taught music?" he said.

"I wasn't. Picked it up here and there."

"Hah," he said, that sound from the back of his throat. "You never studied it? Theory? Composition?"

"No." I cupped my ear. "Just listened and picked it up. Learned the names of the chords, that's about it. Did you? Take lessons and all?"

"My mother studied classical piano, so she taught me."

"You're from out east, then?"

"Why do you think that?"

"Whatever you just said: 'theory,' 'composition.' Don't think they teach that stuff out here. I didn't learn it, at least. And you had a mother who studied classical piano, which also isn't so popular here in Washington."

He laughed. "She was from Indiana. But I grew up in Cheyenne."

"Cheyenne? You ride?"

"Sure."

"Horse do that to you, then?" I asked, pointing to the protruding collarbone I'd noticed.

"Yep. Colt threw me off when I was a kid. My dad was a ranch foreman." That sounded right; Charlie looked to me like he'd spent time in the sun, dark freckles everywhere.

"You come to Tacoma for work?"

"I came here to play country and western music." He said this plainly, and it was the first time I'd heard anyone be so earnest about music, as though it were a legitimate living and not just something we squeezed in on the side. He told me he was the youngest of four sons. His mother taught him to read music and play piano, but it was a ranch hand who'd shown him how to fiddle. Charlie had saved up for a basic fiddle, and his parents thought it was a pleasant enough distraction on the nights when the boys were making camp and helping run cattle, but they expected Charlie to go into ranching like the other sons. He had a different notion. Cheyenne, the only major stop on the Union Pacific's City of Portland route between Chicago and the coast, saw a lot of travelers making their way West. Charlie hung around the Union Pacific depot enough to pick up that Tacoma was the place to be for musicians. "A girl I grew up with, Margery, and her family were already out in Tacoma, so my parents thought they'd make sure I was all right," he told me. He was vague with his parents about his plans out here, and when he got a job at the salt plant, wrote to them about that without mentioning his music. "What about you? Where are you from?"

"Eastern Washington. Walla Walla."

"Isn't that farm country? I thought you hated milk."

"Had my fill of it, I guess."

"Your family there? You have brothers, sisters?"

"One. A sister. Henrietta."

"You must miss her."

I said nothing, thinking of her smirking as the sun hit her shiny brown hair. I knew KVI's range didn't extend to Walla Walla, but hoped she'd heard me somehow, maybe on a trip to Western Washington.

"Why'd you leave?" Charlie asked.

I'd been working on different answers to this. Althea asked me the same thing in my first week at Triton's, and I'd spilled a splash of coffee so I wouldn't have to respond. I needed something that would let me glide over the fact of leaving the farm at age ten, which would raise too many questions. I needed to make it sound like I'd come straight to Tacoma from the farm. I'd settled on a response that I hoped was silly enough to shut people up, so I tried it out now. "We were a farm family with two girls; one of us had to work, and let's just say when it came to brains . . ." I tapped my temple. The next line, I'd perfected with an accent I thought was southern and ladylike, based on Vivien Leigh's in Gone with the Wind, which I'd seen at the Roxy in Walla Walla. I fanned myself, Scarlett-style, and added, "And to think that I was blessed with the intelligence and the beauty, too. My poor, dear old sister."

Charlie gave me a look like I was nuts, but he didn't ask me anything else. We passed the Gibson back and forth, playing different tunes. He talked about music in ways I didn't understand: counterpoints, modes, imitations he heard in fugues. We played until we heard the warning siren of Stewart Spencer, Sales, saying "Hello, Mrs. Hideous," and Mrs. Hideshima's flat reply. Only then did Charlie lift the amp and jog back to Stewart's office, and I followed him with the guitar.

From then on, when Charlie came to Triton's, he gave me lists of jazz and blues records, my own reference library: Freddie Green playing in the Count Basie Orchestra, Eddie Lang with Bing Crosby's band, W. C. Handy, George Van Eps, Eddie Durham, Big Bill Broonzy, Mississippi John Hurt, and Blind Lemon Jefferson. Althea's boyfriend, Claude, teased me about it whenever he picked Althea up: "What's that boy got you listening to now, Lillian?" he'd ask.

When I listened to Charlie's suggestions, they sounded country to me, in a good way: the same topics as the stuff I'd grown up with, like wayward men, hard times, and money problems, but with eerier singing and better guitar playing. Charlie's lists progressed from just names of artists to what seemed like coded messages. The day I wore a crimson dress to Triton's, Charlie scrawled on the end of the list Jimmie Gordon's "Little Red Dress (Mary Usta Wear)." The wheat in my belly swished when I touched his handwriting.

For my part, I experimented more with Stewart Spencer's Gibson, copying licks I heard from country players, too, making them on what we'd soon call electric guitar. I figured out minor chords and chord progressions, and tried to get my fingers moving faster and faster as I picked out melodies. Guitars had been around for hundreds of years, and as much as I loved my Gretsch, it always felt like I was playing catch-up with what earlier players had already mastered. With electric guitar, though, I was discovering this instrument at the same time as the professional musicians, creating a new sound that could tell my story.

Johnny T., flush with money he'd inherited from his grandfather's shingle mills, showed up at one performance with a brand-new amplifier. I asked him what had happened to the other one, and he said he was throwing it out. I went to his house, pulled the amp out of his alleyway trash bin, and brought it to the basement room where I lived. When I told Charlie the next morning at Triton's, he raised his tomato juice in a toast. "Guess what," he said. "I've been saving up for my own Gibson." He bought an ES-150 two months later and brought it to the KVI library so we could play together. When it got to be springtime and the days of gray and cold rain stopped, we met outside at Charlie's place.

Charlie lived in an upstairs room in a house in North End, not far from my place in Old Town but a steep walk uphill, like everything in Tacoma. From one side of his corner, we had a clear view down to the tip of the busy port. A quarter turn to the north and we saw Commencement Bay, as wild as it must have been hundreds of years ago besides a couple of houses dotting Vashon Island. We sat on cement stairs cut into the sidewalk while his dog, a copper-colored mutt named Red with a tail in the shape of a bass clef, patrolled the sidewalk. ("Red?" I'd said when I met the dog, pointedly checking out Charlie's own russet hair and pink freckles. "He looked like family," he replied.) Charlie brought jars of Nalley's pickles. The first time he offered me a pickle from an open jar, I took one out of politeness and ate a bite, and then spit it out when he plunged his hand into the jar and let it sit there.

"What on earth?" I said, coughing.

He tipped the jar toward me. "Want to try it? It thickens your calluses."

"Yuck, and I'm never eating a pickle from one of your jars again." I scratched Red's head.

"I could stay here forever," Charlie said then, and I was thankful that Red distracted us by lunging for a squirrel, so I didn't have to figure out how to tell him that I felt the same.

I spent more and more time at KVI, translating what I'd heard on the library records. I made little money and ate once or twice a day, depending on what Triton's customers left behind and whether Marko was at the dish station. Mrs. Hideshima, who brought in homemade banana bread for the office, seemed to notice my constant hunger. She sliced off the ends of her loaves and stored them for me in the library. In return, I brought her bananas too bruised for the new Bananas Foster Triton's had just added to the dessert menu to appeal to the shipbuilders who'd recently moved here from Louisiana. Realizing, I think, that I was mostly subsisting on her banana bread, Mrs. Hideshima mentioned that I could pick up extra money on weekends by filling in on the better-paid Saturday and Sunday shows. She took the messages when a singer called to say he couldn't come, and gave me notice so I could plead with the weekend manager to let me take a spot.

One Sunday, the regular trio of University of Puget Sound singers for the 11:00 a.m. country show was at a competition in Spokane, and I got to substitute. It would be a long day of work, as I was supposed to cover a Triton's shift and the Paper Boys had booked a show at Pappy's Cabin on Pacific that night, but I didn't mind.

A skeleton crew—just the weekend manager, an engineer, and the DJ—were also working, but the DJ was coming off a drunk and kept dozing off. Though the manager supplied him with coffee, the DJ would introduce records that he hadn't told the engineer to cue up, and the engineer threw such a fit that I ended up carrying most of the show.

For my third song, sitting in an office chair, I'd positioned the mic so it picked up my voice and my Gretsch equally, and I picked my way through "Dusty Old Dust." During the last verse, I noticed the manager on the other side of the glass holding a sheet of paper, his face pale. I hurried up the rhythm and got to the end fast, but the manager didn't wait for my last chord to die out before he opened the door to the on-air studio and fumbled for the mic like he'd been blinded. He practically sat on me before I jumped up. I don't think he'd spoken on air before, because he made a terrible racket as he uncrumpled the paper into the microphone.

"I've got to tell you," he said into the mic. "This is the assistant weekend program manager of radio station KVI, Tacoma, Washington, speaking. We have reports of an attack on Oahu, Hawaii, in the Pacific. From Japanese forces, we are hearing, on military targets there. We are directed to ask you to remain calm, and for military personnel and auxiliary personnel to return to their bases immediately, and for citizen volunteers to proceed calmly to police and fire stations. Again, we have reports of an attack taking place from the Japanese in Oahu, Hawaii." The manager ran out of breath.

I wasn't even sure where Hawaii was exactly, besides somewhere in the Pacific. We'd all been focused on the European war—would we or wouldn't we get officially involved—but this, this was immediate and sure.

From the far side of the glass, the engineer, a telephone receiver sandwiched between his ear and shoulder, made a keep-going circle with his index finger. "Dead air," he mouthed; it was a cardinal sin in radio, because audiences immediately switched stations when they heard silence.

My toes felt cold. "Dead air," I whispered to the manager.

His face was blank as he gazed at the paper he held.

"Dead air," I said, louder. The engineer motioned with the phone receiver in the air: *Do* something. The guitar was still strapped around my body, and I played a C, then an F, and then I used my leg to drag the manager, in the chair, away from the mic. There was only one song I could think to sing then, as I pictured soldiers destined for Hawaii rushing to Tacoma's ports, and that was "I Cover the Waterfront."

I stayed at the station as staff flooded in in their Sunday church clothes, as assistants ran around with cables, as desks filled with producers and newsreaders, as we broadcast a reporter from Honolulu on the roof of a hotel describing the bombs, the fires, for three hours. We would be next, we thought, just across the Pacific, with Boeing and Fort Lewis and McChord Field making us a target. I claimed an empty desk near the library, and when I heard planes, I dove underneath it, laying my body carefully over my Gretsch. Sandwiches came from somewhere; I ate one filled with ham and mustard. I stayed until evening, no one noticing that I was there, and I forgot about my Triton's shift as I swallowed down news like it was whiskey. Soldiers going to guard the Boeing plant. A radio report of "Japanese farmers" down East Marginal Way, just south of Boeing, who could be saboteurs. Blackouts. The radio station was to go off air at 7:00 p.m. The FBI was searching houses of people of Japanese descent, an issue of national safety. Leaders of the Japanese American community were being arrested.

I missed my Triton's shift entirely and remembered the Pappy's gig only half an hour before it was supposed to start, and called Johnny T.'s house to see if it was on, but no one picked up. Charlie's neighbor, who took calls for him sometimes, said he was out, too. Not knowing what else to do, I took my guitar and went to Pappy's, exchanging tentative glances with the few other people on the streets. I found Johnny and the bass player outside the closed bar, passing a gin bottle back and forth, deep in a heated conversation about the attack. As I approached, Charlie arrived from the opposite direction, his fiddle case in one hand, his Gibson case in the other, though he'd never played the Gibson with the Paper Boys. There were a thousand things I wanted to talk to him about—the radio station, the war, would he enlist, who would take care of Red if he did—but I thought we had so much time unspooling in front of us, and instead of saying something important, I said, "You brought the Gibson?"

"I didn't know if we'd play, but I thought if we did, maybe you'd want to use it," Charlie said.

I widened my eyes. "That guitar should be played at an auditorium somewhere, not here, tonight."

"It's a guitar that should be played, period. I guess we don't have a show, but I thought if the crowd heard you play this tonight, it'd give them something nice to think about. Maybe at the next gig." He lifted the Gibson from its case and offered it to me, meeting my eyes with a question. My blood flow seemed to slow, and I forgot how to lift my arms up to take it. Charlie took a step closer, set the guitar against my body, then lifted the strap over my head and lowered it. His hand lingered on my shoulder. I brushed the low E string, and it vibrated.

"Well, well, what's this?" Johnny T. said, clawing for the guitar. "You got a Gibson?"

"It's Charlie's," I said, stepping away.

Johnny looked from Charlie to me, then squatted down to examine the instrument. "An ES-150," he said. "What, one last spending spree before you settle down? Margery let you get away with this?"

"Margery?" I said, not quite placing the name.

Johnny's eyes were unfocused from the alcohol. "Charlie's girl. Wedding's in a couple weeks, isn't it?"

I opened my mouth, but nothing came out.

"Guess it's smart to buy it before the wife tells you not to," the bass player offered.

My temples pulsed. Charlie swished his shoe back and forth on the sidewalk.

"Can I take her for a spin?" Johnny asked Charlie, reaching for the guitar.

"No," I said.

"It's not yours," Johnny pointed out.

"Know something, Johnny? It sure isn't." I yanked the guitar off my body and thrust it at Charlie.

Johnny shrugged. "I'm gonna get out of here. Go find someplace that's serving something tonight. Who wants to come?" He ambled off with the bass player, leaving me and Charlie frozen a couple of yards apart in an Old West standoff, the guitar dangling between us.

"Lillian," he said. "I should've told you. Margery's a friend of the family."

"Yes. I remember now. Her family was supposed to watch out for you in Tacoma when you left Cheyenne."

"See, we've been engaged practically since we were kids; everyone expected us to get married, and that made the whole move here, for me, something my parents were fine with."

"That's a sweet story, Charlie."

"No, it's that—I'm trying to say, you and I started spending so much time together, and at first it seemed strange to mention it, and then it seemed strange that I hadn't."

"Stop. Stop. You don't have to explain. You don't owe me anything."
I shoved the Gibson at his chest, and he reflexively grabbed it. Then
I picked up my Gretsch and walked away. I wanted Charlie to come
after me, to shake me, to tell me that Margery was a mistake and he
and I would play guitar together forever, sitting on his cement steps as
Red sniffed around, but he stayed put.

When I got back to the Old Town bungalow, I felt as worn out as
if I'd been working the harvest all day. The landlady wasn't home yet,
but a rolled-up newspaper was on her front porch from the morning.
I picked it up, let myself in, and went downstairs, passing the other
boarders murmuring about the attack. On my bed, I unrolled the paper. This paper did not know what was to happen at 7:55 Honolulu
time on Sunday morning. This paper did not know that Charlie's and
my time together had to end, trivial as that seemed next to the attack
in Hawaii. This paper did not know what was to come tomorrow. Nor
did we.

What would come: We would obey the blackouts, racing home to
avoid the dark streets and the cars without headlights on. We would
share rumors as we waited for early buses in the black mornings. We
would compare notes on where to find cooking oil. We would divide
up rotting cucumbers at the grocery, since all the Japanese and Japanese American people, including the vegetable farmers who supplied
most of the state's produce, had their money frozen. Merchants in
Nihonmachi put up American flags and signs declaring their US loy-
alty in their windows. Our mayor, Harry Cain, went on the radio, telling Tacomans to "protect the rights of those Japanese who know so
well what it means to be an American," and invited Eleanor Roosevelt, when she visited Tacoma that December, to meet with Japanese
American students.

It didn't matter. The government required anyone of Japanese ancestry to turn in radios, cameras, and other equipment that could be used
to spy. Soldiers who were any part Japanese were reclassified from 1A
to 4C, "enemy aliens," unfit for combat. All over town, the federal

government posted handbills, and soldiers eating at Triton's left behind pamphlets they'd been issued. Beware of the Japanese. How to
tell "a Chinese" from someone Japanese. At work, most of the KVI
men stopped saying good morning to Mrs. Hideshima. I overheard
Stewart Spencer, Sales, telling the station manager it was a danger to
have her so close to broadcasting equipment. When the curfews and
travel restrictions came down, it was hard for me to imagine what the
government was hoping to do by keeping Mrs. Hideshima inside her
house after eight o'clock. I left the bananas in their usual spot at the foot
of her desk, not because I wanted her to make banana bread for the office anymore when none of those men deserved her banana bread, but
because I didn't want her to think my view of her had shifted.

And then President Roosevelt issued an executive order about evacuation and relocation. The rumors came fast: they would take Ger-
mans, Italians, Japanese. I assumed it would be recent immigrants,
those who had the closest ties to their old country, not people born here
or living here for years. They can't be worried about Mrs. Hideshima,
I said to a KVI producer, who didn't reply. In March General John L.
DeWitt announced the evacuation of anyone of Japanese ancestry
from the Western parts of Washington, Oregon, and California, didn't
matter if you'd thought of your family as Americans for generations.
"Evacuation," as though it were for their own safety. Children—the
same students who'd met with Mrs. Roosevelt—nurses, teachers, busi-
nessmen, Mrs. Hideshima. Signs went up telling anyone of Japanese
descent to report to Union Station two weeks from the posting date,
bringing only what they could carry.

The Monday the posters went up, I arrived at work to find Mrs.
Hideshima at her desk, typing more quietly than usual. Stewart Spen-
cer, Sales, told her she was not to speak to anyone that called for him.
She pressed the bridge of her glasses to her nose and kept typing. I
took a couple of fresher bananas along with the brown ones from
Triton's the next morning, and left them in the usual spot, but she

didn't come to KVI on Tuesday, nor on Wednesday. On Thursday, the bananas had started to smell of sweet rot. I asked the morning-show manager where Mrs. Hideshima was. He said she was seeing to her affairs.

I threw the bananas in a trash can, left KVI, and wandered through Nihonmachi, where some merchants put up handwritten signs: "Evacuation Sale. Fifty percent off." Other stores were shuttered, with goods still in them. Cars—bound for who knows where, as people weren't allowed to leave with cars—had suitcases and furniture tied onto them, and their drivers honked and yelled. Outside apartment buildings people piled up stuff, chairs or clothes or books, selling everything for pennies on the dollar. It reminded me of being in Walla Walla when the banks closed, the farmers selling their best stock horses for a fraction of their value. When a young mother set her baby's crib on the curb, I left all the change I had on her doorstep. But it was a useless offering, and I knew it. A man dragging a trunk uphill caught my eye, and called something to me from across the street, and I pretended I didn't hear him.

I did not want to witness any more. I stayed far from Nihonmachi and Union Station on the May morning they left.

Charlie, Johnny T., the rest of the Paper Boys, the male KVI radio singers, they all joined the service, off to training in various branches. At Triton's, Althea developed puffy bags under her eyes and kept mixing up the caf and decaf. Her boyfriend, Claude, had enlisted in the Navy, but she'd wanted him to stay home, she said. When I asked why he didn't just wait to be drafted, she appeared very tired. "He doesn't want them to think we're not patriotic," she told me.

This was all coming, and there, in my hands, was the oblivious morning paper from December 7, 1941. Time would be divided into before and after, as my little world already had been so many times.

★ ★ ★

"Engaged," Althea said, tucking her legs underneath her on a wicker settee. "I wouldn't have guessed that."

"Married, now, has to be," I said. We sat on the porch of her apartment building, now our apartment building. A whiskey bottle and a mug of half-cold coffee sat on a table in front of us, and rain tapped on the roof above. My concrete basement room in Old Town had never been very appealing, and with winter's rain and darkness, it had become impossible. Walking to Triton's during the blackouts for my 5:00 a.m. openings made me worried about getting hit by a car or by a madman, but waiting in the dark for a bus with its lights off meant I missed more rides than I made. I'd asked Althea, whose Hilltop apartment was a short walk from the restaurant, to put me in touch with her building's manager. When a nurse leaving Tacoma for a military hospital moved out, I got her room. The building was three-story and brick, with a covered porch where residents socialized in summer; it being March and drizzling, Althea and I had it all to ourselves.

"Did he say what he wanted me to do with the guitar?" I asked.

Althea had come back from Triton's that day lugging Charlie's Gibson. He hadn't returned to Triton's during my regular shifts, but Althea said he'd stopped by, hadn't ordered anything, just asked her to give it to me.

"Keep it until he's back, I guess."

"Back from where?"

"What do the two of you talk about?" she said. "He said he was taking his dog to his parents' in Wyoming. He's shipping out this week."

I picked up my coffee from the beat-up wicker table and added whiskey to the mug, forcing myself to worry how city dog Red would do in the country. "We haven't actually talked," I said. "Not since he told me he was engaged."

Althea pulled out a pack of cigarettes and lit one. "Were you two . . ."

"No."

"Don't mean offense. I know you're inexperienced."

I coughed into the drink.

"There are other fish in the sea. Other fish out *at* sea, I should say. There aren't going to be many men left in this town soon."

"What are you gonna do with Claude? How long's he got?"

"Finishes boot camp next month."

"Has he proposed again?" Claude seemed to ask Althea to marry him more or less weekly. Once he'd done it in front of me at Triton's, and Althea had just said "Shush" and smoothed her hair.

She blew out a ring of smoke. "Twice."

"He's persistent."

"Let him write letters to me from overseas, pine for me, show me how he missed me when he gets back. You think I want to be a house-wife right now?"

"You'd be bored?"

"Honey." She helped herself to a sip of my coffee. "Being a wife is more work than being a waitress. I'm one of six children, and believe me, I saw it with my own mother."

She offered me the cigarette; I waved it away. "It's bad for my sing-ing voice," I said.

"Mine, too, but that doesn't stop me."

"Hold on. You sing?"

She raised a finger. "No, no, no. I know you've been trying to make your own band with the boys leaving, and I don't sing your kind of music."

"Where do you sing, then?"

"Church."

I looked pointedly at the whiskey bottle and the cigarette, then back at her, and she shrugged. "What? I can't have a little fun because I go to church? I like the music. Less so the preacher. That man does go on."

"Don't you want to sing outside of church?"

"'Don't you want to sing outside of church?'" she mocked. "You think you aren't obvious? No, not if it's hillbilly music."

"Do you have to call it that? Just say 'country.' Anyway, I'm serious, Althea. I was at KVI yesterday, and the station manager was saying how he's losing all his men's groups, and that he'd have space on the Saturday show for a girls' group if I could get a good one together. Saturday has lots of listeners. We'd have a real audience."

"It's . . ." She wrinkled her nose. "It's hillbilly. All those songs are about a man drowning his girlfriend, or a woman drowning herself because the man's with someone else. It's so dramatic, like 'If he be married, my grave is like to be my wedding bed.'" She said this last part in a quavering actress's voice, her eyelids fluttering.

"What song is that from?" I asked.

"It's from *Romeo and Juliet*. You didn't have to read it in high school?"

"Althea, in high school I learned how to capon a chicken," I said. "It's not all grave and wedding bed stuff, anyway. I think you're thinking of old-fashioned songs like 'Banks of the Ohio.' Country and western isn't that. It's dancing, rhythm, fun. You've never even heard it, have you? It's good music with a beat, songs about real people. Wait."

I hopped up, ran up to my room, and returned with my Gretsch. "What's a song you like to sing?" I asked her.

"Oh, I don't know. 'Tea for Two.'"

It was a snappy little song whose melody I knew, and I worked out chords on the guitar. "Ready?" I said, three of my left-hand fingers pressing down to make an A-minor chord, my right fingers hovering over the strings. She stared at the mug, and for a minute I thought she was going to pour it out and leave, but instead she took a sip of the coffee, took a deep breath from her belly—the kind good singers know to take—and sang a slow verse in a rich alto. I accompanied her. When she finished the first verse, I said, "You can sing."

"Yes."

"So, country—"

"Hillbilly—"

"Country, what we'd do is like this." I played the chords again, but gave them a strong downbeat this time, and took the verse once more, making it sound lively and danceable this time. When I finished, I said, "How about it? You and me, in a band? We'd get a couple others, another girl or two. I've heard one of the boarders here fiddling in her room, and I can find out who it is. Then we'd just need someone on rhythm, probably bass, or I suppose someone could hold a tambourine, if it comes to that. It'd be country songs along with whatever you wanted to sing, just a little faster for the crowd. 'Day will break and you'll awake,'" I sang, slapping the Gretsch for percussion. "If we did KVI on Saturdays, we could land other gigs around town, plus KVI pays more on the weekends."

She tapped her cigarette in an ashtray. "KVI pays?"

"Not much, but sure."

"I thought it was a hobby you had. Do the gigs pay, too?"

"Johnny T. never paid me, said I was getting paid in 'experience,' but the band made money, enough to cover gas and food and have a little left over."

"We'd split it? Evenly?"

"Evenly."

"But . . ." She took a deep draw of her cigarette.

"What?"

"Lillian. You don't think that's gonna be a problem? You being white, and us singing together?"

"It's Washington State. Not Louisiana."

"It's gonna feel like Louisiana real fast if they see a Black girl up there with a white one."

"Washington's not like that," I said easily.

To think that I meant it then. When I became a songwriter, I tried to get in people's heads, seeing a stranger at the grocery or the gas station and pulling a life story from his worn shoes, from the swoop of her eyeliner. Yet when I considered Althea, my friend, my coworker, I figured she was more or less like I was, held back like I was, by being a woman, and if we could just confront that, she could choose what she wanted just as I could.

"Lil, look at this place. There's a reason you're on the second floor, and I'm on the third," she said.

"I'm on the second because that's where a room opened up."

"You ever wonder why the manager offered the open room to you, a girl she'd just met, and not to me, who'd been living here two years?"

The second floor was nicer, with oak floors inlaid with patterns, moldings on the ceilings, and a larger tub in the shared bathroom. I took a sip of whiskey from the bottle. "So anybody gives us trouble, we leave. KVI's never had a girls' group before, so this is the one chance we have, while the boys are at war."

Althea stubbed out her cigarette. "You know, I've got a little sister plays bass."

"Why didn't you say so?"

"Because you'd get all . . ." She gestured at me. "Like you're about to twitch."

"Can she play country?"

"Joy's still in high school, and plays in a youth symphony now, but she *can* play anything she wants to. The question is whether she *wants* to play country."

"If her big sister told her how great it was . . ."

"Now I'm a country music promoter? I'm doing it for the pay, let's keep it clear." She took a sip from the bottle. "Joy wants to go to college, though, so she could use the money, and I bet you could use it too. How are you going to keep waitressing when you can't stand the smell of milk? Just promise me one thing. Don't you ever sing 'Tea for Two' in public. You'd better not ruin that song for me."

I picked up the mug and clinked it against the bottle. "Deal."

★ ★ ★

We called ourselves the Snoqualmie Sweethearts, after a mountain near Tacoma. Althea, despite her aversion to hillbilly music, knew a host of songs that sounded country to my ear. The fast-talking fiddler, a pale redhead named Lettie, was a bucker at the shipyards, and called every man she met Mac, a habit I soon picked up. She'd been born in Appalachia and came west when her father got a job paving the Snoqualmie Pass. Althea's sister, Joy, had an incredible ear, and was soon playing country on her bass like she'd been doing it for a lifetime. She was barely five feet tall, and why a girl that small chose an instrument that huge, I don't know, but she could play the bass arpeggios from Vivaldi's "Summer" in one breath and in the next do an impersonation of her big sister, down to Althea's chin juts when she sang low notes, that had us all in tears.

At practice, I saw a connection between the sisters that stirred a memory just shapeless enough that I couldn't quite harness it: Joy poked fun at Althea between songs, and Althea went right back at Joy with a retort that would've shut me up for a week. When Althea sang and Joy plucked the bass, though, the two of them could simply exchange a glance and communicate, shifting into two-part harmony or picking up the rhythm in sync, and despite all the ribbing, when they used the easy "we" to describe themselves, their family, it made me recall me and Hen, though I couldn't think when or why.

In the apartment building's basement on Tuesday nights, we rehearsed, picking some of the same songs, but we knew them differently. We all knew "Midnight Special," for instance, but we all thought it was about a jail near where we'd grown up—I'd figured it was about the Walla Walla pen, with the Northern Pacific line running right there; Althea was sure it was about the Angola prison in Louisiana; and Lettie had heard it was based on Sing Sing. When I called out "Goodbye Liza Jane," and played the version I knew, Joy went into "Steal Miss Liza" and said she'd learned it as a kid.

One night we ran into trouble figuring out how to play Gene Autry's "Back in the Saddle Again," though we more or less agreed on the words. It was our feelings that clashed, a collision of sound. After a few times, Lettie plucked a string hard. "What is this song *about?*" she asked.

"About riding a horse, free as anything," said Joy.

"But riding a horse isn't that freeing," Lettie said. She'd learned to ride as a kid, but instead of galloping like her brothers did, she had to sit a certain way, wasn't allowed to go faster than a canter, and had to be accompanied by her riding instructor on every trail.

"That's true. I never got to ride the range like Gene Autry," I said. "If I was ever on a horse, it was for farm work."

"So maybe that's how we ought to sing it," Althea suggested. "'Back in the Saddle' just means something different for girls."

We tried the song again, and this time none of us sounded happy about the saddle. Instead, we sounded furious. I went at Charlie's Gibson hard, Althea sang mournfully, Joy plucked at her bass with rage, and Lettie sawed like smoke was going to rise from her strings. The song became a parody of all the things we hadn't been allowed to do growing up because we were girls. I spat out my consonants and chewed my r's, and kept driving the rhythm faster and faster to see how fast we could make it. When we finished, I was out of breath. We all looked at each other, realizing that finally the song meant something to us.

As Joy packed up her bass, Lettie and Althea left rehearsal and walked up the stairs ahead of me. Lettie was talking about how she and the other girls at the shipyards had received hard hats that morning, but they'd all been in men's sizes, so they'd kept slipping over their eyes and the girls could hardly get any work done. I bolted ahead of them to my room, my guitar strapped to my chest, though Lettie was telling a lively tale about the girls stuffing the helmets with scarves to make them fit. I had an itch to write a song.

I'd written a couple tunes for the Snoqualmie Sweethearts already, but they'd been cheap approximations of Roy Acuff or Bob Wills, featuring the elements I thought should be in a good country song, like railroads, or trails, or cattle. The songs didn't have anything to do with my own life. But if we could play "Back in the Saddle Again" like we just had, in a way that made sense to us, then maybe I could try writing something different than everyone else.

Some memory tugged at me again, something that felt like the sore below a scab, trying to distract me: the smell of milk, the Bo-Weavil Blues.

I opened my window, sniffed the mud-flat-scented Tacoma air, and made myself focus on what I'd just been thinking about, of being closed in at home while the boys got to do what they pleased. Thinking about how I was hemmed in even when I was a little girl, I pictured school recess. The boys got messy and shouted, while the girls played neat games like jacks or jump rope and chanted simple songs like "Ring around the Rosie" or "London Bridge." I thought that kind of singsongy chant could make a good base for a song, but about housework instead of play. I came up with:

> *Wash it, dry it*
> *Sweep it, dust it*
> *Cook it, bake it*
> *Start again*

I played around with a few different melodies for that until I had something lively.

But the "Wash it, dry it" chant was more of a gimmick, though a good one, than a verse or chorus. On a notepad, I wrote down every saying I could think of about women and men. After some time, I wrote, "A woman's work is never done," and I knew I had my title. The rhythm had the right emphases to translate easy to a song—a *wo*man's *work* is *ne*-ver *done*—and the consonants made it easy to sing fast without sounding slurred.

I picked up my guitar and tried about thirty different ways of singing that phrase. Then I played with notes and rhythms until the "Wash it, dry it" chant could be sung at the same time as "Because a woman's work is never done" line on the chorus.

For the verses, I listed rhymes for *done*: *gun, fun, run*. *Fun* seemed an obvious pairing, and it would work if I made the woman in the song a newlywed, and addressed the song to her man:

> *When it's Friday and you're looking for some fun.*
> *You're off drinking and you're dancing with someone.*
> *While a woman's work is never done.*

The girl thinks that her work is over once she gets married, but it's the same thing it was when she was young. The "Wash it, dry it" chant became a taunt, opening and closing the song.

It took me three days of thinking about it when I was at Triton's and KVI and walking around the city. Working it out on paper back in my room, I settled on lyrics and accompanying chords. When the song seemed as finished as I could get it, I grabbed the paper, the Gibson, and the amp and ran them up to Althea's room. "Listen here," I said, explaining it first.

After I'd sung it once, Althea hummed the opening "Wash it, dry it" back to me. "But," she said, "do that and the closing 'Wash it, dry it' without any guitar or fiddle, so that it actually sounds like girls at a schoolyard. So the first thing you hear is just the voices: 'Wash it, dry it, sweep it . . .'" I joined in, and we plowed through the song.

Althea grinned when we were done. "Now that's some hillbilly music, Lillian," she said.

I titled it "Woman's Work," and the Snoqualmie Sweethearts added it to our playlist for that Saturday's KVI show. Beyond the radio appearances, we spread the word about our group by showing up with our instruments at parks in town, or near the bridge to the ports. Soon we began to get paid bookings, at honky-tonks, at gyms for dances, and at events like store openings or local fairs. On KVI we'd talk up our upcoming performances, and more and more people came to our shows. At first we figured only men wanted to hear honky-tonk music—the women mostly crossed their arms and refused to dance when we played. Then we tried "Woman's Work" at the opening of an Enumclaw furniture store where our stage was the back of a flat-bed truck. This time, the women in the audience clapped along and cheered.

"Like I told you," Althea said to me, taking in their reaction. "Lot of unpaid work, being a wife."

The day after, we played a picnic held in the interior courtyard of a church. When we walked through the nave to get there, I tried to recall the last time I'd been in a church. I'd never gone to services in Walla Walla, though I'd told the Feasleys I attended Lutheran ones. The last time Hen and I went with Mother to a church on the edge of town, I couldn't have been more than four or five. Here, the pastor, or minister, or whatever he was called, was ancient and jolly, and the other girls seemed happy to move as slowly as turtles and talk with him, but I hurried ahead, eager to get away from the stale air, the hard pews, the stained glass depicting clear moral lessons.

In the courtyard Joy and Althea hung to the side while Lettie and I set up and parishioners crowded in. When it was time to play, I noticed that Joy and Althea had been shoved all the way to the back of the courtyard. "Hey there," I shouted, but the crowd was too loud; for shows like this, we depended on the site's equipment, and the church didn't have a mic. "'Scuse me," I tried, but nothing. Then I had an idea: I plugged the Gibson into my amp, turned the volume up all the way, and played the open strings, creating a shriek of feedback. The sound shut people up right away. "Hi there!" I yelled. "We got two more girls in our band, but they're stuck at the back. If you wouldn't mind making a path for them?"

The church folks parted, but Joy stayed behind her bass, and Althea's eyes were fixed on the church's roof. "Come on up here," I said, but the sisters stayed in place. I nudged Lettie, who looked as baffled as I was. "Maybe start fiddling?" I suggested to her, and as she did, I shouted to the crowd. "Guess I'll just have to go get them myself!" I yelled. "Can we give them a little encouragement?"

The audience clapped, and the haphazard applause settled into a steady rhythm. I wound through the crowd, and as I reached Joy and Althea, the rhythm seemed to get louder and faster.

"Come on, then," I said. The sisters stayed stock-still, Althea looking up, Joy looking down. "What on earth? We got a show." I grabbed the handle of Joy's bass case and rolled it forward. The sisters followed me.

The show was weak, me afraid of offending the religious folks, Althea forgetting words, Joy playing like a beginner; only Lettie was half decent. As Lettie drove us all back in the car she'd borrowed from her uncle, Althea and Joy sat in the back seat and whispered about their father's upcoming birthday. At our building Althea got out of the car before it came to a full stop, and I had to ask Lettie to mind the Gibson as I chased her inside, grabbing her elbow as she rounded the landing to the third floor.

"What's the matter with you?" I said.

"What's the matter with me? Why, nothing," Althea said. "You should probably go back to the second floor."

"Come off it, Althea, I've been to your room before."

"Have you now? Then I guess you know everything about me."

"Are you mad about playing that kind of church? Since you go to a Methodist church and all?"

"Because of that *kind of church*? No, Lillian." Althea clicked open the latch on her purse, fumbled in it for something, then shut it hard in frustration. "You didn't hear them?"

"Hear who?"

"You're telling me you didn't hear that?"

"I don't—I didn't hear what?"

She started up to the stairs to the third floor. "It was nothing, I suppose," she said. "Nothing at all. 'Washington's not like that.'" She took prim steps toward her room, though her heels landed with enough force on the uncarpeted wood that they must've left marks.

I left the door to my room ajar so I'd hear her when she came down, which I figured she'd have to do eventually. After a bit I heard her distinct clipped footsteps and the giggles of another girl. I peeked out to see that Althea had changed into a short-sleeved printed dress, and her friend wore a white blouse and bright skirt. I felt I had to move, that perhaps the end of our friendship, the end of the band, was coming unless I acted now. "Althea!" I blurted, running to the staircase and rounding the landing fast, my hand gripping the banister so I didn't fly off. "Althea!"

Althea's friend, tall and elegant, gave me a cool glance from the hallway. "Is this the country girl?" the friend said.

"Bernice," Althea said.

I straddled two stairs, not really understanding. "Where are you going?"

Bernice started to say something, but Althea cleared her throat and Bernice shut up. "To a dance," Althea said.

"I could come," I said. The air was tense and bright. But my own dress was wrinkled and unflattering; I'd dressed modestly for the performance in case the religious folks had rules around that. "I could change, I mean, and could I come?" I said, way too fast.

"It's at the USO," Bernice said, like that somehow barred me from attending.

"I have a clean dress," I said.

Bernice sniffed. "I mean, you said she was country, but—"

"Lillian, it's at the new USO that just opened. The one on Commerce," Althea said.

They both looked at me, waiting for me to get it. I still didn't. I wished they were men, so I could flirt or argue with them; I didn't understand all the things that passed unsaid between women. "So," I said, grasping for something to make them change their minds. "I could change and meet you there later?"

"Lillian," Althea said. "It's for Black soldiers."

I blinked. "Is this because of today?"

Althea straightened her back. "It is not because of today," she said. "It is because I want to go, and dance, and have some punch, and talk."

They moved to the door, and I heard Bernice say the word "hill-billy," and Althea tell her to shush.

I felt nauseated before the next Sweethearts practice, sure Althea wasn't going to come and that Joy would stay home, too. But Althea arrived in our rehearsal room, sat on a stool, and sang her scales; a few minutes later, Joy pulled in her bass case. Neither Althea or I mentioned the social again, and we didn't have another church gig anyway. We were soon playing dances, honky-tonks, baseball parks, and shows at Fort Lewis. Our audiences started to change. Soldiers, sailors, airmen, and war workers in Tacoma came from all over, fresh off their trains from Alabama and Mississippi and California farm country, Black and white boys alike. When word got around that we were popular with the military boys, we couldn't keep up with all the bookings; we gave the apartment manager an extra dollar a month for all the phone requests she handled for us.

Soldiers liked to stump us with their requests, calling out dirty songs, which we'd clean up, or foreign-language songs, which we'd play as instrumentals. Only once did I freeze onstage, when a soldier called out "Y'all know 'Bo-Weavil Blues'?" I reached for the gray metal microphone stand as Joy played the "Bo-Weavil" intro and fed the words to Althea, who sang, and the whole room seemed to close in. "It's 'I'm a lone bo-weavil,'" Joy said to me from somewhere. I wiped my forehead and banged sideways into Lettie, nearly knocking her fiddle to the ground. Althea gave me a worried look and moved in front of me, singing, and I just stood there with my guitar, frozen. She announced we'd be taking a break and pulled me offstage. "Could've just said you didn't know the song, Lil," she said as she sat me in a chair, an attempt at a joke.

After that, I told the girls that we should give the crowd options, ask if they wanted to hear this song or that song, not take any old suggestions from them.

Tacoma became a city of women, filled in sometimes with men who came in from ships or bases during the day and left again at night. Althea and I both got raises at Triton's, with her running the kitchen—now made up of women cooks—and me running the front of house. When new battleships or transport ships anchored in Tacoma, changing the port's skyline with their towers and platforms, we placed bets on what their crews would order if they got shore leave: the *Ainsworth* sounded fancy, so we guessed oysters Rockefeller; the *Funston* was built right at the Seattle-Tacoma Shipbuilding yards, and we thought doughnuts. At KVI I stepped in for the assistant noon-show manager when he went to war, learning to manage newsreaders and plan programs. Girls in coveralls and headscarves bucked and riveted B-17 wings, and girls at the shipyards balanced on high planks and welded. Girls wore big heavy slacks and neat little caps and filled up tanks at the Texaco. Girls wore skirt suits with the epaulets of the Cadet Nurse Corps and addressed their seniors—women!—as Lieutenant or Corporal.

At our apartment building we talked of seaplane tenders and seaworthy ships, aviation fuel and catching red-hot rivets, B-17s and B-29s, transports and destroyers and freighters, sutures and amputations and malarial fever, swing shifts and overtime. We drank coffee mixed with chicory and reused the grounds the next day. We combined our ration coupons to get sugar and flour so the apartment manager could make a girl a birthday cake. We learned to do new kinds of math: three number 5 coupons for four gallons of milk equals what? We saved frying oil in tin cans, reusing the grease, reusing the cans, then donating both to the Salvage Committee when we were done.

We hoarded hairpins, traded aluminum curlers. We examined our stamp rations to buy gasoline or meat. We contributed to used-tire drives. At Triton's, the owner reworked the menu, so that we had a long list of "Yes, we have no . . ." due to war shortages: nuts, shrimp, chocolate, sugar. Any customer who wanted a hamburger or Salisbury steak would order it for breakfast, for we ran out of meat by eleven o'clock. We moved the sugar canisters to back where the line cooks worked, and portioned it out ourselves if a customer wanted some sugar in his coffee.

As training planes circled above, Althea, Joy, Lettie, and I sang to the rich NCO men and the poor enlisted men. We sang to men from Seattle and men from Sarasota. We played for people to dance and forget the war. We played our way out of the Depression. And on weekend nights, when Tacoma's women finally had a couple hours off, they brought the energy of the city to our performances, dancing hard and shaking off their workweek as they sang along with us.

I was too young to know it wouldn't last.

★ 13 ★

Hot Springs, Arkansas
June 1980

Gene Farver stood over a plastic table, waving a chicken wing. "I go after Patrice, so it's my turn," he said, provoking a chorus of defiance from the rest of us.

"No, it goes Kaori, then me, then Tommy Reed," Patrice said.

"You've had three turns already, Gene," Charlie said.

"And you got first pick, too, Gene, and don't eat any more fried chicken or you'll have heartburn all afternoon," Tommy Reed said.

"We all sound like a bunch of second-graders, and anyway, didn't you all skip me in the last round?" I asked, squirting honey onto a biscuit. My bandmates and I were seated in a fast-food joint on the side of a highway, sharing a bucket of fried chicken, a side of biscuits, scoops of coleslaw, and, for Kaori, what passed, in Arkansas at least, as a salad. We'd played that morning at a festival in Hot Springs, and stopped for lunch on the way out at a place with the first decent juke-box we'd found on tour so far. Since we had a full day to get to our next stop in Tulsa, we were taking our time and taking turns on the jukebox.

"No, no, no, no, Lillian," Kaori said, "because you played the Carter Family on your last pick, and then Charlie did Sister Rosetta Tharpe."

I stuffed the biscuit into my mouth. "Can we stop arguing in that case, and appreciate that this jukebox has the Carter Family and Rosetta Tharpe, when we've been hearing the same seven records on the bus this whole time?"

"I do think it's my turn," Gene said, throwing down his wing and running to the jukebox remarkably fast for a man with a belly his size. Before Tommy Reed or anyone else could stop him, he ordered up Johnny Cash's "Long Black Veil," and in an instant we went from eating and laughing to being somber as gravediggers, pausing our meal as we listened to the first verse.

"She walks these hills . . . ," Johnny sang, going mournfully into the chorus.

I figured I should revive the mood. "What do you all think the saddest country song ever recorded is?" I asked. "I'll start. Merle's 'If We Make It Through December.' Because you just know it's not gonna get better in January."

Gene suggested "I'm So Lonesome I Could Cry." Charlie countered with "For the Good Times," the Kris Kristofferson version. Kaori suggested Emmylou Harris's "Boulder to Birmingham," and played that on the jukebox when her next turn came. As we listened to Emmylou's wistful voice recounting the rawness of Gram Parsons's death, I thought we had a winner. Then Patrice said "'Old Paint,'" and the three other men seemed as though they were going to burst into tears.

"'Old Paint,'" they repeated, reverent.

"At the end there—"

"Where the cowboy—"

"The 'Turn our faces to the west'—"

"You can just see—"

"Just riding those prairies—"

Kaori and I exchanged a glance. "'Old Paint'?" I said. "The melody is great, that half step up for the last verse, but what about the horse?"

"The horse?" Charlie said.

"Sure, the horse. 'Tie my bones to his back, turn our faces to the West?' This man's whole idea is his poor pony is gonna drag his dry bones around forever," I said.

"You're being a crank," Tommy Reed said.

"I'm not. I'm not! Think about it: The bones are gonna knock against that horse when he bends to eat grass or drink water, and for what? So the cowboy can become part of the Old West stories? 'Why, there goes old Buster's pony, with old Buster's bones. Real cowboy. He died like a man.'"

"Conscripting his pony to lifelong service," said Kaori. "I'm surprised he didn't require his wife to ride along behind him for the rest of her life."

"There's no wife," Gene said. "The line is 'A cowboy rides single, like it or not.'"

"That makes sense," Kaori said. "'No earthly foot can step between a man and his destiny.'"

"What song is that?" I asked.

"It's not a song. It's a book. *The Virginian*." Kaori had gone to some college fancy enough that Patrice's nephew wanted her advice on how he could get into it. "By Owen Wister."

"Why do men get all the good destinies?" I said.

"Because in the patriarchal structure—" Kaori began.

"What's next?" Tommy Reed interrupted. "You two gonna burn your bras at the next gig?"

She didn't answer, and Gene stepped in. "Now hold on a second," he said to me. "You really want a man's destiny from back then? You're telling me that in the Old West, you'd rather be out fighting warriors and shooting at highwaymen, instead of safe at home?"

"I don't recall where home was very safe then," I said. "There was diphtheria and smallpox and who knows what, and half the women died in childbirth, and anyway the women were stuck in these muddy frontier towns with nothing to do but work until they couldn't work anymore, so, yeah, give me a horse and send me out into the wild any day."

"You want me to tie your bones to a horse, Lil? 'Cause I'll do it," Charlie offered.

"Hell, maybe this really is a farewell tour," Tommy Reed said, and they all laughed.

I picked a piece of meat off a chicken thigh. I've thought about the end, of course, when I go, when my voice goes; same thing, I think. I've already spent days shut inside the Old Hickory Lake house, and I'm sure that won't be where I do it. "Nah, no horse-and-bones for me, even though there aren't that many other things to do with a body, are there? You could put it in water." I've thought about ending in water, perhaps the salt water that I discovered in Tacoma. A working port, cargo ships, black gasoline trails above me, the rich chemical scent of fuel, the slap of water against moss-slimed dock supports. "Fire." Strapped on Douglas fir planks, smoke and resin in the air, flames consuming my body and my hair.

"You get antsy when it's more than seventy degrees outside," Gene said. "Fire?"

I lifted a shoulder, conceding the point. "Or earth." That's where I think I'll end, especially now that I've learned about the Greeks. Coy Ray Dexter, my old producer, in one of his endless attempts to improve me, gave me some poetry and other old stuff to read, including Greek poems, so that I could sharpen how I wrote my lyrics. Nothing stuck with me, except the story of Demeter.

"You're missing a whole host of things you could do with a corpse," Tommy Reed said. "Don't want to put it on a horse, put it on a train. Hell, put it in a truck. Or just set it out in a prairie somewhere."

"Well, now, trains, trucks, and prairies? That's just a country song, Tommy Reed, not a way to get to the great beyond," I said.

The men debated on what elements were, in fact, necessary for a country song, while I kept thinking about the earth, and Demeter, its ruling goddess. Her daughter Persephone was abducted while she picked flowers. Persephone called for her father, Zeus, as she was taken, but in fact he had authorized it, had handed her to his brother Hades. "No one, either of the deathless gods or of mortal men, heard her voice," I remembered reading in a hymn to Demeter. No one heard Persephone, and no one told Demeter, who looked everywhere for Persephone, but silence reigned: "But no one would tell her the truth, neither god nor mortal men; and of the birds of omen none came with true news for her."

I knew what that was like. "Don't speak, you won't remember," Hen had told me before they put me in the milk shed that last time.

Demeter in return brought harsh winters and infertile fields, only letting up when Persephone was returned to her for two-thirds of the year. At last Demeter allowed spring to come, allowed seed to grow and grain to wave. She punishes the earth every year because she is an angry woman. This I understand. Silence provoked fury inside me, too. So I think that when it's all done, when at last I can stop moving, I can rest on the earth with Demeter.

When I tuned back in, Patrice was opining that a proper country song had to reference liquor, and Gene argued that that would exclude all the country-gospel songs that got the genre started, and Kaori was monitoring this debate without saying a word. Finally, at a lull, she speared a black olive covered with mayonnaise dressing. "You interrupted me earlier, Tommy Reed," she said in a crisp voice, commanding the table. "I can't speak for Lillian, but I'm not going to burn my bra at the next gig, because I don't wear a bra."

We all laughed, Kaori, too, Tommy Reed so hard that he spit a mouthful of chicken skin over the table.

★ 14 ★

Tacoma, Washington
1946–1952

I married him because he was handsome. I married him because he parted his hair with a neat comb line. I married him because his friends took me in and, though I never felt like one of the giggling girls, here I was in a bikini on his pal's motorboat off Point Defiance, and there I was wobbling down Mount Baker in trousers and skis in the spring snow. I married him because, for a woman with no family, it offered the simplest route to stability that I could see. Respectability, I didn't care about, but stability, this appealed, not having to pull double shifts all my life.

I married him because I needed somewhere to live.

His parents came up from Lakewood for the wedding; mine were not discussed. And as his girlfriends flitted about me and rouged my cheeks, telling me I was such a peach, so pretty, I wished one of them would take a snapshot so I could write the word "See?" on the back and send it to Hen. I glided through the city hall wedding and the luncheon afterward, my head light, insisting on only one thing, which was that I would remain Lillian Waters and not take his name. I made it through my wedding night, nothing I hadn't done before, with him and with others, and no better with the marriage contract between us. It was the first morning, waking up with this snoring, heaving lump beside me in bed with a whole day ahead of us, that I first felt terrified: this was not stability but a weight tied around my waist, pulling me deeper and deeper into the ocean.

"Morning, puppy," he said, and his breath came at me like toxic gas, and I tugged a comforter to my chin to separate myself from the fleshy body of Johnny T.

★ ★ ★

I had run into Johnny T. again while I was trying to find Charlie to give him back his Gibson. During the war, air-mail letters had come addressed to me at Triton's, full of drawings in pen, always depicting a yokel with freckles and a buzz cut—meant to be Charlie—sweating it out in the Pacific sun or wrinkling his nose over a plate of navy-issued food. The yokel talked to me in a thought bubble: "Durned if I didn't leave my cowboy hat back home, Lil," that sort of thing, far cornier than Charlie ever sounded. When Charlie Christian died in March 1942, my Charlie simply sent a drawing of an ES-150 with the line, "Rest in music." He signed his letters "So long, Charlie," but gave made-up return addresses under names like Ens. Mickey Mouse, so I couldn't reply.

I thought he'd find me at Triton's when the war ended, at least to get his guitar back. In the months after the surrender, after all the boys returned, whenever I saw a figure taking his seat at the counter, I'd check to see we had butterhorns warmed.

He didn't come.

I'd left the Hilltop apartment building by then. When the Japanese had surrendered, every bar downtown passed out beers on the house, and the men streamed up from the port and over from the bases, and we all filled the downtown streets, hugging and kissing and screaming. The war was over, for all of us. But '45 became '46, and the boys came home, and we lost our places. Althea and I were both back to waitressing rather than managing, for lower pay. KVI scaled me back to two mornings a week, singing backup for college boys. The two other Sweethearts drifted off, Lettie marrying and moving away, Joy enrolling in college in Atlanta. Then the building manager decided she could up the rent and attract newly married couples moving to town, so I needed somewhere else to live. Using the classified ads, I found a furnished two-room apartment in Stadium, with a roommate who complained that I didn't make hospital corners on my bed. Althea got a roommate in Hawthorne, a Black section of town at the bottom of Tacoma's U-shaped shoreline. She was still fending off proposals from Claude. He'd hoped to see combat but had been assigned to be a messman in the war, one of the men who cooked and cleaned for the white sailors. He was saving up to buy a house and open a sandwich shop.

One afternoon I walked back to Stadium from yet another fruit-less interview for a job I'd read about in the help-wanted section. It was for a coffee-counter girl, but the owner wanted a Catholic server and asked to see my baptismal certificate. For the first several months after the war ended, I tried for music-related jobs—selling records or radios, working at a station—but the companies filled the positions with men. Then I lost out on housekeeping, retail, and childcare jobs to more qualified new arrivals who'd come through Tacoma during the war and returned to make it their permanent home. That day, on Commerce, I passed a honky-tonk with a sign in the window: "To-Nite: Johnny T. and his Paper Boys."

The last I heard of Johnny T., he was going to officer candidate school in Virginia. I hadn't wondered about him since. My first thought on seeing the sign was, Well, that's just like Johnny T. not to call me to perform, although I had no interest in being a backup player after leading a band during the war. My second thought was, Charlie might be there.

I called Althea, though she'd turned down my last few invitations, and was surprised when she agreed to come out. When I spotted her at the bus stop where we'd arranged to meet, she saw I was carrying Charlie's guitar case and said, "He still married?"

"It's his guitar; he needs it back. Besides, maybe we could line up some singing gigs here. Someone must know someone. You must miss it."

Althea shook her head. "Sometimes I forget how young you are."

"What's that mean?"

"It means it's not the war anymore. I could use a night out, but think it through: no one wants a girls' group anymore, and I can't sing with a group of white boys." We were outside the tavern now, the smell of stale beer pouring out, the music loud. She looked a little nauseated.

"Do you want to do something else first? Get a bite?"

"No, I'm on a diet." She pressed a curl to her head. "I'm getting married in three months."

"Married," I said, feeling like I'd been punched. I'd thought Althea and I would make our way together in this world, but here she was giving in and becoming a wife.

She patted the curl down. "Yes. I gave my notice at Triton's, too. Tips aren't any good these days anyhow."

"I thought you didn't want to be married. You said no to Claude so many times. You said it was more work than a job."

"That was when I thought . . ." A cowboy-booted man scuffed past us and gave her the once-over. "When I thought I could do something else."

"You can sing."

She clenched her jaw. "When someone gets engaged, you're supposed to say 'Congratulations.'"

Another man pushed the door open, letting out a gust of warm-beer air. "Congratulations," I said.

She walked inside the bar, and I followed. It was muggy and dim, and loud from the house band onstage. There were only a handful of women there, and they seemed too shouty for this early in the night. A couple of men stared, initially at me, but then they noticed Althea.

"I should go," she said.

"We just got here."

"I should go," she repeated.

"Just wait, Althea. I lugged this guitar all the way here; let me see if Charlie's here. Please."

Onstage, a band I didn't recognize played a Hank Williams song that the singer twanged through his nostrils. Althea gripped her purse handle tightly, and seeing that, I knew somehow: If I called her in the next weeks, she wouldn't answer, and wouldn't leave a forwarding number once she and Claude set up house. She wouldn't come by Triton's; the days of sharing an apartment building were over, the war finished, whatever we'd had in common dissipated, and she had come tonight out of Louisiana politeness, just to say goodbye. "It's all right," I said. "It's all right. Go ahead."

Her eyes swept the room, which smelled of stale beer and sweat. At the door, a hulking figure of a man shoved his way in, and Althea drew herself into the shadows for a moment. "Good luck, Lil," she said, and she stepped out into the streetlight.

Half an hour later, I'd positioned myself between a wall and the guitar case, so the people shoving past me with beers and whiskeys didn't knock it over or slop liquid onto it. When the manager announced Johnny T. and his Paper Boys, a bigger band than we'd had filled the stage. I couldn't see everyone from where I was standing, but the only person I recognized was Johnny, at the front as usual— no Charlie. They started playing, and I didn't want to stay, feeling exposed for having come all this way. I was making my way to the door when I heard a delicious electric-guitar solo, notes that soon arranged themselves into a simulation of Charlie Christian's on "Flying Home."

I turned. Charlie Hagerty was playing, and shooting me a lopsided grin.

I carried his guitar to the side of the stage, and when the band finished its first set, he jogged down from the platform to me.

"I figured you could play that solo even better with this," I said.

He broke into a full smile, and when he reached for the guitar handle, his fingers brushed mine. "You take good care of her?"

"Tuned her up before I came."

"Thanks. I borrowed Johnny's tonight, but you know how he is." He took a big breath. "How you doing, Lil? You still singing?"

"Here and there. Work's dried up some. What about you? The war for you?"

"Got to see Guam in the summertime. Not many people get to see Guam in the summertime."

"That's where those letters were from?"

"Letters from me? Charlie Hagerty?"

"I think they were from Captain Donald Duck, but they reminded me of you somehow."

"I do remind people of cartoon characters," he said. "Hey, Lil, thanks for bringing the guitar back to me. I figured if you didn't need it when the war was over, you'd find me and tell me so, and probably yell at me some."

"You could've come to Triton's."

"Yeah." He tapped his boot. "I have a son."

"Oh?" I didn't let my face move. "What's his name?"

"Kevin."

"That's a nice name. How's Red?"

"Good. No cattle to herd like in Cheyenne, but he's happy I'm back."

"And Margery?"

"Fine." He blinked. "Fine. Say, you heard the new record from—"

Then a heavy arm slung around my shoulder. "Well, if it isn't our girl singer," said Johnny T.

I was still watching Charlie, and he me. We had so many things to tell one another, about his war, about my war, about music and work and life, but Johnny was pouring me a drink, and his piney gin breath was sharp in my nose. I agreed to go out with him a few days later because the war years had tired me, and Althea and my other friends were moving on, and I took it as a sign that I ought to, too.

After we married, Johnny had me quit Triton's. I joked about it with the other waitresses: I'll be sitting on the couch eating chocolates all day. For the first time since I was five or six, I wasn't up before dawn to start work. Johnny's parents gave him some wedding money, which meant he could buy us a Craftsman in South Tacoma and fill it with all the modern gear a housewife required: a refrigerator, a washing machine, even a radio, my very first one. He pressured me to quit KVI, too, as he felt it wasn't right for a wife to be singing to strange men, letting them imagine sliding a hand up her skirt, but I convinced him that this was wholesome stuff for workingmen, and besides, the extra money allowed me to buy a little more meat at the grocer.

I did spend half of my meager pay from KVI on household items, but kept the other half in an envelope that I taped to the bottom of a bureau drawer. Other girls called this mad money. I called it a set-aside for when, not if, I would need it.

Our money disappeared fast. Johnny had lost interest in reviving the Paper Boys, and worked as a salesman for his grandfather's shingle mill. But he got paid mostly on commission, and he didn't like to work, preferring to be out with his friends or at Longacres betting on horses. Whatever money he had, he spent on gambling or buying rounds of drinks or meals for his friends.

His set of "young marrieds," as they called themselves, were mostly people he'd grown up with in Lakewood, a fancy suburb of Tacoma. Before the girls got married, they had a wildness about them; when we water-skied down at American Lake, they shrieked with joy when they got thrown into the water, forgetting about their hairdos. Once they became wives, though, they preferred to stay in Tacoma and keep their hair curled and set. They followed a script that I'd never even read, playing bridge and hosting afternoon teas. After Johnny and I married, I went to a few of those teas and it was hard to believe that these Washington girls who knew how to canoe and shoot deer were suddenly serving from shiny silver trays and observing etiquette over who should pour the tea given her husband's Army rank at Fort Lewis. I couldn't follow it, didn't want to follow it, never had cause to spend money on a tea set, and the invitations stopped coming, especially once the girls had babies.

Johnny wanted children, too, though I knew ways around that. My Lysol-and-Molex regimen from the time with the Judge had gotten more sophisticated, and though I now used a pessary, I could keep pregnancies at bay.

Sometimes I'd lie and tell Johnny that I was going to the hairdresser. Instead, I'd haul my Gretsch (or, if Johnny wasn't home, his old Gibson electric) on the bus to Charlie's house in the McKinley neighborhood. Charlie's Navy commander had set him up in the logistics office of a shipbuilding company after the war, and he continued to play guitar and fiddle around town for different singers. His freckled cheeks reddened if I talked about Johnny, so we didn't talk much as a result. Instead, we played for hours as Margery, a capable, wide-shouldered farm girl, carted Kevin around and fixed their fence or tinkered with a broken lamp.

Once Charlie asked me why I didn't go onstage anymore. I said, "Oh, I think that's done and gone for me now."

Red nosed at me, wanting more attention, and I rubbed the short hairs, now whitened, along his snout.

Charlie chewed his lip, noodling on his fiddle.

"What?" I said.

"It's not 'cause Johnny doesn't like it?" he asked.

"I don't care what Johnny thinks," I said, but my heart beat fast.

Charlie let the silence balloon. A Steller's jay squawked and dipped overhead. I scooted my chair back, rose. "I should go," I said. "I'll just say bye to Margery."

When I went inside the house, Red trotting beside me, Charlie picked up his bow and played "John Hardy." I only later remembered the opening line: "John Hardy was a desperate little man."

★ ★ ★

The first time:

Neat ranch house, sunken living room, cocktails with olives on toothpicks. Johnny and I were at a party of some friends of his friends, a couple we'd never met. An hour or so in, the husband discovered that I was a girl singer on KVI. "I've heard you!" he said.

"Now, stop, you're going to give me a big head," I said.

Johnny, who'd been debating engineering flaws in the new Tacoma Narrows Bridge with a couple other men, overheard and came over to us.

"Have you met my husband, Johnny?" I asked. Johnny squeezed the man's hand, hard.

"Honey," the host called, and his wife trotted over. "Guess what? This here is Lillian Waters from KVI."

"Oh, I just love your songs," our hostess trilled.

"You're a lucky man, Johnny Waters," the host told my husband.

The wheat in my belly swished.

Johnny pulled me out of the party a couple minutes later. On the drive back to South Tacoma, I tried to tell myself that he hadn't noticed, that he'd just had a few too many. I tried to engage him in a conversation about the Huskies' chances. He stared out the windshield.

We'd fought before, of course, and we both got rough when we did, him gripping my wrists hard enough to leave bruises the next day. This was different. As I walked from the car to the house, slow, the air was heavy with lily of the valley, that scent of graveyards.

"Get inside, puppy," Johnny said.

A blade of grass, brown and bare, scratched at the flesh of my foot in my party shoe.

"Get inside," Johnny repeated.

The hallway was dim. He closed the door, slid the deadbolt, fastened the chain.

A dust mote floated in a shaft of light, and I hoped to God Johnny didn't notice it. He liked a clean house.

"Johnny Waters?" he said.

The woman I'd been at the party was gone, swapped like a playing card for this one, who trembled as she stared at the linoleum, her vision dimming.

"Is that what you want, puppy?" he said.

I stumbled back.

"You answer me. Is that what you want? To take me to a party and humiliate me, let everyone think my last name is Waters?"

My tongue sat like felted fabric in my mouth.

"I saw how you were tonight. I saw how you went around the room thinking everyone wanted to talk to you." He leaned close to me, leering. "They were laughing at you. Did you understand that? A KVI girl singer, same as the day I met you. Nothing more." His face was shiny, his eyes small and hard. He smelled of Aqua Velva aftershave and onion dip and gin. "Now you've got nothing to say?"

I had sworn, when I left the farm, that I wouldn't be that silent again. Those who think loud fighting is upsetting have never experienced the terror of silence, when your words are stored too deep to access, when you try to make noise and find your voice has vanished, when all you can hear is grunts and squeals sewn together with lyrics about bo-weavils played at a crazed speed, where no one would respond even if you could somehow call for help. "Don't speak," I heard Hen saying.

Not anymore.

"No," I said to Johnny. "No. You want to take me home and punish me because someone called you by the wrong last name?"

He twitched. "You're nothing. You know that? Nothing to them."

"Really? Is that why they called you Johnny Waters?"

Crack, the sound before the impact, and then flames on my cheek-bone. Before, I'd retreated, but my fury spiked now, and I trembled with it. "That the best you can do?" I kicked him in the soft part of his knee.

He shouted and bent over, and I kicked him again on the side of his shin. It felt good. Anger as it was supposed to be let out. I'd seen boys punching one another in the schoolyard since I was a little kid, and I understood it now, wanted to erupt like them.

He swung. I ducked. He got me in the side of the ribs. I ran up the stairs. He followed me, lunged for my throat.

"What, you want to make it so I can't sing anymore, so you don't have competition?" I said.

Slowly, he bent one of my fingers backward until I shuddered. "You don't talk to me like that, puppy."

Years earlier, Charlie had taught me how to punch and kick so that it hurt; he figured I'd need these skills if I was performing in bars. I needed them now in my home. I kneed Johnny's groin, and he jumped back. I punched his chest, and he grabbed my shoulders, spinning me so my back faced the stairs. I reared back. "Be a man," I said. "Put me in my place. That's what you're trying to do, isn't it?"

He took one more swing, and I stepped back. I missed the edge of the stair and tumbled down the flight, smashing my head as I fell.

That was the first time.

★　★　★

My days were ridiculous, dusting, reading magazines, pretending I cared about casseroles, trying to keep house on the meager allowance Johnny gave me. I'd lost my KVI work. They'd moved the transmitter from Kent to Vashon so the station would cover Seattle, and then decided just to move the studio to Seattle entirely. Though they kept a lot of the programming, *Sagebrush Serenade* and *Chuckwagon Jamboree* and all that, KVI told me that if they were going to continue with girl singers, they needed *girl* singers, not dried-up housewives, or that was what I heard them say, anyway.

It was 1951. I was twenty-seven years old.

After I left KVI, I stopped listening to the radio. The songs seemed to taunt me. I figured that losing this job meant one less thing for Johnny and me to fight about, so I might get a good night's sleep or wake up without a knot in my stomach about what he had coming.

Things would go calm between us for days at a time. He'd go out with his friends, I'd cook his favorite dishes at night, and I'd think maybe we'd find a rope to pull us out of this cave. But when he was home at night, and I made him a Scotch sour and myself a whiskey neat, another set of drinks followed fast, and soon he'd blurt out something. That my new turquoise skirt made me look like a whoring mermaid. That I was barren, not pregnant when all our set had two children already. That I was frigid, reacting so cold when he moved inside me, his thing like the serrations of a knife scraping off my insides. I'd drink more whiskey to blur what was coming, and the next morning just remember corners and angles and twisting my body so my elbow or knee would hit the floor before my head.

We still went out as a couple with his friends, and I always messed it up. When we dug for geoducks on the coast, he had to pull me out of a hole I fell into. "She's so clumsy," he said to his friends, and then in my ear: "That was dumb, puppy." Or if he wanted me to drive because he was drinking—he'd taught me for that reason—and his friends were in the back seat, and I missed a highway exit, his fist would slam down onto the horn, and I'd almost swipe a car in the lane next to me. "Lillian never could handle machines," he told his friends. The dread of anticipating his violence became almost worse than being hit, for I knew that whenever we got home, he'd have something new to do to me, yet I had to chat to his friends for hours of a command performance ahead of that.

When we got to the house, time slowed. Sometimes, when his eyes glazed and his face tightened, it seemed I could've been a boxer's warm-up bag—no more than an object to absorb his punches. I might've provoked him less if I'd been quiet, pliant, but something elemental took over. My brain pulsed at its edge. My stomach became light and hot. My mouth was minutes ahead of the rest of me, pulling my tongue and forming red words and throwing them at Johnny, knowing precisely what reaction they'd get. A sort of excitement, almost a rush. My eyes glittered at Johnny's slack jaw, his loose face. Go on, I said, opening up my body to him so he'd have a good angle. Go on. And when he did, when the punch landed with a crack, or he grabbed my neck tight, the pain flashed and it satisfied me, because I knew then how much he hated me. And the unfairness of it, that he was built broad and muscular, and I could only pound away with my little fists like a butterfly angry at a bull. I could not hurt him, not physically, and when I tried, rage erupting out of me and needing somewhere tactile to land, he swung back twice as hard.

The next day, I would pretend I was going to the grocery store without makeup, just to see him apologize and ask me all sweetly to cover up the marks.

I pressed on my bruises at night, to feel proof of how we hated each other.

I stopped having time to see Charlie, as Johnny had begun calling home a few times a day and expected me to pick up.

I saw Althea once at Rhodes downtown. She was sniffing a crystal-cut bottle of perfume. I had a bruise that spread from my eye socket to my temple and was trying on a cover-up in a thick peach shade. She saw me. She knew. We both looked away.

I should've left. It's easy to say now. It wasn't so clear then. I didn't know if this was just another part of being a married woman that no one had bothered to tell me about, the way no one ever told me about my monthlies. The last person to give me any womanly advice had been the Swiss governess at the Judge's years earlier. I studied the other wives at the grocery and on the bus to see if they too wore long skirts and sunglasses, and many did. I also had big worries, about money (I had next to none) and work (I'd have to start over now, at almost twenty-eight, arguably worse off than I'd been when I arrived in Tacoma a decade earlier). Then mundane objections entered my mind. *I wouldn't have a couch if I left.* Or reasons to delay. *I just planted a rhodie and want to see it bloom.* Johnny seemed to sense, too, whenever I was seriously thinking of leaving, and then he'd make a fire in our fireplace and fix me a drink and let me play his old Gibson. He'd say we should go hear music together, tell me how pretty I was, how much he needed me.

No one had needed me before, not ever.

The phone rang one Saturday in spring '52. I wasn't supposed to answer unless it was Johnny, who'd ring two times, hang up, then call right back. But I knew he was at Longacres for the day, where he got distracted enough by beer and bets on the four-horse-to-win-and-the-five-horse-to-show that he wouldn't bother calling home. It was the one upside of his gambling habit.

When it rang, I was scrubbing coffee stains out of one of Johnny's favorite mugs. I backed away from the wall phone, wondering if it was a test. I figured the person would hang up, but it kept on ringing, and I finally reasoned I could tell Johnny I'd thought it was an emergency if he did try to call and got a busy signal. My dish gloves were on and sudsy when I picked up. "Trewick residence," I said, as Johnny had instructed me to.

"Lil?" It was Charlie.

Not an emergency. I had to hang up. Johnny might still call. "I can't talk."

"Lillian?"

"I'm washing dishes. Dishes, Charlie." My voice squeaked.

"Are you all right? You've been impossible to reach. I'm just back from California and Arizona. With that new band? Man, I got some good stories for you. I've been calling but never get you. I was thinking of coming by to check on you."

"Don't." I didn't want him to know; to him I wanted to be tough Lil, not some meek housewife who couldn't handle her husband. And if Johnny found Charlie here without his knowledge, without his approval . . . "Please."

He waited a few beats. "Yeah."

"I should go."

"Wait. Lil. There's an audition I heard about. Country and western, and they need a new backup singer who knows guitar. They're holding a real audition, and I've heard these guys play. They're good."

"I've got to go. I didn't turn the water off. When the phone rang? The water bill was too high last month."

"Lillian. I bet a girl singer, and a girl who could play electric, would blow them away. You have a piece of paper? I'll give you the details."

"I don't play electric, Charlie." I'd wanted my own electric guitar since playing Charlie's during the war, but I couldn't afford one. The best I could do was to work on my Gretsch in parks, and practice on Johnny's Gibson when he wasn't home, barricading myself in our unfinished basement and stuffing a quilt under the gap in the door to block the sound in case he happened to come home early.

"You *can* play electric, and it's in two weeks, so you've got time to practice. I'll drop off mine—"

"Please, Charlie, don't."

"Then practice on Johnny's. Come on. Grab a pencil. You haven't played in so long. It'd be good for you." He rattled off the time and place of the audition, in an auto-body shop on South Thirty-Eighth. I didn't write it down the first time, which he figured out when he asked me to recite it back to him. To get him off the phone, I did it, pulling off one wet glove, shutting the water off, grabbing a pencil from a mug that sat above the sink, and writing the details on a scrap of paper. I recited the information to him, then folded the paper and put it back into the mug of pencils, meaning to burn it as soon as I'd finished the dishes; Johnny sometimes searched the trash lately, looking for proof I'd been cheating on him or spending money without his permission.

Then, a couple of nights later, I came home with a bag of discount rice from the remainders store that I expected was half shot through with moths to find Johnny sitting in the armchair of our cherry-red living-room set, strumming a new guitar. It was an electric, its wood the color of banana pudding, with a black pickguard and a devilish swoop at the top. I couldn't breathe.

"What's that," I said, my voice flat, though I recognized it in an instant, as I still lingered at music-store windows. It was a Fender Telecaster.

"New toy. Thought I'd take up playing again." We couldn't even afford full-priced rice, much less a guitar. Johnny said he'd picked it up at the pawnshop, but I knew that guitar had only been out since late '51. No one would've hocked it so quick, and even a hocked Telecaster would be way too expensive. That meant either he'd siphoned off his pay for himself, or his father or grandfather had written him a check. This while I slow-boiled water to save a few pennies on our electric bill, and detached Johnny's collars to flip them and resew them when they frayed. He had stolen from me, that's how I saw it, and he'd bought a guitar, perhaps the only material thing I cared for in the world.

When Johnny left the next morning, I lugged my old amp from our attic crawl space down to the basement, and then took the Tele from where Johnny had left it leaning against the couch; he hadn't even bothered to put it back in its case. In the basement, I plugged the Tele into my amp, turning the volume on both as low as they could go, and sat on an overturned laundry basket, playing the chorus of "Woman's Work." My whole body vibrated with the guitar's sound: moody, sharp, a little angry. I adjusted the knobs, played with the settings, moved my fingers up and down the frets, and tried out other songs. The Tele seemed made for me, the swell of my thigh matching the curve in its body.

A water pipe in the basement clanged, and I jumped up, kicking the basket backward across the room. It skidded to a stop at the bottom of the concrete stairs, and my eyes followed the railing up to where I'd stuffed a blanket under the door.

You did so much to get away, Lillian, I thought, and here you're trapped in another room. No: here you've trapped *yourself* in another room.

I turned the amp as loud as it could go, and played a furious B-minor chord. It bounced off the hard walls of the basement.

Johnny had broken my wrist. He'd made my nose bleed. He'd pulled a chunk of my hair out. He'd held a gun and directed me to crawl on the floor—*Lower, puppy, you can get lower than that*—just a week prior. But it was the Tele that gave me the nerve to go. That night I counted the money I'd slowly set aside and taped underneath my bureau drawer. Enough for a month or two of rent, with some left over for food and bus fare.

On Saturday lunchtime, as Johnny read the comics, I noticed that he hadn't fought with me for several days. He'd been nagging me about my housekeeping, sighing over every out-of-place cup or book in the house, but we hadn't really argued. Maybe things were changing, I thought as I cooked him a tuna melt with sliced green apples, making sure the bread was fried crisp but not black.

When Johnny left for his friend Vance's place to listen to a Florida horse race, I tidied up the newspaper he'd been reading. Seeing the date, I realized it was the day of the audition. I searched for the sheet I'd written the audition information on, but I didn't find it; Johnny had emptied that mug of pencils, and presumably the paper with it, on a recent cleaning spree. I knew it was on South Thirty-Eighth, though, since Charlie had made me repeat the address twice. It would take me near an hour via Tacoma's meandering bus routes, so I'd likely miss the audition, but it was just a ten-minute drive. Johnny was at Vance's apartment, three blocks away, and Vance's building had a parking area where our red Pontiac would be easy to find. I could use the extra set of keys, grab the car, and go and be back before Johnny even noticed I was gone. I'm not sure what I was thinking: maybe that I'd get the job and Johnny would let me do it, or that the band would tell me I wasn't good anymore and I could stop my dreaming.

I ran the three blocks to Vance's to find the Pontiac parked neatly in the lot. After checking for any sign of Johnny, I unlocked the car with the extra key and drove it back to our house. I left it running while I ran inside and grabbed the Tele in its case, then took the envelope of cash from my bureau and tucked it into the Tele case. I had to move; the auditions would be over in an hour.

The audition was at an auto shop whose hard walls promised good acoustics. I wrote my name down on a list and waited my turn. As I practiced on the Tele, my eyes relaxed, so I saw colors around me— the shiny blue paint of a truck, its chrome grille—but not details. Then the heat in the room rose, and a chord from the band's guitar player landed loud and harsh, and the reflection of a man appeared in the truck's glossy paint.

It was Johnny T.

He lifted a corner of his lip. "I thought I'd find you here," he said.

A curly-haired man with rectangle glasses gave Johnny a sympathetic glance and scurried to the far side of the garage, leaving me and my husband alone, yards from anyone else.

The room darkened. Johnny reached for the Tele. I jumped back, moving it over my shoulder so it rested on the Chevy's bumper, my body protecting it.

Had he been able to see my hands, he would've clocked that they were twitching so much they couldn't have played a single chord, but they were behind me. He studied my face instead, and I'd long since figured out how not to let it show a thing. I blinked slow. "You follow me?" I said.

"Oh, I figured you were coming, puppy. You don't cover your tracks so well." He pulled the piece of paper I'd stuffed in the mug from his pocket. "'Audition, March 8, 2–4 pm, 1311 South 38th.' You didn't think you should tell me about it? Lied to me, when you were supposed to be home all day? And then stole my car and my guitar? That's not so clever, puppy. Not when you're dealing with Johnny Trewick."

I shifted, trying to keep the Tele from his reach.

"Time to go home," Johnny said, his voice singsong and soft.

"Next we got Lillian Waters," the band's singer called out.

Now I knew why I'd come, why I'd taken the money and the car and the Tele. Johnny wanted to keep me in frozen anticipation, waiting and waiting for something worse to happen. When I was ten, I left the farm so I wouldn't have to wait anymore, and I kept on moving, and there was still some part of that inside of me.

Johnny edged closer to me. "She's not singing," he called back. My shaking intensified. No one in the room knew me; they'd take a husband's side against a wife's any day, even if he slugged me in front of all these people. Still, I was safer trying to leave from here than returning to our house, where he could pull a gun, smash my head against a kitchen counter, strangle me, do any of the things he'd tried before.

I lifted the Tele. "I'm right here," I called to the singer.

I moved to the oil-stained floor where the band had set up, plugged in the Tele, and told the band what to play. I sang for a gunshot in the ceiling, a highball glass thrown against my legs, cake makeup I layered on to cover my bruises. My fingers flew over the Tele, and it felt like she was alive and shifting in my hands, working with me, telling me how to get out.

I played the last chord, and it careened off the Fords and Nashes in the shop. I didn't check for Johnny T. I just saw a clear path to the open garage doors, and I grabbed that guitar and its case, ran to his car, slammed down the lock, started the ignition, and I drove.

★ 15 ★

West to Arizona
July 1980

I'd felt it since that diagnosis in Nashville, of course. Pain pulsing between my ears, a feeling like a lump in my throat, hoarseness, scratch-
iness. When I heard myself rasping near the end of an Oklahoma
City concert, I said we'd finish with instrumentals and hoped no one
noticed.

We drove west and farther west. Patrice's map promised the cool
blue stretch of the Pacific, but the ocean seemed to be a tale someone
made up. Cracked cement at filling stations, bathrooms with brown
water coming from the taps, bathrooms with no water at all. Dust
and trails and the beating orange sun, pushing open the windows in
the Green Giant and closing them again as fine dust settled into our
teeth and the inner corners of our eyes. Brush and dust, red dust
and brown dust and gold dust, the road so hot that the pavement
appeared liquid.

"Whose idea was it to tour in summer, anyway?" Charlie asked as
sweat dripped from our foreheads, as we flapped our hands at one
another to move air inside the bus.

It was mine, and he knew that, but I did not tell him why, why it had to be these months, these highways, one more time.

We loaded out, we played, we loaded in. Me and Charlie changed the set list to show off his harmonica and Kaori's fiddle. I wrote another song, and Charlie added a banjo accompaniment. We taught everyone the new song, took Tommy Reed's advice on changing up the rhythm.

We were becoming a group.

As the bus left Wichita, Kaori mentioned that she'd written a new song called "Workin' on a Heartache." It was good. We added it to the playlist, me and Kaori trading verses with an anything-you-can-do-I-can-do-better approach. The crowds loved it, I did a couple more interviews, we got a few reviews. Stanley sent telegrams: NW ARKANSAS TIMES: "IT'S CLASSIC COUNTRY WITH AN EDGE AND WATER LIL AND BAND ARE IN FINE FORM; IT'S CALLED THE FAREWELL TOUR, AND THIS REVIEWER, FOR ONE, IS GLAD THIS FIRST LADY OF COUNTRY IS BACK FOR ONE LAST GO." GOOD FEEDBACK FROM PROMOTERS. TICKET SALES UP. ADDED DATES IN DAVIS, MEDFORD, AND SEATTLE. KEEP GOING. STANLEY.

Donna the Dip sent Charlie a telegram, too, which a venue promoter accidentally gave to me. BALLROOM BOOKED FOR SEPT! CORAL AND MINT FOR COLORS? MINT TIE FOR YOU? DRESS FITTING TOMORROW. LOVE, DONNA. I monitored Charlie's face when he read the message, but he appeared neither glad nor sad.

The bus kept rolling, and outside it, oil rigs pecked at the earth and trucks moved soil from here to there. Dark nights with neon signs, sunrises over low-slung motels, and then the sun baking the earth, the road divided only by brown telephone poles and yellow yield signs.

Norman, Fort Worth, Abilene, Lubbock, El Paso. The Farvers and Charlie didn't even talk about going over the border for a night out, which wouldn't have been a question a decade or two ago. As we drove into New Mexico, the playing cards grew soft at the edges, thumb-greased and brown. Signs to Indian reservations, Mescalero and Zuni and Navajo.

Another telegram from Stanley. COMING TO SEATTLE—BOOKED ALASKA CRUISE—WILL STOP BY WALLA WALLA. It was very Stanley to think that Seattle, the departing port for cruises to Alaska, was around the corner from Walla Walla. People from the East never got how big a western state could be; Walla Walla was six or so hours from Seattle, over the mountains. I'd have fun telling off-color jokes onstage to make his cheeks get red.

Amarillo, Alamogordo, Las Cruces, Tucson. We slept when we could, I drank honey-laced hot water for my throat, Kaori did calf raises, Tommy Reed spit tobacco into pop bottles, Gene complained of heartburn, I bought Cokes for Patrice and let them go flat, Patrice gave us math problems (driving 62 miles per hour with 122 miles to the state line, how long would the bus take at a rate of increase of . . .) that none of us except Kaori could solve, Charlie brined his hands in pickle jars.

When the Farvers and Kaori went to bed and Patrice was absorbed with driving, Charlie and I would keep talking. We played albums on the bus's record player, trying to figure out where B. B. King was doing his bends. "He's doing it down the fretboard," I said, "listen"; "No," Charlie said, "he's got to be up the fretboard; don't you hear that ping, that F?" I said, "Let's have one more drink," and what I meant was, let's keep talking like this, until the first birds cackle and we have to rest.

The night before Flagstaff, as Charlie was intent on teaching me the mandolin, an ear zap lit up my skull. His outline wavered in front of me. I went to my room, took four aspirin, opened my mouth, and tried to sing. My voice cracked.

I threw the aspirin bottle across the room. It rolled under the bed.

★ 16 ★

Tacoma, Washington
1952–1960

My instinct was to go back to the South Tacoma house I'd shared with Johnny T and get what I needed, but then I thought, What was that? Some trousers? A teapot? I had the guitar, I had some money, and that was enough. If I had to leave my Gretsch behind, the Tele was a beautiful replacement. I drove around Tacoma, the windows down, smelling the fishy stink from the port, watching red-and-white tugboats lined with tires, until it was late in the night and I was low on gas. I drove to Charlie and Margery's. I'd never told them about the fights Johnny and I had, but at least Margery must've noticed my painted-on peach face. I knocked on their door. Charlie, in blue pajamas, opened it, and a half-blind Red shuffled out of a back room and gave my leg a lick.

"Lil," Charlie said, seeming as though he'd just been waiting for me to ring his doorbell at 1:00 a.m., for me to get to the same conclusion he'd come to long ago about Johnny T. Behind him, in the hallway light, Margery wrapped a robe around herself, and I wondered what I'd interrupted, how tired she was of my shenanigans already.

"I just need a place to stay for the night," I said. "I'll get back on my feet tomorrow."

Charlie and Margery exchanged a glance, something unspoken and tender passing between them. I wondered, if I had had wavy hair and big blue eyes and could iron things and raise a kid, would I get soft looks like that, too? He opened the door wider, so I could come in all the way, and she took neatly folded sheets from a hall closet and began making up the living room couch.

"We got a call for you this afternoon from the band you auditioned for," Charlie said. "I'd mentioned to the singer that you might be trying out, and he was trying to find you. Said they liked you but you ran out without leaving a number."

"Johnny found out about the audition and showed up. I can't worry about the audition now. I left him, Charlie." I clutched the Tele case's handle and came in, and though Charlie gently tried to take the guitar from me, I wouldn't let go. "This is all I took," I said with a hollow laugh. "And Johnny's car, actually."

Margery made coffee, Charlie poured me a whiskey, and we all talked in the kitchen, deciding that tomorrow Charlie should leave Johnny's car and keys outside our house to stop him from going around looking for it. Margery gave me some old clothes of hers to sleep in, and some more to wear in the coming days, along with a pan and cup and fork and plate, and Charlie tried to slip me some money, but I wouldn't take it.

I kept my promise to my hosts, staying just the one night. Instead of sleeping, I read through the Rooms to Let section of the paper.

The next day I got a cheap furnished apartment in Stadium. The building was crumbling yellow stucco, with stained green carpeting in the hallways that smelled of mushroom soup. I told the landlord I could only cover one month's rent upfront and didn't have a deposit, so I did what I had to do. He came by my place once a month, when rent was due, and gave me a break on the rent in return for a quick tug. When he unbuttoned his pants, I set my hands and mouth at making him finish fast while going somewhere else in my mind by reciting song lyrics. Each time he left, the neighbor ladies would gossip about me, cigarettes hanging from their mouths, wearing faded housecoats and scuffed slippers past noon. I didn't make eye contact with them. They were going to be stuck here the rest of their lives; I wasn't. They could've done with some lipstick, anyway.

Margery put me in touch with a lady from her church who'd gotten a divorce. When I told the lady I didn't want Johnny finding me, the lady said I'd better use her lawyer. He was a nice old man who had a daughter about my age, and he seemed to understand how out of luck I was without me having to explain it. When he listed everything that I could claim from Johnny, even furniture and books, I said, "I only want the Tele." He then launched into how complex a divorce court case would be, and how it all depended on which judge we got, and then he mentioned something about fraud and annulment.

"What do you mean, fraud?" I asked.

Under Washington divorce law, he said, you could get an annulment—no court appearances, marriage dissolved, that's it—when fraud had occurred.

"What if I didn't use my real name when I married Johnny?" I asked. I'd put "Lillian Waters" on our marriage certificate, I told him, but I'd never legally changed my name from Lena Thorsell. The lawyer filed for an annulment, which was granted, and the lawyer then called in a favor to a law school pal working in Walla Walla, having the pal legally change Lena Thorsell to Lillian Waters in Walla Walla court. "Don't want to worry about fraud when you get married again," my lawyer told me.

I assured him I was not getting married again.

Meanwhile, I fished help-wanted sections from trash cans on the street and lined up jobs: night desk clerk at the Winthrop Hotel, tray girl in the dietary department of Washington Minor Hospital, clerk at a floral shop, fill-in waitress at Frisko Freeze. A carpet company wanted a "housewife" to address advertising postcards, which I did during my bus rides. I snuck most of my food, eating canned mandarin sections from hospital trays or leftover fried prawns from Frisko Freeze customers.

My feet throbbed. A toenail blackened and fell off. My hair smelled of grease and seafood, but I didn't have time to wash and set it, so I sprinkled it with talcum powder instead, which left it smelling like diapered prawn. I took home my pay in greasy coins and moist dollar bills. I was never anywhere, had no focus. If I was carrying a double cheeseburger and vanilla malt, my mind was on whether I'd mixed up the violet and iris deliveries from the flower shop. My fingers got stiff and sore, and I think it wasn't from all the work, but because they no longer moved around the strings. The Frisko Freeze jukebox sometimes played country music songs, and I felt like I'd heard them on a three-day drunk, like it couldn't possibly have been me performing them once. Music became a memory: Did I really sing? Did I once listen to records? There was no time; there was no me; all my force was bent toward keeping me alive and fed.

No matter how bad things got, though, I didn't hock the Tele. It would cover several months' rent, if not more, but when I picked it up, sadness swelled in my knuckles and I had to wash dishes, sweep up, make my bed, find another job that would get me out of this hole.

My schedule was unpredictable, given the competing hours of different places, and most positions didn't last long. The manager would decide that I wasn't valuable enough to make up for me being late from the job I was working just before or missing the prior Tuesday due to a bus breakdown. Other work went on for longer. One manager pretended my breasts held milk, that he could squeeze them and suck it out. I let him; it made him finish faster and I could get back to earning tips. I began carrying a fifth of whiskey in my purse, and learned to work with a buzz, hoping for a locked door and a cool day so the managers would not sweat on me, along with the continued success of my pessary. When the managers finished I took some pleasure in using extra-thick wads of toilet paper to wipe their mess from my body, satisfied that the paper came out of their budgets. Then I went back to work. Charlie did not know, and if he had, he would've gone and pummeled the men into the ground, and I'd be out of a job, so there was no point. Pride was a joke. Tips were not.

★ ★ ★

I knew, because I overheard the casual talk of the other employees while I worked, that there's a point where whatever you dreamed of doing becomes just that, a dream. So what, you wanted to be a teacher; now you sterilize hospital trays. That kind of thing. Waitresses and grill cooks, bicycle-delivery men and movie-theater vending girls—so many of them once had other plans. I thought music was going to be that for me. I thought I could box it up, put it away, try to attend to whatever my life was going to be without it, maybe listen to a record now and then.

But here is the thing about music. When you need it, you need it. Like a pill, like a slug of whiskey. There's no way to moderate it. Charlie, feeding the addiction, gave me his old record player one Christmas, three or four years after I'd left Johnny. If I put on one record, I put on another. I played, I picked, I sang, I wrote. At the coffee shop where I'd landed a job as "steam table lady, Christian preferred, under 35," I took home *Tacoma News-Tribunes* that customers left behind and read about country and western being played around town: at the Play-Quato dance hall in Chehalis, at Steve's Gay '90s on South Tacoma Way.

In early '57, Charlie dropped by one afternoon, fresh off a tour of Ontario. He'd been playing fiddle for a bluegrass group, performing at high school auditoriums and town hockey rinks. As he leaned against the doorframe, waiting for me to canvass my place for change so I could pay for my own apple fritter, he noticed my Tele's case was open. "Been playing," he said.

"A little."

He crossed the room and picked up the guitar, then cocked his ear to the body as though it were a phone receiver. He nodded. "Right." He thrust the guitar toward me. "She says she wants to be played more."

"Tell her once she starts contributing to the rent, she can do anything she wants." I opened a kitchen drawer that held a single butter knife and a few pennies.

"Lil, come on, how long you gonna do this?"

"Do what?" Underneath the pipe of my kitchen sink, I found a nickel.

"Just work and not play music. In public, I mean."

I stood up so fast I banged my head against the counter. "Just work?" I said. "*Just* work?"

"You know what I mean. Your music."

"I don't play because I don't want Johnny to find me."

"Lil, Johnny could call me up if he wanted to, and he hasn't come looking for you. He's not contesting the annulment. Maybe he wants to move on, too."

"Maybe. How much do fritters run these days?"

"You had your group during the war, but that's more than ten years out, and at some point, if you're not playing, if you're not performing, you'll lose it."

"Okay, Mac, that's enough." My voice sounded tense, and I felt tense. Charlie didn't seem to think that me just being here, in Tacoma, on my own, surviving, was enough. He didn't know what I did for my jobs; he didn't know that all this was a miracle, didn't know where I'd come from, didn't know how far I'd already run. "We don't all have a wife running the show so that we can take off for Canada for a few weeks."

He set down the guitar in its case. "That means I have to support a wife, too, Lillian, and a child, right? It means I work weekends and nights so that I can take three weeks off for a Canada tour for penny-ante money, because at least I can play, try stuff out, see an audience."

"It might not be much money, but at least you get good gigs, Charlie. Best I could get is backup singer, and it's not worth missing shifts to play backup."

"Then play lead."

"Sure, Charlie. Nothing but ladies at the top of the charts these days."

"Patsy Cline?" She'd just charted with "Walkin' after Midnight."

"She's got to be ten years younger than me and has a voice that sounds like silk, not like cigarette smoke."

"She's got a heck of a voice, sure, but she doesn't write her songs, or play guitar, like you do. Kitty Wells?"

"Kitty Wells, as the radio DJs remind me every time they play 'It Wasn't God Who Made Honky-Tonk Angels,' is actually a happy housewife in real life, not a hellcat bachelor girl like me." I counted out the meager change I'd found, then flung a penny at the counter in frustration.

"Check your coat pockets. You always find something in there."

I searched in the pocket of a fuzzy orange overcoat I'd taken from the hand laundry where I worked three days a week ironing; after a customer had left it unclaimed for months, I'd smuggled it out in a grocery bag. Charlie was right; the pocket held two quarters and a dime. I showed my palm to Charlie. "Jackpot. But, Charlie, it's not the same when you're a woman."

"It's not the same," he said. "But it's not as different as you think it is. Guess the fritters are on you anyway, rich girl."

I ate two fritters and a cruller from a doughnut hut as we wandered around Stadium, asking Charlie about Margery, asking him about shipping logistics, asking about everything, in fact, except music.

That night, playing alone in my apartment, I whirled my usual carousel of excuses as to why I wasn't out there playing, but this time, I heard responses to each of them. Johnny would find me. (*But Charlie is right, Johnny doesn't seem much interested in finding you.*) I didn't have time. (*You can make the time.*) It wouldn't pay enough. (*So what?*

You'll keep your other jobs.) I'd do it sometime soon, but not now. (*You're chicken, Lillian, and you're not getting any younger.*)

The next day at the hand laundry, as I ironed and folded one of the "bachelors' bundles" the place specialized in, I heard Patsy Cline singing "Walkin' after Midnight" on the radio. As I clutched a hot iron, I realized that the work I was doing at age thirty-two was the same work my mother had come to Walla Walla for when she'd been a teenager. Patsy Cline, meanwhile, was doing what I was supposed to be doing.

I finished my shift, and that night I took a bus to South Tacoma Way, taking my Tele with me.

Steve's Gay '90s had a blinking arrow outside and was themed like the 1890s inside, where the owner had installed pieces of old Tacoma mansions, like a giant mahogany staircase. You could sit in fringed surreys or in cable cars, and the all-you-can-eat lunch smorgasbord in the surrey room cost less than a dollar. The real pull of Steve's, though, was its stage, which might have a floor show or a melodrama or can-can girls, depending on the night.

It also had country performers.

I downed a couple of whiskey shots, found the manager, and sang for him with all I had, picking at that guitar so hard I could almost feel the old calluses forming. He offered me a regular hour-and-a-half set, two nights a week.

At home I studied the new music that appealed to me, studying to update my old-fashioned repertoire. I liked Elvis's voice, but it was his guitar player, Scotty Moore, with his jazz and blues chords, that I was really interested in. Merle Travis, Chuck Berry, Sister Rosetta Tharpe, Little Richard, Buddy Holly and the Crickets: I learned something from each of them. I couldn't quite figure out how to make it work for me, though. Nationally, country didn't sound like country anymore. Elvis was melding into a pop sound, while Nashville producers made records with violins and church-choir singers, overdone and sweet.

But then one night in '58, just before I went on, I spotted the night manager talking with a big-nosed, brown-haired man drinking a Coke.

I learned that the man was Buck Owens, a California country player who'd just moved up here and poached one of the best fiddlers who played Steve's, a teenager called Don Rich, for his band. Buck had also become co-owner of a little radio station, KAYE Puyallup, and was DJing there, the manager told me later that night.

I listened to Buck's radio show that weekend. Buck played a Johnny Cash record. I had heard Johnny Cash for the first time not three weeks before and loved how he was clipped and short and angry, his words almost spoken instead of sung. Now that, I thought, is the kind of music I want to play.

"You're listening to KAYE-AM, 1450 on your dial, and I'm Buck Owens," Buck said. "Up next is my own record, though you wouldn't know it from what the record company did to it. This is 'Come Back.'" The song wasn't great, but the electric guitar on it sounded sharp. If what the Nashville labels were putting out was all satin and velvet, Buck's was a rocky road and a tree stump.

I took out the phone book, found KAYE's address, and spent way too much on a taxi down to Puyallup, bringing my Tele. When I arrived, the secretary said Buck Owens was on air. I said I'd wait until the next song and then see myself in. "You can't, ma'am," she said, but the station was about the size of my foot and I could see Buck. I opened the studio door as soon as he put the next record on.

"Why aren't I on your show?" I said.

He leaned back in his chair. "Who're you?"

"I'm Lillian Waters. I play at Steve's Gay '90s. I sing. I play electric guitar. This is my kind of music you're playing, and I'm as good as these records you've got on."

He let out a loud chuckle. "Play me something. You got your own guitar there?"

I unbuckled the case. "I got a '51 Tele," I said, enjoying how he blanched in envy as I plugged it into his amp. I was so tired of the girl-singer songs with the same flounces and winks I'd done for two decades that I did a version of Buck's "Come Back," which I'd heard just the once. Making up the words I didn't know, I got in most of those crisp guitar notes and added some more besides.

When I finished, he leaned back, a smile playing at his lips. "Right now, we got a special visit from Miss Lillian Waters, here in the studio," he said, leaning into his mic. "Thanks for stopping by."

He probably expected me to clam up, but I hadn't spent all those years on KVI and KUJ for nothing. "Very pleased to be here," I told the mic.

"She's a honky-tonk singer from Tacoma, and I expect you may have heard her playing around town from time to time," Buck said, as though we'd rehearsed this entire thing. "It seems only fair that if she takes the trouble to come to Puyallup to visit old Buck, I let her play. Lillian, tell them about your song today, honey." His tone was somewhere between flirtatious and challenging, and I set my mouth right back at him.

"Well, Buck, here's a song I wrote some time ago called 'Woman's Work,' and I hope you listeners out there like it," I said, and tore right into it.

Buck would soon go back to his hometown of Bakersfield, California, an oil town in the middle of a dry valley, and help shape the rock-tinged Bakersfield Sound, a hard-driving West Coast answer to Nashville country. He and Don Rich and the other Buckaroos would become international country music stars, with twenty-one number 1s, among them "Act Naturally" and "Together Again," and he'd host the TV show *Hee Haw*. For now, though, Buck was a small-time DJ, and I was a small-time singer, and we became friends.

As soon as Buck started regularly putting me on his KAYE program, I began to book gigs around town. Finally, at the age of thirty-six, I was singing lead, I was playing electric guitar, and I had men backing me up. When Buck needed a steel guitar player, I suggested Charlie, who'd been trying out that instrument lately. He and I and the rest of the band sat around nights in the backyard of Buck's house in Fife, a Tacoma suburb, drinking and playing. Red the Second—though he was black and white, he had inherited the name—sniffed around for treats and pats, while Charlie picked up a banjo or an accordion or anything anyone brought and figured it out. On percussion, we had Buck's second wife, who slammed the back door regularly to let us know how she felt about all the carousing.

Buck, who could strike a great business deal as easily as someone else could tie his shoes, soon added a TV show called *The Bar-K Jamboree*. I got spots on that, too, and had the fun of hearing Charlie, Don, and the others playing stuff I'd written. A young singer called Loretta Lynn, whose husband was working timber in Washington, came on the show with a confident twang and a great old honky-tonk sound. Other Tacoma acts were getting traction, too, like the rock and roll group the Ventures. It felt like the city and I were catching fire at the same time, and those snobby folks in Nashville had no idea what they had coming once we mastered the Washington sound.

We hated Nashville, in part because Nashville never took our music seriously. The Grand Ole Opry, their country music showcase, decided who mattered in the official history of country music and who didn't, and this got our crew riled up. The Opry would have on performers from Nashville who didn't even have a single out yet, but West Coast players were only welcome once they were at the top of the charts. Nashville was old; we were new, and we genuinely felt that our sound was better than theirs.

On a May afternoon in 1960 just before he returned to Bakersfield, Buck gathered all the Bar-K regulars for one last show on Vashon Island, in the San Juans. I'd never been to the islands, though I'd seen Vashon every day when I lived in Old Town. On the ferry ride over, I stood on the deck, the wind whipping my hair as Tacoma got smaller. On those nights in Buck's backyard, I'd talked about maybe going to Bakersfield with the rest of them, starting over one more time. I'd never planned on staying in Tacoma for good, but I figured a woman had to be more established than I was to go to a new town in a new state and not have managers, promoters, whoever, expect the usual casting-couch stuff from her. So I'd decided to stay in Tacoma for a little longer. I figured Charlie, with a kid in school here and in-laws down the street, would do the same.

When we docked, Charlie asked if I wanted to check out a cove before sound check, and I agreed. We tottered down a hill, grabbing vines and branches so we didn't slide to the bottom, and arrived at a pebble-gray beach, rocks rising on either side of us topped by evergreen trees. Clear gray water stretched in front of us, and in the distance, the blue outline of another hilly island was streaked with low-lying clouds.

"They don't have this in Bakersfield, I bet," I said.

"I heard it's real flat there." He leaned forward, unlaced a shoe, scrunched off a sock, and placed his bare foot back on the sand. He had gold-red hairs on the knuckles of his toes.

"You're not going, are you? To Bakersfield?"

"Nah. I don't want to keep working for Buck. He's tight-fisted and has a mean streak."

"You don't say." I'd heard Buck lay into his musicians, sometimes in front of live audiences, and tales about how he'd screwed one songwriter or another out of royalties were as plentiful in Tacoma's bars as Rainier beer. "He puts out good music, though."

"Sure, but none of it is that different from the next. I also don't want to just keep doing steel guitar."

"I keep thinking you'll settle on just one instrument."

He took off his other shoe and sock and drew his foot across the sand. "Back home all of us kids worked the ranch with my dad once we were old enough. Depending on the time of year, we'd help out with setting up the winter pen, or halter-breaking the colts, all of that. The first year I pitched in, I thought it was about the best thing I could imagine, all that time in the outdoors. Second year, too. The third year, when I was putting up the pen, the fence wire cut my hand in the same place as the year before. I was ten, eleven years old and I could see exactly what I'd be doing for the rest of my life." He reached down for a mussel shell and tossed it at the water, where it made a mild splash. "I want to go from picking up a harmonica and thinking, How the hell does that thing work?, to knowing how to play it. I want to listen to whatever's just coming out, the rhythm guitar and the solos on 'Kansas City,' and play them, and make something. Make something new. With guitar, with harmonica, with whatever I'm working at. Do you know what I mean?"

A whip of wind came at us, and I shivered, though I didn't feel cold. That was it: to make something, to try to put something into the world—however ugly the process, however much we struggled to make it, however harsh the reception might be. It was more than a living; it was life. Our eyes met briefly, and I felt a zap in my stomach and wanted to say something that rose to the level of what he'd just told me. But instead I bent down and lifted an open clamshell. "I think any Tacoma singer will be glad to have you try whatever instrument you want," I said, maneuvering the clamshell so it appeared like it was talking.

He sighed. "Actually, Lil, I got a call from Bill Anderson in Nashville. He saw me play a couple of months ago. He's going on tour, and he needs a rhythm player."

"I hope you told him where to put it."

"I'm going to go, Lil. Bill Anderson's a good man."

I let the shell fall. "But he's in Nashville."

"We play country, Lil; that's where country is happening. If I want to do this as a career, that's where I've got to go. I'm tired of fitting playing around my job." Charlie was still working a nine-to-five at the shipbuilding company, using his vacation time to tour.

"But Tacoma . . ." I fumbled for what I wanted to say about the Washington sound, but with Buck and Don leaving, there wasn't much of an argument to be made that Washington was going to outdo Tennessee. Charlie going to Nashville seemed to betray the music we made together, though, and I wasn't sure how to stop him. "In Tacoma . . . ," I tried, but again I couldn't find an end to that sentence.

"I'm going to Bakersfield," I said abruptly, the words out there almost before I knew what I was going to say. "By myself. On my own. I'm fine on my own. You'll see. I'll visit Buck down there, maybe, but I'll make my own way."

He waited a while, then sat down. "I suppose you will," he said.

"I will." I sat down too, hugging my knees into my chest as the sun sank toward the water, creating a cone of reflected light that sank deep and stretched long at the same time. The sky tinged orange and pink, the flat clouds and the island in the distance shifted to purple, and the sun dropped slow, slow, and then slid away from us, gone.

I tightened my sweater around me. "Guess I won't be seeing you for a while."

"We'll hear each other on the airwaves." His toes made an indent in the sand.

"Better get back up there soon or Buck's gonna shave some money off of our take." I rose and took a couple steps in the heavy sand.

"Lillian," Charlie said, his voice lifted by the wind. I looked at him in the twilight. He faced that cold Washington water. "Promise me you'll keep playing."

Charlie didn't need to give me the same assurance; I knew he'd keep going with music no matter what. I said it anyway, though: "If you promise me you'll keep playing." The wind stung my eyes, and I walked back up toward the trees, which angled from the hill, grasping toward the sea.

Flagstaff, Arizona
July 1980

Flagstaff hadn't originally been one of our tour stops, but as we gained momentum and good reviews, Stanley added a night there with back-to-back shows. We were playing the Orpheum, whose more than two thousand seats made it our biggest venue yet. The promoter sent word that he expected gate receipts to be strong, maybe a sellout. He requested we open with "Workin' on a Heartache," Kaori's song, which the *Amarillo Globe-Times* had called "a crowd-pleasing take on classic country themes."

When we arrived in Flagstaff, I was hoarse, and talked in a girlish whisper on my morning radio interviews. The Orpheum had a good backstage setup, and I'd spent the rest of the day in a dressing room there, resting my voice. I sucked on cough drops, ate spoonfuls of honey, and did scales and vocal warm-ups, but my voice was rough and my throat sore. I could cover it up well enough when I spoke, but when I sang, I cracked and frayed on notes that were usually well within my range.

Lately, before we went on, we'd done a backstage routine, getting into a circle and linking arms. The Farvers and Patrice prayed, Kaori led us in a few deep breaths, Charlie gave last-minute instructions, and I tried to rev up the band so they'd give the audience a terrific show. That night, though, when Patrice knocked on my door at fifteen minutes to showtime, I told him I was having costume problems. At five minutes I left the dressing room and hid in the wings, watching my band do the routine, afraid they'd figure out what was wrong with me if they heard me without a mic. I only moved into their view when I heard the promoter onstage. "Please welcome Water Lil and her band on the Farewell Tour!" he called out.

"Where you been?" Charlie said to me as we came on, waving to the audience.

I didn't answer, heading for the mic. "We're so glad to be here in your city tonight, and we got a special show lined up for you," I told the audience as quietly as I could. I'd been hoping for a stroke of magic, some richness back in my voice, but it wasn't there. There was no way I could start with "Heartache," which required me to sing in a high key. "Well then," I said, trying to think of a song that I could manage in a low key. All I could come up with was "Old Paint." "Well, then, we're gonna start with a number that I think you'll enjoy, a Western favorite called 'Old Paint.'" I mumbled "Key of C" to the band and pulled a pick from my makeshift dress pocket.

It was a sad number to open with, and the rest of the early show suffered for it; we had low energy, my voice sounded fried, we were sweltering under the stage lights, and I saw an audience member wince when I cleared my throat for the fortieth time.

After I signed autographs, I was heading to the backstage ladies' room to fix my melted makeup before the next show when Kaori passed me, moving so fast she almost left a tailwind.

"You late for something?" I croaked, expecting a laugh.

She shoved the bathroom door open. The light inside was dim. "Do you know how far they drove?" Kaori asked, facing a mirror.

"Who?"

She held her own gaze in the mirror. "I asked you for five minutes. Five minutes. That's all 'Heartache' takes, but you, you . . . I guess in a venue as big as the Orpheum, five minutes is too much for someone else."

"Pete's sake." This little girl on her very first tour was throwing a fit about not having enough of a spotlight? She, a college girl who was the daughter of a doctor? When I'd started from nothing, had struggled for everything I got, when me making it in country music with all I'd overcome was a goddamn miracle? "You don't need to get so worked up. You'll have plenty of time to sing 'Heartache' on this tour."

"It's not about singing it this tour! It was about singing it tonight, when my uncle and his kids were here."

An uncle: that's right, Kaori had said something about her family coming to the Flagstaff show. I flipped on a light switch and pinched my cheeks, trying to add some color despite the fluorescent glow. "Well, do 'Heartache' at the late performance, then. Sing the whole thing yourself, even. I'll just play guitar."

Kaori whirled around to face me, dots of red on her pale cheeks. "You actually don't listen to anything anyone else says, do you? My uncle runs a restaurant in Las Vegas and needs to be back to close it up tonight. This was my one chance for him to see me, for him to tell my parents that I can perform for a crowd, that I'm not wasting my entire life with country music."

Las Vegas was a good five-hour drive from Flagstaff, meaning her family had spent the better part of a day coming to see this kid fiddle and sing. I tried to imagine any relative of mine coming that far to see me, but could only picture dainty Hen saying she'd rather spend the evening filing her fingernails than see a country show.

Kaori looked back at the mirror. "You've never played with a woman before," she said.

"What's that?"

"You heard me. You've never had another woman in your band before, have you?"

"There weren't many women players. They called me a girl singer well into my fifties—"

"You've talked about that. You go on and on about how hard it was, it is, to be a woman on the country scene, but when I showed up you nearly lost it. I think you like being the only woman onstage, that whatever leg up you have you keep for yourself."

Anger replaced the twinge of guilt I'd been feeling. "Now hold on a second. Whatever leg up I got, I scrapped for. I came up on my own, from nothing."

Kaori drew close enough that I could see the straight pale line of her part. "And you make sure everyone after you has to do the same," she said, and stormed out.

I fixed my lipstick and waited until her footsteps faded to go out myself. Charlie was in the hallway, arms crossed, surveying Kaori's dressing room with its shut door.

"Don't tell me you're sore at me, too," I said.

"Come on, Lillian. That was a low move."

"It wasn't a move. I forgot, that's all."

"This is the only thing she's asked for this whole tour, and you forgot?"

"You're now Kaori's defender?" A scythe coming through the wheat fields. "Wait, do you—you and Kaori? You're— She's young enough to be your daughter. Your granddaughter, really."

He slammed a hand against the cinder block wall so hard I jumped. "Christ, Lillian, you think that's the only reason any man's got interest in any woman? I think Kaori's a promising musician. And I think she deserves for her family to know how good she is. But I guess it's always going to be Water Lil first, and her band second."

Stale air came through my nostrils. "You're angry about being in my band?" I said. "Go out on your own then. Make it 'Charlie Hagerty and His Band.' Except then you'd have to face the fact that you don't want to be fronting a band. You don't want to be the one all the reviews are about. You don't want to have to fail in front of an audience. You want to play good, solid guitar, and good, solid everything else, and be respected by everyone in the business but never have to put yourself out there, not really."

"That's what you think of me?" he said, his jaw muscles clenching. "That's good to know, Lillian. Wish I'd known that earlier. I canceled a session where I could've made a lot more money and frankly had a much better time to come on this tour."

"A session with Sylvia."

He balled up his fists. "Who's kind and generous instead of trying to grind everyone into the ground with the heel of her boot so she can feel better. Nope, I came out here, leaving my fiancée behind— that was a big argument because I'd just been working for months straight and promised I'd be back for at least two weeks so we could visit her parents at the lake, and you never asked if I had anything else I might be up to, didn't even occur to you. And why'd I have to help you out one more time? Because you didn't bother to hold one rehearsal before you hit the road, didn't even try to get your band to play together. Why should you? You're Lillian Waters. You do what you want and damn the consequences. No problem, you can leave the scene for years, hole up in your house like a hermit, and the moment you decide you're through with all that, snap, on come the lights."

I let out a cackle. "Oh right, because—"

But Charlie wasn't done. He shook his head like he was arguing with himself. "And here's old Charlie again, giving you the thumbs-up, handling the band and the tempo and the phrasing and every other damn thing so that you can be the lead guitarist and the star of the show and not have to bother with any of that boring grunt work. It's fine, Lillian, I'm used to how it goes with you by now."

I wanted to scream at him, and had to grab my throat to stop myself from hurting my voice further. "Guess you know me perfectly, Charlie. Isn't a thing left to learn about old Lillian," I said.

He didn't move or react, just glared at me until I stalked back to my dressing room with only a little time before we had to gather for the next show. I redid my makeup, smashing blush against my cheekbones.

When Patrice gave me the five-minute warning, I joined the band, kneeling to take the Tele from the case where I'd put it after the first show. Kaori, her fiddle clasped against her chest, didn't respond when I said something to her about the crowd. I tried a joke with Gene, but he just gave a nervous laugh. Was I really such a miserable old thing that everyone assumed I'd edged her out on purpose?

"What's your uncle's restaurant called?" I asked Kaori.

"Why do you care?" she said.

"'Why Do You Care' is a strange name for a restaurant. Come on, humor me. What's it called?"

She pulled her fiddle in close. "The Buffalo Grill," she murmured.

The promoter called us on, and I greeted the crowd again, introducing "Heartache." "It was written by our fiddler, and a good singer, too, Kaori Tanaka," I said. "Now, some of her family came earlier tonight and didn't get the chance to stay for this second show, because they run a restaurant not far away, in Las Vegas. It's called the Buffalo Grill. If you're impressed with Kaori, and I think you will be, maybe you'll drop in to the Buffalo Grill, tell them all about it. Here's Kaori Tanaka, taking it away. One and-a-two and-a-three and-a-four."

I got through the rest of the show, barely, sniffling and coughing whenever I was away from the mic so I could sell the band a story about how I had a cold. After the show and another round of autographs, I went to the alleyway where the Green Giant was parked and saw Charlie ambling in from the other direction, carrying a sack of McDonald's.

"Shoulda let her play when her family was here," he said to me.

"I know that."

"Was nice of you to mention the restaurant, though."

"I know that, too."

He opened the bag. I took out a fry. "About earlier," he said.

"Don't. Me, too. By the way." I coughed. "You should pick a couple tunes to play lead on. I can back you up sometimes."

Patrice opened the bus doors as I wheezed. "You all right?" Charlie asked.

"Just a cold."

"You caught a cold in July?"

"You know how it is on the road."

"But offering to play rhythm?"

I winked. "You know how it is on the road."

Kaori thundered by us then, holding a bottle of orange juice. "Wait, Kaori," I said. "I was thinking, maybe you all should figure out a name for the band. 'Water Lil and Her Band' doesn't have much of a ring to it."

She pivoted to look at Charlie.

"From Lillian, that counts as an apology," he said.

She sipped her juice. "Actually, I'd like something else from you," she said crisply.

I glanced at Charlie, but he was studying a French fry with fascination, which meant I probably had to do whatever Kaori asked. "Go ahead," I said.

"I was talking to Patrice, and he said there's time for an extra stop in California, but that I needed to check with you," she said.

This wasn't what I'd expected. "Fine, if Patrice says we can fit it in. Where?"

"Tule Lake."

"Tule Lake?" It took a second, but I placed it: an internment camp on the California-Oregon border where a lot of Washington Japanese Americans had been sent. "Why?"

"My mom lived there."

"In the war?"

"Yes, in the war. I told you, my mom's family was from Kent?"

"I didn't know they were . . ." I grasped for the word. *Evacuated* was the word government had used, but that didn't seem accurate. "I didn't know that was what you meant."

"No. They had a farm, a berry farm, in Kent, and after . . ." She lifted a shoulder. "It was gone. So they moved."

"Kaori," I said, but then Gene maneuvered in between the two of us, shaking off sweat. "Arizona's real hot," he said, and I had to jump back so he didn't fling any droplets on me. Once he'd moved through, I continued. "I guess you're not so happy with me, but listen anyhow: are you sure you want to visit the camp?"

"Why wouldn't I?"

"Well, there's just no real reason you have to see it, especially if it would upset you."

She jutted her head forward, and underneath the alleyway's lights, I could see the fine hairs between her eyebrows as she studied me, her eyes darting left and right. "I don't care if it upsets me. I have to confront it. I have to face that what happened, happened."

Though I willed the wheat in my stomach to be still, it waved and blew, the heads whispering. I pressed a hand against my belly, hard, and I said, "I'll ask Patrice to add a stop."

★ 18 ★

Bakersfield and Pasadena, California
Reno, Nevada
1960–1963

The big bald dome of an oilman named Frank, matched farther down by his big white belly, poked out of the murky Hart Park plunge. I kicked my feet and churned the silt-heavy water, moving myself farther away from him, wondering how long it would take both his belly and head to turn a burnt red and how long a reprieve I'd get before he'd dogpaddle over to me and start talking again.

I'd gotten a new bathing suit for the occasion, a bikini that I could fill out pretty well, even at my age. In flat Bakersfield, I wasn't walking anywhere near as much and had started to lose my figure, so I gave up the fried things that I used to eat and switched to a green apple for breakfast, cottage cheese for lunch, and canned soup for dinner followed by a square of Jell-O to satisfy my sweet tooth.

The bikini, a bright white, was now covered in bits of algae, and would likely need several ammonia rinses to get clean. I'd need to reset my hair as well, for I could feel the smooth silt settling into its roots though I was trying to keep my head above water.

A little kid, his teeth missing, shrieked about a crawfish pinching him as I flipped onto my stomach. I was used to swimming in American Lake near Tacoma, which was deep and refreshing and lined with tall evergreens. I was expecting the same when Oilman Frank asked me on a swimming date at this plunge, but it was actually a hole dug into the earth and force-fed with river water, so that the water was barely cooler than the air and certainly less clean. When I left a changing stall, I had to douse my feet in an antiseptic wash; given that the shallow end was slippery with moss, I wondered why there wasn't an antiseptic wash on the way out, too.

The sky above was bright blue; the sky in Bakersfield was always bright blue. The earth was so hot it cracked. Behind Oilman Frank, a sad attempt at a hill had thrust itself up and out of the earth. It was covered in dried-up scrub, with a few dark green trees that were attempting survival in this sun-beaten climate.

Well, welcome to Bakersfield, Lillian.

I'd been in town two months so far. I hadn't asked Buck Owens to introduce me around. I didn't like owing anyone anything, and from the way he'd described the place, I thought the bars would practically be busking for singers, not the other way around. Plus, the one time I did mention his name at a club, I could tell I was about the tenth person that day to say I knew Buck Owens, as his records were selling so well by then.

It became clear to me pretty quickly that there was a reason Buck had come back here when he'd been floundering some in Washington. Everyone in Bakersfield had known everyone else for the longest time, and had played together in certain groups, and this band played Doc's Club and that one Green Door and these fellows Club 409 and those fellows High Pockets, and me and the rest of the newcomers hauling our guitars and basses and fiddles around were told the schedules were full up, had been for some time, and unless one of the regular players got caught up in jail they wouldn't need a relief player, and no, no need to come back tomorrow.

Pete's sake, Bakersfield. I'd come all the way to California to find a town that looked like Walla Walla, but surrounded by oil derricks instead of farms. In the day, the light was harsh and flat and brought out the scuffs and dust. The whole place seemed as though it had sprung up overnight, which it basically had during the oil boom, a bunch of worker ants hustling to build the wide flat streets and the wide flat buildings. I took some solace in the Sierras in the distance, but Bakersfield's flatness with the Sierras' height and texture made the mountain range seem like a backdrop painted by a set designer for a high school play.

I could do without the landscape, but I liked the people. Men in oil-streaked hard hats and boots came to drink after their shifts, and women drank after their shifts, too, and that wasn't frowned upon. Pretty much every woman there was making money one way or another, if not at a regular job then by sewing piecework or selling brownies or babysitting kids. Some spoke Basque, and some Spanish, and those who grew up speaking English in Bakersfield had a strange California accent, where *morning* became "marning" and *Washington* "Warshington," as though the sun dried out their speech, too.

At night, when the heat receded and the sky grew dim, Bakersfield came alive in neon and rhythm guitar. I got daytime work at a luncheonette on the east side of town and said yes to any man who wanted to take me on a date in the evening, sometimes getting a dinner out of it, sometimes a shift at a club, usually in exchange for a fumble in the back seat of his car and pretending he wasn't married. When I did this with one bartender, I landed a semi-regular time slot at Club 409, where I'd try out new things I'd written. I'd go out to the clubs when I wasn't working, too, to learn what the other performers were doing, and I listened to the Grand Ole Opry, broadcast from Nashville on Fridays and Saturdays, to see what those singers were up to. Merle Haggard was starting out then in Bakersfield, going from a stint in prison to playing backup at the Lucky Spot, and Rose Maddox was scandalizing everyone outside Bakersfield but entertaining all of us inside it with her hot rhythms and racy lyrics.

Yet I had not come to California to beg for a night onstage at a club, which is what I'd been doing in Tacoma. I saw how Buck made his money and his name, and I needed to do the same: recording and touring. Those, and not bar performances, would get me out of the roach-motel apartment where I'd tacked up a sheet to pretend like I had two rooms.

First, though, I needed money, which I wasn't going to get from luncheonette tips and irregular shows. I asked around to find out where the oilmen ate lunch, and was directed to a Basque restaurant called Wool Growers. I gave myself a fresh round of dye, so my chin-length hair was a bright blond, and teased it high off my head, using a curling iron to flip the ends. I put on a tight dress, unbuttoned it to just below where I ought to, put on my rouge and lipstick and powder, and set out like I was a Tacoma lady shopping for a new fur at Rhodes downtown.

I surveyed the restaurant when I got there. I needed a man without a wedding ring; I'd made a rule of never getting involved in long-term dramas involving wives. He shouldn't be too handsome, either, as I didn't want to work that hard. I noticed a balding man gesturing over a plate of red octopus tentacles. When he signaled the waitress for another round of drinks for his guests, I figured he had to be someone important. I asked the hostess to seat me right where he could see me.

I eavesdropped on his conversation, about blowout preventers in an oilfield between Taft and Maricopa, and after listening further, found out that he was named Frank and was a salesman at a refinery. His head was round and bald in the middle, with brown strips of hair on either side just above his ears. He was polite to the waitress, though, and left a tip; this mattered to me.

I signaled to the waitress for a coffee, which was the only thing I could afford, then caught his eye.

I used to think reeling in men was a great art, when I was a kid observing the Wa-Hi girls do it, but I've since learned it is nothing complex. What I did with Frank was I gazed up over my coffee cup, eyes wide; then down behind the cup, all shy; then I made eye contact and licked the rim of the cup, nice and slow. The women who are best at this game can really make themselves feel it. I didn't feel it, but I could mimic it well enough, at least to where someone like Oilman Frank would be interested.

He introduced himself, we chatted, he asked me on this swimming date, I accepted. And now I was paddling around in the muck at Hart Park, flirting and biding my time until we could get to the second date and sleep together. After that, I could hint at what would really make all the difference in the world for a little gal like me, alone in a new city: money for a demo record.

★ ★ ★

Oilman Frank sat on an office chair at KUZZ, a Bakersfield radio station, beaming from the other side of the studio glass as I recorded my first demo. He'd happily paid for studio time at the station and for an engineer to help me lay down the demo track, which I'd decided would be "Morning Sun," an up-tempo song I'd recently written. I blew a kiss at Oilman Frank through the glass as I asked the engineer to adjust the soundboard, since I knew the big, cheap type of records used for demos couldn't tolerate a heavy bass.

A few weeks later, I was the proud owner of three dozen acetates. I had no intention of sending my hard-won records to a Nashville label; I imagined secretaries there putting them straight into trash cans. Instead I drove north and south from Bakersfield in a dinged-up Chevy I'd bought when I was leaving Tacoma, dropping them off in person at every music label I could find listed in the phone books, with what I hoped was a dose of charm.

The only nibble I got was from Bradley Cuthbert, a producer at a small label in Pasadena, who said he wanted to meet me.

I drove to the Sugar Records office, where Cuthbert worked from a small suite above a dentist. This seemed strange, but what did I know about record labels? The office had tan wall-to-wall carpet, dark brown file cabinets, and a pine table, and Cuthbert was also dressed in tan and brown and beige, with a signet ring on his pinkie. He asked what else I could write. I told him, anything you want. He went into another room, I heard a muffled conversation and the clacking of a typewriter, and he came back with a two-year contract that included an advance payment that was more money than I'd ever had at once in my life. Trying not to scream with excitement, I signed without reading a word.

Afterward, I shook Cuthbert's hand, gingerly, as I'd noticed his habit of scraping underneath his hair, edging a piece of something off it, rolling it, and dropping it on the ground. He said, "Why don't we go out for a drink to celebrate?"

I was about to say yes, to do whatever Cuthbert wanted me to do. At least I had a signed contract already.

I stopped myself. *I had a signed contract.*

"I've got to get home, but I'll be happy to meet for lunch the next time I'm in Pasadena to discuss business," I said, and left him and his scalp extrications in Pasadena. It felt pretty good.

A couple days later, I told Oilman Frank I couldn't see him anymore, that he deserved a woman who could make his house a home, not an itinerant singer. His low energy worked in my favor; he sent me a couple bouquets of roses, then gave up.

Cuthbert soon had me come back to cut my first single. I drove my Chevy back down to Pasadena, navigating the yellow-brown roads with signs advertising cigarettes or hot coffee or girls, all products to be sold, I figured. In a rest stop outside Pasadena I changed into a short, ruffly gingham dress that I'd bought at a discount ladies' wear shop in Bakersfield for the promotional photos Cuthbert wanted to shoot. The girls on Sugar's label wore real spangly, gingham outfits, fresh off the farm by way of a whorehouse, especially women like me who hadn't seen girlhood in some time. ("The short skirts will take attention away from your age," Cuthbert assured me.) Though I was wary of spending any of my advance money, especially on costumes, he promised I'd make it all back in royalties and bookings. I made only one alteration to the costume, as I didn't care that much about fit or length: adding a pocket for my guitar picks.

I'd be recording at KIKK, a radio station that went off the air at midnight, and if it wasn't exactly Nashville's Music Row, it was a genuine studio. We'd have an hour to set up and work out the mic balance, three and a half hours to record, and half an hour to clear out before the 5:00 a.m. newscast. Cuthbert, waiting in a lobby, introduced me to the session musicians who'd be backing me. I thought we'd record "Morning Sun," then maybe "Woman's Work" for the B side. Instead, Cuthbert announced that we were cutting two other tracks that day. He handed me sheet music, which I'd already told him I couldn't read. At the top of each was a writer's name that wasn't mine.

I'd heard that Sugar was a music publisher in addition to being a label, but I hadn't understood what that really meant. In my contract, we'd agreed to record "mutually agreed upon" songs, and now I saw that the upshot was that I had to record whatever Cuthbert picked from his stable of dreadful songs as he tried to make money from them.

When my first record came out in late '61, the single was a hokey one called "The Ranch I Love"; the B side was "Under the Starry Skies." Both could've been written for *Barn Dance* in the '30s. The songs got radio play on the one Pasadena station where Cuthbert bought the DJ regular steak dinners, and that was about it. I didn't even bother writing Charlie about it; I knew the record would be impossible to find in Nashville.

Worse, Cuthbert sent me a royalty statement showing that I actually owed *him* money. Sugar charged me for studio time, the musicians, breakage fees (they put that in automatically, that they were gonna make however many records but charge me for 10 percent of them breaking) and then Cuthbert took out 10 percent for management, and another 5 percent for running a fan club I'd never heard about. I'd thought the contract was my salvation, but it was a con, and I still could barely pay the rent.

I kept playing around Bakersfield, tracking Buck and Don with envy. In '63, the two of them had the number 1 song in the country, week after week, with "Act Naturally." Lord, was that a good song. Catchy, twangy, just right. I'd have loved to record something similar, but it wouldn't work for me: the only stuff women seemed to get on the charts was maudlin, about death and heartbreak. I listened to the radio and tried to mirror Skeeter Davis's sweet sadness on "My Last Date," but I couldn't sound that cut up over losing a man. I kept writing, but Cuthbert said my songs were too brash, too honky-tonk, for a woman.

Well, I thought after a while, Sugar wants sad stuff, I'll give 'em sad stuff. I needed to write a hit for myself so good that they'd have to record it, one that I could make actual money from. I'd been jotting down ideas late at night and trying to form them into a good song, mostly working on that when I stayed over at Willie Pearson's place.

Willie was a young DJ who I was seeing. I'd met him at a Bakersfield bar; he was twelve years my junior, young, optimistic, and happy. Neither of us had any interest in something serious, but we enjoyed each other's company. "Warrior Willie" was his on-air name. He was half Tillamook, and the station owner had come up with the moniker and the war whoop Willie had to do at the opening and closing of his show. The Tillamook, who'd lived on the Oregon coast before being pushed onto a reservation, had had more than enough salmon and berries to go around and had been pretty peaceful as a result, not needing to do war calls even a hundred years ago. It made my teeth hurt when I heard Willie do that whoop, but I never asked him about it because I didn't want him to have to justify it to me any more than I wanted to defend my gingham getup to him. Willie was friendly with Buck and Don, and often had them over with whichever women-not-their-wives they were seeing at the time, and we'd all talk and play music until dawn, despite the fact that Willie's place was hardly set up for hospitality. The living room had a few folding chairs and a salvaged coffee table, and the fridge held grape Shasta pops and a single hunk of deli ham that I'm pretty certain had been there since the first time I'd come over.

After Willie and I fooled around one night, he went to the radio station while I stayed behind to try to gin up a hit song. That particular night, I'd brought a letter from Charlie with me, meaning to jot down a response. Charlie's letters still depicted himself as a rube, straw in his hair, saying "Goll-lee" about the Opry stars playing the Ryman Auditorium in Nashville. He and Margery had divorced a few years back—all Charlie said was that Nashville didn't suit her—and she had taken Kevin back to Washington. I'd stashed his latest note in my purse, meaning to dash off a reply at Willie's. When I took his note out, though, the drawing reminded me of all Charlie's sketches during the war. I put the paper down. "The Letter," I wrote on my notepad, tapping my pen on the words.

The shape of the song came at me fast. Letters back and forth between the narrator and her man stationed overseas.

No, not her man stationed overseas. Too obvious. I crossed that out. Her friend stationed overseas, her best friend from growing up, and they stayed close, even though she was a girl and he a boy. He's sent overseas by the Navy, they write letters back and forth, she falls in love with him but doesn't tell him, and then she runs into his mother in town. The mother says he's about to propose to a mystery woman, and the girl, heartbroken, sends him a letter cutting off their correspondence.

Soon after, the boy's mother knocks at her door, giving the girl a sealed letter with her name on it, in the boy's handwriting. The girl doesn't understand. She reads the letter, in which he says she's the only girl he ever loved and asks if she'll marry him when he comes home. The mother says the Navy sent it back with his things after he was killed in action.

A little grave-and-a-wedding-bed, as Althea would say, but it could work.

I added some detail, thinking of the letters Charlie had sent me during the war, after we'd had that silly quarrel about him being engaged to Margery. What if he hadn't come back? If I knew it was too late, that what I had done I could not undo, that I would never see my friend again, that we would never again argue over whiskeys whether Merle Travis's version of "Sixteen Tons" was better than Tennessee Ernie Ford's?

He always signed his letters, then and now, "So long, Charlie." I thought the boy in this story would do the same, even in the final letter.

Willie didn't have any whiskey, so I took a can of Shasta from his fridge to keep my energy up. For my imaginary hero, I didn't want to use Charlie—Charlie would have a laugh and a half about that, and his name didn't rhyme with much, anyway, so I started with John. I thought about the letters the two might have sent each other over the years. Loose-leaf paper folded into triangular hats in high school. "Wait for me after practice? So long, John." "You'll do great on the math test. So long, John."

No, it couldn't be John. Jean Shepard's "Dear John Letter" charted in the fifties, and besides, I didn't want to go giving Johnny T. any reason to believe I was thinking about him, wherever he was.

If not John, then Jack. That would be easier to rhyme, anyway.

Jack's mother is talking to the girl now, explaining the circumstances of his death, but for the girl the mother's voice is radio static. The girl can't imagine their town without him: he's there, at the ice cream stand, there, at the path on the side of the baseball field, there, beneath the sign on the road into town that says "A Great Place to Live."

Not without Jack, the girl thinks.

I opened another Shasta, the sweet hit of its syrupy grape taste making me feel like I was getting a lump in my throat just like the girl. Jack, her friend, her one true love, her great regret.

You had someone that loves you, but so long, Jack.

By the time Willie returned at dawn, I'd written the song.

★ ★ ★

A long honk jolted me from my sleep.

"What's that?" said Willie from underneath the single sheet that constituted his bedding.

"Must be teenagers," I said, shifting so I didn't roll off the mattress and onto the floor. A couple months before, in the excitement of re-cording "So Long, Jack" in Pasadena, I'd bought him a bedframe on the way back; it leaned, unassembled, against his wall.

We heard a car roaring past again, honking like Willie's pea-size house was on fire.

"I'd better go see," he said.

The honks continued, someone's car screeching out circles in front of the driveway. Willie pulled on his undershorts and opened the front door.

"Hey," Willie said, and then, "Yeah, she's here. Lil! It's Don Rich!"

"Don," I hollered, "it's the middle of the night, ain't no party hap-pening now."

"Come out!" Don yodeled. "Come out!"

I knew that Don was drunk and would go away sooner if I did what he asked, so I wiggled into my sweater and skirt and walked to the door behind Willie. "What on earth," I said, unable to see much beyond the glare of Don's headlights.

Don pounded on his horn in glee. "Lillian!"

"You're going to get arrested, Mac," I said. "Or you're going to get me arrested."

"Who cares! Tell 'em you're the singer of 'So Long, Jack!'"

Sugar had put out my single two weeks earlier. I'd asked Buck and

Willie and everyone else I knew in the business for advice on how to promote it. I mailed notes to DJs across the country asking them to play the song and stopped at radio stations all the way up to Portland and down to San Diego to do appearances. I did as many performances as I could handle in those two weeks. I had to get that thing to hit the Top 100 country charts; without that, I knew I'd be stuck with Sugar for a lifetime, making records that no one listened to.

Don smacked the horn again. "Number one and number seventeen. Can you believe it?"

Number 1 meant him—Buck Owens and the Buckaroos, at the top again with "Love's Gonna Live Here." And 17 . . .

"Seventeen?" I said. "You mean me?" The newsstands weren't supposed to get new copies of *Billboard*, *Cashbox*, and *Record World* for another few days.

"Buck's got a guy in New York, gets the charts early," Don said. "You, Lillian Waters, have the number seventeen country and western song in the country. It's seventeen with a bullet! Not bad for a couple of kids from Washington, huh?"

"Get out of the car!" I said. "Get out of the car and come on in. Willie, switch on the lights. We've got to celebrate. Number seventeen!"

The next week, it was number 11, thanks to territorial breakouts in Phoenix, Sacramento, and LA. I wondered if Charlie had heard it in Nashville. I did radio interviews. I booked top clubs all along the coast. An overseas promoter called, asked if I was free in June, as he was putting together a package tour, ending in Edinburgh. Edinburgh! I couldn't even pronounce it, but now I was going to play there. I searched for mentions of "So Long, Jack" in newspapers, entered record stores and asked how it was selling, talked not just to DJs but to engineers, station managers, program directors, secretaries, anyone who could offer an opinion. "You think it'll break top ten?" I asked. I imagined swanning into Nashville—I pictured it as a dusty Main Street town, not unlike Walla Walla—and saying hey to Kitty Wells and George Jones. When Nashville's Grand Ole Opry asked me to join them, I'd say, Thanks, but I'm from the West, and we don't need the Opry where we live.

And in her fine house in Walla Walla, Hen would turn on her radio and feel sick. She'd hear Lillian Waters, but some tug of our sisterhood would alert her that it was me, now, cracking the top ten.

The next week, the song stayed at 11. The week after, it was down to 25, then 57.

The calls slowed. I reached out to the overseas tour promoter, but his secretary said he was in a meeting. He never called back.

So that was it, I figured, that was all I got: a quick burst and then back to being nothing.

* * *

A woman can outrun her body only so long, and I was no fool, no doe-eyed girl who finds out in shock at twenty, thirty weeks, that she's pregnant. One of Willie's rubbers must've given out, and when I suspected, I bought a dime-store ring and slipped it on my fourth finger, then made an appointment with a new doctor. "At thirty-nine, it's really a blessing. Your husband must be so happy," he said.

I let myself consider it for only a day, understanding all along what the ending had to be. I'd seen what happened to women the moment looser dresses could no longer hide their bellies. They were fired, and that was from a job like grocery store clerk, or secretary, and those were women with husbands. Asking my audience to accept me knocked up, without a ring on my finger? Popping a hip for sex appeal mid-song when my stomach was swollen? No.

That night, lying in bed in my own apartment, I thought about holding a little child against my chest. A kid with thick lashes like Willie's, putting a trusting hand into mine. Crayon drawings with yellow-yarn hair. Hugging me with simple need, so that perhaps in return I would learn to touch, to be loved, to love. But that wouldn't be me. I knew how I would be as a mother. Love was a language others spoke, and not only could I not interpret it, it landed in my ear harsh and irregular, chirps and clicks where others heard lilting phrases, poetry. I could barely tolerate touch, squirmed out of hugs. I couldn't respond like that to a child who'd done nothing wrong.

An image of Hen's children popped into my mind, as clear as though I'd seen a photograph: tintypes of her, girls with shiny brown hair in perfectly pressed dresses standing outside their grand Walla Walla house. And then I thought of my mother, how she'd been to me. When I calculated it, I realized I was now far older than my mother had been when I'd left home. I thought she'd been so wise, back then, as she talked to the bank man in the city hat, as I glimpsed the shocking sight of her yellowed brassiere, a button I was supposed to fix dangling from her blouse.

Bo weavil's here, bo-weavil's everywhere you go.

I slapped my cheek to erase that line of thought, then poured myself a drink to the same end.

I'd heard about a surgeon in Las Vegas, but I learned he only did "therapeutic procedures," which meant he'd only operate on married women who could claim a psychiatric reason and who had their husbands' sign-offs. Through a waitress I knew at Club 409, I got the name of a place in Reno instead, and made an appointment; the woman on the phone said it would be $300.

I made $30 from my next three performances at the Blackboard, and got Sugar to pay me an upcoming $120 check early. That left me $150 short, and the only person I could think of who had that kind of money and might lend it to me was Charlie Hagerty.

I worked up a story about needing a new car, downed two shots of whiskey, and called Nashville information. When Charlie picked up, I heard the *a-roo, a-roo* of a dog in the background.

"Couldn't hold on to Margery, but you still got Red the Second?" I said.

"That's Red the Third, actually," he said. "I would ask who this is, but there's only one person who'd call me after all these years and not even start with a 'Hello, how are you.'"

"Sorry about Red the Second. He was a nice dog."

"He was. Wasn't gonna get another one, but this stray found me when I was out fishing and seemed to think he belonged to me, so."

"Smart dog. It's good to hear your voice, Charlie. I heard you on the new Bobby Bare single that just came out. Didn't even realize you were backing him, but the minute I heard that soft picking, it was like you were talking to me."

"You mean that line when Bobby sings about the sun sinking low? That picking, there?"

"That picking, there," I said. I twirled my empty shot glass; I hadn't needed it after all. Once I heard Charlie's voice, I'd relaxed, remembering how easy it was for us to pick up where we'd left off.

"Hah," he said. "I was actually thinking of Vashon Island when Bobby sang that line. When we played that last show together with Buck and all. The beach, when we talked. I was trying to get the guitar to capture that."

Currents of warmth moved low in my belly. I couldn't figure out how to say anything as nice back to him, so I said, "I guess Nashville's working out?"

"I'm getting a lot of work as a session player. I like to fit in touring, too, when I can; most people choose one or the other, but . . ."

"Right. You can't stay in one place."

"Say, I don't think you called to talk about my licks on the Bobby Bare album, Lil. What can I do for you?"

I twisted the phone cord around my finger. "I hate asking you this, Charlie, you know I do, but I need some money, and I'm not sure who else I could borrow it from."

"You *are* in trouble if I'm the only person you can borrow from. How much?"

"A hundred fifty."

He whistled. "Lil."

"I wouldn't ask, but I've scraped up what I can otherwise."

"What's it for?"

I had the explanation right there, that the label wanted me in a nicer car for my image, but I found I couldn't lie that way, not to Charlie. My voice lowered. "It's for a procedure."

"A procedure? Is everything all right?"

"A *procedure*," I repeated.

"Oh."

I waited for it, waited for the lesson I knew the world would deliver to a woman like me somehow, whether it was from Charlie now, or a week from Wednesday, from the person doing the procedure in some dark and dank Nevada room.

An edge in his voice, Charlie said, "Who is he? He won't help?"

"No, it's not like that. He's a boy, practically; I'm pushing forty. If I thought he had a buck fifty to spare, I'd take it, but he's living on Saltines and I don't want to have this conversation with him."

He was quiet for a minute. Then he said, "I'll get you the money. You sure it's safe?"

What was I going to tell him? Of course I wasn't sure it was safe. I had heard the stories, had read the newspaper articles, a woman's life reduced to three paragraphs in the *Tacoma News-Tribune* or the *Bakersfield Californian*, the explanations of a perforated uterus or an air embolism or an amateur performing surgery. But I wasn't rich, I wasn't married, and I didn't have another option. "Yes," I said, and about this I found I could lie.

"Will you call me when it's done? Let me know you're fine?"

"Charlie, it's not necessary."

"Maybe not to you, Lil."

He wired me the money, and on a November Tuesday, I drove through the desert, up through the Sierras, and back down into the desert until I reached the neon playground of Reno. In the passenger seat, I'd piled a sanitary belt, Kotex napkins, menstrual rags, old towels, dark trousers, and other supplies that the woman from the clinic had told me to bring. On Wednesday morning in Reno, I put the dime-store ring on and drove to a one-story brown building on the outskirts of town, next to a liquor store and an abandoned grocery. Thoughts piled in my mind, of hangers, of filthy sheets, of this practitioner spreading my legs ever wider, of him demanding something more than money in return from me.

It was only when a teenage couple, both young enough to have acne breakouts, came out that I made myself go into the building.

The reception area was clean, and a nurse in a crisp white uniform led me to the back. The person who'd do the procedure, I was startled to see, was a woman, a stout matron. She asked me only medical questions, and didn't seem to care about my ring. The nurse counted three-two-one and jabbed me with a needle a few times, and when she asked if I could feel anything, I said no. She and the matron spoke in low voices. I counted the ceiling panels, their tools tinged and blew and whooshed, and then the matron said I was finished and that everything went fine. The nurse instructed me to wait in a recovery room for a few hours, and not to leave Reno until Friday morning in case there were complications. When she left the room, I sat up and watched the matron scrubbing her hands. "Thank you," I said, my voice dry. "Thank you for doing this."

She dried her hands on a cloth towel, and for the first time, we looked directly at each other. "Thank you for saying that," she said. She dropped the cloth into a bin and left.

Afterward, at my motel, I stayed in bed for several hours with the cramping and bleeding I'd been told to expect. On Thursday I was feeling better, and picked up the phone in my room. When a woman answered "Hagerty residence," I nearly dropped the receiver.

"Who's this?" I bleated, as I knew Margery was long gone.

"Why, this is JoEllen Hagerty," she said in a feathery voice, dragging out the "Hagerty." "Who may I say is calling?"

I jerked the receiver away from my ear. Charlie had gone and gotten married again, this time to a girl with a southern accent? JoEllen, for Pete's sake? We had strange names in Washington, and I figured it was because some girls' mamas could hardly read and chose strange spellings, like Pheona or Sharlet. But at least we weren't in the habit of adding "Jo" to the front of a perfectly fine name. He hadn't mentioned he'd remarried, but then, had I asked him about anything but music?

"This is Lillian Waters," I said.

"Yes?" I expected that she'd recognize my name, but it didn't seem to mean anything to her. Charlie, who I'd known since he was practically a kid, had never thought to mention me to his new wife?

"Calling for Charlie."

"Mr. Hagerty is not at home right now."

"Mr. Hagerty": now I was getting annoyed with this JoEllen. She was living with Charlie, after all, meaning she was surrounded by a mess of guitars and harmonicas and dobros and an electric organ, and Red the Third, who, if he was anything like his predecessors, liked to romp in mud and roll in manure, meaning that despite her affectations, JoEllen did not live in a land of doilies. "Tell Mr. Hagerty," I said, pronouncing the words with her same southern inflection, "that Lillian Waters called, and everything's fine."

"May I ask what this is in regards to?"

"He'll be aware," I said, parroting back her voice. "Thank you, Jo-Ellen, and I just hope Red the Third doesn't knock over too many jars of pickle juice. Those can be a real mess to clean up." I hung up, feeling small and rude, sore that I had played such a minor role in his life when he was the only person I knew I could ask for a hundred and fifty bucks.

* * *

Still a little fuzzy from the pain pills, I left Reno on Friday morning, after a stop at the clinic where they cleared me to go. As I drove high enough into the Sierras that my radio signal got staticky, I shut it off.

In the silence, I found myself chuckling over the idea of writing a Sugar-sanctioned song about the experience. "Call it 'Woman Problems,'" I told the empty mountain pass aloud, my window down so the cold air would keep me awake. I cackled at a loud volume; not a lot of people were crossing the Sierras on a Friday in November. "'She's got a woman problem, 'cause her man done her wrong . . .' No, 'Her man knocked her up . . .'" I hooted, entertaining myself. At a viewpoint near a peak, I pulled over to snack on some raisins I'd brought. I checked my trousers; the bleeding wasn't bad. I kept driving. When I got over the Sierras a couple hours later, I needed a coffee or Coke, but the foothill towns struck me as empty, spooky. People appeared dazed, like the ghosts of miners.

In Rocklin, I pulled over at a gas station for a Coke. When I came into the store, "So Long, Jack" was on the radio, echoing off the store's tin roof. "Couldn't afford Buck Owens?" I said as I pulled a bottle of pop from a cooler. I took out a quarter, expecting a laugh, but the cashier appeared frightened. I checked my trousers, but no blood had come through, so I didn't understand his reaction. I didn't wait for my change, just got in my car and pumped the accelerator. Once I'd reached a good speed, I tried to shake off whatever had been going on in Rocklin and realized that my radio was still silent. I switched it on.

"So Long, Jack" again.

Now everything seemed wrong, like I'd gone to Reno and returned into an unsettling dream. In Roseville I saw a woman throwing up into a garbage can, and a postman crumpled over his bag of mail.

When I landed on the next radio station, I was happy to hear someone who wasn't me. A man with a Texas accent was being interviewed about his opinion of President Kennedy and what he had done for small businesses. I grinned, thinking about Kennedy's visit to Tacoma two months earlier, where he'd given a speech about conservation. He'd opened with a joke about not being much impressed with Mount Rainier—"Mount Ruh-Neah," he pronounced it—given the wonders of the "blue hills of Boston," which he described as all of three hundred feet high. One hand was on the wheel and the other on the radio dial when the announcer said, "That was our reporter from Dallas, Texas, interviewing citizens about the death of President Kennedy. President Kennedy died of his bullet wounds at approximately one p.m. Central Time . . ."

I jerked the car against a curb and opened the door without shutting off the engine. "Is it true?" I said to the first person I saw, a woman pulling along a little girl whose tin lunch pail was the color of rain. "Yes," she said. She picked up the little girl and ran, the girl's pail banging against her mother's shoulder blades. I slid down against my car, my head dropping between my knees, not caring that I was slumped in the middle of a road.

So long, Jack.

★ 19 ★

A series of thumps slipped into my dream. My Appaloosa had galloped past the penitentiary, his hooves clattering on the street, and reached downtown Walla Walla, but he only responded to his Indian name, and I'd forgotten what the Nez Perce woman had said *Appaloosa* was in her language. *Maa . . . Maa . . .*

More sounds, and they were knocks, and my eyelids were sticky, and I was wearing a motel bathrobe and wasn't sure what town I was in.

"Lillian," said a voice from outside. Charlie. He knocked again. "You up?"

Bakersfield. I was in Bakersfield. And there was no way I was opening that door.

We'd arrived the day before, checked into the motel as a treat so we could indulge in hot showers, and played back-to-back shows at the Blackboard. We were now Water Lil and the Stock Horses—Charlie, a Wyoming boy at heart, had come up with the name. He'd taken me up on my offer and was now playing lead on a couple songs, and I had to admit he sounded pretty good. The next day, I did interviews on KUZZ and KZIN, both now owned by Buck Owens, then a record-signing event downtown, and finally a show at the Bakersfield Inn. My voice seemed stronger after I'd rested it for a full day and a half, and I didn't rasp onstage like I had in Arizona.

After the show, Charlie and I had dinner with some of our old friends. It was odd to see Buck without Don Rich, who'd died in a motorcycle crash in '74. Buck and Don, meeting by chance at Steve's Gay '90s, had been two strangers who miraculously spoke the same musical language, and Buck without Don was half gone. His hair was dyed beige, and though he had all the money in the world, he struck me as an empty walnut shell. Willie Pearson still went by Warrior Willie, DJing a morning drive-time show and hosting auto-mall openings and the like with that signature war whoop. When I did the math, I figured that our kid would've been seventeen by then. It was so evident how badly the two of us would've messed up a seventeen-year-old that I ordered a round of whiskey shots to stop thinking about it. We'd become old men with sunken cheeks, we'd become aging women whose scalps shone pink beneath our thinning hair. The only one with any verve left was Rose Maddox, who'd moved to Oregon but had come down to see me. She'd had health problems and appeared the worse for them, her hair white-gray. But her laugh was just as loud as ever, and when she burst into a phrase of one of her songs, she sounded like the same untamed Rose. Even Rose and her dirty jokes couldn't enliven the conversation, though. We didn't laugh. We ate fast, and Buck, the richest man in town, told us what we each owed and I dug through my wallet for the right number of dollars, dimes, and pennies to cover my chili verde and whiskey-and-Cokes. We said our goodbyes, no one lingering.

Charlie and I walked in silence back to the motel, where we found our bandmates in the pool. The Farvers were dead drunk on rum, Kaori was singing doo-wop, and Patrice did cannonballs off a diving board. Neither Charlie nor I had swimsuits, and though I wasn't drunk, what I'd just witnessed, that time had passed and friendships had faded and we weren't getting any of it back, made me think what the heck, so I stripped down to my bra and panties, and Charlie followed my lead, shedding everything but his underwear. I shouldn't even have looked at him, but my eyes wandered to the lift of his hipbones, jutting below his pale chest with its strawberry-red hair, as he gave me a sideways grin and jumped in the pool with a shout.

When the stars came out, he sat next to me as I shivered under a thin towel on a deck chair and Kaori and Patrice did crawl-stroke races. Charlie asked if I was ready to see my sister in Walla Walla. I said I wasn't sure I'd ever be ready. When the Farvers peeled off, I said it was time I went to my room. "I'll walk you," Charlie said.

In the motel bed now, I touched my hair, stiff from the chlorine.

"Lillian." Charlie's tone was louder.

"Don't want to talk about it," I said. I got up to brush my teeth. The lights in the motel bathroom were harsh, and my skin appeared as though a vindictive illustrator had crept in during the night and added gray to my hairline, dark shading to my crow's feet, purple under my eyes. This was what Charlie had seen last night, then: no wonder he'd been so put off.

I could see how it would unfold from here: we'd go stiffly through the rest of our tour, me shutting myself in my bedroom, him switching bunks with Kaori so we didn't have to hear one another breathe at night.

He rattled the door handle. "Lil, open up, or I'm getting the motel manager to let me in, and you know that's somehow going to work its way back to Stanley, and he's gonna lecture you about knowing your limits with whiskey."

I pulled on the pink minidress I'd been wearing the day before and opened the door. Before he could really see me, I made for the bed, where I sat with my legs slung over one side, my back to him.

"We've got to talk," he said.

"Had too much to drink and you know what that can do."

"You weren't drunk, Lillian."

He was right. I hadn't been drunk. He'd accompanied me to my door, and then, underneath a buzzing hallway light, we both hesitated, and I meant to say something to him about Buck, about Bakersfield, but he stood there, hands in his pockets, deep lines on his face, my old friend, and instead, I said, "Charlie, it goes so fast," and I moved toward him and my lips were on his, and he tasted like salt and chlorine, and he leaned into me—that was the thing, he responded, his hip pressed against mine—but then he said, "No. Donna."

I'd gone inside and locked my door.

Now Charlie made his way to the window and pulled open the curtains. I winced in the light. "Lillian, it's . . ." He twitched like something wanted to bust right out of his skin. "Last night, a wild night, a sad dinner, getting together after a night like that, that could've been anyone, see? Any two people on tour, or, hell, at some accountants' convention, who threw back a few too many, regretted it in the morning. I don't mean that we would've regretted it, but what I'm saying is, you and me . . ."

He was addressing the hills in the distance. "About Donna. We might not be all that suited, Donna and I. Since I proposed, she—well, it doesn't matter, but marriage is a long train ride, and I'm not sure she and I are gonna make it. But one night, while I'm engaged: that's not it."

A vein in my bare foot throbbed.

"I walked you to your room last night because I had this strange idea of putting you to bed. That's it, just bed. So I could pretend, for a couple minutes, that that's how it was, that you and me were together, that everything else had fallen away and it was my job to take care of you, and I imagined it, Lil, as you went to sleep and I sat there in the armchair, and once you were asleep and couldn't hear me, I could tell you how I felt, and I could see how it would've been, could've been, if we—imagine, if it were thirty, forty years ago, nothing but life ahead of us, and we hadn't married other people yet. That we got to wake up together every morning, and fight like dogs over something silly like what to have for breakfast just to get the fight out of us, and then write and laugh and play music all day, and you'd help with my riffs and I'd get you unstuck from some rhyme that wasn't working, and when I was out on the road you'd give me a hell of a time when I called late and I'd do the same when you did, and maybe we'd have a couple of kids and a dog and at night I'd get out my guitar and we'd play together while they were all running around in the yard."

He said all this without moving a muscle in his body, his broad back dark against the bright window. There wasn't a sound from outside.

"Last night, I wanted to say yes, but you and me, Lillian—we deserve better than that." He turned, and now that my eyes had adjusted to the light, I saw in his small blue eyes a kind of gentle question that I had rarely seen from a man.

I saw that he was asking for something, and I knew that I could not give it to him.

I pulled my arms around my knees and began crying, wet warm patches forming on my dress, because it was impossible to look at him any longer. He came to me, I felt the heat of his hand above my back, and then the warmth receded, he walked away and closed the door behind him, and I fell onto my side, the morning sun through the window fixing me in an unwanted spotlight.

★ 20 ★

Nashville, Tennessee
1964–1971

A man's thumb brushed the outside of my breast. Another man sloshed a drink that smelled of oversweet pineapple on me. My whiskey spilled onto a woman's shoes. We zigzagged between suites at the Andrew Jackson Hotel in Nashville, in search of the RCA Records room, which we heard had pigs in blankets, and Mercury's suite, rumored to have gin martinis.

It was October 1964, and it was the annual DJ convention in Nashville and my first time in that city. Sugar flew me out; my contract was expiring, and Cuthbert suddenly wanted to keep me, given what "So Long, Jack" had done for his ledgers. In the East they mourned Kennedy with Chopin's funeral march, with "Dona Nobis Pacem." In the West, though, we felt Kennedy, with his jokes and his youth and his relaxed spirit, was more like one of us than any president so far, and the sad and casual farewell of "So Long, Jack" was how we said goodbye. With all the play it got in the West, the song went to number 3 nationally and stayed there for a few weeks. I did my first TV appearances, singing it on LA daytime shows and evening variety shows. I helped a puppet called Mr. Bubbles explain the president's death to children on a San Francisco morning show. Sugar rushed out an album with some of my other terrible recordings for it that also featured "So Long, Jack." I received royalty payments that were substantial, even after Sugar's generous self-accounting. I sent a check for $150 to Charlie, and though I wrote and rewrote a letter to him, in the end I just enclosed a card that said "Thanks." I made an appointment at Nathan Turk in Hollywood and had him work up custom stage costumes for me. The checks kept coming. I opened a savings account. I remembered good harvest years, and I remembered the ones that inevitably followed, and I knew not to spend next year's cash on this year's costs, not to invest in a mule combine when the age of engines was arriving.

There was only one place left to go if I really wanted to be a country music star, and that was Nashville. Even I had to admit that I'd bet on the wrong horse when I'd predicted that the West Coast would become the center of country music. Buck Owens was doing great; the rest of us weren't making an impact. I had to move to matter, and as much as I disliked the idea of cozying up to Nashville, when Sugar asked if I wanted to attend the DJ convention, I said you bet.

At the Andrew Jackson, A&R men squired around girls half my age with big lips and mascara-coated eyelashes, who blinked lazily as DJs said things like, "When you come through St. Louis, honey, you stop by KMOX and we'll visit." They were my competition, but I wasn't theirs, not with the wrinkles below my eyes. The Sugar salesman accompanying me had gotten distracted by a pair of harmonizing sisters with waist-length braids, leaving me to roam free a couple of suites earlier.

I got pulled into a decent-sized group of singers and musicians, all of us bloated from the salty food and free drinks. We swept out the door to Tootsie's Orchid Lounge, an industry hangout popular with Opry stars, as it shared an alley with the Ryman Auditorium. I crowded inside with the others, moving from a room off the alley into a bigger, lower one. There Tootsie, the owner and bartender, barely tall enough to see over the bar, crabbed at people as she filled drink orders and simultaneously lined up work for her regulars. "Del," she shouted at one of the people I'd come in with, "you go talk to that boy in the back there, he's got a gig in Maryland next week and needs a drummer. Says he pays scale." The room, the people, made me a little jumpy. They all wanted to be in music just as bad as I did, but they were younger, better rested.

I was pushing my way to the door when I heard a voice I knew: Charlie Hagerty, asking Tootsie for a glass of water.

The last time I'd seen him was four years before on Vashon Island. He'd sent me letters, I'd written back, but we'd only talked on the phone the once, when I needed the loan and when I'd learned his new wife had no idea who I was to him. I wasn't sure how to start talking to him, what I should open with.

He rested his left hand on the bar as he waited, palm up, fingers stretched and curled, and I saw he was playing a barre chord. The people between us faded into shadow; we were the only ones in color. I was next to him before I knew it, as though my body had glided there independent of my mind. "A-major seven?"

Charlie's chord hand paused. He pressed his lips together. Without looking at me, he said, "B-major seven."

It was a guitar player's joke: both chords called for the exact same finger position. I rocked back on my heels, wondering if that was all I was going to get in response from him, and if he'd rather I just left him alone. Then he took that chord-playing hand and grabbed my shoulder. "Lillian Waters. I thought good western pickers never set foot in Nashville."

"I heard there was at least one other good western picker here," I said. "That, and a lot of free drinks at the Andrew Jackson."

"You're doing the DJ convention rounds."

"On Sugar's dime. I thought I might see you there."

"Nah, DJs got no use for me. I'm meeting up with a couple of buddies here."

"Still doing session work?"

"Yep, and trying to tour when I can, though JoEllen wants me to be on the road a whole lot less."

Of course old JoEllen, of "Who may I say is calling" fame, didn't get what we musicians were all about. There were still some things I could do better than regular ladies.

He let go of my shoulder and shoved over so there was room at the bar for me. "What instruments you working on these days, Mac?" I asked.

"Mostly rhythm guitar. Harmonica, a little. Fiddle, if they're real hard up. Violin, if I'm real hard up."

"Ah, that was you on all those croony numbers? 'Love is no excuse for what we're doing?'" I sang the line from the Jim Reeves and Dottie West hit.

"I'd be rich, but no. Glad that you still got your Washington chip on your shoulder, though. What about you? 'So Long, Jack' was a real nice song."

I flicked away an abandoned napkin, embarrassed both that he might figure out he was the inspiration for it, and that it was the only one of my songs he would've heard out here. "Say," I said, wanting to tell him the story of the trip back from Reno on the day Kennedy was killed, but stopping myself before I could say, *You know that time you gave me the money for an abortion?*

"Say . . . ?" he prompted. Tootsie set down a water glass for him.

Beehives and bolo ties bobbed at me, and sweat trickled from my underarms. "Excuse me," I said. I elbowed my way through the crowd to the alley door and hurried out, pressing my back against the brick wall outside and sliding to the pavement. The alley lifted and rolled. I gulped back a burp.

"Lillian?" Charlie crouched next to me, holding his glass of ice water.

"I'm too hot," I said.

He dipped his fingers into the water and took out an ice cube. I reached for it, but he pressed my arm down, his calluses cool against my clammy skin. My heartbeat slowed a little. He put the ice cube over one of my eyebrows then the other, then on the back of my neck. "I believe it cools you down faster this way," he said, still crouching.

The ground ceased shifting, and I took a ragged breath and started to get up.

"Take a couple minutes. You're not missing anything in there besides a bunch of record people telling each other how great they are."

I settled back against the wall, and Charlie sat next to me.

"You asked me what I'm doing," I said. "What I'm doing isn't any good. Sugar's choosing almost all the songs I cut, and they're penny-ante versions of Nashville songs from ten years ago. Only good thing I did was 'So Long, Jack,' 'cause I wrote it myself and made it a hit." I reached for the glass of water and took a few gulps. "This tastes like pickles," I said, giving it back to him.

He examined the ice bobbing in the glass. "You're writing, though?"

"Sure, but nothing much better than what Sugar gives me."

"What do you really want to write?"

I watched the trash cans a few feet away. "I don't think anyone wants to hear the songs that I'd pull from my own life. You think I could have a hit with 'Lord, My Producer Only Cares about Money?'"

Charlie snorted so hard I thought he was going to choke. He bent over, and when he sat up he was red-faced with laughter. "'Why's Buck Owens So Rich When I'm So Poor?'" he suggested.

"A honky-tonk favorite. 'My Rent's Past Due So Please Buy My Single'?"

"'My Kid Just Sent Back My Christmas Present'?" His smile flickered.

"Aw, no, Charlie. Kevin?"

"He and Margery live in BC now. She married a Canadian fellow up there. With the touring and all, I guess Margery doesn't want Kevin

getting too worked up if I can't see him much. So, return to sender."
A beat passed, and he jerked a thumb in the direction of the Andrew
Jackson. "What about here? You getting any interest?"

"You know how it goes. The DJs are all from around here: Missouri, Oklahoma, Texas. They're polite enough, tell me to look
them up if I'm passing through. I'm not passing through: I've barely
been farther east than Las Vegas. My Sugar contract's up in a month,
and I'm thinking—don't laugh—maybe it's time for me to move to
Nashville."

He took a sip of water. "You think so?"

"You like it, don't you?"

"The music, yes, but the angling for everything, the who you have
to know, that I don't like. And it's a fine city, but the more I play country music, the further I get from the actual country."

"You mind . . ." I pulled out a pad and pencil from my purse and
wrote "further from the country" on it.

"So you *are* still writing."

"If you're not going to use it . . ."

"Take it. Why Nashville now, though?"

"I can handle it now," I said simply.

He swished water around his mouth. "You know what they say; to
make it in Nashville, you got to have a lot of luck, or you got to be
hell-bent on success."

"I've never had much luck, but hell-bent?" I started laughing, and
spanned my hands like I was showing off a theater's marquee. "Tonight," I intoned in a low announcer's voice, "Lillian Waters appears in
'Hell-Bent on Success.'" Charlie caught my giggles, and we were both
cracking up again. "Lord," I said when I caught a breath, "did I ever
tell you how I picked my stage name?"

Charlie gasped in mock surprise. "Don't tell me you weren't born
Lillian Waters."

"You think any of the women in this town are using their real
names? Kitty Wells was born Ellen Muriel Deason! No, I got the name

from a movie poster, and boy, will you laugh when you hear what the movie was: *Hell Bent for Love*. It was plastered up at the Roxy the day I left the farm, starring Lilian someone. I figured if she was determined enough to be hell-bent, then it had to be a good name." I waited for Charlie to boom out his laugh, but he'd paused with his cup of water in midair. "What?" I asked.

"'Hell Bent for Love?'" he said.

"Some B movie. Walla Walla didn't exactly get first runs."

"It played in Cheyenne. I'd just turned fifteen. I went to see it with my friend Tommy. We thought it was a Western."

"With a title like that?" I said, not getting his point.

"You said you saw the poster the day you left the farm. But the movie played in '34, Lil."

"Oh, you're thinking about 'Water Lil'? That whole story about how I was born during the Walla Walla flood of '31? Let's just say there was a little taken off my age along the way."

"No, I knew that was just a tale; we met in 1940, after all, and I remember you mentioning once you were born in '24. But you'd always said you left the farm when you were a teenager. If you left in '34, you would've been nine, ten."

My fingers fluttered, landing on his cup of water, which I lifted from him. "A lady never tells her age," I said weakly.

His hand was curved as though he were still holding the cup. "I don't care how old you are. I'm asking—are you saying you left your family when you were that little?"

I pressed my back against the rough brick of the building and drained the last of Charlie's water. I set the glass upside down on my knee, turning it once, twice. "Don't tell, Charlie?" I said, my voice sounding young and thin.

"I'm not going to tell, Lil." He took the glass and set it on the ground. "Why'd you leave so early?"

"Two girls and . . . The brains . . ." But the words of my standard explanation refused to come out. My breath came too rapid and shallow now, and though I was already sitting, I had to press on the pavement to keep from tipping over.

"That's all right," he said. "That's all right." He pressed a thumb against the glass, then smeared the smudged print, about to say something else when some of the crowd from the Andrew Jackson lurched into the alley. A bass player called out, "Lillian! We're all going back for the WSM party!"

Charlie and I both stood up.

"It was real good running into you, Charlie," I said.

"You got my number, but in case you lost it, seeing as you forgot to call this time—" He grabbed my notebook and wrote down a phone number. "Here's hoping that out here, they figure out you should be singing your own songs. Promise me you'll keep playing."

I held the notebook tight, thinking of that Northwest afternoon on Vashon, those big green trees and dark sand. And though he didn't need the spurring from me, I said the same thing to him that I'd said then. "Promise me you'll keep playing," I said.

As I was pulled into the tide of performers, I heard him call, "So long, Lil."

★   ★   ★

"We're selling this old girl for parts," I yelled to a salesman as I leapt out of my run-down Chevy in a dealership on the outskirts of Nashville, slapping the hood. I was buying myself a new Cadillac.

I let the Cadillac salesman give me the full pitch, and I settled on an Eldorado in Cobalt Firemist and arranged a payment plan. This was not me being extravagant: I molded soap slivers onto new bars and steamed off postage stamps that hadn't been marked. This was me making sure I upped the ante enough so that I had to succeed here. I didn't want to scrape by on waitressing jobs yet again; I wouldn't do the Lower Broadway honky-tonk circuit; I was forty and had put in my time, and I couldn't and wouldn't charm a bartender half my age into letting me perform somewhere for free. I would not tug at men's things in the neighborhoods and nightclubs where their wives would not go, nor in the industrial kitchens, the restaurant bathrooms, the alleyway walls three feet from a trash bin. I wouldn't use Oilman Franks anymore, tossing them out when I was finished with them.

That Cadillac said to me: Lillian, you're going to make it on your own.

I drove straight from the dealership into town, figuring I'd take in the city before circling back to the motel where I'd parked a U-Haul full of my stuff. It was late December, but I took the top down anyway, shivering as I sang along to the radio. In Nashville, I hoped, I'd find that women had real say. Jean Shepard, a singer who'd worked in Bakersfield, had come here and become an Opry star; she was also raising her sons alone after her husband died in the same plane crash that killed Patsy Cline in March '63. Loretta Lynn, who I'd met back in Washington, had put out a couple of catchy singles that sounded way more honky-tonk than most Nashville productions did. Dottie West, a terrific songwriter with a pretty alto voice, had just charted with "Let Me Off at the Corner." Despite the backing chorus that made it sound like a church hymn, the song was about a cheating woman. Sure, I'd read the fan magazines where the female stars were all portrayed as happy Holly Homemakers, but I figured those were figurative aprons tied on by a press manager. They were like me, I thought, and we'd all knock back whiskeys together at Tootsie's, trading tips on which producer couldn't keep his hands to himself and which promoter would run off with a performer's take before she even finished a show.

Charlie Hagerty was on a three-month Australian tour when I arrived in Nashville, so the first person I looked up was Jean Shepard, who suggested I meet her at Tootsie's at five on a Thursday, after Opry rehearsal.

I figured I'd better dress Nashville if I was gonna survive in Nash-

ville. The morning I was to meet Jean, I got my pin-straight hair set
and curled at a beauty shop. "You want to look like a country star,
darlin'?" the hairdresser drawled through a cloud of cigarette smoke,
and I said "Do it big, and make it last." I could've hidden a ruler in my
hair when he was done. That afternoon, I put on a Nathan Turk costume—a skirt and jacket in white suede with red fringe—and brand-
new cowboy boots.

Tootsie's was fairly empty when I arrived, the few customers
mostly men. Go ahead and look, but that's it, I thought when they
checked me out. Soon they'd know who I was because of my songs.
I sat down at the bar and ordered a whiskey, double, tapping my stiff
boots against a barstool.

A New York–looking girl came in, her blond hair slicked flat, in
a sleeveless turtleneck dress with a big belt buckle at the waist and
pumps. It was Jean. "You come from a gig?" she said warmly. When
I'd last seen her, it was in a fan-magazine photo from an Opry performance; her hair had been half a foot off her head, and she'd been
wearing a prairie-style dress with a ruffled collar.

I greeted her, then drank a sip of whiskey.

Her face puckered when she leaned over my drink and smelled the
alcohol, but she didn't say anything about that, instead ordered herself
a Dr Pepper.

One person after another from the Opry came into Tootsie's after
that, clearly having ditched their gingham costumes. Jean introduced
me to performers whose voices I knew but whose faces I couldn't
keep straight, not after a third and fourth whiskey, especially because I couldn't square how they'd sounded in my head to how they
appeared in person. The women had nice small hairdos and nice
small breasts and nice small waists, and instead of shiny brand-new
cowboy boots, they wore muted pumps. The men wore thin ties and
sports coats.

I kept the whiskeys coming till Jean squeezed my arm and said she
had to go home. "You all right to drive?" she said.

The casualness that she touched me with—I wasn't easy like that with women, not physically—threw me for a loop, so I slapped her on the back. "Course."

"Maybe . . ." She leaned in, lifted one of my heavy curls away from my ear so she could whisper to me. "Maybe it's best not to drink so much here. It's not like Bakersfield."

Down the bar, one of the Stoney Mountain Clogger boys had made a pyramid of his shot glasses. "Doesn't seem all that different," I said.

Jean perched on the edge of the stool next to me. "Women don't drink much here," she said. "It's not looked too kindly on."

I flicked the whiskey glass to make it go *ping*.

"Just a piece of advice, and I mean this real friendly," she went on. "I was never a drinker, but I've seen girls come through here and disappear real quick because there were rumors that they had a problem, and everyone here knows everyone."

"I don't have a problem. I'm drinking a whole lot less than those fellas."

"It's the South. The labels hear drinking, or pills, or what all, they get jumpy. Anyway, I'd better get home to my boys. I need to straighten up before dinner."

Marion Worth, another Opry star, overheard this last part, and she said, "Oh, it's half past. I'd better git, too—on Thursdays I make apple cake."

Despite my ridiculous getup, despite hair so high that I'd hit the top of the doorframe on my way in, despite Jean's warning about drinking, I had been feeling all right until this point. Hearing those two women, though, that feeling evaporated. In Tacoma or Bakersfield, the couple of other women musicians I knew had let go of cooking and housework altogether; if we had a can of beans for dinner, or dusted once a month, we were doing fine. That Jean and Marion were going home after a full day's work, with the live Opry show ahead of them tomorrow, to clean and bake? I had run so far, fought so hard, to get here, and yet here, like before, like everywhere, the women were cooking, and cleaning, and raising kids. I slid my whiskey glass hard down the bar, so it rammed into the pyramid of shot glasses, which cascaded down with a crash as I slipped out the door.

★ ★ ★

Leave your number, leave your name, leave your record, someone will get in touch, the receptionists at the record labels told me. No one did. The few times I did meet producers, I'd mention "So Long, Jack," and those that could place it nodded vaguely and said "What've you been doing since?"

Singing and picking, Mac.

"Anything I've heard of?"

Guess not.

I was old goods, a product that might've sold a year earlier but now sat dusty at the back of a shelf.

I'd need to try something else. At the plain East Nashville ranch house I rented, I listened to the radio nonstop. Whenever I heard a song I liked, I wrote down its title in my notepad, and then went to the record store and read the credits to see who'd produced it. One morning I heard a song with a syncopated beat and double stops on the fiddling, and discovered the producer was named Coy Ray Dexter. I found his address in the phone book, located it on my city map, drove there, and parked across the street. Like I was a kid again following the Judge through Walla Walla, I monitored Dexter's house, which was small and modest. This was good for me: I didn't need a producer who had lots of money, I needed a producer who wanted to make lots of money. I waited until I saw his wife walk out. She was sunny-faced and plump, wearing what looked like a hand-sewn dress, and didn't seem like one of those Nashville society types who thought musicians were no-good hillbillies.

I followed her car to the A&P parking lot, and inside the store I shoved my empty grocery cart down an aisle so it crashed into hers. "I'm real sorry," I said, and began chatting. She mentioned she was buying juice for a church event, and though I could barely distinguish a Baptist from a Roman Catholic, I told her I was brand-new to town and planning on attending that church myself. Nashville's southern hospitality worked in my favor, and she invited me to her house, saying she'd get me sorted out not only on church but the best dress shop, the best grocer, all of that.

I visited a week later in the afternoon, and stayed on well past my welcome, asking for one more cup of coffee, shooting her questions about Altar Guild duties and butcher-shop quality and anything else I could come up with. I remained in her living room even as she started making dinner and cleared her throat twice and said she hated to cut this short. I wasn't sure how much longer I could stall when the front door opened and in came Coy Ray Dexter.

He was a funny-faced man, a widow's peak on his forehead, eyes a little close together, ears so big they resembled tuba bells. He mumbled hello to his wife, who was in the kitchen to the left of me, the door open. He barely took notice of me until I blocked his way and introduced myself.

"Coy Ray Dexter," he said in response, giving me a quick handshake.

"No," I said. "Coy Ray Dexter? Oh, you have to be joking."

He tugged at his earlobe.

"Well, if this isn't a coincidence," I said. "I've been listening to your new record just about nonstop. I'm a singer and songwriter, you see."

His wife, at the kitchen door, dried a head of celery with a dish towel, watching us; it must've been clear to her, now, why I'd shown up and refused to leave.

Coy Ray, too, seemed to have heard this before; he tried to maneuver past me to the kitchen. I didn't care, not if I made his wife steamed, or if I got kicked right out of there. "Out of Washington

State and Bakersfield," I continued, falling into pace with him. "You may've heard 'So Long, Jack'? Charted at number three? As it happens, I'm new in town, working on some songs, and I've been talking to labels. I wonder if I could play you a song or two."

He stopped at a curio cabinet in the living room, flipping its brass handle, then glanced to his wife. She must've given him a we've-got-no-choice look, because he said, "I've only got a couple minutes."

Coy Ray dipped into another room, came back with an acoustic, and stood at the back of an armchair. I kept chattering as I tuned the guitar so he couldn't interject and tell me to leave. I didn't want to do one of my own songs; the few auditions I'd had, my original stuff had been as well received as a topless act on the Opry stage. Instead, I played a new Loretta Lynn song, "The Girl That I Am Now," about a woman who feels unworthy of her man after she cheats. I thought of Jean Shepard's comments at Tootsie's, and tried to summon the spirit of a sorrowful, cake-baking wife while I sang.

I finished. Coy Ray scratched his nose. In the kitchen, I could hear his wife chopping celery. "You're not Loretta Lynn," he said.

"No," I said.

"Your voice is good, and your playing is fine, you've got some good riffs, but I just don't think it comes together," he said.

It was a version of what every producer had told me since I'd arrived here, and it wasn't anything I could fix. Nashville believed in a vague idea of who was in and hot, and who was out and not, and no one offered clarity on how I could get from the out to the in. "What do you mean it doesn't come together? Why not?"

"It's too—you got no—" He gazed at the ceiling. "Look, where'd you say you were from?"

"Washington State by way of Bakersfield."

"And you're what, forty?"

On the nose. "Early thirties," I said.

He lifted an eyebrow, but let it pass. "Married?"

"Was once, not anymore."

"Well, there's the problem, now. Loretta Lynn, she's got her story. Married as a teenager, sings her way out of coal-mining country, cuts 'I'm a Honky-Tonk Girl' for her first single, and we understand exactly who she is. Her songs tell her man to shape up and for women to leave him alone. You can sing the Loretta song fine, but I don't get the sense that you really regret cheating on your fellow. Also, Nashville's got the actual Loretta already. My label, GMI, is new, and I got room for only one girl singer on my roster, and I don't think I can sell a forty-year-old—excuse me, early thirties—divorcée. If you were—" He stopped himself and nodded, apparently satisfied with this explanation. "I wish you the best of luck, but I'll have to—"

"To pass." To my horror, my lips quivered, but I dug my nails into my palms and told myself I was not going to cry in this man's living room. I wasn't even a divorcée, technically, but correcting him at this point wouldn't help; a forty-year-old annullée, if that was even a word, wouldn't be any more appealing. I approached Coy Ray's wife, who was cleaning up vegetable scraps, and made a graceless bow. "Thank you for the hospitality, Mrs. Dexter," I said to her. To Coy Ray I said nothing.

Back at my rental, I bought a newspaper, circled some classified ads, went into a dry cleaner, and got a job. Hadn't I done this in all my other lives?

I still made the monthly payment on the Cadillac.

A couple weeks later, I was getting ready to leave for a shift at the cleaners when someone knocked at my door. "Lillian Waters?" a woman's voice said.

I opened the door to see a pert little thing with a giant bun.

"Well, ma'am, you sure are hard to find," she said. "Ain't got no telephone?"

I'd expected to set up phone service once I got signed, but that hadn't happened. "What's the problem?" I asked.

"There's no problem, ma'am. I'm Rosalie, the secretary to Coy Ray Dexter, at GMI Records. He'd sure like you to come in for a meeting."

I ran to my neighbor's house, which did have a phone, and called the dry cleaner to say I'd be late. Then I sprinted to my Cadillac with my Tele and sped to the address she gave me, an office a few blocks from Music Row. My hair was a mess, I had no makeup on, and I was in the moth-eaten sweater and pedal-pusher pants I'd been planning to wear to work.

On his desk, Coy Ray had a mess of handwritten papers, plus stacks of books, records, and sheets of music. A Hammond B3 organ, the kind that Booker T. and other Memphis Sound musicians made famous, sat to one side, and an amp on the floor. The shelves behind him were piled with tapes in cardboard boxes, with "Safety" or "Dupe" scrawled on them; they were backups of sessions. To the side, other shelves were thick with books, including a full set of *Encyclopaedia Britannica*, a bunch of Shakespeare, and some by authors with one name only, Hesiod or Plato.

"Lillian Waters," Coy Ray said, shaking a cigarette from a pack. "I listened to a few of your albums. There are a couple good cuts on there besides 'So Long, Jack.' You have a good voice. It's just your sound is all over the place. I'm not sure what I'm getting when I put on your records. What'd you do after 'So Long, Jack?' You charted top-ten since?"

"I've been on the road a lot."

"That's a no. What happened with Sugar?" He lit the cigarette, sucked on it, and huffed out a breath.

"Contract expired. I didn't renew."

"Yeah, Cuthbert's a thief." He reached to the organ and played a couple notes. "I shouldn't have sent you off like that. It'd been a long day and I don't know that I gave you a real shot. My wife wasn't very happy with your scheme, by the way."

"No, I wouldn't think so."

Coy Ray tapped some ash into a brass container shaped like an upside-down cowboy hat. "It showed you want it, anyhow."

"Heard you need to be hell-bent on success to make it here," I said.

"You brought your guitar?"

"Yes." I unbuckled my case and pulled out the Tele.

"Whoa. 'Fifty-two?"

"'Fifty-one."

His eyes widened; these things were collector's editions now.

"Ran out on my husband and this was all I took," I told him. It wasn't a joke, of course, but I made it sound like one.

"Well, you got your priorities straight. Plug her in and play me something you wrote. Not Loretta Lynn, not . . ." He waved his arm to indicate other female singers.

I started playing my Snoqualmie Sweethearts song "Woman's Work."

Three lines in, he took a drag of his cigarette, "It's about a newly-wed. Too young for you these days. You got anything different?"

I'd written a song a couple weeks back about arriving in Nashville and getting so many rejections. It had reminded me of something Buck Owens always said, that Lady Limelight only shines on a person for so long, and then she's gone. "Lady Limelight" was a tongue-twister, so I'd changed the title to "Lady Luck's Light." I played the chorus:

> Don't know how she picks who she chooses
> But I know that it's me who always loses
> Why don't Lady Luck's light ever shine on me?

He shifted forward on his chair, his energy changing. When I finished, he muttered, "If we could add some strings . . . the divorcée . . . down on her luck . . ." He stamped out his cigarette in the cowboy-hat ashtray and held his hands out like a frame. "If we could change your look and your sound, add strings: violin, maybe even a harp. You could be a divorcée, not heartbroken, but world-weary. Kicked around. We'd need to change your look, since we got enough blondes, and Loretta's a brunette, so maybe a redhead. A redhead, but still got her looks. You could lose some weight; talk to Rosalie out front about that. And 'Lillian Waters' doesn't work. Sounds like a librarian. 'Lil Waters.' 'Lily Waters.' I'll think about it. Where did you grow up?"

"A town called Walla Walla, Washington."

He stretched for the organ, playing a minor chord. "Never heard of it. Sounds country enough. We can keep that. As for age, how old did you say you were?"

"Early thirties," I said.

"Your real age."

I sighed. "Forty. I was born in March '24."

"As I think you've figured out already, if you're a forty-year-old woman in this town, you might as well be dead. We'll say you're thirty-four. So born in March '31 in Walla Walla."

"The great flood," I said.

"What's that?"

"There was a flood in March '31 in Walla Walla. Came close to washing away downtown."

"Wait a second. Wait a second. A flood. Water. Water lily. Water Lil. Can you write me a song about that? You know, 'I was born in a flood, now I'm called Water Lil.' Can you do that?"

"Give me a day," I said.

I began humming "Water Lil" on the drive back to the house and finished it that night.

> *When I was born, the water filled the streets*
> *My mother cried at another mouth to feed.*
> *My father cried ain't this a bitter pill?*
> *We'd better call this baby Water Lil.*

Water Lil cries all the time, gets teased by other kids, but then meets her sweetheart. To the bridge:

> *And when I met you, darling, you said please don't cry.*
> *I'll keep you smiling 'til the day I die.*

And when I see a teardrop then I will
Know you're crying 'cause you're happy, Water Lil

Back to the verse:

When you walked out, I thought that I would weep,
The tissues would stack up a mile deep.
But I sit and stare with eyes so dead and still:
No more water in this world for Water Lil.

Up a half-note for the last verse:

I think about the girl I used to be,
And crying seems to be a memory.
I took your name, you laughed, you used me ill
You've gone and you've dried up your Water Lil.

When I sang it for Coy Ray Dexter the next day, he came as close to a smile as I'd seen from him. "'Water Lil,'" he said. "See, that's something an audience can remember. Water Lil's no ingenue, she's lived some. Ten years ago we couldn't have sold it, but I think we can now. Let's give it a try."

★   ★   ★

"Water Lil?" said Charlie.

"It's a gimmick," I said. "Figure I'll do this one song, make Coy Ray Dexter happy, and then leave the silly name behind."

We sat over midday hamburgers at Rotier's. Everyone went out to lunch in Nashville. Ladies took other ladies out to lunch to celebrate babies and engagements and tennis victories. Men took other men to lunch to toast business deals and golf scores. When men took a woman to lunch, they went to one of three places: the Andrew Jackson dining room, if they wanted formality; the Pie Wagon, which was near the *Tennessean* and *Nashville Banner* newsrooms, if they wanted coverage; or Rotier's, if they actually enjoyed the friendship, because the burgers were that good.

Women didn't take men to lunch, since we weren't paid enough.

When Charlie got back from his Australia tour, he'd invited me to his house to meet JoEllen, his new wife. They lived in a quiet neighborhood on the south side of Nashville. I'd expected a southern version of Margery, all efficiency and can-do attitude, but JoEllen prattled on about everything on her mind, from her mother's tendonitis to her tennis partner's serve. I'd frankly been more interested in meeting Red the Third, a blond dog with ears like a German shepherd's. This Red approached me with a low growl, but once he concluded that I was not likely to take off with Charlie in my jaws, like a bobcat would a chicken, he returned to his sentry post by a front window.

I thought it'd be just Charlie and me when he invited me out for a late lunch at Rotier's and the Friday Opry show, but here we were with JoEllen, too. Her yellow hair was set in sausage curls, and her wide nostrils and round brown eyes made her look perpetually surprised.

"Dexter isn't unsophisticated, Lil," Charlie said. He was sunburned from Australia, and his freckles had doubled, the combined effect making his face brighter red than his hair. "You don't think he might have something there? That audiences will remember Water Lil?"

"I've been performing for, what, twenty-five years now? Don't you think I might know something about this business, too?" I stacked onions high on my bun.

"But you came to Nashville . . ."

"And?"

"Nothing." He shook his head. "Nothing."

I took a bite of my burger, onions falling out the side, as JoEllen said, "I think Water Lil sounds like a lovely perfume."

I followed them to the Ryman in my Cadillac, which JoEllen complimented; Charlie didn't say a word about it.

At the Ryman, an employee directed the crowd outside with his megaphone. I was supposed to meet back up with Charlie and JoEllen in the alley which the theater shared with Tootsie's. I'd passed by the Ryman several times already, but I hadn't been inside yet, and I wanted to see it up close now that I was going in for my first Opry. I stood off the curb, so I wasn't blocking the audience getting in line, and examined it. It was brick with white-lined windows that were narrow and pointed at the top; I'd heard it had once been a church.

So this was the place I'd hated and envied for so long. This was where Hank Williams sang, memorialized in a black-and-white photo wearing a pale cowboy hat and behind a microphone with WSM on it, the radio station that had broadcast the Opry since its start in '25. This was where Chet Atkins played guitar so fast it sounded like he must have extra fingers, and Kitty Wells won over her audience, and Johnny Cash met June Carter.

"Lillian!" Charlie whistled from down the alleyway, where he and JoEllen stood by a back entrance to the auditorium. He'd recently written a jingle for Mary Carter Paint, and since Mary Carter was sponsoring this part of the show, Charlie had arranged backstage access for us.

The door that Charlie stood by was busy, musicians running in pulling basses and holding guitar cases. Charlie maneuvered us into the back of the theater, and I peeked out. I wanted to hate it. I expected to hate it. But the place was filling up with eager audience members, many with clothes and suntans like they'd come from out in the country for the show, and instead of hating it, I wanted to be on that stage.

Technicians bumped against us, and musicians' cases whacked me on the legs. The stage manager, Vito Pellettieri, a white-haired man in owlish glasses, rushed by me, carrying a pad of paper. "Archie Campbell to the stage, we're on in two, then the Browns," he shouted to someone, not taking any notice of me. My cheeks flushed; I realized I could be any old fan, and nothing about me signaled "musician" to these folks.

The house lights dimmed, Archie Campbell jogged onstage, and the stage lights brightened as he sang an intro song. "This portion of the Friday Night Opry is brought to you by the Mary Carter paint company," the announcer intoned as soon as he finished. Then Archie spoke, his mustache twitching over his remarkably white teeth, to introduce the Browns: "the best trio in the business." The three Browns came out from stage right, Jim Ed handsome in a suit and his two sisters, Maxine and Bonnie, with picture-perfect hairdos and nice modest dresses that covered their shoulders, then started into the Bob Dylan song "Blowin' in the Wind" in mellow harmony.

"What do you think?" Charlie whispered as we watched.

I was wondering why Maxine Brown, who was younger than me, got to stand in front of that mic and I didn't. "I think Dylan would be surprised to hear that his song is now a hymn to Jesus," I said.

Next up was Connie Smith, and if Maxine had upset me, I wanted to throw my shoe at Connie. She didn't even have a record out yet—it was coming out Tuesday, she told Archie—and yet here she was appearing on the Opry. It was clear to me, or I thought it was clear to me, why she'd gotten this slot on the show: she was adorable, around twenty years old, with huge eyes and shiny strawberry-blonde hair. Archie practically tripped over his words in praise of her. "You're a pretty little booger," he told her, and she giggled. "You sure got a face I'd like to shake hands with."

"If she can even hit a single note, I'll be darned," I said to Charlie.

Then she sang, and I shut up: she was more than good. Her voice reminded me of Patsy Cline's, with smooth phrasing and an edge of heartbreak to it, especially on the high notes, and she was backed chiefly with a steel guitar rather than the throw-every-instrument-in-there orchestra that was so common in Nashville.

"So?" Charlie asked me when she was finished.

"So if I was twenty years old and giggled that much, I guess I'd be on the Opry too."

Archie Campbell, who wasn't much of a singer, was up next with a religious song, and I tapped Charlie on the shoulder to tell him Archie should pray that he sticks to comedy from now on, but he fixed his eyes to the stage.

When the segment ended, Charlie took JoEllen's arm and pulled her toward the alley door in fast, stiff steps, saying brief hellos to different players and singers but not stopping to chat. I had to jog to catch them. He burst into the alley, JoEllen practically cantering to keep up with him, and he said, "Well, that's the Opry; good night, Lillian."

"Good night, Lillian," JoEllen echoed, as Charlie practically dragged her toward the street.

"Wait a second!" I ran in front of them, cutting them off. "Where're you going so fast?"

His face was stony. "Home."

"What's gotten into you?"

He threw up his arms. "What do you want me to do, Lillian?"

"What do you mean?"

"You sat at lunch, making fun of your Nashville record contract and how GMI and Coy Ray Dexter actually want you to succeed, and when you see actual Nashville, actual players, you tear them apart, too?"

One of the Browns' backup players hurried by. "G'night, Charlie," he said.

"G'night, Hully," Charlie said.

I waited until the man was out of earshot. "You're mad I don't bow down at the altar of the Opry like the rest of Nashville?"

"You're the one that chose to move here, didn't you? No one hauled you here by the scruff of your neck?"

"Last I checked I wasn't a cat."

Charlie tipped his head back. "It's easy, Lillian, for you to tear things down. You thought Bakersfield wasn't good enough for you, and neither was Tacoma, or Walla Walla, and now Nashville. Yeah, the Browns slowed down 'Blowin' in the Wind' some, but you see how the crowd responded? They loved it; that's why they played it; that's why audiences love them. Have you ever—" He stopped himself.

I knew what he was going to say. No, I'd never had a crowd roar like that for me.

I stepped back hard, accidentally landing wrong so my ankle pinched, but kept my face serene.

"If you want to complain about Nashville from the West Coast, that's one thing, Lillian. To come here and tear it down, though? Where's that going to get you? You want to come here, spit in their eye, tell them to go to hell with their Opry, and still be invited onstage as an honored guest? You can't be here and also be too good for it. At some point you've got to trust that someone else knows something about country music, or selling records, that maybe you don't. At some point, you've got to listen," he said. JoEllen extracted an embroidered handkerchief from her purse and dotted it at her forehead, while Charlie slid his arm around JoEllen's waist. They turned the corner onto Fifth Avenue, disappearing before I could say another word.

★ ★ ★

"Has Coy Ray decided what I'm recording yet?" I asked on my daily call to his secretary, Rosalie, at GMI.

"He'll tell you at the session, Miss Waters," she replied, pleasantly.

"I need a demo, though, or lyrics, or something," I pleaded, same as I had on the preceding days.

"He'll tell you at the session, Miss Waters," she said, this time a little less pleasantly.

Coy Ray had booked my first recording session for two o'clock on a Friday afternoon, two days from now. We were laying down "Water Lil" for the A side, but for the B side, I wasn't sure what he had planned.

"Rosalie, could you please ask him?"

"He'll tell you at the session, Miss Waters. Have a blessed day." She hung up.

"Talk to you tomorrow," I said to the dial tone.

I'd prepared as best I could. I'd laid off whiskey and drunk coffee and water and poured honey down my gullet. I'd gone to bed early. I'd stayed away from crackers or nuts, thinking they could scratch up my throat. I'd done scales and breath exercises. But Coy Ray refused to tell me what I'd be singing other than "Water Lil," so I couldn't do the most important preparation of all: learning the song.

The day of the session, I styled myself carefully. I thought about what Water Lil, a world-weary divorcée who still had sex appeal, would choose. I settled on a plain black dress. It hitched up when I put my guitar strap over it, but I was Coy Ray's only girl singer; I didn't want to draw extra attention to myself by wearing pants or, at the other extreme, something tarty. My hair was not yet red; Rosalie had given me a hairdresser's name but I didn't have the money to have it done. I styled my hair as best as I could, slicking it down like Jean Shepherd's.

As I pulled into the lot behind the recording studio at ten minutes to one, the door to the studio banged open and out burst a mess of heavy-bellied men. They ran around the lot, clapping and shouting, as I stared. They didn't seem to notice me in my car, and, wanting to keep my Tele safe, I waited for them to run back inside before I got out of my car.

Inside the studio, Coy Ray was waiting for me in a tiny room, a pile of boxed tape reels and acetates spread in front of him. "I was thinking the B-side could be 'Lady Luck's Light,'" I said after setting down the Tele case.

He said that song was depressing without being sexy, and anyway we couldn't start out with two songs from an untested songwriter and an untested singer.

Untested, I thought: I'd been doing this two and a half decades. But I thought of what Charlie had said the other night and didn't push back. "What are we cutting, then?"

"'Water Lil,'" Coy Ray said.

"What else, Coy Ray? We got three hours in there."

"We're paying for it, too."

Sugar had taught me my lesson, and I'd read every word of my contract this time. "I know. Studio time, plus tape, plus scale for the players. Coy Ray, what game are you running? What else am I gonna record? Where can I rehearse?"

"That's just it, Lillian. When you practice, you don't sound fresh; when you sang that Loretta Lynn song, it was overplayed and overdone, but when you sang new stuff, it worked." He slid three acetates, four tapes, and several sheets of lyrics toward me. "We've got enough time to lay down tracks today that we can use on future records, so you should learn all of these. For the 'Water Lil' B-side, the best option is called 'Away from Home,' but we'll cut three or four tracks today just in case, so get familiar with the other ones, too. There's a room down the hall where you can listen to the demos, but don't overdo it."

I picked up an acetate, baffled. "You want me to be ready to record three or four brand-new songs in an *hour*? I can barely read through the lyrics in that time. And guitar licks—"

"Don't worry about that."

"Coy Ray."

"I said, don't worry about that."

I opened my mouth, then closed it. I was recording whether or not I threw a fit; I didn't have the time to be angry. I took my Tele down the hall, where I worked through the songs, including "Away from Home," a basic song about a girl moving to a big city and missing the town she came from. It was saccharine and dumb, and I couldn't get any emotional heft in my voice for the word "home."

At two o'clock on the dot, Coy Ray took me into the studio. An engineer made final adjustments to the microphones and instrument placements as the men I'd seen jogging around the parking lot waited with their steel guitar, bass, acoustic guitar, and electric guitar. Session players; they would've played the morning session, too, and the jog, I realized, had been to energize themselves for the afternoon.

The engineer joined Coy Ray in the control room, then, through a window, I watched him put on headphones and adjust the soundboard. Coy Ray looked over all us musicians, then pressed a button and his voice came over a speaker. "We're here for three hours, we're gonna get at least three, maybe four tracks laid down. Listen up to the first one, 'Away from Home.' We'll be doing it in C."

I set my Tele case at my feet. "Hi there, I'm glad to—" I began, but the players signaled me to be quiet. Each of the musicians had a piece of paper ready. As Coy Ray played the demo, the men scratched out markings as fast as a secretary taking dictation. I knew they used the Nashville Number System here, but their scribblings made no sense to me: diamonds and symbols, rows of numbers like 1 5 4 5. The demo finished. Coy Ray said "Again," and replayed it, and this time the players went through and corrected what they'd written before. I didn't understand their notation. I didn't understand Nashville. And I couldn't stir up any feelings about this song.

I opened my Tele case and strapped on my guitar as the demo singer warbled "The last time I saw home, I was raring to be free, but now that I'm away from—" But Coy Ray stopped the demo there. His speaker crackled, and the steel guitarist froze his pencil in midair. I looked left and right, trying to figure out what was wrong.

"What's that around your neck?" Coy Ray said.

I touched its body. "My Tele."

The bass player, whose name I'd learn was Gene Farver, scooted closer to his instrument.

"You're not playing guitar," Coy Ray said.

I pulled the Tele close to my body. "I do play guitar."

He spoke louder. "I'm aware of that, but you think we don't have enough of an uphill battle launching a forty-something divorcée who isn't from these parts and doesn't listen to me when I tell her to get her hair dyed red, without dealing with the fact that she's a lady guitar player—a lady *electric* guitar player? I don't care if you can pick better than Grady Martin, you'll take that thing off and I don't want to see it again."

I didn't move.

"I said, put it away," Coy Ray said.

I could leave, but I had nowhere left to storm off to.

I tugged the strap over my head, pulled the strap across the guitar body, and laid the Tele carefully in its case while the other musicians averted their gazes.

"Let's rehearse it," Coy Ray said.

He gave a beat of and-a-one-two-three-four as I dashed back to my mic, and the musicians started. My voice quavered on the first verse, thinking about how Coy Ray had made me put away my guitar, how he might as well have asked me to take off my dress and stand naked in front of all these men. Like the girl in the song at her city job, I was stuck, no other options, couldn't run any longer. I went at the last verse and final chorus hard. I knew Coy Ray was going to chew me out again, and I wanted to give it to him good before he could switch on that speaker and tell me I wasn't worth a thing.

We finished. Everyone was quiet. "Golly," said the steel guitarist, who went by Tommy Reed.

The speaker came on. "Good thing I was rolling tape. That was all right," Coy Ray said.

At this, Tommy Reed's shoulders visibly dropped, and he gave me a wink.

★ ★ ★

We used my vocals on that take of "Away from Home" as the B-side cut. It blasted onto the charts at number 11, and "Water Lil"? "Water Lil" made it to number 1. Newspapers and trades, at Coy Ray's urging, dubbed me Water Lil, and though Lillian Waters still appeared in small print on my records, it was Water Lil on the album covers. Coy Ray was right. People remembered the name.

He enrolled me in what he called comportment, and what I called charm school, a clinic run by a frighteningly elegant woman from Uruguay. She'd been a founding member of that country's national ballet, and taught me how to move, dance, and stand with panache. ("You stand," she told me at our first meeting, "like a furious soldier. You must embrace your hips.") Rosalie made an appointment for me at Harvey's, the downtown department store, where a stylist dyed my hair a deep red. I was sent to a makeup artist, who showed me how to contour my nose and enhance my eyes, and a nutritionist who put me on a diet of cabbage soup. Rosalie arranged a fitting at Judy of Nashville, where I ordered up stage dresses with outrageous fringes and spangles; when I visited LA, I stopped at Nudie Cohn's for suits and dresses in tropical colors, made of satin and velveteen, covered in rhinestones and embroidery. Coy Ray, who'd decided to read through a whole college-literature course a couple of years earlier, assigned me classic stories of wronged women he thought could inspire my own songwriting: ancient Greek poetry, *The Scarlet Letter*, Shakespeare. (When I finally read *Romeo and Juliet*, I wanted to tell Althea that caponing a chicken was a heck of a lot simpler.)

Only then did Coy Ray think I was ready for the road. He had me open for a more established country singer on his roster, one who kept calling me by the name of the last girl singer he'd toured with. With him, I played the Deep South for the first time. The stark segregation of Nashville had already unnerved me when I moved there. I hadn't noticed it on my trip to the DJ convention, thinking the streets held pretty much the mix of people I was used to seeing in Tacoma or Bakersfield. Once I lived there, though, I realized that any indoor space I was in, whether it was a movie theater or restaurant, was filled with only white people. And when I toured farther south, the color lines were so clearly drawn as to be a shock. My first time in Mississippi, it hadn't been a year since Medgar Evers was murdered in Jackson, and in Alabama, Selma hadn't happened yet. If there weren't technically separate waiting rooms at bus stations anymore, or separate water fountains, it sure felt that way in practice. At hotels, white guests, Black bellhops and maids. At restaurants, white diners, Black waiters. On trains, white riders, Black porters. If I met Black musicians on the road, we'd trade the names of places we could meet up and have a beer together and play and talk. There were only a couple of joints in each town, usually a motel or a low-key dive bar, where we could do that without hassle or worse; for their safety, I had to bring one of our white male band members with me, as we all knew what could happen if someone in those states spotted a white woman socializing with a Black man.

I toured throughout the South, and then beyond it, adding package shows until my sales and radio play got high enough that I could headline my own tour, where I sold out crowds of three hundred, then eight hundred, then two thousand.

I can tell you tales of hot coffee slopped into mugs, of teeth gritty with the night's beer and the morning's dirty water, of the relief of the first sip of whiskey and the regret of the fifth glass. I lived in a bus when I didn't live in a camper, and when I didn't live in a camper I lived in the back seat of a car. I bought stacks of sugar cones at ice-cream parlors so I'd have a snack ready when I was hungry.

Flamingo on the twenty-third. Bishop on the eighth. CBS and Glen Campbell on the tenth.

Thank you, all, I'm so glad you came here.

Thank you, all, for giving me this welcome.

Gonna tell you a story 'bout my Daddy's mule operation.

Goodnight Kansas City and good morning Broken Arrow.

St. Cloud, St. Croix, St. Peter, St. Paul, St. Charles, St. Clair. South to Texas and west to California and another set of saints. San Juan, San Jacinto, San Gabriel, San Marco, San Pedro. Did "Pedro" mean Peter or Paul? We didn't know.

I stopped opening my show with a greeting like "Hello, Louisville" after I said "Hello, Louisville" when we were actually in Kokomo, Indiana.

We played the Hidy-Hody Ranch Bar, and the Circle-M Saloon, the Round-Up Rodeo and the Boiler Room, the Gunshot Lounge and Gunshot Bar and Gunshot Club.

Road and road and road. Brown and buildings and occasional green. Road and signs. Road and motels.

Old Yellers for energy. Speckled Birds to stay thin. Seconals and whiskeys to calm the high after a show so I could sleep.

Bladder full, empty, full again, empty again. Pissing in bushes. Pissing on dust.

Calling Coy Ray from pay phones to sing him new songs I'd written. Coy Ray told me, "Stick with who Water Lil is." That meant: no songs about the road, about ambition, about men I tumbled into hotel beds with when I was drunk enough. (Once, when I ended up at a house party after an Ohio show, a curly-haired blond woman planted one on me as I was pouring myself a drink. The kiss didn't do anything for me, but I half wanted to write a song about it just to get Coy Ray's hackles up.) He let me record my own songs when they were about lost love, missed opportunity, poor choices, bad women—like "Three-Quarter Time," written from the point of view of a mistress who only gets her man one quarter of the time. When Coy Ray told me to write about motherhood from a divorcée's point of view, I wrote "Mommy, Won't You Come Upstairs?" It stemmed from an evening at Tommy Reed Farver's house; Tommy Reed and Gene Farver, the steel guitarist and bassist from my first GMI session, were brothers who had become my regular session players at recordings, and sometimes came on the road with me. The little Farver boy had his first nightmare, and he called to his mother, "Mommy, will you come upstairs and tell me what is happening?" It was such a grown-up wording, but a child's way of being bewildered by a nightmare. I wrote the phrase in my notebook and made it into a song about a broken marriage, where the kid doesn't understand where his daddy's gone off to. Got to number 8.

Awards. Ceremonies. Photographers: "Lift your skirt, Lillian." "Chin to the left." "Eyes up at the camera." Drinks with DJs. Drinks with promoters. Drinks with distributors.

Water Lil sold, and I sold that version of myself, giving answers to interviews that people wanted to hear. At KTYL, in Mesa, Arizona, a radio station with huge glass windows and speakers along the exterior so people could drive up and watch while they listened to the radio broadcasts, the DJ asked me about "Water Lil." "Now, you were born during a big flood in '31," he said.

"Sure was. Water rushing in all over the place."

"I'm sure that's the truth. But—"

The wheat in my belly rustled. But you lied about the year. But you weren't born in a flood. But you left home at ten. But I talked to your mother and sister, and they know, and what you did was—

"But that can't be the case about your mama and pop fretting about a new baby. They must've been glad to have you join the family."

"You're right, we had as nice a family as you could imagine," I said. The DJ, sounding almost reverent about my ideal family, asked me to sing a piece of tripe from my Sugar days, "When My Mother Smiles on Me." I even managed a tear at the end for the audience.

Sometimes we fumbled through, the crowd restless, the songs routine.

When we played well, though.

When the music flowed.

It is a feeling I first had when I waded into our clear stream in Walla Walla as a child. My feet supported by smooth pebbles, water swirling around my ankles. Onstage, we picked up one another's notes, and the swish of a snare and the pick of a guitar string swelled into something that didn't even seem like a song anymore, shimmering like it wasn't meant for this world. I hit every target with my rifle and aimed at the next, *pop*. The room floated, cigarette smoke and creaking wood floors and heat of the lights and the ripe rich smell of the audience lifting up and away. There was so much in my life that I couldn't talk about, that people couldn't know about, yet when I was onstage the audience clapped and called for more, sweat on their foreheads and boots on their feet, and it wasn't just that I felt good, but that they saw me, and they heard me, and they thought I was all right anyway.

And when they yelled my name—Water *Lil!* Water *Lil!*

And when my eyes scanned the crowd and I could see Hen, I pictured her realizing that whatever she'd built for her life could not compare to this, no matter how tidy her house, how pretty her children, how impressive her husband, however many Annas she employed, she could not do what I could do.

I belted out the last song of the night, my hips swayed to the rhythm, all of us onstage stomped and the crowd danced and everyone shouted and bottles broke and fights started and I loved it.

Just one more song before we go. And a one, and a two, and a one-two-three-four.

★ 21 ★

Tule Lake, California
July 1980

"Where exactly do you want me to go?" Patrice asked Kaori, who was leaning over the driver's seat on the bus, surveying the road.

"They should have a marker or something." She took a sip from her own flat Coke; Patrice had converted her to the drink somewhere around Albuquerque.

"We're supposed to be in Medford by five."

"Why don't we drive for ten minutes more, and then we'll stop if we don't see anything," I said from the table at the front where I was tinkering with lyrics.

Patrice kept going, but we didn't see any signs, and ten minutes or so later he pulled the bus to a stop and opened the doors. "Here good enough?" he said.

"I guess so." Kaori walked off the bus and entered a flat plain of nothing, red-brown grass and succulents, hard earth, green scrub brush. A flat-top mountain lay squat in the distance.

Gene rolled out of his bunk and yawned. "Why're we stopping?"

"Kaori's family lived here during the war," I said, crossing out a word.

"Who the heck would live here?"

"Wasn't by choice, Gene. It was one of those internment camps."

He looked at me blankly.

"When the government took the Japanese people from the coasts and sent them to camps?"

"I was in Arkansas," he said. Whether he meant it as an excuse for why he hadn't heard of them or an explanation as to why it didn't affect him, I wasn't sure, but it annoyed me either way.

Patrice closed the bus door and wiped his forehead with his sleeve, checking the air conditioning, which was already on high. "Hotter out there than in here," he said. "We got to keep on to Medford, though: how long does she want to stay?"

"Don't ask me," I said. "Why don't we play a round of rummy?"

The boys gathered around the table, except for Charlie. He was in the back of the bus pickling his hands. I'd seen, when I'd gone to the bathroom, that he had a telegram on the table in front of him; he'd received it at the venue we'd played in Redding. I couldn't imagine that Donna the Dip's questions about the wedding were that fascinating, but then, we'd barely exchanged a word since Bakersfield, except for a few gruff comments about set lists. I couldn't look him in the eye, communicating with his forehead instead, and tried to shut my ears off when Gene, who was about to celebrate his fortieth anniversary with his high school sweetheart, quizzed Charlie about his wedding plans. Onstage and on the Green Giant, Charlie and I stayed as far apart as physically possible.

Gene took out playing cards, shuffled them, and laid them out, slap-slap-slap.

We played a round, but when Gene picked up the cards to shuffle them for another, Patrice took them from him. "Can't be waiting on her much longer. We got to get going."

We all looked out the windshield. Kaori remained in the red plain where she'd stood, unmoving, this whole time.

"Not it," Tommy Reed said, his mouth full of chewing tobacco.

"Not it," Gene and Patrice said in chorus.

"Pete's sake," I said. I motioned at Patrice to open the door again. The dirt made scratching sounds against my shoes as I walked over to Kaori; I could tell I'd need to sop off my ankles with a washcloth later. Kaori's eyes were closed, her back to the flattop mountain, the sun on her face, her arms stretched out.

"We got to get moving to make Medford," I said.

She widened her arms.

"Kaori, we got to go," I said.

Sun reflected in her eyes when she opened them. "There's nothing here," she said. "Nothing to mark it."

"Maybe there's another spot somewhere near here with a sign."

"There is. A memorial, a plaque, somewhere around here, that Japanese Americans pushed to have put up, and the government only installed it last year. But no one seems to know about it. When Patrice stopped at the gas station on the way in, I asked three people where the Tule Lake camp had been, where the memorial is. No one knew. No one cared. There's not even a lake."

She was right. There was nothing beyond arid land.

"What did you think?" she said, raising a leg and pointing a toe.

"Of this place?"

"No. What did you think back then? You were in Tacoma during World War II. What did you think when all the Japanese Americans were taken away?"

"Oh, now, Kaori. It wasn't me who ordered it."

"But what did you think?" The relentless sun gave her hair a red glow.

"I thought . . ." I recalled the sickly smell of the rotting bananas I'd left for Mrs. Hideshima, and how I'd hightailed it out of Nihon-machi after leaving a few cents in change. "I felt bad for everyone," I said.

"You felt bad." She flexed her foot. "Right. Did you do anything?"

"Lord, Kaori. Why are you asking me? Ask Charlie, or Gene, or Tommy Reed, why don't you?"

"I will ask Charlie, and Gene, and Tommy Reed. Right now, I'm asking you."

I didn't have a good answer for her. My generation didn't protest like hers did, but I wasn't sure if it was because we weren't aware that we could, or because we were scared to risk what we had, or we—I— just didn't care enough to get involved. "I didn't know what to do," I said.

"Something would've been better than nothing." She kicked her heel hard into the ground. "Forget it. We'll be late for Medford." She started for the bus.

I followed several paces behind, running my tongue along my teeth. "Your mother," I said. "What does she say about it?"

Kaori swiveled, waiting a while before she spoke. "My mom won't talk about it," she said. "The camps. She was just a kid. My grandparents won't discuss it either. 'Shikata ga nai.'"

"What's that mean?"

"'It can't be helped.' It's what everyone from that generation says. Like the camp was an earthquake or a snowstorm, not a place with barbed wire that people, Americans, thought up. My uncle, the one in Las Vegas, is the only one who's told me anything. He was fifteen when they went. They had two weeks to get rid of everything they had. Their tractor, his cat, even. He loved that cat. He still has nightmares where he's got to leave and can't find the cat. They get to their first camp, Pinedale, in Fresno, and they're not sure if they're going to be shot or stuck there for the next eighty years or what. When they were transferred to Tule Lake, my mother's whole family, six of them, were in one room. They had straw for mattresses. No toilets, just pits in the ground. There were watchtowers and guards, and if you went beyond the barbed wire you got shot. It was a prison."

I knelt down and plucked a yellow wildflower, twirling its rough stem. I'd known the bare outlines of the story, from reading the newspapers after the war ended, but I hadn't heard any of what Kaori was describing.

"I mean, no one in Minnesota learns about it, but I thought out west it'd be different. I'll bet it's hardly in history books, even here. Everyone would rather forget."

A phrase from long ago surfaced in my mind. *Washington's not like that.* I placed the flower on the ground and patted it into the dust. "Have you ever been to the mountains in the West?" I asked. "Hiking, skiing?"

She shook her head no.

"There are mountains in Washington, in the Cascades, at Baker, Rainier, where climbers who don't know what they're doing die every winter. There are parts that look like an open field of snow, but it's a trick of the eye. The snow settles into crevasses made of ice and the surface seems smooth, solid, but the crevasses are just wide enough for a hiker or an animal to plunge into. Do you see?" I traced a pattern in the dirt. "That's the West. People want it to be beautiful, majestic, to be the future of this country, and they just see the surface and think it's perfection. They don't see the cracks. They don't see how people can disappear here."

Kaori reached for a small, flat stone, and a second of the same shape. I saw she was making some arrangement, moving faster and faster. I gathered some that seemed to match, offering them to her. One for Mrs. Hideshima. One for the mother with the crib. One for the man with the trunk. One for Nihonmachi. One for what I could have done. One for what I did not do.

When Kaori set her last stone, she tossed a handful of dirt toward the sun, but a breeze blew it back toward her sandaled feet. "We have to talk about it," she said. Her eyes were pulled down by weight. She grabbed my hands between her palms. "We have to talk about it," she repeated.

We walked, slowly, to the bus, our feet kicking up clouds of dust.

Nashville, Tennessee

1971–1974

The Water Lil Fan Club Newsletter

Edition #18

Summer 1969

This week we have a special treat, an interview with "Water Lil" herself! Sincerely, Peg Cupertino, Fan Club President, Alpharetta, Georgia

What is it like to appear onstage at the Grand Ole Opry? Do you hope you'll be inducted?

Of course every country music singer would love to be a part of the Opry, but my touring schedule doesn't allow for that many performances there. It is a thrill, though, just to be on that stage. To think about standing in the very footsteps of Kitty Wells!

Do you have a favorite drink?

I do not drink liquor, of course, but I do enjoy a virgin daiquiri on tour. I first tried one in Las Vegas. Oh my!

What is your favorite hobby?
I love to bake cakes for neighbors and church pic-
nics. (See "Water Lil's Strawberry Extravaganza,"
below.)

Have you ever wanted to play an instrument?
Sometimes I have thought of taking up the guitar
again. But I'm not sure my fingers would still know
all the chords!

★ ★ ★

On a winter morning, I was packing for a flight to Tulsa, where I'd
be playing Cain's Ballroom for a week straight, an audience of almost
two thousand a night. My bedroom, its walls painted a chartreuse so
intense it hurt my eyes, was covered in clothes and jewelry. I'd traded
my East Nashville ranch for an Edgehill bungalow, then left that for a
historic Victorian near downtown and hired a designer to do an outrageous interior overhaul. We'd covered the place in fluffy white wall-
to-wall carpets, graphic wallpaper, and bright paint. When a fancy
neighbor told me it was a shame I hadn't chosen more historically
appropriate colors for the interior, I had the outside repainted purple.

The phone rang as I was folding tissue paper around a Nudie skirt
suit, mustard velvet with snakes and bluebirds appliquéd onto it; the
lively audience at Cain's would want to see the biggest and brightest
costumes I had.. "Lil," Charlie said. We'd seen each other at awards
shows and industry parties over the past few years, but between
chaotic touring schedules and him and JoEllen moving out into the
country, we hadn't gotten together much. Still, I had a stack of all
the albums he'd played on in the living room; sometimes I listened
to them at night, placing the needle back to hear a certain riff of his
again, wondering if it was meant for me.

"Hey, Mac," I said, wedging the receiver against my shoulder. "Talk
fast, I've got to be at the airport in an hour."

"I'll let you go, then."

"No, I've got a minute. What's going on?"

He waited a beat, then said, "I've got to put Red down."

"Aw, Mac, that's no good. Isn't he pretty young?"

"He was a stray, so no telling his age, and he's in pain. The vet says there's nothing they can do, and he's not eating. I made him a last meal of steak and kidney, and he doesn't even want it."

"You're giving your dog steak and kidney?"

Charlie didn't answer, and I held up two rhinestone necklaces to see which one sparkled more, then noticed he'd been quiet for a while. "You still there?"

He cleared his throat. "Yep. No. I'm just—I'm about to take him to the vet. Over near you, actually."

"Thought the vet said they couldn't do anything."

"I'm gonna have him put down there."

"The vet's got a shotgun?"

"Christ, Lillian, no. They give them a medication that stops their heart."

"Oh." I tried on a chunky yellow-quartz ring. "Sorry. At the farm, we'd always shoot the animals once they got that bad."

"Yeah. The ranch, too. I just—I just can't do it."

"Say, do you and JoEllen want to stop by on the way? I can fix you some coffee, and I could rustle up a treat for Red?"

"Nah. Nah." He cleared his throat. "JoEllen's got a tennis game."

"Tennis? She's not going with you?"

"She's not a dog person."

I held the receiver away from my mouth and huffed out hard. I wasn't sure if there was a later flight to Tulsa or not, but the performance wasn't until tomorrow afternoon; I'd drive if I had to. "Well, then, I'm coming."

"You've got a flight."

"There'll be other flights. I'm coming."

"Lil, you don't need to."

"Know what, Charlie? I do. Give me the address and I'll meet you there."

I waited in the vet's parking lot as Charlie pulled in and parked his truck. Red the Third lay in the pickup bed. When Charlie let down the tailgate, Red, who'd usually jump right down to suss out his surroundings, didn't move.

"Hey, Red." I moved to him and reached in, let him sniff me, and scratched his chin. "Not doing so good, friend?" I studied Charlie, whose eyes were wet. "You need help getting him off the truck?"

"Maybe you could pick him up and move him to the edge. I can lift him from there."

"Sure." I hoisted myself into the truck bed and lifted Red. He was heavy, sixty or seventy pounds, and his legs splayed in panic as I pulled him up, yet when Charlie took hold of him, Red relaxed against his owner's body like he was a child, his front paws over Charlie's shoulders.

"All right, boy," Charlie said. As he carried Red into the vet clinic, he wiped his eyes with his sleeve. "Christ. I'm sorry. He's just such a good dog."

"Yeah." My throat tightened. "I'll go check in, all right?"

The waiting room was lined with cages of cats and dogs, meowing and whimpering. A severe receptionist, whose thick bangs nearly covered her eyes, sent us to a back room, where Charlie set Red on a metal table. I pulled a dog treat from a glass jar on a shelf and offered it to Red; he sniffed once and moved his head away. I rubbed his head. "Well, goodbye, old fellow." To Charlie, I said, "I'm thinking you've got things to say to Red, so I'll wait outside, okay?"

Charlie pressed his lips together and gave me the barest of nods.

When Charlie came out to the lobby, his freckles popped magenta against his pale skin, and his head hung low. Seeing the receptionist, he fumbled for some cash in his pocket, but I steered him to a bench by the door. "I can settle the bill. You sit there a minute," I said.

He sank down.

While I waited for the receptionist to finish a phone call, I eyed a big brindle dog in a cage. It had soft, floppy ears, and a short coat, with a shock of white fur at the collar. The dog lifted bloodshot eyes to me and then lowered his head, resigned.

When the receptionist hung up, she handed me the bill and I asked her what kind of dog it was.

"Oh, her?" the receptionist said, suddenly animated. "That's a mutt of some sort. A vet tech found that one on the street and brought her in. She has a little mange, but she's healthy otherwise. We have to bring her to the pound later today, actually. I'd take her home myself, but I've already got three dogs and a baby."

The dog raised the skin above her eyes, then rested her head on her paws.

"Handsome dog, anyway," I said, signing a check and sliding it to the receptionist.

From the bench, Charlie said, "This dog goes to the pound, she'll have two days, three days, before they put her down. How old is she?"

"We think maybe three, four," the receptionist said.

"No one's gonna be taking home a full-grown mangy dog with a sad face in the next two days."

"Charlie," I said, making an I'm-sorry face at the receptionist. "You don't know that."

"Yes, I do."

The receptionist bent down to get her receipt pad. When she got up, Charlie said, "I'll take the dog."

"Really?" The receptionist beamed. "She's a sweetheart. A good dog."

"I'll take her," Charlie repeated, walking to the row of cages.

"You sure?" I asked. "You just put Red down. You ready for another dog? And a girl dog at that?"

He slid his fingers between the front bars of the cage, and the dog's nose twitched. "There isn't always time to do things exactly when you think you're ready. This dog's here, I'm here." He signaled the receptionist. "Can I let her out?"

The receptionist took a leash from the wall and passed it to Charlie. "On the house."

Charlie opened the cage. "Come on, now," he said. The dog slowly rose to her feet and took a tentative step out of the cage and toward Charlie, who dropped to his haunches so he was face-to-face with the animal. "Hi, there," Charlie said. "Hi, friend." The dog moved its nose toward him, took a sniff, then shook herself out, skin wriggling, and jumped down. Charlie leashed her, and the dog tentatively followed him. When they reached Charlie's truck, the tailgate still down, Charlie said, "How 'bout it, Red?"

The dog leaped in, settling herself into a contented circle.

★ ★ ★

After so many years when opportunities didn't come, I vowed not to say no, not to any offer: Lady Limelight was finally shining on me, and I was going to stick with her as long as I could. It was yes to a European tour, yes to the Wembley Country Music Festival in London, yes to Ontario and Manitoba and Saskatchewan. Yes to a duet with Loretta on the Opry, a call-and-response mix of her "Fist City" and my "When You See Him in the Morning," yet another song I'd written from the point of view of the other woman. Loretta and I put it out as a single, and it held number 1 for five weeks straight.

People want to be near you when you get famous, and you talk yourself into thinking they like you for you. I'd done all right without a manager for the first several years in Nashville, because I didn't want to give away any of my money, but the scheduling and payments and contracts got so complicated that I hired one. Then the more I toured, especially on package shows with glamorous women like Tammy Wynette or Dolly Parton, the less my dyed-hair-or-wig and self-applied makeup held up. So I hired a hairstylist and makeup artist to travel with me. Men who'd just spent five days on the road drinking gin from a personal cooler could slap some water on their faces before a show and have the audience think they looked rugged, but if I were to show up with bags under my eyes after three hours' sleep jammed against a car window, the crowd would think I was sick or using pills or drinking too much. When I did have to use pills to stay up, or drink to come down, the hair and makeup ladies were able to hide that, so they earned every penny. Their gossip drove me crazy at first—who was doing well, who was sinking, who the producers loved and who was about to be dropped by their label—as did their habit of buying *Billboard* on Wednesdays to see where everyone was charting.

That is, until I began charting top ten consistently. There I was, up with the singers I'd envied for so long. Here was my own tour bus. Magazine profiles. A sprawling house on Old Hickory Lake, outside of the city, after I got bored of scandalizing my downtown Nashville neighbors. Song-of-the-year awards. Hours-long lines for autographs. I always took the time to do autographs. Always. These people had come to hear my songs, and that meant something real to me.

A week at the Playroom in Atlanta. Two weeks in Las Vegas. An Army base in Georgia. Another album. Another single. *Hee Haw*, which Buck hosted and starred on with Don Rich. *The Porter Wagoner Show*. *The Johnny Cash Show*. *The Tonight Show*. At the other end of those cameras, always, I pictured Hen, in her fancy living room, calling Mother in a panic. "It's her," she'd say. "She's a star now. We were wrong." At the CMAs and the Academy of Country Music awards shows, after I took the stage and accepted my trophies, producers from Decca and Columbia and Capitol waylaid me in the hallway. "If you ever get the urge to move on from GMI and Dexter," they said, "please think of me."

I hardly had time for my old friends. *Hee Haw* filmed in Nashville, so I saw Don Rich from time to time; Buck I avoided, as he'd gotten ornery as he'd gotten older and more successful. Don and Charlie would get together at Charlie's house and play music, but between my touring and public appearances and the drinks I needed to get to sleep, and the sleep I needed to handle the drinks, I kept missing their meetups. In '74 Don Rich died in a motorcycle crash in California after a late-night recording session. I didn't go to the funeral. I was playing the Golden Nugget in Vegas, five 45-minute sets per night with only 15-minute breaks in between, and you didn't cancel on the Golden Nugget. My makeup gal later gave me a newspaper clipping with a picture of Don in his coffin, like he was asleep, his hands folded and covered in white gloves. Something about the picture bothered me, but I didn't have time to think on it; I was performing at the wedding of a Texas oil baron's daughter that afternoon.

I drank, more and more. This was how the men passed time on the road. They liked that I could keep up with them, and I did, too: I was one of the boys, sure, and the drinking unfurled my tongue, let me relax, let me not think about things I didn't want to think about. If it was a good show, we celebrated with a drink; if it was a bad one, we erased it with a drink.

I got colds and flus and headaches from not sleeping enough. I worked weekends and holidays. I had my bus driver dip into Mexico to get refills on my pills, which I kept in a silver case with plastic dividers. I kept charting. Number 1. Number 2. Number 10.

I picked up other musicians' guitars to see if my fingers could still work the fretboards, and put them down before I got up enough nerve to play a single note.

Always, whether I was playing the Roxy in LA, or Mr. Lucky's in Phoenix, or a package show at the Mid-South Coliseum in Memphis, I gave my audience a show. I gave them all of me—or as much as I knew how.

★ 23 ★

Tacoma, Washington
August 1980

The second Patrice's turn signal indicated that we were getting off I-5 in Tacoma, and I mean the very second, the Tacoma Aroma pushed in strong through the open window of the Green Giant. That smell of gasoline and sulfur and kelp and oily seawater made the others pinch their noses, but Charlie and I glanced at each other and giggled, and then the giggles became laughter, and the laughter full-on howls, both of us bent over and gasping.

"Y'all lived here?" Gene said. "How?"

This made me guffaw so hard I couldn't talk, so I pointed at what was outside the bus: Tacoma spread out before us, the busy port, the icy white and blue of the Cascades behind it, the lift of downtown Tacoma's hill rising from the water.

"We in Tacoma?" Tommy Reed asked, yawning as he opened his bunk curtain, fresh off a nap. "It's pretty, but that smell!"

This set me and Charlie off again, and when we were done, tears pooled in both our eyes, he flipped his palms up, a concession, and I tilted my head to tell him I was sorry that it had become so strange between us.

It was Wednesday. We'd played a packed house in Seattle on Tuesday, and the Washington State promoter had wanted us to stay there another night, but I'd insisted we keep Tacoma. I was right: we'd sold out a theater downtown, the city's biggest. Then the promoter had been on us to add another night in Tacoma, but I said no. I wanted to get to Walla Walla on Thursday, give myself a little time there before our final show on Saturday.

The beginning of downtown appeared the same, with Union Station, the railroad tracks, and the port visible from one side of the bus and brick buildings from the 1800s on the other. It took until Patrice pulled into an alleyway behind the theater and we got off the bus for me to sort out why the city felt so different. "Where *is* everything?" Charlie said, loping down the bus steps behind me. I glanced uphill, where I could spot the blank marquee of what had been Triton's, evidently taken over by a tattoo shop and then boarded up. I looked downhill, to the office buildings that had been thick with workers and now stood empty. The storefronts were almost all vacant, except for a few selling secondhand clothes or used books. Charlie and I started up the half block to Broadway together, and I scanned the street, looking for the view I'd memorized from seeing it through Triton's windows every day. The glorious sprawl of signs and stores and shoppers was gone. A lone neon sign for LeRoy Jewelers remained. "And where is everyone?" I asked. We used to have lines outside the restaurant every morning, and now the town resembled an abandoned movie set.

Patrice had come up the hill behind us. "The promoter said he was surprised by the sellout for a downtown show, but he figures everyone who used to be a fan must be coming in from the suburbs," he said.

Downhill, the port appeared the same as ever, packed with cranes and smokestacks and cargo ships. "The port's still so busy, though."

"I guess people are driving in from the suburbs for work there," Charlie said.

"It's a shame," I said. "I always thought that maybe someday I'd try living in Tacoma again, but not if no one else is around." The Triton's marquee was now missing letters and read "RIT NS—Bargain Tattoos." "Hey, Patrice, wanna see where I used to be a waitress?"

"Where she used to be a waitress that had to serve me butterhorns and coffee," Charlie added.

"And tomato juice. The number-two special," I said.

Patrice laughed. "Now that sounds like a tale, but I actually have a second cousin out here who I'm meeting for lunch. I need y'all back here at four for sound check, all right?" He headed back to the bus, throwing his arms out for counterbalance so he wouldn't fall down the hill.

"How about you?" I asked Charlie. "Care to see what Triton's looks like up close these days?"

"I was hoping you'd ask," he said.

We crossed the intersection, which used to be so clogged with cars that I had to dodge them to get across. Now, you could stand in the middle of it and sing a ballad without a car passing by. Most of the Triton's windows were boarded up, but one had a break in the plywood. We covered our eyes and peered in to see only a couple cracked chairs and curling posters of tattoo art on the walls. I tried to summon me and Althea in our cute sailor hats, serving and laughing, but I felt the same sadness that had pulled at me in Bakersfield. That time was gone, and there was no getting it back.

Charlie was gazing toward the port, and I couldn't tell what he was thinking.

"Well, Mac, I'm off," I said. "I'm gonna try to track down Althea."

"That right? Give her my regards. Say, Lil. That telegram I received in Redding."

"Uh-huh?" My gut knotted; I didn't want to hear about whatever wedding details Donna had chosen.

"It was from Kevin." Color flushed his cheeks. "He says I can come see him in BC after the tour ends. Got a kid of his own, now. Says the kid's got rhythm, and he's already thinking the boy's gonna be a drummer."

"Mac!" I wanted to hug him, but I punched him in the arm instead. "That's the best news I've heard in a while."

"I just kept writing to him, figuring one day . . ."

"You write good letters, Charlie."

"Yeah." His entire face was pink with pleasure now. "Yeah."

"Grandpa."

"Hah." He rolled back on his heels. "Guess I am."

"That's one lucky drummer boy, your grandson." I could feel my face reddening with emotion, too, so I gave an awkward salute good-bye and walked across the street to the theater's business office. There I borrowed a Polk's city directory and looked up Althea Williams, but there were too many "Williams, A" listings, and I realized I should be looking under Claude's last name anyway. It reminded me of a stomach condition, I knew, with a -gas in it. Prendergast, Pendergast, something like that. I found an A. Pondergast. Though other listings held details on people's lives—"Ponce, Debra A, counterwmn; Pond, Michael, plant wkr Nalley's Fine Foods," this one had just an address in Hilltop and a phone number. I dialed it and a woman answered. I said "Althea?" When the woman said "Yes?," I hung up. I needed to see her, not just talk to her.

I changed into walking shoes, then trekked uphill to Althea's street. After three blocks, I was huffing and sweating, forgetting just how high Hilltop was; the one time it snowed when we lived there, Hilltop stayed dusted for days after the snow melted in the rest of the city. When I reached the neighborhood, I saw parts of it were the same as when I'd lived there, with neat houses and tended gardens, but there were also boarded-up stores covered in graffiti and old men slouched outside a liquor store.

Althea's place was a tidy one-story brick house with a neat wood fence in the front and geraniums in flower boxes. Next door, though, was a house with a wet rug slung across the front-porch rail, and in the yard, piled-up cinder blocks, bags of trash, and three beat-up chairs facing in different directions. A platinum-haired woman in slippers and a loosely tied bathrobe stood in the yard as a dog did its business. I waited for her to go back inside, then opened Althea's gate and knocked on her door. She opened the door and left the door chain attached. "Yes?"

"I—" I didn't quite know what to say, but I hoped that she'd recognize me and we could go from there.

"I think you have the wrong address," she said politely, and shut the door just as I said, "Althea."

Of course she didn't remember me; she was something to me, my first female friend, arguably my only female friend, but I was nothing to her, I thought, just some coworker from decades ago. I flexed my toes, so the pressure of the shoe leather stopped me from getting all worked up. Well, Lil, forget it, I told myself. I was already at the fence when she said, "Wait." She'd opened her door fully this time, without the chain, and stood in the frame. "You said 'Althea.' Pardon me, but do I know you? My memory isn't what it was."

I came toward her, taking in this Althea, whose hair was thin and scraped into a bun, who wore wire-rimmed glasses, but who also had on lipstick and a shiny pair of heels in the middle of the day. "My name's Lillian Waters. From Triton's? And the Snoqualmie Sweethearts?"

"Why, Lillian," she said. "Water Lil from Nashville, Tennessee: I've heard you on the radio. I wouldn't have recognized you in a million years. Your hair, your . . ." Her fingers waggled, but she didn't elaborate. "Come in. I'll fix you some coffee."

She moved around her kitchen with her old grace, though her shoulders had rounded. "I'd ask if you take cream, but I expect you still hate it," Althea said as she stirred coffee crystals into hot water and passed me a mug.

"I still do," I said.

She opened a cupboard and picked a few pecan turtles from a

candy box and arranged them on a plate, then gestured for me to follow her to a sitting room with wall-to-wall carpet in brown with orange diamonds. I sat in a green-leather chair that I figured was Claude's while she perched on a couch. I hoped she might start the conversation, but she seemed equally off balance. After I'd drunk half my coffee, she said, "How long has it been?" at the same time I said, "I suppose I wanted to say thank you."

She raised her brows. "For what?"

"You taught me how to waitress, and how to get tips, and got me a spot in the apartment building here, and showed me how to get around in Tacoma."

"You needed a hand," she said. "I don't know how old you'd told the manager you were to get the Triton's job, but I knew you were just a child."

"You talked to me. You sang with me. You were . . . nice to me."

"Nice to you?" Her tone was between amused and puzzled.

"Well, yes. Women usually aren't."

Althea picked up her mug and took a sip. "That's right. You and women." She made a noise like a hiccup, but I saw she was stifling a laugh.

"What is it?" I said.

"I'd forgotten all about that, but you always were talking about how mean other women were. First that sister of yours, and then pretty much everyone else who passed through, but Lillian, what woman did you ever treat kindly? I saw you with male customers at Triton's, all big eyes and pouty lips, folding yourself over the counter, Tacoma's Hedy Lamarr. But if a couple of women ever asked for a cup of clam chowder, you'd forget about their table until that soup was cold and then slam down the cup so hard the chowder about flew out of it. In the Sweethearts, you told us what to do, and if we had an idea of our own, you'd talk us into the ground until we gave up and did it your way."

I set my coffee cup on a coaster. "Well, anyhow," I said. I got up and scrutinized her backyard through her window. Zinnias about as tall as Althea, yellow and orange and white, bordered the far side of a neat square of grass. Closer in I saw pastel snapdragons that bowed to the ground, pale pink peonies with magenta borders, and bright blooms in purple and yellow. "Are you or Claude the gardener?" I asked.

"Claude passed."

I turned. "Oh, Althea. I'm sorry. He was so nice."

"Thank you. It's been four years now. He was a good husband." She patted her hair. "I'm the gardener. I had to learn for my job."

"Your job? I thought you were going to be a homemaker. That's what you said, that last time I saw you."

The pecan turtles had sat untouched thus far, and Althea took one, bit into it, and pulled it away, neatly avoiding the caramel strings hitting her chin. "I do domestic work," she said.

I thought of Althea on the porch of our apartment building, swearing she'd never even become a wife, because she hated cooking and cleaning so much. And the present-tense *do*; she must've been in her mid-sixties. "I see."

On the other side of Althea's zinnias: a chain-link fence, weeds in a garden, and a boarded-up house. "Did you live here this whole time?"

"Claude hoped to live in Narrowmoor. After the Navy, he liked to see the water every day."

"Pretty views from out there."

"We couldn't buy there. We weren't allowed." She said how she and Claude had tried other areas, Tacoma's outer neighborhoods that were getting built up thanks to the GI Bill, but banks wouldn't give him a loan. So they bought in Hilltop, which was at least close to the sandwich shop he opened up downtown. The minute the Tacoma Mall opened in 1965, though, downtown died, and soon Claude closed his sandwich shop, and Althea, who'd hoped to retire after twenty years of both raising children and working twelve-hour days, kept on working.

Washington's not like that, I'd told her forty years earlier: a lie.

I thought of what Kaori said to me in Flagstaff, that I always thought I had it harder than anybody.

Althea had had a beautiful voice, I remembered. Yet she'd refused to even consider pursuing singing professionally. And I hadn't thought about why.

Snow over crevasses.

Althea and I talked a little more. About Claude, about her children, about Joy, who'd become a chemist in Atlanta. Then she wanted to talk about me. "I saw you downtown. At the cosmetics counter at Rhodes, when you . . ." She patted her cheekbone, her eye socket. When I had Johnny's bruises on me, she meant. "I should have helped you."

I gazed out the window again. "You didn't know how. Heck, we all should have helped each other, but none of us knew how."

"I hope you left him," she said.

"Took me too long, but I did," I said. A robin pecked at the grass outside.

"Lillian, are you an alcoholic?"

"Why?" I'd only had a single whiskey the night before; I was certain I didn't smell like booze.

"I figured that's why you've come. Isn't it part of the alcoholics' program, to come and make amends?" She picked up a second pecan turtle.

"I'm not—," I protested.

"There are no amends to make. You and I, we were fine. We are fine."

"I'm not an alcoholic, I think, unless the papers are saying something new about me," I said.

"It must be strange to be famous. 'So Long, Jack' was the first one I realized was yours. It was pretty. When the announcer said your name. I figured there couldn't be too many Lillian Waterses out there singing hillbilly music."

I rolled my eyes. "Hillbilly."

"Are you performing here? I'm too old to attend one of your shows, and I work most evenings anyhow, so I hope that's not why you've come." She dropped her pecan turtle on her plate. "Oh, no, you're not going to write a song about me, are you? Is that why you're here?"

"No. No! Althea. I'm not writing about you. Don't worry." There was movement outside the window, and we both followed it, a yellow bird hopping around the zinnias. "I suppose, Althea, I suppose I wanted to come see you again, and see if you've had a good life," I said.

The bird fluttered its wings. Althea adjusted the plate. "It's been a life," she said. "That's about all we can ask for, isn't it?"

★ ★ ★

When I returned to the theater, I was glad to see some street action in the form of two men huffing uphill on South Ninth. Both wore sweatshirts, stiff but wrinkled jeans, and work boots; they moved in the way a lot of the longshoremen had when I'd lived here, sore from lifting and stacking bags of grain or planks of wood all day. One read the theater's sign. "Water Lil's playing here?" he said. "I like her stuff."

"Don't bother," the other said. "You wouldn't believe how much tickets are."

I dashed into the box office to see about house tickets for them, but by the time I returned they were gone. From the theater's office, I called Stanley in Nashville. He was packing for his Washington-to-Alaska outing, thrilled with how the tour was turning out.

"Listen, Stanley," I said. "What if we add a free show in Walla Walla? We can do it the day before the final concert, at whatever time the fairgrounds can handle it, but I want a show where anyone who wants to can come."

He objected, as I knew he would, and I won, as he knew I would.

The Tacoma show was great: the interior of the theater so ornate it was like playing inside a lace dress, three encores, a line of fans buying up old records of mine, telling me they used to hear me at Steve's Gay '90s or the military bases around town. After, all of us went to the bus for some rest, but I was nowhere near wanting to sleep, and we weren't leaving for Walla Walla until the morning.

I asked Charlie if he'd take a walk with me.

We made our way down to the Eleventh Street Bridge, which Charlie used to cross twice a day to get to work, joking about how our legs were no longer used to these steep angles. Beneath us, stacks of office paper bound together on flat railroad cars slithered in a snake-spine formation along the tracks. We stopped to look south to the pointed white triangles of the Union Pacific bridge at Fifteenth Street, and north, where we could see the solid outline of a container ship against the horizon. Though it was near eleven p.m., lights were on all over the port, and metal was clanging, and steam pouring from factories.

"Where to?" Charlie said once we'd reached the port.

"Let's find somewhere we can sit and see the town," I said. We picked our way toward the City Waterway, crossing a parking lot and maneuvering around the side of a chain-link fence. At the edge of the lot, a set of steps over the water led to a floating dock.

"We're probably trespassing, but a night in jail couldn't make my reputation worse at this point," I said. "Come on." I took off my heels and we navigated down. On the dock, once I got my balance, I wriggled up the tight-fitting bottom of my dress to free my knees. "What do you think? Are we going to get some infection if we put our feet in the water?"

"Let's chance it." He took off his shoes and socks and rolled up his pant legs, and we both sat and dangled our legs in the chilly water.

We looked across the blue-black waterway to the silhouette of Union Station on one side and the square clock tower of Old City Hall on the other. It smelled of salt and seaweed and gasoline, my Washington.

The water licked at the wood of the dock.

I shivered.

He lifted his hand, hesitated, and then placed his thumb lightly on my knuckle.

He smelled of guitar-strap leather and dill-tinged vinegar.

The wheat waved in a different way, stirring close to the root.

A tugboat horn sounded.

What life could have been, if we'd figured out to sit here with each other near forty years earlier.

As though even that would've been far enough back to give me a fresh start, as though I weren't already bearing thick-tissue scars all over, as though I was then young and simple and believed in the kind of easy love I sang about in my songs. That I had ever shared a strawberry-stained kiss, that I had felt love without fear. That I didn't stiffen when I was touched, that sex was something I discovered growing up, a nervous encounter with a boy my age that led to a choice I got to make.

That this touch of his finger to mine, so tentative, could be just the start.

His thumb on my knuckle, this was all, yet it made me tremble. My pulse directed only to that vein, blood pulled from my head and my feet as it rushed to meet him where he was, where I wanted him to be.

Lightly, I placed my palm on his broken collarbone.

His breath caught.

But I knew what awaited me when I returned to Nashville: a stripped vocal cord, the end of my career, and from there, a repetition of those years on Old Hickory Lake when I'd woken and drunk and slept and dreaded waking again. The few times I was happy in my life happened when, for a moment, I could forget who I was and where I was, when I was onstage and singing and the harmony hummed and the lights showed a person in a far-away row and I saw I was stirring something in them. I knew these were almost gone, memories that would exist for no one but me. I had no notion that Charlie and I could be together, not in a real sense: I would not conscript him to the pale, sad life I was resigned to.

What remained. That longing still existed. That dreams died. That the touch of a finger pad against a knuckle, a palm on a knotted bone, proved more arousing, more intimate, than anything I'd done with the dozens of men I'd been to bed with. That at this age, at last, I felt an ache, my heart muscles squeezing around themselves, my skin asking for more, my body and I working in tandem, and me unable or unwilling to do anything about it.

★ 24 ★

Memphis and Nashville, Tennessee
1975–1979

I was playing Memphis, Tennessee, on the final night of a four-week tour when I got the letter.

My bookings had been slowing lately, and I knew why. Crossover singers like John Denver and Glen Campbell were at the top of the charts, and Dolly Parton had just left her longtime musical partner and struck out on her own with "Jolene" and "I Will Always Love You." It was '75, and my stuff was feeling outdated. I wanted to talk to Coy Ray about pushing the Water Lil image some, going beyond the mistress-and-divorcée songs, letting me write music that was rawer and more authentic, even bringing back my Tele and surprising the world with how well I played it.

I'd decided to raise the issue at this Memphis tour stop, which Coy Ray was attending. I'd loved Memphis the first time I'd played there, just after I'd moved to Tennessee. Maybe it was because it was pouring rain that first time, but it reminded me of Tacoma, with its low-slung brick buildings along Main Street. The city's great blues scene had melded into country and soul with Memphis players like Booker T.

and the MGs and the wailing energy of Otis Redding at Stax Records, while Sun Records—Johnny Cash, Ike Turner, Jerry Lee Lewis, early Elvis—was also founded in the city. On that first trip, I wrote "Room Service," about a woman wondering what her man's up to while he's traveling for work. On my second visit, I came up with "Memphis Bound," about—no surprise—a cheating woman, but I snuck in some flourishes borrowed from Stax and Sun recordings.

After Martin Luther King Jr. was assassinated, though, I didn't write about Memphis anymore, and didn't much like to visit. He was killed at the Lorraine Motel, where I'd spent time; it was one of the few places in town where my band and I could socialize with Black musicians without trouble. After King's assassination, I could only think of Memphis as a place where so much had been lost. The city reflected that when I returned: its hotels and theaters were now empty shells, with girlie dancing and liquor stores replacing Beale Street's great clubs. Sun had been sold, and Stax was now on its last legs.

I'd have rather stayed in an outlying neighborhood, but my itinerary showed I was staying at the Peabody Hotel downtown, a fusty old place with chandeliers. I was playing the Lafayette Music Room, a music hall a few miles east, and after the show, I was cohosting a fundraising telethon on WMC-TV. The Peabody suited Coy Ray's purposes, too, as he wanted to have a sit-down breakfast with me and his new English boss the next morning. GMI had just been sold to a British company, and he figured a Peabody breakfast was formal enough for even an Englishman.

Coy Ray called me in my hotel room a few hours before the show. "You're gonna put on a great show, right, Lillian?" he said. "Really give it all you got, show what country music and Water Lil's all about." He even asked to go over my set list, something he never cared about, and had me add a couple English folk tunes to it. "Give 'em hell," he said.

I didn't need the pep talk. I was ready to show this Englishman, Oliver Hughes, how good I was, as I wanted him on my side by the time we went to breakfast, when I was going to pitch them both my new vision for Water Lil.

That was the plan, anyway.

Except one of Coy Ray's minions, who'd driven him and Hughes to Memphis, had the bright idea of bringing along my fan mail. I'm not sure why the trainee thought to haul it all that way, except I guess he wanted to impress the new boss with his initiative, or maybe Coy Ray asked him to do it to show Hughes how devoted my fans were. Regardless, the kid knocked on the door of my room at the Peabody, dropped off a sack of mail, and scooted off to the elevator.

I didn't have much to do that afternoon, and a game show played on TV in the background as I read through the letters. They were nice, made my head tingle with pleasure. A couple from kids, which I always set aside to respond to personally. Some requesting a signed photograph, which I piled up for my manager to handle.

And then. The logo I knew too well from my childhood, an intricate line drawing of a sun rising over a craggy mountain. Below it, in the same heavy font as I'd last seen decades earlier, the words "Bank of the West."

Branch address, West Alder Street, Walla Walla, Washington.

Same as when I was a kid.

Same as the letter that came to our farmhouse.

Same as the mortgage.

That logo felt as tangible as a hot brand on my skin. Only when I heard the minor piano chords introducing *The Edge of Night* did my eyes slide to the address line.

It was addressed to Lillian Waters, a/k/a Lena Thorsell.

I dropped the envelope on the rug, toppled a chair onto it. Went to the pint of Calvert whiskey I'd uncapped the night before, drank some straight from the bottle, and drank again until my heart slowed and the envelope's edges wavered. Clutching the whiskey bottle, I bent down and read the letter again.

Bank of the West, to Lena Thorsell.

I told myself to open it.

I drank some more. I splashed my face with water. *The Edge of Night* ended, and another soap opera came on.

I drank so that all I could taste was the alcohol, so that the traces of raisins and caramel in the whiskey faded and I might as well have been pouring Pennzoil down my throat.

The bottle was empty, far too fast. I grabbed my purse, and went outside, the Memphis heat as thick as cotton stuffing, into a liquor store. I found the clerk there was having trouble understanding me when I asked him for Calvert. "Cherry Heering?" he said. "Cointreau?"

I got back somehow and then sat on the closed toilet lid in the hotel bathroom, uncapping the Calvert and pouring it into a water glass from the sink. "I take my whiskey neat," I said to it. I downed the liquor, counted to three, and circled the letter, still lying on the rug. I squatted down and opened it.

"Dear Mrs. Waters," it read. "I represent the debt-due department of Bank of the West, Walla Walla, Washington. I write concerning those certain parcels of land on the W 1/2 NW 1/4 of section 30 in township . . ."

I knew those numbers from the mortgage paper. Our farm.

"Periodically, as part of our ongoing collections operations, we examine county court records in conducting due diligence efforts to reach clients and clients' families, and found that you are now going by Lillian Waters."

County court records. My annulment, the one time I'd linked Lena to Lillian; my divorce lawyer, thinking he was doing me a favor, changing my name in Walla Walla court. If the bank had found me, then my family could know where I was, then Hen could know. "The realized fair-market value of the property did not meet or exceed the deficiency in the payments due from Erik and Alma Thorsell, which thus remains on our books as an unsecured debt." The language was too financial for me to entirely understand, but I knew it had to do with money that my parents owed the bank. "As next of kin, you assume moral responsibility for the debt . . ."

Next of kin. How had Henrietta avoided this? Next of kin meant—and there, a few lines down, it was in black ink: "At the time of deaths of Alma Thorsell . . ." So Mother was dead; I should've felt sadness and shock, but instead felt a bare flicker of interest, no other reaction.

". . . preceded by Erik Thorsell . . ." Father, though: when I thought of him, I always imagined he was out singing timber shanties somewhere far from the farm, where he'd gotten free of all of it, too. Yet he had died even before her.

". . . preceded by Erik Thorsell, the mortgage payments had been in arrears for some time, and thus we write you with a polite request to submit the following past-due amount as soon as possible to . . ."

The mortgage. My God. She said she'd have the payment, two more weeks, end of the month, and she hadn't, despite what I'd done for her and the family. What I'd sacrificed.

I ripped the bedspread off the bed, crushed the letter underneath it, then dumped the rest of the fan mail on top. All this, money, fame, adoring strangers writing to me, but I'd never gotten away from home. She'd let Hen go free but had stuck me with the bill, in the end. I punched the mattress hard, pummeling it, but it did nothing to calm the sparks my body was throwing off. I fell onto the bare sheets of the bed.

According to the bank, I owed $500, the amount my parents had never paid, plus annual compounded interest, for a total of just over $11,000. The money wasn't the issue; I could cover that with a few shows. It was the rest. Father dead, Mother dead, Hen somehow free of all the consequences, and Bank of the West after me after all these years, because Mother left me with the mortgage, in the end. Gave Hen a way out, married her off to a rich man, likely told the bank to track down Lena, but not Hen. Never Hen. Pretty Hen. Perfect Hen.

No, but Mother loved me, in her way, and if it wasn't for Hen, she would've loved me better.

The Calvert bottle was emptier than it seemed like it ought to be.

I must've napped. The girls came to do my hair and makeup and get me dressed. They clucked over me and placed ice in a towel on my eyebags. I poured myself another glass. I sent the hairstylist out for one more bottle.

The show comes in flashes:

Me frowning at a sheet of lyrics, sure that the road manager had played a trick on me, as they swam and bubbled off the page and would not line up no matter how much I blinked. Me trying to tell the band that we should play "Memphis Bound" with a rockabilly sound drawn from the Sun artist Carl Perkins's "Blue Suede Shoes," but I forgot the full title of the song. "Like shoes, make it sound like shoes," I kept insisting to the baffled electric guitarist.

The crowd, their arms up and waving, singing "Water Lil" along with me.

A story I began about Johnny Cash where I lost the thread halfway through and couldn't recall who I was talking about.

I don't remember anything after that.

The Peabody's front desk phoned at eight the next morning. I supposed I'd asked for a wake-up call for my 8:30 breakfast with Coy Ray and Hughes. My ears had a mosquito hum in them, my head felt thick and heavy, my face was puffed and sallow, my hair matted, but I did what I could, wiped a washcloth over my face, underarms, and privates, sprayed on perfume, and put on a peacock-colored dress to distract from my face.

Suddenly I had a flash of another blue dress, one that an anchor at WMC-TV had worn the night before when I'd done the telethon after my show. Four of us clustered around a table with a telephone on it, with a big "Come On Memphis Stand Up to Cancer" banner behind us. It'd been me; the WMC anchor; Tennessee's "Mother of the Year," a gentle older lady; and a low-energy building-and-loan president. The WMC anchor in her blue dress answered the phone and held it to me: "Miss Waters, why don't you take this one?" I tried to think of what I'd said to the caller, but could only picture fumbling for the black phone receiver.

The Bank of the West envelope poked out from below the heap of bedspread, and I kicked it back underneath.

Coy Ray waited in the hotel restaurant with Oliver Hughes. As I got close, I saw Coy Ray had creamy coffee and Hughes's cup held a tea bag. I smelled milk and had to cover my mouth with my hand so I didn't burp out stale whiskey. I slapped Coy Ray's back. "You started without me," I said.

"Lillian." Coy Ray didn't smile, nor introduce me to Hughes, which I took to mean that I had met him the night before. "Nice to see you," I said as I sat down, hoping that covered the situation either way.

"Lovely to see you as well. That was quite a lively performance last night," Hughes said, dabbing his lip with a napkin.

"Thank you," I said, though I wasn't sure it was a compliment. "I'm glad you're both here, because I wanted to go over some thoughts I had about what's coming next for me."

Hughes rose. "If you'll excuse me, I have a meeting in Nashville. Coy Ray. Miss Waters."

His teacup was full.

I waited for him to leave, then said, "Wasn't breakfast for eight-thirty? I'm not late. You mind if I order?"

"Why don't we stick with coffee," Coy Ray said. It wasn't a question. "Lillian. Last night."

"I meant to bring these for Hughes to see," I said brightly, pulling a couple of fan letters from my purse. "Here, you can pass them along. 'Dear Lil, I can't tell you how much your music means to me'—now, that one is from a woman in New Mexico, isn't that something?—and here's one from—"

"Lillian. The label's making some changes. The Englishmen who bought GMI are finance people, not music people, and they have a different approach to management, especially creative management. Hughes was visiting from England to make some assessments, as he called them. He wanted to see some of the label's acts that were, that are . . ." He pulled out a cigarette. "Underperforming."

He struck a match, and we both watched it burn almost to his fingers before he lit his cigarette. "You haven't charted top ten in a year or so now, and your album sales on the last release weren't very strong. But you know that. You see the royalty statements."

I plucked at my turquoise sleeve.

"And that telethon? My God, Lillian. Country music fans will stick with an artist through just about anything, even drinking, but you going on about how the fans themselves are foolish? Are you out of your mind?"

The conversation with that caller suddenly resurfaced. She'd just come from my Lafayette Music Room performance and said she'd enjoyed it so much and was nervous to talk to me. "Wouldn't be nervous if you knew me," I'd slurred. "You, fans like you, you think you're seeing the real thing up onstage, but it's all makeup and a wig and lighting and fairy tales. Nashville sells it and you all buy it, because you're that simple; you ought to be smarter than that." I'd taken off my wig to make the point and flapped it at the camera as the Mother of the Year looked on, aghast. "It's all a dumb game to gin up ticket sales, and you all eat it up," I'd said.

"At least it was live," I said in a small voice to Coy Ray.

"They were recording. The local stations rushed it out for their breakfast shows, and it's getting national pickup. One of the hosts has dubbed you 'Poison Lil.' GMI's already getting calls from fans. Former fans. And DJs who say if that's what you really think about the business, there's no need for them to support you any longer."

"It's not what I really think. I was . . . ." I pressed my lips together as nausea seemed to rise from my toes up through my body. It really wasn't what I thought, not of the fans, who were one of the best things about this life and who made it worth it, people excited about stuff I'd made and sung and put out into the world. I was furious, sure, but not at them.

"You were drunk," Coy Ray said.

I held a spoon that had no coffee to stir. Coy Ray was discussing a statement I could work up to say that I was retiring after many productive years of making music, and was excited about gardening, cooking, and spending time with friends and family. This was not how it was supposed to go. I'd been about to tell Coy Ray how he needed to change, and I expected him to listen, to nod, to say, Lillian, we never appreciated you. Lillian, we'll give you the best promotions man we've got, why, I'll go to the record stores myself. It was supposed to be me, on my terms, telling him how it needed to be, not him pushing an already final decision on me. After the money I'd made for him, after the way I'd hustled, the days in cars and the nights at clubs, after the visits I'd made to radio stations, the interviews I'd done, the mess of wigs that had made divots in my scalp. "What if I say no?"

He twirled the cigarette, glum. "It's not a matter of you saying yes or no. The label's not renewing your contract. You were on the cutting-room floor, so I brought Hughes out here and hoped he might be able to get a sense of you, but . . . last night's show and that interview, Jesus. He gave me the final decision this morning."

"So, so . . ." I grasped for something. "So Waylon Jennings can get so loaded he can't get through 'Luckenbach, Texas,' and Mel Tillis can go on a six-day bender and end up in another state, and I can't have a drink or two to relax before a show?"

"You couldn't speak. You couldn't sing. And you criticized your fans, Lillian. You just don't do that. Ever. *Ever.*"

"So you're firing me."

"Don't make this worse than it is."

"I'm making it exactly as bad as it is." I got up, clutching the spoon. "I'll find someone else. I'll find another label, and they're gonna see that one mistake shouldn't end me, and they'll see that my fans love me, and they'll let me record the stuff I want to record. You'll hear me out there, Coy Ray. You'll hear me out there and you'll know you were wrong. I'll sign with, I'll sign with Decca. Capitol. RCA. I'll sign, and you'll hear me, and you'll know, and they'll all know, Coy Ray. They'll all know." I threw the spoon down, and it ricocheted off the table and landed on the carpeted floor.

I had the hotel arrange a taxi to drive me back to Nashville, and left a message for the road manager that I'd had a family emergency, and to please pack up my costumes from the tour bus and send them to my house on Old Hickory Lake. I drank the entire four-hour ride back, and when the taxi dropped me off, I closed myself inside my giant house, thinking it wasn't over. My fans would rally, and Coy Ray would figure out he made a mistake.

But no one called, not from Decca, or Capitol, or RCA, none of the producers who'd tried to poach me a few years before. The papers ran stories quoting fans who said they'd been misled about who Water Lil was and it didn't feel right listening to me anymore. My manager dropped me too. I stopped answering my telephone after that.

I put limits on when I could take Seconals and when I could take Old Yellers, and how many of each I could have, and how much whiskey I could drink before dinner, and blew past those limits and swore not to do it the next day and then the next day thought I was being too hard on myself and I might as well have a pill or two, wash it down with a whiskey; I deserved it.

I went to just enough Nashville events that rumors wouldn't spread about me, like that I was hooked on pills or liquor or worse. I kept the drinking private, and at events, had only one or two whiskeys. Sometimes I saw Charlie at those, and we'd talk briefly. JoEllen had left him for her mixed-doubles partner, and he had a new girlfriend named Donna. Red the Fourth was working out well, protective and gentle, and Charlie invited me over to visit. I went once, tossed a ball to Red and learned she liked belly rubs. Donna didn't want Charlie on the road so much, he said, and Charlie said at his age it was about time he learned to settle down, so he'd mostly given up touring to be a session musician. He said it was a lot steadier than touring, and he was enjoying it. I let him get away with the lie, as I wanted him to allow me mine: that I was busy writing and playing.

I wasn't playing, and I couldn't write. Had forgotten how to. Had a near-empty notebook. "River," I'd write. "Shiver. Liver." A five-year-old could do better. The only lines I could seem to produce were lyrics from "Bo-Weavil Blues," the song my father taught me and Hen. I'd find lines scrawled on envelopes, margins of books, grocery store coupons. "Some of them so evil, I'm 'fraid they might poison me." "I'm a lone bo-weavil." It was my handwriting, but I had no memory of putting pen to paper.

On the bad nights, in an act that reminded me of Mother pouring rubbing alcohol on my foot after she extracted my splinter, I read that letter from Bank of the West, trying to glean clues from it, as though it would tell me if Father had ever been happy, if anyone went to Mother's funeral, what easy fate and fine Walla Walla house Hen had been delivered into. I'd paid the check already, sending it in a letter instructing them never to contact me again, but I couldn't throw away their note. I fell asleep clutching it and woke up in the past. On the farm, needing to go fetch eggs. Waiting for Mother to come back from the bank. The sickening smell of sweet, rotting dairy in the milk shed. Hen in her blue dress: "All girls sacrifice for their families." And "Don't speak, you won't remember."

The days bled. I woke up late, shuffled out in my housecoat to get the paper, ate toast to settle my stomach. I'd once experienced a time when the days were too short, when I couldn't get everything done, and now I prayed I would sleep until it was light and then waited for the afternoon to come so I could dull myself with whiskey.

This went on through winter, through summer, one season rolling into the next. 'Seventy-five, '76, '77. I was nauseated most of the time and had bad headaches. The only time I bothered being sober was on Tuesdays, when my housekeeper came and I went grocery shopping. I didn't need a disguise; with my short-clipped graying hair and no makeup on my face, I was practically invisible, like any other woman beyond childbearing age.

One Tuesday in January '78, I went out to the Piggly Wiggly before a rare snowstorm. Due to the forecast, there were long lines, everyone panicking and buying milk and canned fruit. When I came out into the frozen asphalt of the parking lot, carrying my bags of TV dinners and bread, I realized that while I did have a snow shovel at the Old Hickory Lake house, I didn't have warm gloves. I drove to a nearby Penney's, where people were buying up snow gear. The store was sold out of anything useful in ladies' gloves; there was only a kidskin pair left, more suited for a night at the opera than for snow shoveling. They were better than nothing, though, so I bought them. Outside, I got into my car, shivering, and as the Cadillac heated up, I unwrapped the gloves from their tissue paper and put them on. They were so stiff that I could barely grasp the wheel. "These aren't working gloves," I said aloud.

An image slid into my mind, the one of Don Rich's body at his funeral. That was what had been wrong with that photograph, I understood now. His hands, those talented hands, had been stuck in gloves just like these.

I pulled them off, flexing and bending my fingers, and drove straight home, where I phoned Charlie from my kitchen. "They put Don in gloves for his funeral," I said as soon as he answered.

"Christ, Lillian, when are you going to learn to say hello like a regular person?" Charlie said.

"Don never wore gloves," I said. "We didn't need them in Tacoma or Bakersfield." It had never been glove season in California, and in Tacoma, where 42-degree drizzle was the winter norm, gloves would just get soggy and make your hands colder.

"I figured his hands must've been scraped up from the motorcycle accident," Charlie said. "But it did seem strange to me, like the funeral people had put gloves on him and nobody told them that Don's hands were how he made a living."

The first time I'd met Don, a dimpled teenager at Steve's Gay '90s, those hands had been moving, and the last time I'd talked to him, at a *Hee Haw* taping, they'd been moving, too. That final time, I'd been expecting to see the Don of our Tacoma and Bakersfield days, and instead he had a paunch, and I could tell from his face that he was drinking too much. He would've thought the same about me, no doubt. His eyes twinkled, and, my God, could that boy work a guitar, but it'd felt like time was bearing down on him. He'd had—I did the math—just two months left at that point. "He wouldn't have wanted to be buried in gloves. He would've wanted to go out playing," I said.

"Don't we all," Charlie said.

I spread out my right hand, the fingers moving awkwardly, then wedged the receiver between my ear and my shoulder so both hands were free. I slid my left hand to the neck of an imaginary guitar, forcing my fingers into the simple G, D, A chord positions that had been my standard warmup. With my right hand, I tried a basic picking pattern, moving swollen knuckles over invisible strings.

"Why're you talking about Don now, Lillian?"

"I got these gloves," I said, but didn't finish the thought. I wriggled my fingers and thought, Girl, you gave up everything for music, and now you're just letting it go? Because Coy Ray Dexter and some Englishman said so? Because you got a letter from Bank of the West? You got hands, and they're not in white gloves, Lillian. Write a song. Play a song.

"I should've gone to that funeral, huh? I bet it's rough, sometimes, being friends with me," I said to Charlie. Outside, the first flakes of snow fell onto my lawn. "I'm not sure what your recording schedule is these days, but if you feel like coming over, noodling around. . . . I'm a little rusty on the guitar, but I'll try to get back in shape."

"Yeah," he said. "Yeah, that'd be fine, Lil."

Once I got off the phone, I poured all my whiskey down the drain, plugged in my Tele, and ripped up the letter from the Bank of the West, stuffing it underneath a coffee jar in my trash bin.

★ 25 ★

Walla Walla, Washington
August 1980

"It looked nothing like this." I leaned over Charlie as he drove the Green Giant down Main Street in Walla Walla, shoving a wig curl off my forehead as I peered out of the windshield.

We followed the elbow curve of Main Street in Walla Walla, the bend of the old Nez Perce trail. Rather than Seil's shoe shop and the ladies' hat emporium, the two-story shopping palaces of Jensen's and Gardner's, all I saw was empty storefronts and discount shops. I thought at first I must be recalling it wrong—was it Alder that was the shopping street? But no, this was the right place, they were just gone, all those small stores that supplied our lives, the drugstore, the billiards hall, the soda fountain, Bendix.

I'd spent real money for these last days of the tour, springing for rooms at the Marcus Whitman Hotel for all of us, though KUJ didn't broadcast out of there anymore. Charlie had dropped off Patrice, the Farvers, and Kaori at the hotel, but he'd taken the wheel of the Green Giant and insisted on doing a tour of my old hometown with me before we checked in. It was Thursday; Stanley had added a free concert

Friday afternoon at the fairgrounds like I'd asked, and we'd have our final show there, too, on Saturday.

Charlie turned down Third, and I thought of when they'd strung the first streetlight in town at Main and Third; it whipped so hard in the wind, they had to refasten it so it didn't come flying off. Now the town had crosswalks and mounted lights. I was thinking about that when I saw that Charlie had pulled into an intersection and was signaling another right, which would put us onto West Alder. "No," I said.

"No what?" he asked.

Bank of the West was on West Alder, as I knew, since I'd sent the check there, and I would not take any chance of passing that place, of seeing the man in the hat. "Don't go right here," I said. "Keep going straight."

"Patrice deserves sainthood for driving this thing," Charlie said, changing gears.

"Charlie," I said as I glanced at the *Union-Bulletin* office, where they used to put up a Play-O-Graph during the World Series. "About Donna. She's a nice girl."

He adjusted the steering wheel but didn't respond.

"She loves you," I said. "What do you think a place called 'Your Truly Western Store' sells?"

St. Mary's Hospital, gone. The turreted Stencil & Baumeister building, gone. We saw seedy motels and a drive-in ice cream stand with dirty windows. Charlie didn't answer.

"I might not go to the wedding, if that's all right. I said I would, in Owensboro, but I might not. I'll raise a glass to you that day. Health and happiness."

Charlie jerked the bus forward and drove in silence to the eastern edge of town, where rundown shacks dribbled out, then the Blues took over and it was nothing but mountains.

"Let's go back to the hotel," I said.

He maneuvered the bus around, and within blocks we were on

Boyer, near Whitman College, lined with the fancy houses where I'd always pictured Hen living. At a giant brick house the front door opened, and I ducked beneath the windshield.

"What are you doing?" Charlie asked.

"I dropped my . . ." I rummaged around the bus's filthy floor. "Nickel."

"I'll spot you five cents. Stand up, won't you?"

I stayed down until we reached Whitman College. Charlie gave me an appraising look as I stood up. "You find your nickel?" he said, amused.

"You know I'm a tight-fisted old thing," I said. We'd almost reached the intersection where he needed to turn for the hotel. "Should we get lunch at the hotel?"

But Charlie didn't turn. He was still driving west.

"Charlie? Hotel's up that way."

"I'm not going to the hotel. I'm going to your farm."

"You don't know where it is."

"No, but I figure that nickel thing had something to do with avoiding your sister, and if I drive around town long enough asking folks where your old farm was, either someone will tell me or you'll get embarrassed enough that you'll tell me yourself. You need to see her."

"She's not at the farm."

"I know small towns. Whoever lives there now will know where she is. You planned this whole tour to finish up in Walla Walla so you could see her, so get your courage up and stop hiding on the bus floor and go find her." He slowed at a red light.

"Charlie, this is ridiculous."

"Where is it, Lillian?"

"Go to the hotel. Please?"

"I warned you." He opened the doors to the bus and flagged down a woman passing by. "Excuse me, ma'am? Do you know the old Waters farm?"

"Charlie. Charlie! Shut the door."

"I will if you tell me where the farm is." He spoke to the woman again. "The Waters place?"

"That wasn't her name, Waters. That wasn't my name," I said.

The woman cupped her ear toward us. "Say that again, please?"

"Shut the door," I said.

"Which way?"

"West," I said. "Head west."

He closed the door and drove.

★ ★ ★

As I steadied myself on the run-down fence marking the edge of what had been our farm, I heard a steady rhythm, the crash of a drumstick against a cymbal.

Stop, Lillian, I told myself. There's no drum here.

But it kept going, *one*-two-three, *one*-two-three.

"You want to ask?" Charlie said.

I looked at him, confused.

He pointed. "The person hammering up a storm over there?"

I let out a snort. I couldn't even place the sound of a hammer, I'd been gone from the farm for so long.

The racket was coming from a chicken coop, and Charlie and I followed the fence until we could see who was making it. It was a skinny old man in overalls and a faded blue button-up shirt. His spine made a C, a testament to a life spent bent over feeding animals and tending crops.

"Hello," I called.

He raised his hammer to his eyes to shade them. "Yup?"

"I'm trying to find someone," I said.

"You with the county?"

"No, nothing to do with the county. I'm trying to find someone who lived here, that's all. Did you know the Thorsells?"

"Thorsell!" Seeming to decide something, he hooked the hammer claw onto a loop of his jeans and moved toward us, holding out his hand. "Gus Sorenson."

Gus Sorenson. The high school neighbor who used to give me rides to town, who spent his afternoons playing billiards. We shook hands, his dry, mine clammy, my heart lurching, my mind disconnected. I felt certain that he knew where Hen had gone. "Lillian Waters," I said, counting on him not recognizing my face. "This here's Charlie Hagerty. So you knew the Thorsells?"

"Some. It's been a while."

"You farm this now?"

"Yep. Live just over there," he said, nodding to the north. "Bought this tract with the farmhouse, oh, I don't know, years ago, at auction. I can't get much from the soil, but I thought Hunter Fruit might want to buy it from me. No interest, though. I never was much of a businessman. Now I keep chickens here, hope someone wants it from me someday."

I looked to the run-down farmhouse, its chipped paint. "You don't use the house?"

"Haven't been inside it in some time."

"What about the rest of it? There was a garden, just there. Carrots, beets."

He sniffed. "It was roots, overgrown when I got it."

"No, the garden was always tended."

"Not by the time it went to auction."

"To auction? The bank foreclosed?"

"Yep, that's what sent the Thorsells into the wind. Hop that fence, come take a gander for yourselves." He pulled the hammer back out and balanced it on his palm, humming, and we followed him, Charlie going first, then helping me over the fence that I used to vault in one easy leap. "Went to auction," Gus continued as we reached the farmhouse, with an orange Ford truck outside it. "Didn't follow what happened to the Thorsells, but we figured she went to join family somewhere. Heard the father was, what was it? Working timber?"

I inhaled. My father hadn't come back, then, at least not before the farm was sold, and my mother had been evicted, then disappeared. I leaned on the truck to steady myself, startling a cat that was napping in the cargo bed. The cat flicked its tail, leaped to the ground, and strutted through an open door into the farmhouse. Slats had fallen off the house's sides, and shingles were missing from its roof. "Can I go in?" I asked Gus.

"I s'pose, but it's pretty run down. Can't go upstairs; the stairs are clear rotted through."

The farmhouse door was off its hinges. I moved it aside, then stepped inside and saw broken windows, empty beer cans, sticky patches on the wooden floor, spiderwebs, a brown-fringed lamp cracked at the base, a swollen ceiling above it. I couldn't quite grasp that I'd ever lived here. The smell of cat urine was strong. One of our old upholstered chairs, stuffing bursting out, was scratched up and down its sides, and a crumpled and empty pack of cigarettes rested on the seat.

A memory nagged at me, and I went into the kitchen, thinking maybe I would find what I was looking for there. The board that Mother hung our pots on was still on the wall. A time-browned needlepoint showed a green-and-white farmhouse, not ours. *"Borta bra men hemma bäst,"* read the stitching underneath it. Home is best, something like that; Mother used to say it when Father was on the road logging. This was closer, but it wasn't it.

"Never could figure out what to do with all their things. Bank didn't bother with them, sold the place as-is," Gus was saying to Charlie as they entered the house.

I scanned outside. "The shed," I said. I don't know if I spoke the words aloud, though it hardly mattered, for they didn't have meaning to anyone but me. My legs moved me toward the back door, the shortest path to the milk shed.

"She all right?" Gus said to Charlie.

"I have to see the milk shed. I have to see it."

"What milk shed?" Charlie asked, his voice fading, and I didn't wait for Gus's answer. The back door banged, and I saw the chicken coop, where Gus had been hammering, then the foundation of the outhouse, now grassed over and covered in weeds, and there it was. The milk shed.

The door was boarded up, the metal bar gone. I tugged on a board. Its nail was rusty, barely attached, and the wood came right off the doorframe, soft as cork. I went at it then, and got those boards down in minutes, pitching the last one against the ground.

I heard Hen walking toward me.

"No," I whispered. There was no door left. She could not shut me in here.

I forced myself to step inside.

The faint smell of rotting milk, clotted and spoiled.

My head surged with blood.

Bo-weavil's here, bo-weavil's everywhere you go

The mortgage due.

"All girls sacrifice for their families," Hen had said. "Don't speak, you won't remember."

I don't want no man to put no sugar in my tea—I don't want no man to put no sugar in my tea—I don't want no man to put no sugar in my tea.

★ 26 ★

Walla Walla, Washington
1934

Here is ten-year-old Lena in her work dress in the kitchen garden. I float up above her, observing her dirt-smeared face. Lena is looking for something she has lost. She scrabbles at the soil, and it's not clear if even she remembers what she hopes to find.

She should go to town now, the floating figure thinks. She should not go inside.

She did, though.

I did.

Entering the house through the back door, I sang "Bo-Weavil Blues" under my breath, hoping that Hen might hear and join in, though she never sang anymore. "I'm a lone bo-weavil, been out a great long time," I was singing as I came inside. Curious about the visiting man whose back I could see from the doorway, I forgot to wipe my feet, then used my dress hem to clean up the dirt before Mother noticed and put me in the shed again. The man wore a hat, not a farm hat but a town hat, and a suit worn thin at his elbows. The back of his neck was flushed red, and short yellow hairs bristled from it.

Mother stood at a strange angle in the parlor, resembling a paper doll. Next to her, I saw Hen in her larkspur-blue dress with its lace collar.

The man said something, and his voice reminded me of a rusty zipper, no melody or intonation. He used the same adult words that Mother had been saying to the neighbors for months. *Receivership. Assets. Liabilities.*

Mother said words back to him. *Loan officer. Liquidation.*

He interrupted. "I read your file, and I see that you liquidated livestock and farm equipment and some of your household goods to make the other payments, but that puts you in a more precarious position, don't you see? There's not much left to liquidate besides the farm itself."

"Not the farm. This is all we have. We can't."

"As I told you Monday last, when you came into the bank, I could give you seven more days and no more to come up with the money for the note come due, ma'am. Those seven days are up."

"If you could just wait until my husband sends pay—"

"If I were to wait until all the husbands searching for work were to send pay—"

"Two more weeks. The end of the month. Please. He's due back pay from the logging company. He sent a letter to me saying that, end of the month, he said. I'll show you the letter. My husband's word is good, just ask anyone in town."

"Wouldn't help, ma'am. The bank is based in San Francisco, so his word in this town does me no good."

It was a warm day, and the room pulsed with rectangles of heat from draped windows.

My mother pulled a strand of hair from her head and it drifted to the bare floor. "There must be some way," she said.

The man didn't answer.

Here, all sound disappeared, and I felt as though I were looking through the stereo viewer that my teacher used to show us slides of the St. Louis World's Fair. Instead of those wonders, this is what I saw.

The man taking in Hen, with her bare legs.

Mother moving to block Hen, her eyes half shut, her face lines deep and tight as though she were tasting something sour.

Mother, her hand at her chest, the top button on her dress loose on its thread. I was supposed to fix the button last week and had forgotten, had lied and said that I had done it and she would know and she'd put me in the shed and the wheat moved in my belly.

Her brittle nail was the same yellow as the second button on her dress as she unfastened it and I saw a stained beige garment underneath.

I must have taken off my boots and knelt on all fours, trying to keep my breath inaudible because I knew I should not be there.

I thought Mother was selling the man her shirt. I thought he would give her less for it because of the loose button.

Sound returns now.

Mother's shirt is open and she has tugged down her beige garment so a mound of sallow flesh pokes out.

"Them's sow's teats," he says. He has lost his city politeness, is talking like a hired man.

I don't understand the exchange, don't understand what Mother is doing.

"How about that one there," I hear. It's Hen. She means me.

Now my vision blurs; I can see only dark outlines against the light of the parlor.

"That one there looks like a boy," he says.

He is talking about me, and something is wrong. I am in a hand-me-down work dress made from a feed bag that's worth nothing, is unsellable. On all fours, I crawl backward toward the door as though I can erase myself from this picture. The floor creaks with each movement. I hear this and not the words the man and Mother and Hen are saying, and then he says, "All right."

Hen gives me a look. Her hair is curled, perfectly curled. Mother must've used the hot rod to set it that morning. Hen's eyes are satisfied. She has won.

Mother's palms against my cheeks, pressing heat hard into them, lift me up. "Come," she says, spurred on by Hen. Hen's idea, Hen's doing. "Come, Lena." Her voice is shaking, her body, too. "Be a good girl."

I look back to Hen, scared. She doesn't stop Mother, doesn't stop the man when he gets up from the chair and comes toward me.

My sister does nothing.

Mother takes me outside, to the milk shed.

"No," I say. "Please. I'll mend the button now."

Hen is behind her. The man follows.

"Please," I say again.

I hear Hen. "All girls sacrifice for their families," she says. "Don't speak, you won't remember."

The thin cloud of Mother's hair falls around her face as she reaches for the door's bar. She smells of vomit and the stale sweet smell of aquavit. Her blouse remains unbuttoned. She guides me in. Yet she leaves the door open.

I spin around. Mother's figure fills the door, and through a space between her ribs and her arm I see Hen, a smug smile on her pretty face. "Hey, hey, bo-weavil," she sings. I haven't heard her sing this verse for years. Not since the mule combine, not since everything started going wrong. And while it once was a song of sly fun, now she's singing it like it's a curse.

I try to ask a question, but I find I cannot talk.

Then Mother moves to the side, and the man comes in. I step back, pressing myself against the lip of the galvanized tub. I see the milk canisters, on the ground beside me, and worry I will knock them to the ground and make too much of a ruckus and Mother will lock me in here overnight. The smell of sour milk is unbearable. The man's face looms at me, bug eyes, protruding lips, and he takes something from his pocket and whacks at it and he is too close to me.

The lyrics careen in my head like someone has moved the speed dial on a Victrola far beyond what it could handle. *I don't want no man to put no sugar in my tea-I don't want no man to put no sugar in my tea—*

I hear Hen shut and lock the door from the outside. The only light is from the uneven spaces between the wood in the boarded-up window above me. The man pushes me down so I hit the cement floor hard. I try to make noise but I remember I cannot, for Hen had told me "Don't speak." *I don't want no man—*

He grunts, screeches, like he is a pig at slaughter, and I try to get away and he digs his fingers into the back of my rib cage.

My mouth opens, and nothing comes out. I need to scream. I need to get help. But I know, I *know*, that no one will listen, and my voice goes silent, my mouth gapes for words.

He forces me apart and everything goes blue and I am silent.

The milk shed arranges itself around me. He is gone. The door is open. It is still light outside. Something drips out of me. I touch the liquid. It is dark red against the lines of my finger. My voice finally returns with a shriek, strange and broken.

Mother enters the milk shed, reaches out as if to lift me. I, who have longed for her touch my whole life, shove her away. I do not want to be touched anymore.

I stumble out. Hen stands there, her dress ironed and fresh. "Hey, bo-weavil," she repeats.

I fly at her, but she steps to the side and I smash against the ground.

"Don't sing the blues no more," Hen chirps.

I scoop up a handful of red-brown earth, shot through with gravel, and smash it against my face, dragging my palm from forehead to chin.

I don't recall how long I stay there. At some point Mother brings me to the kitchen and heats water for me and pours it into the tub, and I can't tell if I am sleeping or waking when I step into it. She tries to use a washrag on me, and I grab it from her and hurl it across the room. In the tub, I leave a trail of blood that curls like a garter snake as it dissipates.

He returned a week later. You said two weeks for payment, Mother said. I said one week, he said.

Some of them so evil, I'm 'fraid they might poison me.

★ 27 ★

Nashville, Tennessee
1978–1980

Here is what I heard from managers, producers, and promoters, once I picked up my Tele and decided to play again: My albums weren't selling. My image wasn't right. My track record wasn't strong enough to support my absence from the scene. People had forgotten about me. My songs were passé. The new girls coming up in Nashville had crossover appeal, and their slow ballads that had only a bare whisper of country in them could play on pop radio, too.

Enjoy your retirement, everyone said.

I'd never retired—I'd refused to make a statement like Coy Ray had suggested—but I guess they'd heard otherwise.

Finally, I called Stanley Sacher. I found him in the yellow pages, having decided to search out a small-time manager who didn't have enough money to take out an ad, or even get his name bolded. He answered the phone himself, sounding about as desperate as I felt, and said he'd be tickled to meet. He was from Minneapolis, and he wore tiny glasses that only covered half of his eyeballs.

"I haven't got a secretary yet," he said when he met me at his office, on a hallway with a carpet-sample showroom and a news-clipping service. Meaning, he didn't have enough clients to afford to pay a secretary.

"Aren't we all," I said. "Say, you told me you'd begin making calls about me after we spoke. So? What you got for me?"

He opened a little leather-bound notepad, and I saw neat lines of capital letters, most of them crossed out. "While of course everyone's happy to hear you're back in the mix, the demand isn't quite where we want it to be." He directed these remarks to the notepad rather than me. "The feedback I'm hearing is since you don't have a new album out, you're not getting a lot of jukebox or radio play, so you're not foremost in people's minds, and ticket sales may be, ah . . . There's also a question of reliability."

"I've never missed a date in my life," I said.

"The last date you played, though, in Memphis . . ."

"That was one time."

"It's just that there's a kind of response, when I call club managers and so forth, that maybe you're not quite up to the job. Now, you are, but part of combating that talk is getting out there and singing."

"'Not up to the job,' like they think I'm a drunk?"

He took off his glasses.

"How bad is it, Stanley?"

He polished them on his shirt.

"Surely somebody can put up with Lillian Waters," I said. I tried to dissolve the catch in my throat.

"We got interest from one venue," he said.

"One." I rearranged my skirt. I thought about the club managers I'd charmed and flattered, the thousands of postcards I'd written to DJs and station managers and club owners, hoping that by working harder than everyone else, I'd end up on top. But I was only as good as the last thing I'd done, and the last thing I'd done was implode in Memphis. "Where?"

"It's a promoter in Oklahoma. Two-night gig; he just had a cancellation and needs to fill the spot."

"Oklahoma's a big state, Mac. Where's the gig?"

He opened his notebook to a blank page and picked up his pen. "Sallisaw. A Pentecostal church," he told the page.

"I haven't played a church since I lived in Tacoma."

The apples of his cheeks were red as real ones. "Lillian, I'm new to Nashville, but I'm not new to booking, and I will get you back on the road and back on your feet, but you've got to start somewhere," he said. "This fellow oversees not just Sallisaw but a lot of gigs in eastern Oklahoma. You get there on time, you charm the crowd, you tell the fans how much you love them, you thank the promoter, and that's how you get more gigs. It's not fair, but it's how it works. Sort out your set list and figure out how to get yourself to Sallisaw in two weeks, and think about back when you were just starting out in this business, what you would've given for a church filled with people listening to you sing."

Stanley flipped to a new page and wrote something down, and I waited, and he waited, and finally I gave in. "Fine, but I'm going to play electric guitar," I said.

"Good idea."

My plan was to let my career bloom again, spend a few years reestablishing myself, and then, when I was charting with new hits, clip an enormous red wig to my head, arrive in Walla Walla as a star, and see Hen once again.

It started out as embarrassing as I thought it would be. Me in a church or a restaurant, one grayhair in the audience, two. It got better. Johnny Cash, George Jones, and other old friends heard I was touring again and asked me to open for them in small venues. They were throwing me a life preserver, and I was grateful for it. Charlie, on tour with Mel Tillis, lined me up an opening stint in five cities. I loved seeing Charlie onstage, doing tricks with his guitar that he wouldn't've tried a few years ago. I was starting to fill tables at cabaret joints, and floors at honky-tonks, and the audience that attended was a lot nicer to me than they should've been, forgiving me for the telethon episode and the absence that followed. I'd throw in flourishes on the Tele like rakes and hammer-ons, like I had done years earlier. Then I booked Fan Fair, and my throat got so dry and sore I almost couldn't get through my numbers. The doctor's diagnosis followed. I knew then that I couldn't wait, that my last chance to return to Walla Walla, and see Hen, was now here.

★ 28 ★

Walla Walla, Washington
August 1980

The milk shed was yards away, white and blurry, and my hands were bloodied from tearing the place up. I was on the ground, my knees rough against soil and roots, my skirt's magenta polyester unnatural against the brown earth.

Inside the shed, I'd seen the walls coming closer, and the door shutting, and heard the slide of the bar, and seen the man's shadow coming close. I'd burst out before Hen could lock me in again, running, running outside where I collapsed by a fir tree. I'd pieced together what had happened to me in some kind of linear way, one thing leading to another, though it had not worked like that then.

Gus Sorenson stalked over to the tree where I'd taken refuge, shouting at Charlie. "What'd you say your name was, now? I'll be goddamned if I'm going to let some pair of strangers come in and tear up my property. You get her up and get her out of here and you'd better not come back, you hear me?"

"Sir. Sir." Charlie spoke in a low tone. "We'll cover any damage she did. I wasn't expecting all that. She lived here as a kid. She hasn't been back since."

"Like hell she lived here as a kid. Thorsells had this for decades, the grandparents before the parents. What kind of game you running here?"

I shoved myself up off the ground and dusted off my knees. "Gus," I said, stepping out from under the tree. "The Thorsells had two girls. I was one of them."

His mouth opened.

"Lillian Waters is what I go by now, but I used to be Lena Thorsell. You used to give me rides to town. You liked to play billiards at whatsit, that place on West Main."

He tilted his head to the right, evaluating me like I was a prize heifer and he a county-fair judge. "Lutcher's," he said.

"That's right, Lutcher's."

"I'll be doggone," he said under his breath. He glanced back to the shed, then to Charlie. "Still need to pay for the damage," he said.

"I'll send a check," Charlie said.

"You think I'm foolish enough—"

"We'll get cash to you," I said, adjusting my wig, which had slid over one ear during my fight with the shed. "I'll have someone drop it off in person. Listen, Gus. We'll get going. I'm sorry about that. It's been a long time since I've been to this place."

He flattened his lips. "Your hair never was red."

"Time and tide and wigmakers." That I could make a joke seemed a minor miracle. I started for the Green Giant, Gus and Charlie falling in alongside me

"They sent you away?" Gus asked.

"That what they told people?" I asked.

He sucked in his cheeks. "Yuh, yep. To live with an aunt, grandma, something? My mother had me drop off a loaf or two of her bread for your mother every few weeks after you left. Mine always said it was a curse to have a farm with no children."

My stomach dipped. "So Hen left here, too?"

"What's that?"

We were almost past the farmhouse now, the absurdly large Green Giant glinting on the side of the road.

"You said a farm with no children. Henrietta. The older sister. She must've gone, too. Before the parents left, I mean."

Something passed over his eyes.

"What? You had an eye for Hen?" I tried to smile. "It's all right. I think every boy in town did."

He pulled his lips up; his gums were dark brown where they met his teeth. I wanted to fill the silence, or else something I couldn't take back would happen. "I figured she went to high school somewhere else, came back and married some rich fellow in town. Even when we were driving through, by the college, I figured some brick house or another . . ." I was talking too fast.

Gus Sorenson's Adam's apple bobbed. Quickly, almost violently, he grabbed Charlie's arm and pulled him to the chicken coop. They were too far away for me to hear them. Gus pointed near the shed, Charlie rubbed his forehead hard, and then Charlie put an arm around Gus's shoulder and they both leaned in. When they separated, Charlie walked back to me, cautiously, his hands up as though I were pointing a gun at him.

I started moving, wanting to make it to the bus before he reached me, but I wasn't fast enough.

"Lillian," Charlie said. His face was colorless. "There's something you need to see. Where exactly?" he called to Gus.

"Behind that old outbuilding she tore up," Gus said. He stayed by the coop.

I wasn't supposed to go behind the shed. "I'm not allowed," I said automatically. Something to do with ghosts, with poison ivy, with death.

Then Charlie was steering me like I was a bass case on wheels, unable to go anywhere but where he moved me, and I tried to break away. I was not to go behind the milk shed, I was not to go there, I was not allowed. I resisted Charlie's pressure, but he sent my feet onto a path they were not supposed to take, to the back of the milk shed, to where purple thistle spiked around a western juniper, large, dry, struggling up from the yellow ground and choked by ivy. I could not move. Charlie stepped around me, knelt at the base of the tree, and lifted a vine from a rock.

I didn't want to see what he was going to show me: "Baby, 1918" and "Baby, 1919." I'd seen those once, and that was enough.

The ground lurched beneath me, and I lost my balance, reaching as I fell and steadying my hands on a rock next to the two small gravestones.

Not a rock.

A gray rectangle, weather-beaten.

I could hear Mother fighting with Father. She'll stay here, Mother said, she'll stay with me. The stone's corners were smoothed and rounded, its words washed by the seasons, but still I could read:

Henrietta Ester Thorsell
Born February 10, 1920
Died August 2, 1928

★ ★ ★

I was sitting on the floor of the Green Giant, pulling a finger over its filthy rubber overlay, as Charlie shut the door with a gassy whoosh.

"Can you drive?" I said. "Anywhere. Please."

He turned on the ignition, backed up, then shifted to drive and made a left, not back toward Walla Walla but west, into more farmland. Eventually, he pulled off at the side of the road. We were somewhere out Frenchtown or Lowden way. Out the window I saw a small brick schoolhouse, its windows broken, its old school number etched over the entrance. He opened the bus doors, and I hobbled around to the back of the place, to a schoolyard that now held just a rusty swing set. I sat in a swing while Charlie leaned against the frame, his back to me.

August 1928.

The night of the mule combine and the fruit smash.

Sent away, returned.

My memory was foggy and disjointed, I could recognize that, but Hen had been there that day. We had been together, and then I'd been sent to that place with the hard floor and then I was returned, and later, so was Hen.

Wasn't she?

But: why would she be returned so long after me? Why would Mother have us in a single bed? Why did she never walk to school with me? Why was there no record of her at Wa-Hi?

The answer to the equation was obvious. What was muddled was what I was supposed to add together to get it.

Think.

I held out my hands, still torn up from the boards over the doorway of the shed.

The milk shed.

"All girls sacrifice for their families," Hen had said. "Don't speak, you won't remember."

Remember, Lena. Think.

I squeezed my eyes shut. I summoned her from memory. Hen in her larkspur dress the day she was returned. Hen in her larkspur dress, saying "*Arga katter får rivet skinn,*" when I cooked with the Nez Perce woman, when Hen told Mother to put me in the milk shed for the first time.

That dress.

I grimaced.

Charlie turned to me and started to speak. I held up a hand to ask him to wait, my eyes still shut. That dress: When was the last time she'd worn something else?

I thought back. When we'd explored the milk shed and found those babies' gravestones. She'd hugged me when I screamed, and I'd touched a dot on her sackcloth dress. When was that? I was not yet in school, so I must've been four. There had been flowers, and Mother was picking mustard weed, so it would've been spring. We still had two beds. It was before I was sent away to the place with the hardwood floor. Go forward in time, then. Later on in the spring, the sun warmer, a memory of Father buying us ice cream in town and Hen dripping chocolate onto her gingham dress. Keep going. Summer, yes, summer and the Boves' party and the "Bo-Weavil Blues," and me and Hen in our gingham. More. A summer morning when we reached for the gingham dresses again because we thought another ice cream outing might be happening and Father said to wear work clothes instead, so we put on our sackcloth dresses and rode Father's draft horse to see the great mule combine. We returned. Went to the creek. I made fruit smash, went to put away the abandoned pitchfork outside.

The images stopped.

"The fruit smash," I said, opening my eyes.

Charlie's back broadened and narrowed with his breath.

The fruit smash that Hen and I ate the night we saw the mule combine. August 1928. Hen and I at the creek, gathering water, Hen pulling fruits off a bush. I knew we were not to eat berries from the creek, but she ate one—I thought she ate one. I wanted to be like her but was a fraidy-cat, so I brought some home in my pocket and told her I'd do it later. When I found the fruits in my pockets, warm and muddled, and supper was fruit smash on bread for me and Hen, because Mother was busy feeding the men in the fields, I knew how I would make them taste good. I mushed up the berries into the fruit smash that Mother had already spread over toast, then got distracted, for I always got distracted, could never concentrate like Hen, and went out the back door to retrieve the pitchfork from the kitchen garden, playing there until dusk, when Mother came back from the fields, and Mother scolded me for getting so dirty and Mother went inside and Mother screamed.

"It was me," I said to Charlie.

Charlie gripped the swing set frame tight.

"Hen dared me to eat the berries from by the creek. I thought she'd done it too, but she must have tricked me, and I meant to eat them myself, but I left them on bread, in fruit smash, and forgot, and she must have eaten them. Hen ate them. Oh, God, Charlie, she ate them." My heart felt like it sat on an ice block, and the hot tears on my face didn't make sense to me with my insides so cold. "She ate them," I said, and now the air was heavy and thick. "I gave them to her. I gave them to her. I did it." My Hen. My sister.

I tripped off the swing onto the school's asphalt, where faded yellow paint still outlined a kids' four-square court.

She was only eight years old. I convulsed; the pavement scraped my limbs. I had done it, and this was why I was put in the milk shed, this was why all of it happened.

Charlie was on the ground with me. His hands wrapped my wrists. "You were four," he said. "It wasn't your fault."

"I put the berries there. In the fruit smash."

"Lillian." Charlie squeezed tighter. "It's not your fault. It was an awful accident. It's not your fault."

The lines of yellow paint swam into curves. "I remember her. After that day. How can that be, Charlie? She wasn't there. I made up a ghost?"

"Maybe. Maybe she was someone you needed."

"I didn't need her. She was mean to me."

No, that wasn't right, either. Hen had helped me mend my dresses, taught me to read, shown me how to spoon the cream from our milk jars for a treat, and how to replace the lid so Mother wouldn't notice. She was not the terror I later feared. She was not the awful ten-year-old, not the avenging twelve-year-old, that I had pictured. She had been eight years old. She had made me laugh. We had played Annie Annie Over and ridden Father's horse. Afterward—but why would I have made her so cruel, if she were a ghost?

Charlie pulled me up. "Most people don't leave home at ten. Why did you?"

"Two girls and one of us had to work," I said automatically.

Charlie shook his head slightly.

It couldn't be. Hen hadn't been there. She was gone, my sister, and I was left.

I was left.

My body went stiff.

In the milk shed, taunting me . . . I thought it was Hen doing it.

If Hen hadn't been there to suggest the milk shed, if there hadn't been a Hen then, it was not my sister who had hated me. It was not my sister who had locked me in the milk shed.

And then I shuddered. The day I had fought to forget, when Hen had told me all girls sacrificed for their families, that I shouldn't speak, that I wouldn't remember. When she volunteered me in her place. How did it start? Me coming in, singing "Bo-Weavil Blues," noticing Hen.

In her larkspur dress.

No.

Hen had not been there.

I had thought it was Hen, all these years, that she had suggested me to spare herself. "What about that one there," I'd heard her say to the man in the city hat.

But it had to have been Mother who'd said that.

Arga katter får rivet skinn.

It had always been Mother.

★ ★ ★

The band left a note for me and Charlie at the front desk of the Marcus Whitman, with the name of a burger joint in town where we could find them. I barely stopped to read it. "Tell them I can't come," I told Charlie, who asked if he should bring me food. I said no. I had work to do. Time was speeding up, getting away from me now, my voice running out, and I needed to tell my story while I still could.

I had the front desk send up a pot of coffee and a stack of toast.

I wrote. I wrote like time was expiring, because it was. I wrote at the desk, on the bed, sitting on the toilet when I had to use it. I wrote on coffee-splattered paper. I put myself back on that farm, and I wrote.

My whole life, I had thought of home as something that I was not worthy of, and the West as a perfect setting where I had no place. But it had been flawed since Juan Pérez and Charles William Barkley thought it needed to be discovered. Since Vancouver and Gray sailed in, and Lewis and Clark came overland and started naming things in their own language, after their own people. During wars and treaties, during promises unkept, during unfair trades and deadly diseases. During Narcissa and Marcus Whitman. During the creation of reservations. During Chinatowns and Japantowns, immigration caps, internment camps. During all-black regiments and redlined neighborhoods. "Washington's not like that," I had told Althea once. But Washington was like that.

I thought my story was the only one that didn't fit here, but how many stories had I missed? How many of us didn't just want to be daughters and sisters and mothers and wives, but people, too, women with names, women whose stories might not yet appear in primers, whose work might not yet fill up history books, but who still belonged in the West? Mrs. Hideshima. The Annas. Kaori's family in Kent. The girls from the Whiskey Row brothels. The Nez Perce woman who'd let me help her make bread, who put up with being called a name that wasn't hers. Althea. Hen.

And me? Broken? Yes. Drunk? Often. Mean. Tart-tongued and ambitious and hard. Not friendly to other women. Not suited for motherhood. A little girl who made fruit smash with poison berries. A little girl who was not allowed to say a word about it. A little girl who knew, at some level, what the time in the milk shed was really punishing her for. A little girl who was made into a sacrifice. The mortgage for the girl.

Althea had asked if I was going to write a song about her. I'd told her I wouldn't. Of course, that is what I always did, everywhere. I pushed and pried, extracted, borrowed phrases, imagined feelings that others felt, found meaning behind what people said, studied the flick of their eyes, the set of their mouths, to find the untruths and the things they longed to say. Yes, I could find a song in Althea's zinnias and a chain-link fence. But that was Althea's tune, if she wanted to write it, her story, if she wanted to tell it. What happened after she said goodbye to me at the honky-tonk club, her husband coming home from mess-hall duty in the navy, the jobs she got, the jobs she didn't get, buying that green-leather chair, planting the snapdragons, children, dogs, cats, holiday parties, cold rains and summer evenings that stretched until the last kid on her block had bounced the last ball off the street. I could picture it. Maybe I'd get it right. More likely I'd get it wrong.

But what I could do was show that they—we—were here. That this was our place, too. I could brush the snow from the crevasses, and show how we, imperfect, broken, lost, gone, silenced, were always part of the story.

"We have to talk about it," Kaori had told me at Tule Lake.

Yes. Or sing.

"We Were Here": I wrote the title at the top of a fresh page and picked up my Tele to figure out the chords.

Someone knocked. Charlie, with his guitar. He came in, saw all the papers, picked up one from the floor. He absorbed it in a second, took a pen from the desk. "Do you want me to start working on fiddle and steel and bass?"

We'd rarely been inside a room alone, the two of us. When he held that paper, I had a flash of a memory that had never existed, the two of us on Vashon Island, the radio on, Charlie holding a map, me holding a mug of coffee, deciding together what to do with the open day in front of us.

"Please," I said.

I wrote, he fixed, I wrote more, we played. We ordered more coffee, I ate cold toast, he wrote down number-system charts, I tried out riffs, he worked out harmony, I wrote some more, he suggested new chord patterns and transitions. I asked him to run to the Book Nook for more paper, he left and came back and said the Book Nook was gone but he'd found a five-and-dime and bought me four notebooks and fresh pencils. I cracked a window for the cold summer air, he did Kaori's calisthenics routine to stay awake, I splashed water on my face, and he ordered another round of coffee plus a few sandwiches.

I kept writing. Didn't ask anything of writing because when writing came to me it was enough. It was enough when my fingers cramped holding the pencil, when words flowed in, when I shut my eyes and re-arranged phrases and unearthed a song and translated it to my guitar. That night, I wrote. The farm, Hen, that milk shed, the girl I was, the girl Hen was, and the fruit smash made with poisonous berries. Like so much in my life, I'd never talked of it again. I hadn't been allowed words, nor music, nor space to mourn.

I wrote about a little girl named Henrietta Ester, who could tiptoe the entire length of a log, who snuck me the last of her peppermint sticks, who believed in kind baby ghosts, who climbed into bed with me on cold winter nights and told me stories about fairy castles in Oregon. Who never hated me, never locked me in a milk shed. Who was my big sister. Who I would always sing to, even now, especially now. When I wrote for her, I pulled in lyrics from our song and made them ours again: *Hey, hey, bo-weavil, don't sing the blues no more.*

Charlie picked up my work, made it better, played the songs with me till they sounded beautiful. He made them beautiful.

The hardest one to show him was the one I wasn't sure I could write. But I did it. I titled it "The Mortgage." I handed it to him and then locked myself in the bathroom, turned on the sink, and flushed the toilet over and over so the noise would drown out any reaction he might have.

When I'd stalled too long, I left the bathroom, fidgeting with a tiny hotel soap.

"'Lena,'" Charlie said. "Call it 'Lena.'"

I dropped the soap.

After a few minutes, so quietly that I later wondered if I had imagined it, he said, "I would've loved you then, Lena."

"Charlie," I said, but I did not move, my feet gummed to the carpet.

A bird twittered as it flew by the window. Icy light filtered in from the Blues. A wave of nausea, the effect of a night without sleep, rolled through my body.

"We've got the free show at four," Charlie said. "We have to rest."

I picked up the soap and pulled at its wrapper. "Do you think we can sing these at the show?"

"We'll run through them with the band, but they're ready. 'We Were Here' is in good shape. We'll do that up-tempo."

"I was thinking of giving it to Kaori, see what she'd do with it."

"She'll be great. And on 'Lena,' 'Lena' . . ."

"Maybe a solo."

"I was thinking so."

I leaned against the wall. Charlie moved toward me. "Lillian," he said. "These songs. We'll do this again."

I let his nearness wake my body, electrify it.

We wouldn't do it again, though he didn't know it. We were far too late.

"Charlie," I said. "Charlie, you're . . ."

A friend, a musician, a person who stood by me and I don't know why you did. A person I can talk to. My person. Someone I love. I plucked the bare soap from its wrapper, because the feeling was too much, and when I looked up Charlie's hand was on the doorknob.

"You, too," he said.

After he left, I wrote one more song. I would sing it for him that afternoon.

★ ★ ★

"Hello, Walla Walla," I said from the stage of the Southeastern Washington County Fair, calling out the words I'd imagined saying so many times, "it's your Water Lil."

A big cheer from the grandstand, and from the grass in front of me, which was crammed with blankets. The free concert had drawn a giant crowd, and it was early enough that all ages could come, the babies toddling around, the older fans finding shade under trees.

Two hours earlier, after a brief and deep sleep, I'd strapped on my guitar and gone to Kaori's hotel room, where I gave her the lyrics I'd scrawled for "We Were Here" and played her the tune. "But you take it," I said, gesturing at the fiddle placed on her bed. "You do what you want with it. Rewrite it. Change the melody. Heck, if it's no good, don't sing it at all."

She hardly responded, already lost in the sheet of lyrics.

I stopped by the bus, where all my trunks with my costumes and my spread of makeup were set up, meaning to pin on a wig, slather on some face paint, and pack myself into a Nudie dress. In my bus bedroom, inspecting myself in the mirror, I patted my crow's-feet and traced the lines from my nose to my mouth. So what, I said to myself: you're fifty-six. You can powder yourself into oblivion, wear a too-small girdle and a sweat-stained dress, but you're still fifty-six and you've earned every line on that face, every gray hair, every inch of soft belly.

Instead of a bright red wig and a sparkling evening gown that would bust open if I moved too much, I fluffed up my real hair and put on an orange minidress. I could move, spin, bow, without worrying about my wig or my corset.

I did wear lipstick, of course, and rouge, and foundation, and eyeshadow, and eyebrow pencil. Couldn't go on without any face at all.

Before the performance, Charlie and I ran through two of the new songs with the band, leaving two others. The first of those was "We Deserve Better Than That," which I'd written after he'd left and hadn't shown to him, and the second "Lena," which I'd sing, accompanying myself on guitar, if I could work up the nerve. We adjusted right up until it was time to go onstage, Charlie and me, scratching out words and replacing them, working in progressions that drew from folk and blues and jazz, trying to make our music sound like the wind over the Cascades and the clang of metal from the Port of Tacoma.

At the fairgrounds, I spotted Stanley in the first row of the grandstand. He'd shown up at our hotel in Walla Walla dressed for his Alaskan cruise, wearing waterproof waders, hiking boots, and a brimmed hat that made him resemble an old-timey archaeologist. "You sleeping on a glacier, Stanley?" I asked. We were east of the Cascades, so it was near a hundred degrees in the afternoon, and I had to ask the boys in the band to lend him summer clothes. This meant that tidy Stanley wore Tommy Reed's sweat-stained khaki short-sleeve shirt with Charlie's jeans, ones I don't believe had been washed even before the tour. He kept the archaeologist's hat on, though.

From the stage, I said to the crowd, "It's good to be back here. If you were unlucky enough, you heard me hollering on KUJ back in the late thirties, and I'm gonna do some songs from that time, and also some of my hits. I got something new for you, too, something special, a couple of numbers that no one's heard before. In fact, the Stock Horses learned them just now, but that's why I have the best band in all the land. We're gonna start off with a little song called 'Water Lil,' about the Walla Walla flood of '31. Anyone here remember that?"

There were a few whoops from the crowd, and we jumped into the song, good and fast. "Water Lil" had been popular even when I wasn't allowed to play guitar on it, but now, with Charlie on rhythm and me adding little bluegrass figures into my playing, it sounded rip-roaring.

The crowd was lively, and because it was free, we got people we didn't always get, people who appeared more run-down and tired than our usual audience members, and who seemed to like the music even better as a result.

We finished "Water Lil." "Wasn't I right about my band?" I asked. The crowd clapped. "They're called the Stock Horses, and since you're farm people, you've got an idea of how hard they work." More cheers. "While we're talking about that, I want to introduce you all to them. First, we got Patrice Aguillard—Patrice, come on out here, he's not playing an instrument but he's kept our heads together and our tour on schedule and driven our bus to boot, and that's no easy job." Patrice jogged out, gave a flourish of a bow, loped back. "We've got Gene Farver on bass," and Gene played a run. "Tommy Reed Farver on steel, great player and those brothers are both serious rummy players. Charlie Hagerty, on guitar right now but you throw that boy a tree limb and he could make it into a musical instrument, and he's also our bandleader. And Kaori Tanaka, fiddler and singer and starting on writing songs, too."

The crowd roared. "Three-Quarter Time" was supposed to be next; I'd loaded up the top of the set with Coy Ray–era favorites so the crowd would give me leeway later. Then my eyes landed on a woman about my age sitting on a picnic blanket, her hair dyed blond, her eyes narrow and intense, her skin tanned to a nut brown. She sat alert and serious, like it was just me and her having a conversation and she was one minute from lecturing me: Don't mess around, you've been places, and I've been places, too. She held a shiny green apple. I wondered how it'd feel, now, to tell her and all these people just what had gone on in my life. I'd lied and dodged all my life, smiled and hustled, shut my mouth and opened my legs, as Johnny T. put it once. To tell a story straight was the thing, and these people, who were from where I was from, who'd lived how I'd lived, maybe they'd want to see what it was like when I didn't cover over the bruises.

I pulled my Tele close. "You all know I write most of my songs, and a lot of them come from a pretty straightforward place, like I heard somebody say something funny on the street, and I thought, Well, that sounds good, and I went home and added some chords and wrote it up. I've also written some that came more plainly from my life and what I've seen and heard. Here's one I want to start with." I grinned at Kaori. "I wrote about some ladies I've met here in Washington State and handed it over to Kaori Tanaka just a little while ago, and my guess is she's fixed it up her way. This one's called 'We Were Here.' Kaori?"

She'd given the band an updated chord and verse structure before we went onstage, as she'd changed my upbeat song to a minor key and slowed it down. As the band got going, Kaori stepped to the center mic, and I retreated to play backup. She'd changed the lyrics, too. She kept my chorus about the women of Washington, the women of the West, but had replaced my verses with specifics about women I figured she knew or imagined. Her voice was strong, and her fiddling mixed in grace notes and pizzicato from the Mexican tradition, a few bars from an Irish-sounding jig, and one-string runs from Cajun music. From in front of me, Charlie twisted his head back and a look passed between us: both of us had been aware she was good, but not this good. With her playing, she underlined the song, incorporating all of these styles that were never assumed to be Western and laying their claim to the West, just like the song itself was meant to do.

I moved farther downstage, seeing Kaori in the sunlight, fiddling, singing, never short of breath thanks to all her exercise, making the song into what she wanted it to be. She closed with a trembling phrase from "This Land Is Your Land."

There was an eerie quiet then, and I felt a spike of nervousness for Kaori, a worry this crowd might respond with indifference despite what she'd just pulled off, and I moved toward the mic to get applause going. Before I reached it, though, the blond woman placed her apple on her blanket, stood up, and clapped, and in half a second, the rest of the audience was on its feet, too. The clapping became shouting, and the shouting became roaring, and the women, especially the women, stomped and screamed, and Kaori, flushed, flung her arms wide to the audience.

What I wanted to do was to shake Kaori in excitement and tell her what a hell of a performance she'd just given, but I was onstage, and I couldn't. I told the crowd instead: "Remember the name Kaori Tanaka. You'll be able to say you saw her back when." We followed with an old up-tempo number, and I took a sip of water that I'd brought on with me, trying to moisten my throat, which ached. The floor of the stage was covered in bits of tape and white streaks where the soles of our shoes had dragged against it. Charlie adjusted his guitar, and pain flashed in my rib, my body realizing before my head did that after tomorrow, I wouldn't play music with Charlie again. I didn't want him to remember me like I'd soon become, voiceless, sad, done for.

"Well, they call me Water Lil," I said. "What a nickname, right? I hardly had time to sit around and mop my tears, but that's Nashville for you." My eyes focused back on the blond woman. "I used to think that wasn't me, I thought that was just what my label was selling. As I get older, though, I find that there's something to the name. As much as I love rhythm, electric, a great beat, a good song's got to have one thing, and that's wanting. Something we lost, or never had to start with. Something we shouldn't have ached for." My breath caught, and I could hear through the sound system how worn I sounded. "Now, don't you worry, I'm gonna end with fast songs, the ones you know real well, 'cause you all didn't come out on a day that's this hot to hear somebody older than the hills sing sad songs."

Applause, laughter.

"Before I get to those, I got two more new ones for you. For the first one, I'm hoping that Charlie Hagerty will come up and help me on the chorus."

He knit his brows together, confused, and I could barely force out the words. "What do you think, folks? Brand-new song, but he picks up things real fast."

There were a few cheers, and when he acknowledged them, the crowd roared. I stamped my feet, making sure they could hold me up when Charlie reached me.

I gave the band the chord pattern and rhythm, which was easy: three chords and the truth, as the songwriter Harlan Howard used to say. As Charlie neared, I pulled a wrinkled sheet of paper from my pocket. "The words," I mouthed, and I didn't allow myself to touch him as I handed the paper over, as I would feel every ridge, every callus, and then I would throw myself against his body and ask him, without speaking, to squeeze me so tight that maybe I would finally know what it was like to feel safe.

I fixed a capo to my guitar's neck and played a slow arpeggiated B-flat in 4/4 time. Gene adjusted his tuning and joined in with a bassline. Charlie studied me as I played, figuring out where I was going. "This song's called 'We Deserve Better Than That,'" I said, watching only the audience, because I couldn't have stepped another inch toward Charlie if the stage had caught fire.

I sang of what Charlie and I could have had, had we not been ourselves. I sang of when we were young and we stood on the Eleventh Street Bridge watching a tugboat go by and his hand inched toward mine, nervous and unsure, and then his fingertip rested on my knuckle. I sang of the sunny autumn day when we married, and Tacoma's hills glowed bright, and Mount Rainier slid out for a cameo. I sang of the music we made together, the calls from the road, the person at the other end of the line who always picked up and always understood. I sang of us sitting out back in our white rocking chairs, sprinklers catching the morning sun, our big-pawed dog at our feet. I sang of waking on Vashon Island, him holding a map of the place, me still in bed, the day before us, life before us. I blurred the sketch enough that no one else would recognize it, but when Charlie joined in on a low, deep harmony in the chorus, his jaw quivered. Together, we sang, "We deserve better than that."

We held that last note for as long as we could, in harmony here if never in life. The crowd cheered. I swallowed over the lump in my throat and stepped away from Charlie without glancing at him one more time.

"Charlie Hagerty, ladies and gentlemen," I said, keeping myself composed by focusing on Stanley's ridiculous hat. "And the rest of the Stock Horses. I'm gonna let 'em go offstage now before they come back for their final round. While they're back there drinking up a storm, I got one last slow song for you before we get back to some foot-tapping tunes." I strummed a few chords on my old, beautiful Tele. "I got to give you some history here. I wanted to end this tour in Walla Walla because that's where I came from."

A chant of "Walla Walla!"

"What I didn't tell you is I started this concert this afternoon with a hello, and I'm ending it with a goodbye. Now, I've never been one to get too into personal business, but it seems like I might as well start. I got one more concert tomorrow night, here at the fairgrounds, and after that, I'm gonna go back to Nashville, because this isn't just called the Farewell Tour: this really is my last tour."

Stanley, who turned pink when he got upset, had become a tiny fuchsia firework, jumping out of his seat and waving at me.

"I saw the doctor a little while ago, and he said that my . . ." I touched my throat. "My voice is running out. Too much singing and not enough shutting up, I guess. Funny thing is, I guess this'll shut me up for good, and there'll be no more touring. Time for me to be put out to pasture."

The blond lady was still staring at me. She took her apple from the blanket and took a bite, unimpressed. I knew that my band would come back on any second, and if I ever wanted to try this, it had to be now. "The story I always told about 'Water Lil' was that it was about the flood at the time I was born, but I was actually born in 'twenty-four. My family was Swedish; we lived out near where Old Highway Twelve is now."

I tried to relax my constricting throat so I could get the words out.

"I left when I was young. Just ten. I never told anyone how or why, but I guess I might as well say it while I still can, and you can think of me what you want to, but I know who I am and why I did what I did."

Now the blond woman rested her apple in her lap and leaned forward.

"This song here, this one's called 'Lena,'" I said.

"Don't speak, you won't remember," Mother had told me. But I did remember. And onstage, for the first time since it happened, for the first time in my life, at last, out loud, I sang what I could not say.

★ ★ ★

After the concert: audience members asked for signatures. Stanley hopped around like a nervous crow as he placed phone calls to newspapers and GMI and Coy Ray Dexter and throat surgeons. The Farvers said they wouldn't have heckled me so much if they'd known this was really my last tour. Patrice said I should rest. Kaori gave me a gentle hug and suggested I add turmeric to my diet. Charlie said to Stanley, Why don't you follow up on interviews tomorrow, because right now we're taking Lillian back to the bus.

Patrice drove us back to the Marcus Whitman from the fairgrounds, and though we all had hotel rooms to sleep in for once, none of us wanted to leave the bus, even though it smelled of sweat, pickles, and French-fry grease. We didn't talk about my voice. We didn't argue about how MCA was producing Merle Haggard. We played hand after hand of rummy. We sang old songs. Patrice drank flat Coke, the rest of us emptied out the couple of liquor bottles we had remaining. We didn't get maudlin; we didn't say goodbye. At a decent hour, we said we would go to our rooms and get some sleep. Charlie had his guitar in his lap, and when I said I should go to sleep, he caught my eye, touched his low E string with his finger, and lifted it toward me the way someone else would blow a kiss. He was sending me music.

The hotel telephone woke me at seven the next morning. It was Stanley. "I've lined up a surgeon at Vanderbilt," he said.

"I don't need a surgeon, Stanley. If I go home, rest up, at least I'll be able to talk for the rest of my life, even if I can't sing. Surgery? The doc sneezes and his scalpel slips, I'll never speak again. I'm not doing it."

"You're really retiring?"

"Don't see another way to go."

"Oh, dear," he said, but his voice trembled with excitement. "That's terrible, but if that's the case, I've got some good news for you."

"Thanks for the sympathy, Stanley."

"The final show: it's a great hook."

"Before you figure out how to sell me one last time, I got a question for you first. Kaori Tanaka. She was your neighbor, learned country from your collection. You must've heard her play or sing before you lassoed her for this tour. Why haven't you signed her yet?"

"Kaori? She's a good fiddler, but . . ."

"But nothing. She can fiddle and sing, and she can do it for hours without getting tired, thanks to those darned exercises she's always doing. She also writes; 'Heartache' should be released as a single. She's young, she's pretty. Nashville's always wanting a hot new thing. Why not her?"

"It's just not the kind of thing Nashville would go for, Lillian. I suppose that kind of novelty is all right if you're Charley Pride, but I—it's just not what the business wants."

Charley Pride was a big-voiced country singer, but that's not why Stanley was referencing him. He was bringing him up because he was the only Black country singer who'd broken into the business in my time. The inference was clear: Kaori, Japanese American, didn't belong in country, couldn't make it, not going through the front door. I turned that over in my mind, not knowing what to do about it, and missed whatever Stanley said next before he finished with "I don't think we can turn it down." I had to have him repeat himself.

"I said, I called Coy Ray Dexter last night," Stanley said. "He'd heard your news already; there were reporters in the audience yester-day. Coy Ray just arrived here in Walla Walla, Lillian. He's waiting for you in the hotel lobby. GMI's recording the whole thing tonight, one last live record for this legend of country music."

"I haven't been signed with Coy Ray's label for years," I said.

"He's bringing a new contract. We've talked about money and he's willing to pay up."

"If he's so excited about this live album, then I want the whole band to have a piece of the sales. Equal shares. I mean it. Patrice, too."

"Patrice is a road manager."

"I don't care. Coy Ray's not gonna mind, as long as he's getting his cut, and you'll get your regular percentage."

Stanley sighed. "Fine. But I want to make sure that what we talked about, the pills and the drinking and all, is under control tonight, espe-cially for a live record—"

"I've been a good little girl this whole trip, Stanley," I said. "Don't you worry."

In the lobby Coy Ray was waiting for me, holding a briefcase. I'd thought of him frequently as I'd wandered around the house on Old Hickory Lake, arguing with him in my head, though I never won; Coy Ray had the last word even in my imagination. These days, he resembled an action-figure version of himself, skin pulled back and shiny-smooth over his forehead. The face-lift almost made me feel sorry for him.

"What sin did I commit to get you here?" I said.

"Hi, Lillian." He kissed me on the cheek, smelling of cigarettes. The strange thing was, I always thought I'd slug him across the jaw if I saw him again, and instead I was kind of happy. We were two old coots now, and we'd made some good music together.

"You got clearance from GMI to have more than one girl on the label?"

He laughed. It was a real laugh. "See you haven't faded with time."

"You either." He was wearing a white suit and bright-green tie; in

Walla Walla, dressed up meant a shirt with buttons. "What are you doing here, Coy Ray?"

He patted his briefcase. "Heard that was some clambake last night, so I got a present for you. A fresh new contract."

"You came in person to give me a new contract? I was too old at forty, but now you think it's time for a revamp?"

"A live album. *The Farewell Tour*. Deluxe treatment. Liner notes about your home in Walla Walla—"

"All of a sudden we're gonna change what we've been telling people about me all these years? What about the beat-up-but-sexy divorcée?"

"Now people want authenticity. They want to feel like their idols aren't idols but people living with the same problems as them. I got myself a *Union-Bulletin* on the way in, and hear what they had to say. 'Waters brought a packed crowd to tears with her—'"

"I don't read my reviews anymore."

"'Honest, raw songs about—'"

"I said I don't read my reviews anymore."

"'Her bleak childhood, including the heartbreaking "Lena," that hints at—'"

"Stop, Coy Ray. Stop reading that to me." I didn't want to hear what they thought of what I'd done, what I'd said, who I'd betrayed, who'd betrayed me. I could sing it, and that was all.

He folded the paper in two. "By the way, I'm real sorry to hear about your voice problems." It wasn't coincidence that he gave me his condolences, such as they were, after his plans for the album. "In the state—predicament—you're in with the vocal problems and all, I think a last live album'd be appealing to you. It'll be your legacy."

Now I had an image of me in a coffin surrounded by my record covers, and I started laughing, thinking of the one I despised most—1969's *The Night Before We Met*. On the cover I'd worn a wig with feathered wings and a cherry-red prairie dress that seemed to drown me in fabric. I held a fiddle skyward, though I didn't know how to fiddle.

"Lillian?"

I was laughing. "Coy Ray Dexter, try as you might, you're never gonna contain my legacy inside an album. You got a pen?"

He passed me the contract, then extracted a pen from the inside of his jacket. "Sure do. You can sign on page—"

I crossed out a line in the first paragraph, and then a clause in the second. "I'll take an hour to go through this word by word," I said. "I've learned a thing or two over the years. And, by the way, I want to split my take among my band."

He drew a cigarette from his jacket and lit it. "Don't care if you want to give it all to a hog farm; the important thing is that we get it out there."

Back in the room, I crossed out lines, and added words, and went over the contract once again and signed it, leaving it for Coy Ray at the front desk.

Then I went out for a late breakfast by myself at a diner. A couple came up to me in my booth, introducing themselves as farmers who grew Walla Walla Sweets on a plot just east of town. They'd attended yesterday's performance. "I liked the one about Lena," said the man, who had tobacco-stained teeth.

"Real sad and real good," said his wife.

I thanked them, added more maple syrup to my remaining pancake, and cut a soggy triangle from it.

I had come to Walla Walla for things that I did not find. I thought I'd been running toward something all this time, one final concert with an awed Hen in the audience. Instead, I'd met my past. I'd seen who I was. And I'd sung about it for my audience, performing something that these two farmers were moved by.

I slid the pancake away with my fork, thinking of Kaori onstage last night.

"Anything else?" asked the waitress.

I said I suppose I'd had my share.

★ ★ ★

We had three and a half hours before the concert. The contract was signed. I knew what I needed to do.

I asked the front desk for Kaori's room number, and when I knocked, I heard fiddling. She opened the door. "Kaori," I said. "Can you break for a little bit? I could use your help."

She held the bow in one hand and grasped her fiddle in the other, balancing on one foot as I explained my plan to her.

"I've already got my costume change and everything ready in my hotel room," I said. "And I amended the contract so they'll record the show however it goes, and so everyone gets equal shares in the sales, if you're worried about that."

"I'm not."

"Then what?"

"I won't lie to them," she said. "Patrice, the Farvers, Charlie. And they won't believe it."

"You can tell them the truth. They'll understand, I think," I said. "The story is for Coy Ray and Stanley and the label, so they can't get out of the live recording."

She touched the bow against her leg, considering. "What about you? Everything you said last night? Your voice? You said you don't want to talk about surgery options, but that means at least for now, this is your last concert, Lillian. It's a sold-out show in your hometown."

I gazed behind her, out her hotel window, to the low storefronts of the town I thought I'd known. "I figured it would mean everything," I said. "Turns out even I can be wrong from time to time."

She stepped close, her eyes dark and intense. "Are you sure about this?"

"I don't need it. You do." I cleared my throat. "Now listen, on 'Heartache,' you've really got to make those 'm' sounds pop on 'Woulda made him mine.' It's a big crowd and the acoustics aren't as good outdoors as you're used to indoors. Oh, and on 'Three-Quarter Time,' if you do a little violin-y waltz in the bridge—"

"I've got it." Her voice was quiet. "Lillian, you'd better go."

"I could use a drink."

"Sounds like you could. Better tell the barkeeper who you are."

"I'll tell 'em I used to be Water Lil," I said, and winked.

Her eyes shone. "She's a trailblazer."

"She was all right. Had her flaws." I tapped the body of her fiddle. "Kaori, one more thing. Can you tell Charlie for me—can you tell Charlie, keep playing?"

She held the bow up to me as though she were a queen about to knight me, and let it fall on my shoulder, a benediction. "I will," she said.

I made my way to the hotel bar. "Double whiskey," I told the bartender. I swished a sip all around my mouth, then emptied it while the bartender turned his back to dust off bottles. I ordered another. "I'm performing tonight," I explained. "Water Lil and the Stock Horses, at the fairgrounds."

"Oh, that's you?" he said as he cut limes into quarters. "I missed the show last night, but my friends said it was far out."

"Water Lil's always far out," I said, downing the second drink. "Keep my tab open, will you? I have to run a little errand."

I tottered to the front desk, where I leaned too close to the clerk and asked him to deliver a message to Patrice: I wasn't taking the bus over, would meet them all at the fairgrounds. Then I inquired where the nearest liquor store was.

En route, I stopped at a drugstore to pick up some pills. When I got to the liquor store, I opened the door too aggressively, almost sending a tinkling bell above to the ground, and asked for a fifth of Calvert. "I'm Water Lil. I'm performing here this afternoon," I told the cashier. "You mind if I open it here?" I offered him a taste, but he didn't want any.

At the hotel, I staggered past the front desk clerk and the bar on the way to my room. There, I took a pressed powder compact from my purse and knocked it against a wastebasket to empty it, then carefully refilled it with the pills I'd just bought. I took off the sparkly pants and metallic tunic top that I was wearing, replacing them with a yellow A-line dress. Then I removed my wig, unclipped the stocking cap from my head, and scratched my itching scalp. I tucked my hair under a scarf and put sunglasses in my purse.

Back at the bar, I ordered another double. "I'm incognito!" I told the bartender, slurring. "But it's me. Lillian Waters. Water Lil? I'm a singer." I burped. "Just a second." I took out the compact from my purse, opened it, and sent yellow and red pills skittering across the bartop and to the floor, then knocked over what remained of my drink. "Oh, now, look at the mess I've made," I said, pulling the fifth of Calvert from my purse. "Can I give you some of this to make up for it?"

"Ma'am, you can't bring your own liquor to the bar," the bartender said, picking up the overturned glass and throwing down napkins to sop up the whiskey.

I tipped sideways off the barstool. "That's fine. I'm going to . . . I'm going to . . . What do I owe?"

"Three dollars," the bartender said.

I plucked a twenty from my purse and slapped it down. "Here's a five," I said.

"Ma'am, that's a twenty," the bartender said.

"That's fine, I'm fine, and I'll tell you what I'll do," I said, wobbling off the stool and waving at the mess. Instead of finishing my thought, I left the bar, taking the hotel's back staircase to the street, where I put on my sunglasses and walked south and west toward the fairgrounds, just before Walla Walla town ceded to wheat and rye fields.

I paid the entrance fee to the fairgrounds attendant. He said that a singer called Water Lil was on in half an hour. The seats were all sold out, he said, but if I wanted, I could hear the show from the area in back of the grandstand.

I moved in no pattern, my heartbeat shushing in my ears, as I passed the exhibits of bushels of tomatoes about to burst and tender peas displayed on curling vines. In a barn, men groomed their Herefords and untangled their black-faced sheep's coats, and little children spoke in solemn voices to their rabbits and pigs before a 4-H contest. I threaded through a pavilion where the women's competitions were held: canning, baking, sewing. I ended up, as I always would, at the grandstand. I made my way to the back of it, where several clutches of people who hadn't gotten tickets were settling in for the show. I found a space under a thick black walnut tree and sat, waiting, watching its light-dappled leaves.

Where is she, the people around me said, what's happening.

I heard she always had a problem with pills, said a lady in a straw hat.

They began to twitch, scratching themselves, saying they needed water, that it was too warm out. I had asked too much of the band, I thought. I had asked too much of Kaori.

Then I heard scattered applause: the band was taking the stage. They dipped straight into an upbeat, instrumental "Water Lil." When it ended, brave Kaori's voice came through the mic. "Ladies and gentlemen," she said. "I'm very sorry to say that Lillian Waters is indisposed and can't play today."

Boos.

She got louder. "We're still going to give you a terrific show," she said. "All of Water Lil's songs, including the ones some of you heard yesterday for the first time. Now, GMI's recording a live album here, so let's show them what Walla Walla can do. All we're asking is that you give us a chance. Here's one that you know and love."

The crowd murmured, unhappy, but then Kaori opened her mouth and began to sing. It was "Three-Quarter Time," and her voice sounded full and young and sad. The crowd quieted. I closed my eyes. Spots of light danced in the darkness. She sang.

★ EPILOGUE ★

May 1981

A salty breeze blew through an open window as I padded inside barefoot, the screen door banging behind me.

When I thought about the future that remained for me, I'd composed a repetitive melody with a dull bass beat, but life is not like that. Music is not like that, either. It speeds up, then lingers, and just when you think you know a song inside and out, you play it one more time and it transforms into something new.

I filled a kettle with water and turned on the radio. It was a country station, and my favorite DJ, a sleepy-voiced woman who knew the music as well as a carpenter knows wood, was on. I opened the fridge and evaluated its contents: Jell-O, apples, homemade gooseberry jam that a neighbor had dropped off, and a half-eaten jar of Nalley's pickles. I opened the jar, took a sniff, and put it back with a laugh. Waiting for the kettle to boil, I listened to the radio. Good tracks. Emmylou Harris, Reba McEntire. They weren't all bad, these kids. Merle Haggard came on as the kettle whistled, then Loretta as I stirred Folgers into a mug, and Rosanne Cash as I blew on the coffee. Then the DJ's calming voice was back on. "Up next, we have the guitarist

and musician Charlie Hagerty, who's one of the more spectacular musicians I've seen. He's now headlining his own national tour, and will
be playing all around town in June, followed by a few shows in the
islands. Here's Charlie Hagerty covering Willie Nelson's 'On the Road
Again,' from Charlie's first solo album, just out from RCA Records,
Hillbilly."

I spun the volume up to its loudest level and hurried outside to the
porch, where I set down the mug and clapped three times for Red. My
Tele was already out there, plugged in to my amp, and I picked it up,
keeping pace with Charlie's sounds. As I played, Red the Fourth trotted up to the porch, her paws covered in dark sand from where she'd
just been digging on the beach. She cocked an ear.

The road was no place for a dog, he'd written me a few months earlier, after I'd sent him a note about where I'd landed. Could he bring
Red to stay with me while he toured?

You don't want her to stay with Donna? I'd replied.

He'd sent back a drawing of his hands soaking in pickle jars, with
an arrow pointing to the bare fourth finger on his left hand. "Ay yup,
marriage ain't for me," his drawing of rube Charlie said via a thought
bubble.

I'd stocked up on pickles. He'd gone through three and a half jars
during his visit to settle Red in. "Better tell the store to get a few
more for when I'm back," he'd said.

After he'd left, with my voice near gone, I'd played my Tele day
in and day out. Heck, I thought, I guess I can talk with this thing if it
comes to it. So I'd gone to a surgeon and asked for my odds. I'd asked
how many of these he did a year, what might happen, what could
happen. I'd sung "The Night the Lights Went Out in Georgia" as he'd
put me under. He'd said we wouldn't have the results until I was fully
healed, and that I was not allowed to speak for four weeks.

I was now on week three of four.

On the radio, Charlie launched into a guitar solo, and I decided
to outdo him, adding in a flat seventh and a bluesy third. He'd hear

my version when he came through in a couple of weeks, when I was guesting on his island dates. I wouldn't be able to sing, I'd warned him. Well, what I need is a Washington girl who can really tell a tale on a Tele, and I've only ever met one of those, he'd responded.

The DJ was back. "Charlie Hagerty last played out here, of course, on Lillian Waters's farewell tour, and for anyone who missed either of those Walla Walla shows, all I can say is I'm sorry for you. Waters was a treat, and when she couldn't play the next night, her fiddler Kaori Tanaka stepped in for her. Maybe you've heard of Tanaka? Just kidding. The live album Tanaka headlined is one of the best of last year, I think, and here's her first single from that album, 'Workin' on a Heartache,' which hit number two last fall."

A familiar intro started, and I lay the Tele in my lap and listened.

For the night of the final Walla Walla performance, I took no pills. Downed no whiskey. At the bar, I'd poured all my drinks into a wastebasket. The pills that I'd scattered were over-the-counter ones for congestion and colds, not Seconals and Old Yellers, but I figured regular folks couldn't tell the difference, and I was right. The *Union-Bulletin*'s story detailing my bender that day, with interviews with the hotel clerk and bartender and a liquor-store owner, was picked up nationwide. I knew DJs and reporters and promotion men would love the story of the fading star Lillian Waters, unable to control her demons, and of the talented young fiddler stepping in to save the day.

Kaori wouldn't get in through the front door on the country scene, Stanley had made that clear. And I knew how the back door worked, all those things I shouldn't have had to do. So I built a trapdoor.

The live GMI album was Kaori Tanaka's debut as a country and western star. It charted at number 4.

After Walla Walla, I'd returned to Nashville only briefly. I had my Cadillac fixed up and packed it with my Tele strapped into the passenger seat and my amp in the back. I paid a neighbor girl to keep an eye on the Old Hickory Lake house, telling her I wasn't sure when I'd be back. I drove east as far as I could, following signs to any place

that sounded interesting, ending up at a river near the North Caro-
lina coast, where locals warned me about black bears and alligators
alike. That was enough for me, so I spun the Cadillac's nose north and
made my way up to Boston. As I drove, I thought of the real Hen and
what we did together. I wondered about Father, who I'd never thought
to blame, but who must have known what he was conscripting me
to when he left, for he knew what Mother could do. And I thought
about Mother, Mother who I had been running from all these years.
I considered what I knew of her life: her own childhood cut short,
sent away to America as an unwanted daughter at age five, working
in Oregon and then at the laundry and then at the farm, bearing and
losing children, her husband gone, the farm the one thing left. She had
offered herself, but she was old before her time, the man with the hat
wouldn't take her, and she was broken and half-crazed and believed
there was no other choice.

But there's always another choice.

In early October I made it to Boston, a city I'd never visited before,
all hemmed in with buildings jammed together and narrow streets. I
wasn't sure where to go from there, but I figured I should check in on
my house in Tennessee. I called the neighbor, who told me that two
trunks had arrived along with a note, which I asked her to read to me.
She recited: "For Water Lil. I thought you could use these still. I hope
you will use these still. P.S. Charlie said he'll keep playing if you keep
playing. Kaori."

"Is that Kaori Tanaka?" the neighbor girl asked. "I have her tape.
Do you think you could get me her autograph?"

I said I could pull some strings.

I couldn't sleep that night, and Boston's cobblestones seemed to be
closing in on me. I got onto I-90 and followed it west. Buffalo to Erie,
Cleveland to South Bend, Chicago to Sioux Falls, Missoula to Boze-
man. This was the kind of travel I liked. When I stopped the car, I ate
at diners and talked to people. I heard my voice declining. I wrote late
into the night, sitting on scratchy motel bedspreads, and let myself

sleep until checkout if I wanted to. I no longer had to make the next town for sound check. I wrote a stinker of a song about Rapid City and a pretty good one called "Vivian," after a South Dakota town with just a couple of one-story wood buildings that seemed very Old West to me.

I left the silver-mining town of Wallace, Idaho, on an October morning. It was drizzly and gray, green pines edging against the Coeur d'Alenes. The border with Washington was barely marked, but I could feel it once I made it, as the mountain mist gave way to the sun-colored fields of Eastern Washington. I wouldn't be driving through Walla Walla, as I-90 didn't go that way and my business there was finished. But the landscape was so similar that I could picture, on the side of the road, the Boves' house, the Melgaards' place—the Thorsells' farm.

In October all the land turned gold, the farmland to hay and the trees to orange, and Hen and I would keep our window open and watch it all. Winter was far enough off that we didn't fret about a freeze; summer, where we'd breathe in dust behind drawn shades to avoid heat, was a memory. In October the sky was calm and streaked with clouds, the Blues dignified in the distance. The land was quieting itself, the green tucked away for the next spring, and the air was clear. Hen gathered rosehip pods and black walnuts and picked comfrey for poultices. I raked leaves and stored them to use in the henhouse for spring. In October the mornings held dark and night closed in early. The workday shortened. The earth rested, and so could I.

So could I, I thought, driving through Spokane and its outlying towns that, with their names of big dreams and little ones, sounded about as Washington as it gets: Ritzville, Fishtrap. In Wenatchee, I drove over the Columbia River, and I sang "Roll On, Columbia." And then I knew where I would go, what I would do.

For in the end, I had sung my song.

I would return to the West, and this time, I would make it my home. Outside my cabin on Vashon Island, Red sniffed something in the air, dense with the smell of brine and kelp, then settled her head against her paws and exhaled. Across the bay, the orange cranes of the Port of Tacoma bobbed and pulled, and its smokestacks puffed. The Cascades rose high behind the port, their snow mostly melted from the warm spring, just revealing jagged cuts of earth.

I warmed my toes in Red's fur, and there we sat, the Tele warm against my body, watching the sunlight fade over Washington as the waves lapped back and began again.

AUTHOR'S NOTE

My first job out of college was as a magazine fact-checker, I spent almost a decade as a reporter at the *New York Times*, and I continue to write nonfiction magazine stories. Old habits die hard, so while *The Farewell Tour* is not a work of historical fiction in the strictest sense, I infused the story with real events and people, and with as much accuracy as I could.

Many of the musicians and performers Lil crosses paths with in the novel are pulled from real life, including Bill Anderson, Bobby Bare, Debby Boone, the Browns, Archie Campbell, Johnny Cash, June Carter Cash, Patsy Cline, Crystal Gayle, Merle Haggard, Waylon Jennings, George Jones, Loretta Lynn, Rose Maddox, Barbara Mandrell, Buck Owens, Dolly Parton, Charley Pride, Don Rich, Jean Shepard, Connie Smith, the Stoney Mountain Cloggers, Sylvia, Mel Tillis, the Ventures, Kitty Wells, Dottie West, Marion Worth, Tammy Wynette, and more. So are almost all of those Lillian listens to as she studies music, including Ma Rainey, Lulu Belle and Scotty, Patsy Montana, Spade Cooley, Jimmie Gordon, and the electric-guitar pioneer Charlie Christian. Don Rich really did play at Steve's Gay '90s in Tacoma; Buck Owens plucked him from there for Buck's own band; and Buck was indeed a DJ in Puyallup, Washington, and featured a young Loretta Lynn on his Bar-K Jamboree. These are some of the giants of music, and I approached them with humility, deep admiration, and, I hope, authenticity.

The members of Lil's 1980 farewell tour band, Johnny T. and the Paper Boys, and the Snoqualmie Sweethearts members are fictional. The songs Lillian writes are made up, as are the songs by other writers that she records while signed to Sugar and GMI (which are fictional labels, and Cuthbert and Coy Ray are fictional producers). The radio stations Lil works for existed at the time, as did many of the radio programs she listens to, including the Barn Dance and, of course, the Opry.

As is the case with all writers, I relied on the hard work and generosity of people who've gone before me, including original sources, archivists, sociologists, and historians, to learn about my subjects—in this case, Washington history, farming, country music, and much more. I'm grateful for all their efforts, and hope I've done them justice. Here's a partial list of what I turned to for each section of the novel:

Walla Walla: *Walla Walla: A Nice Place to Raise a Family, 1920–1949*, by Robert A. Bennett (Pioneer Press Books, 1988); *Personal Stories of the Great Depression*, by Robert A. Freeman (publisher unknown, 2017); *A Good Day's Work: An Iowa Farm in the Great Depression*, by Dwight R. Hoover (Ivan R. Dee, 2007); *A Homesteader and His Son*, by Alexander Joss (Ye Galleon Press, 1990); *Cornbelt Rebellion: The Farmers' Holiday Association*, by John L. Shover (University of Illinois Press, 1965); *Walla Walla Valley Memories: The Early Years*, by the Fort Walla Walla Museum and the editors of the *Walla Walla Union-Bulletin* (Pediment Publishing, 2006). Joe Drazan's Bygone Walla Walla site (last accessed fall 2022 at wallawalladrazanphotos.blogspot.com) offered a carefully indexed visual account. I based my depiction of Walla Walla in the twenties and thirties on items from Whitman College's Penrose Library, including contemporaneous fire maps, photographs, newspaper accounts, railroad maps and directories, along with the archive's Feagins, Jones, and Laidlaw family papers; Avery Hailston Cornell's

"My Life Story," in box 57 of the Walla Walla photographs collection, 1849–2017; the D. W. Ramsaur diaries; the Ella Baker Zumwalt scrapbooks; and the Northwest Ephemera, Walla Walla Ephemera, and Munnick Northwest Ephemera collections.

Tacoma: The digital collections of the University of Washington and the Tacoma Public Library; the collections and exhibits of the Washington State History Museum, the Tacoma Historical Society, and the Port of Tacoma; *Images of America: Vanishing Tacoma*, by Caroline Gallacci and Ron Karabaich (Arcadia Publishing, 2013); the UW's Tacoma Community History Project interviews (last accessed fall 2022 at https://content.lib.washington.edu/tacomacommweb/communities.html); the Library of Congress's Veterans History Project interviews (last accessed fall 2022 at https://www.loc.gov/vets/). For the lives of Japanese and Japanese Americans in and around Tacoma in Lillian's time, the extraordinary repository of oral histories and primary sources from Densho, a Seattle-based nonprofit documenting Japanese Americans' experiences under incarceration during World War II, was invaluable (last accessed fall 2022 at ddr.densho.org). As Densho says on its website, "Our interviewees, or narrators, share their life histories to preserve history, educate the public, and promote tolerance. We urge our users to approach these materials in the same spirit."

Bakersfield: *The Bakersfield Sound: Buck Owens, Merle Haggard, and California Country*, by Scott B. Bomar et. al (Country Music Hall of Fame, 2012); *My House of Memories: An Autobiography*, by Merle Haggard with Tom Carter (It Books, 2011); *The Birth of the Bakersfield Sound: A Honky Tonk Attitude*, by Lawton Jiles (Yorkshire Publishing, 2018); *Proud to Be an Okie: Cultural Politics, Country Music, and Migration to Southern California*, by Peter La Chapelle (University of California Press, 2007); *Billy Mize & the Bakersfield Sound*, directed by William J. Saunders (Old City Entertainment, 2014). The Kern County Library and California State University, Bakersfield's interviews with Kern County residents who lived there in the midcentury (last accessed fall 2022 at https://archive.org/details/kerncountylibrary; https://archive.org/details/csubakersfield; and https://hrc.csub.edu/oral -history/sjvohp/), and Cal State Bakersfield's oral-history project on the Bakersfield Sound (last accessed fall 2022 at https://hrc.csub.edu /oral-history/bakersfield-sound/) were enormously helpful.

Nashville: While music always does, and should, come first in country and western, several books were helpful in shaping Lil's life in song: *Whisperin' Bill Anderson: An Unprecedented Life in Country Music*, by Bill Anderson with Peter Cooper (University of Georgia Press, 2016); *Looking Back to See: A Country Music Memoir*, by Maxine Brown (University of Arkansas Press, 2005); *Finding Her Voice: Women in Country Music, 1800–2000*, by Mary A. Bufwack and Robert K. Oermann (Vanderbilt University Press/Country Music Foundation Press, 2003); *Never Look at the Empty Seats: A Memoir*, by Charlie Daniels (W Publishing Group, 2017); *Bus Fare to Kentucky: The Autobiography of Skeeter Davis*, by Skeeter Davis (Carol Publishing Group, 1993); *Singers & Sweethearts: The Women of Country Music*, by Joan Dew (Dolphin Books, 1977); *The Grand Ole Opry: The Making of an American Icon*, by Colin Escott (Center Street, 2006); *The Storyteller's Nashville*, by Tom T. Hall (Doubleday, 1979); *Sunshine and Shadow*, by Jan Howard (Eagle Publishing, 1987); *Every Night Is Saturday Night: A Country Girl's Journey to the Rock & Roll Hall of Fame*, by Wanda Jackson (BMG, 2017); *Producing Country: The Inside Story of the Great Recordings*, by Michael Jarrett (Wesleyan University Press, 2014); *Smile When You Call Me a Hillbilly: Country Music's Struggle for Respectability, 1939–1954*, by Jeffrey J. Lange (University of Georgia Press, 2004); *Fifty Cents and a Box Top: The Creative Life of Nashville Session Musician Charlie McCoy*, by Charlie McCoy (West Virginia University Press, 2017); "'It Wasn't God Who Made Honky-Tonk Angels': Women, Work and Barn Dance Radio, 1920–1960," by Kristine M. McCusker (2000 doctorate in history thesis from Indiana University); *Behind Closed Doors: Talking With the Legends of Country Music*, by Alanna Nash (Alfred A. Knopf, 1988); *Buck 'Em: The Autobiography of Buck Owens*, by Buck Owens with Randy Poe

(Backbeat Books, 2013); *The Selling Sound: The Rise of the Country Music Industry*, by Diane Pecknold (Duke University Press, 2007); *Pride: The Charley Pride Story*, by Charley Pride with Jim Henderson (William Morrow, 1994); *Buck Owens: The Biography*, by Eileen Sisk (Chicago Review Press, 2010); *Down Through the Years*, by Jean Shepard (Don Wise Productions, 2014); *Stutterin' Boy*, by Mel Tillis with Walter Wager (Rawson Associates, 1984); *Ramblin' Rose: The Life and Career of Rose Maddox*, by Jonny Whiteside (Country Music Foundation Press / Vanderbilt University Press, 1997); *Stand By Your Man*, by Tammy Wynette with Joan Dew (Simon & Schuster, 1979). The hymn to Demeter that Lil is so taken with is from the 1914 translation by Hugh G. Evelyn-White, last accessed fall 2022 at https://www.gutenberg.org /files/348/348-h/348-h.htm#chap37.

As much as I've tried to bring country music into these pages through my words, there's no substitute for listening. For playlists of the songs Lil studies, plays, and enjoys, as well as book club resources, head to stephanieclifford.net/TFT. You can contact me through that website, too; writing is solitary work, and hearing from readers is one of the biggest rewards of publishing a book.

ACKNOWLEDGMENTS

Lisa Grubka, my agent: calm, smart, and a true professional with exceptional literary insight.

Emily Griffin, my editor: both a careful line editor and a brilliant big-picture thinker, a rare and wonderful combination.

The Harper team: Milan Bozic and Sara Wood for designing the beautiful cover; Miranda Ottewell, whose copyediting saved me from errors small and large; Micaela Carr, hardworking and efficient; Katie O'Callaghan, such a smart marketing executive and supported by social pro Amanda Livingston; Maya Baran, bringing that Seattle magic to publicity, and the lovely Karintha Parker.

My film agents, the sparkling and savvy UTA team of Jason Richman, Mikey Schwartz-Wright, and Akhil Hegde.

Craig Havighurst, whose Nashville, Opry, and musical expertise made this book richer and better. Craig's beyond-interesting podcast with country and roots musicians, *The String*, is addictive, and the lucky people who live in and around Nashville can also hear him on WMOT Roots Radio, 89.5 FM. And big thanks to Karen Hayes at Parnassus Books in Nashville for connecting me with Craig. (When you need help? Ask a bookseller.)

Dr. Paul E. Kwak of New York University Langone's Voice Center, who was generous with his time and expertise in helping make Lil's vocal problems realistic. Pam Sakamoto's and Peter Keane's careful reads helped fix errors and add perspective.

(Of course, any errors are mine alone.)

Herb Pedersen, for graciously allowing me to use an excerpt from his and Nikki Pedersen's "Old Train." I've listened to his music for so many years, and it was a thrill and a privilege to correspond with him about the song.

The estate of Carolyn Kizer, and Copper Canyon Press, for permission to use an excerpt from Kizer's poetry, which was searing and far ahead of its time.

The librarians of the New York Public Library and the Brooklyn Public Library, who handled my nonstop book and research requests with patience, good humor, and insight. In particular, I'd like to thank Felicia Boretzky, Danielle Cordovez, Jonathan Hiam, and Jessica Wood at the NYPL's Performing Arts Library, who spent an afternoon taking me through their incredible collection so that I could better understand the recording technology that Lil would have been using and radio programs she would have heard.

Jennifer Kleffner, a Walla Walla farmer, who took time from a typically busy day at her farm—she was rubbing a newborn blackbelly sheep with its mother's placenta as we spoke——to show me around and discuss crops, farm maintenance, and more. She chronicles her work at MilesAwayFarmWW.com, a must-visit for those interested in local agriculture, sustainability, and everything from broccoli growing tips to mustard recipes.

The librarians at Whitman College's Penrose Library archives, an indispensable resource for Northwest history.

Several people read early versions of this book and offered valuable comments: Francine Chew, who approached this with the care and intelligence she brings to everything; Kate Axelrod, whose perceptive comments made the book sharper; Daisy Garrison, whose feedback helped shape a key scene (she knows the one); Erin Autry Montgomery, my sister in country music, who made me feel like I could keep going when I wasn't so sure; and Jessica Silver-Greenberg, my person, always.

My parents, Steve and Judy, offered encouragement, feedback, and support, and gamely put up with another novel about wayward parenting.

This book would not have been started, much less finished, without the people who looked after our children, especially Germaine, Taylor, Audrey, Lexi, Anna, Mian, and Emily. Thank you. Our kids are better people for your care, as are we.

My grandmothers, Bette and Kay, were inspirations for this novel in more ways than I can count. They are gone, but their battles paved the way for my generation and those after me. We'll keep up the good fight.

Our cats and dogs were constant companions during the writing of this book, and listened to my out-loud mumblings and occasional groans of frustration without judgment and with (at least feigned) interest. Thank you to them, and to A New Chance Animal Rescue, Animal Haven Shelter, and Badass Brooklyn for saving their lives and those of so many other animals.

My children, S and E, bring joy, laughter, excitement about reading, and thought-provoking questions and observations to each day, along with interesting facts about Athena and archery from the one, and about Artemis and octopi from the other. I'm so proud of the kind, inquisitive little people you are becoming.

My husband, Bruce, handled a thousand crises, both real and anxiety-fueled; helped with musical questions; provided deep and thoughtful feedback on the book; and, most of all, kept me believing in this creative life that we're making together. Thank you.

ABOUT THE AUTHOR

STEPHANIE CLIFFORD is an award-winning investigative journalist and a bestselling novelist. As a *New York Times* reporter for almost a decade, she covered business and law. She now writes long-form investigations about criminal justice and business for the *Times*, *The New Yorker*, *The Atlantic*, *Wired*, *Elle*, *The Economist*, *Bloomberg Businessweek*, and other publications. Her accolades include the Loeb Award in Investigative Reporting, the Deborah Howell Award for Writing Excellence from the News Leaders Association, the Society of American Business Editors and Writers in Explanatory Reporting, and the Deadline Club Award in Magazine Profiles, among others. *Everybody Rise*, her first book, was a *New York Times* bestseller and *New York Times Book Review* editors' choice. She grew up in Seattle and lives in Brooklyn with her family.